11 / 3 / 11

11 / 3 / 11

by

AE Merrick

DOUBLE ‡ DAGGER

Library and Archives Canada Cataloguing in Publication
Merrick, AE. author
11/ 3/ 11 / AE Merrick

Issued in print and electronic formats.
ISBN: 978-1-990644-10-8 (soft cover)
ISBN: 978-1-990644-11-5 (e-book)

Editor: Phil Halton
Cover design: Pablo Javier Herrera

Double Dagger Books Inc.
Toronto, Ontario, Canada
www.doubledagger.ca

To P.D.S.

Not only must the Conspirators work in secret, they must make every effort to insure that their plans are not made public. The first task of a conspiracy, then, becomes that of convincing the people that the conspiracy itself does not exist.

—A Ralph Epperson, *The Unseen Hand*

Some will sell their dreams for small desires
Or lose the race to rats
Get caught in ticking traps
And start to dream of somewhere
To relax their restless flight
Somewhere out of a memory of lighted streets on quiet nights …

—Rush, *Subdivisions*

1: Conform or Be Cast Out

[Transcribed from *Full Disclosure with Gilbert Emmerich*, AM 710, September 21, 2015.]

Gilbert Emmerich: Okay, we're back on. Coming out of the break, that was Rush, with their 1982 prog-rock hit, Subdivisions. Kind of a theme song for Full Disclosure, you dig? Be cool or be cast out, my fellow truthers. Be cool or be cast out. That's exactly what the system wants you to do.

Anyhow, this next hour of the program is brought to you by X-Y-Zeus patented male enhancement supplements. All organic, all natural, and let me tell you, all powerful. X-Y-Zeus works. Your wife or your girlfriend, she won't know what hit her. And I mean that in a good way.

Okay, whether you're a longtime listener, or this is your maiden voyage with us, you know what we're all about on Full Disclosure. The abnormal, the paranormal, cover-ups, conspiracies, questions. We talk about the stuff the lamestream media doesn't want you to think about. I've been doing this a long time, man, thirty years now, and I've encountered a lot of craziness out there. But my next caller is …

Well, listen, truthers, if you're just tuning in, I need to give you the context here, before I introduce the caller. Although if you don't already know the context, then you've been living under a rock, that's all I can say.

As you all know, we're almost at the fourth anniversary of something called 11/3/11. That means four years of police-state laws gripping our fair city. Four years of fascist government overreach. All in the name of public safety.

What's the official story with 11/3/11? What does the mainstream media and the government want you to believe? Well, in a nutshell, you get some disgruntled has-been televangelist, calls himself a patriot, Doctor Richard Declan. Declan surrounds himself with a couple likeminded folks, they hatch a plan to carry out one of the biggest acts of domestic terror we've ever seen.

Everyone's seen the surveillance photos. The cargo van, looks like your standard delivery truck, parked outside the Van Lathan Building on the morning of November 3, 2011.

And what's in the back of that van? Well, as the official story goes, there are six plastic drums back there. Apparently, those drums are full of a nice cocktail of ammonium nitrate and diesel fuel. Two thousands pounds of the stuff. Officially, they're all wired together with a couple hundred feet of primer cord. Officially, this whole nasty thing can be set off two different ways. One is by cellphone. The other is by failsafe, a little timer device, not much more complicated than a cheapo stopwatch.

Officially, they find the guy who is supposed to be driving the truck. One Ronald T Fortin. Goes by Ronnie. Former skinhead. We all know what becomes of Ronnie Fortin.

But for truthers like us, you know we've been talking about the other side of the story, all those inconvenient little details that just don't add up. I've personally heard countless different interpretations and expert opinions, and what it all comes back to is this.

John Doe.

The official story gives us the main players, but there's one more guy also believed to have been at the scene on 11/3/11. The guy who drove the damn truck in the first place. The guy the mainstream media won't talk about, the guy the authorities deny altogether. Johnny Doe, truthers. Fact or fiction? Conspiracy or crackpot?

Well, with that introduction, let me come back to my caller. Caller, sorry to keep you hanging like that. I just needed to set the stage. Alright. Go ahead.

Caller: Is this ... am I on the air, Mr Emmerich?

GE: Yes you are. Live and loud.

Caller, laughing: Well, thank you, Mr Emmerich. It's an honour to speak with you. Can I just say I used to listen to your show all the time. All the time. My granddad had your show on every night when I was growing up. I lived with him, my granddad, and he was—

GE: I'm sure your granddad was a gent, caller, but in the interests of time, I want to focus on what you told my producer Paul a few minutes ago.

Caller: Oh, yes, of course. Well, here's the thing. I'm not really supposed to listen to your show anymore, because of where I am now, and what I'm doing, which is being quote-unquote a productive member of society. Which is all part of what I agreed to do. With the authorities, I mean. What the authorities had me agree to do with my life. To straighten out, I guess you'd say. But this is almost the fourth anniversary of what happened, and everybody thinks they know what's what. So I tuned into your show to hear your thoughts, because I knew you'd have a different, like, take on it, than everybody else. Other words, I knew you'd be after the truth, Mr Emmerich..

GE: I appreciate the vote of confidence. The truth is what Full Disclosure is all about.

Caller: So, in any case, I can't really give you my name. I'm going to have to use a codename or an alias or what-have-you, because the authorities, they're still keeping tabs on me. Anyway, I'm calling in to set the record straight. To give you the true facts of the whole thing. Ronnie Fortin, Doctor Declan, the Patriot Bloc, everything that happened on 11/3/11. I think it's important to get the story out there. Officially I shouldn't be telling you any of this, because of my being a quote-unquote productive member of society, but the truth matters. The truth matters.

GE: And how is it you know the truth, caller?

Caller: Because I'm him, Mr Emmerich. I'm John Doe.

The man who comes to be known as John Doe doesn't like the term conspiracy theories. Theories imply fallacy. Theories can be disproven. John Doe prefers the term conspiracy. Full stop. Conspiracies are real, about the realest thing there is. Conspiracies are how the way the world.

John Doe (how about Johnny, caller, or JD? you okay with that?) knows all about conspiracies. JD knows the moon landings were filmed on a Hollywood backlot. He knows JFK was shot by a second gunman, on orders from the CIA. Or the FBI. Or the EPA. Or some other secretive acronymic agency.

JD is 38 years old. Apart from driving his granddad's ice cream truck, he hasn't been saddled with a job in a few years now. He spends a lot of time reading, uncovering the truth, unravelling the conspiracies.

JD knows the British Royal Family are reptilian shapeshifters from Planet X.

JD knows Paul McCartney has been dead for decades, replaced in public by a crude imposter. JD knows vaccines and fluoride are population control drugs.

JD knows subliminal messages come out of your phone and TV. Mind control on extremely low frequency waves, ELF. That's why he stays away from computers. Google, YouTube, Facebook – they're all giant emitters for ELF mind control. He sticks to books from the library or used bookstores.

He knows the attack on the World Trade Center was an inside job.

The Freemasons have a lot to answer for.

There are massive inconsistencies in the story of the Holocaust.

JD is a white man. JD knows conspiracies explain how the game is rigged. These aren't theories. Nothing ever happens just because.

Another thing JD knows about is persecution. Much of his life has been one persecution after another.

Late one evening in early fall, he's persecuted by a couple of night-shift cops. Persecuted right into the Bayfield City Jail. The reason for JD's persecution is false, of course. A frame-up. Part of the conspiracy.

They – the amorphous, unidentified They, the conspirators themselves – are out to get him.

It's Friday, September 23, 2011.

Persecution on Friday means JD won't be able to stand before a duly-appointed magistrate until the courts open on Monday morning. But this isn't the first time he's been locked up. He knows the drill. He only needs to keep his head down. Do his own time.

By the time he's booked and processed, it's past midnight. His clothing and wallet are confiscated. Also confiscated is JD's pendant, the small teardrop of blue orgonite he wears on necklace. Never mind the clothes and the wallet – it's the confiscation of the pendant that fills him with unease bordering on panic. But still he keeps his mouth shut.

JD is strip-searched. Given a shapeless orange jumpsuit. Two burly, ill-tempered guards escort him to one of the short-term ranges. The range is vacant at the moment. All the other guests are in their cells.

The guards open the cell on the end of the range and deposit JD within. A moment later the steel door is shut fast behind him. The cell is narrow, not much wider than the span of his arms. There are two metal bunks, one above the other, mounted to the cinderblock wall.

JD's cellmate, also a white fellow, is lying on his back on the bottom bunk. The man's hands are composed together at his midsection. It almost looks like he's meditating instead of sleeping, except for the quiet snores. He doesn't stir as JD climbs onto the top bunk.

JD stretches out as best he can. The thin plastic mattress is not comfortable. There's a light behind metal mesh on the ceiling. The light is dimmed, but not turned off. He can hear the electricity buzzing in the wires. He can't sleep. All he can do is replay the evening's events.

He only wanted to see his son. Check on him. Ensure his safety. That was all. What was the harm in exercising his fatherly duty?

He squeezes his eyes shut.

The light buzzes. There's a low tone of ELF coming from it. The ELF carries messages. Commands. JD doesn't like what they say. He would be shielded from them if he still had his pendant. Orgonite is a powerful ward against mind control. Instead all he can do is roll on his side and stick his fingers in his ears. This is beyond persecution. This is torture. This is conspiracy of the cruellest kind, directed at none other than him.

Wakeup comes at 6:00 AM. Six hours before JD is used to rising.

Despite the ELF coming from the light fixture, he must have fallen asleep at some point. The guards' yelling brings him around with sore eyes and a confused head.

He looks down and sees his cellmate doing a set of pushups on the concrete floor. JD watches him do twenty-five. Then the man stops. Stands up. He's a tall man. Lean. His hair is shot with silver, and there are lines at the corners of his eyes and mouth. But his eyes are bright and clear. Somehow lit from within. JD finds it hard to look away.

"The martyr cannot be dishonored," says JD's cellmate. "Every lash inflicted is a tongue of fame. Every prison a more illustrious abode. That's Emerson, my friend. A true pillar of individualism at a time when this civilization was something we could take pride in. Heh." The man's mouth quirks. It looks like he wants to spit on the floor, but he doesn't. "They tossed you in here sometime after twenty-four-hundred hours, yes?"

"Twenty-four …," says JD. "You mean midnight?"

JD's cellmate nods. "Twenty-four-hundred hours," he says. "I was only half asleep. Still vigilant." He scoops some water into his mouth from the shallow stainless steel sink mounted on the back of the toilet. Then he says, "You must always be vigilant in this place."

That's the extent of their interaction that morning, but JD is still struck by the way the man's eyes seem to have an inner light.

He thinks they're in the same cell for a reason.

There is no just because.

After the cell doors open, the guards do a count. There are twelve persecuted men on the range. Misfits. Drunks. Drug addicts. The rest of the prisoners are the gangster and hoodlum type. They have lots of tattoos. JD supposes their bark is worse than their bite, but he intends to ignore them.

After the count is breakfast. A tiny omelet, soggy hashbrowns, sad-looking baked beans. Watery orange juice. Weak coffee. JD hears one of the other men on the range say the breakfast comes from a nursing home kitchen down the street. JD has his doubts. He's certain this … food … has been prepared in a laboratory somewhere. Somebody's using it to test various drugs or chemicals on human guinea pigs. Not unlike what They do with fluoride.

After breakfast there's nothing to do but kill time. JD finds himself a concrete bench where he can sit and keep his head down. The air is rank with smells of piss and sweat. An endless buzz of ELF coming from the lights, whispering insidious commands if he would just listen. It's hard not to.

The hoodlums take over the best viewing spots near a TV mounted in the corner of the ceiling. JD has no interest in the TV. All that brainwashing. Consumerist garbage. Even looking at the screen causes the ELF in his head to spike.

He does his time. He even drifts off.

Then he snaps awake. There's a commotion. He looks up. Sees that his cellmate is in trouble with the hoodlums. Something to do with the TV.

JD listens to the rising voices. It seems his cellmate has told the hoodlums to turn the TV off. Told them their minds were being polluted by the reality show they're watching. The cellmate is a man after JD's own heart.

"Who the fuck do you think you're talking to, you little cocksucker?" says one of the hoodlums. "Do you know who I am?"

"I was only telling you for your own good," says JD's cellmate.

JD closes his eyes. He feels dizzy. Untethered from the world. Must be the ELF.

Then there's the unmistakable noise of a scuffle. JD looks again. Four of the hoodlums are on their feet. JD's cellmate is sitting on the floor, his back to the wall. Hands up to cover his face. The hoodlums have knocked him down, but they haven't started punching or kicking him. Yet.

On the wall above is a surveillance camera. JD is sure the guards are watching the range, but so far the heavy steel door leading out remains shut. At best the guards don't care what happens in here. At worst – and most likely, JD decides – the guards are entertained by a four-on-one beatdown. Elsewhere on the range, the other persecuted men are studiously paying no attention.

The hoodlum standing closest to JD's cellmate asks again, "Do you know who I am, motherfucker?"

JD's cellmate mutters something.

The lead hoodlum kicks him. "Louder, motherfucker."

"I-I don't know who you are," says JD's cellmate.

"I'm who you stepped to is who I am."

The lead hoodlum and his three friends crowd in closer. JD sighs. He can't sit by any longer, not when one person alone is about to be set on. It's dishonorable. But so much for minding his own business.

He stands. For a moment, the dizziness intensifies. He can hear his cellmate whimpering. As JD gets close, the hoodlums all turn to look at him. Dark faces, black eyes. JD puts on a stony expression. It's a look he's practised in the mirror at home.

"Leave him alone," JD says flatly.

The lead hoodlum shows his teeth. They're all capped with gold. "Do you know who I am?"

"I don't care who you are," says JD. "This battle isn't worth it. You may or may not know it, but the game is rigged. That's why we're all in here. It's the prison-industrial complex, and we're just stuck in it. We're all stuck in it. Don't you see that?"

The range gets quiet except for the chatter of the TV. The lead hoodlum keeps his eyes fixed on JD's. JD doesn't waver. At last the hoodlum looks away. He kisses his teeth and spits on the floor beside JD's cellmate's feet, but that's all he does.

JD nods, helps his cellmate up. A moment later, the dizziness subsides.

"Dr Richard Declan," says JD's cellmate. "It's good to meet you. You never know where networking with the right people will happen."

They're back at the bench JD had claimed earlier. Declan's handshake is firm and direct. Three pumps. His eyes are glowing again.

Declan looks left, then right. Leans in. "First off, I want you to identify if you are an employee of the federal government."

JD laughs. "What? Am I an employee of the government? No, man. No way. I don't work for the government. Do you think those slave drivers would have someone like me?"

Declan sits back. Smiles coolly. "You're the kind of man who understands, aren't you. That pleases me. Like attracts like. These days, in the waning of what our forefathers built—" he looks over at the hoodlums "—that's more important than ever."

JD nods. He's not sure what Declan is talking about, but he can't deny how he is drawn to the man.

With the introductions out of the way, there isn't much to do but kill time again. They make small talk. Declan keeps that cool smile throughout. Back in the day, JD's granddad had a buddy who was good at chess. Talking to Declan reminds JD of the few times he played – or attempted to play – chess with Granddad's buddy. Almost as if every interaction is a test, a gambit.

The endless morning turns into an endless afternoon, then an endless evening. The hoodlums stick around the TV. They stay clear of Declan and JD. Good policy on their parts. After another nursing-home-kitchen meal for supper, the guards do an evening count. Then everyone is locked in their cells for the night.

By now JD is comfortable enough with Declan to talk about the grander failings and injustices and hidden schemes of the world. He tells Declan about some of the latest conspiracies he's studied. The way paper currency is a front for human trafficking. The way celebrities are all controlled by the illuminati. The way the Great Pyramids were built to conceal UFO landing sites.

Every so often, Declan says "I understand" or "Fascinating." At one point, Declan says, "Truth will ultimately prevail, as George Washington reminds us."

There's no judgment in Declan's tone. Declan is the best listener JD has ever met. JD almost mentions the ELF emanating from the light overhead, but he catches himself. He doesn't want to sound crazy.

There's a lull in the conversation. JD has been speaking without a break for an hour. Then Declan says, "So, my friend, what do you do to make ends meet? What's your line of work? When you're not shackled in this pit, of course."

JD smiles up at the ceiling. Normally he doesn't like answering this question, but he doesn't begrudge Declan. JD tells Declan about the various fields he's worked. The service industry, for example, where JD performed labour for a professional junk removal service. The arts and entertainment industry, where JD worked in a video rental place. JD's most recent occupation was Chief Helmsman of his granddad's ice cream truck.

"You drove an ice cream truck?" says Declan.

"Yeah, I did. One side of this piece-of-crap city to the other. It was my granddad's operation, but he was sort of the big boss. The executive. I was the one who basically ran the operation."

"Fascinating," says Declan.

"And yourself?" says JD.

"I too have had many occupations," says Declan. "But there's only one I'd have engraved on my tombstone after I go. Patriot. Dr Richard Declan, Patriot."

"Patriot."

Declan yawns as he answers. "Indeed. Perhaps I'll tell you more tomorrow. I sense that you're a man who can be trusted with classified information. A fellow patriot. I invite you to consider it."

A minute later, JD hears light snoring from the bottom bunk. He looks over the edge. Declan is in that meditation-like repose again. That vigilant half-sleep. His eyes are closed.

JD rolls onto his back, laces his fingers together behind his head. I invite you to consider it, he thinks. He smiles. He doesn't get invited to much. Most sheeple find his intelligence intimidating. He blinks, surprised to find his eyes heavy. For the moment, the ELF isn't bothering him.

There's one phone mounted on the wall in the range. JD has seen a few people using it throughout the weekend. Calling lawyers or family. JD doesn't call anyone. The only person who would understand his situation is Granddad, but Granddad is out of reach for now.

Declan meanwhile makes one phone call. In fact, he needs JD's help with it. It's Sunday after lunchtime. Declan is looking at the hoodlums, who seem to be ignoring him. For now at least.

"My friend," Declan whispers. "I need you to watch my six while I contact one of my associates. I don't want the beastmen to launch a flank attack. Can I trust you?"

JD nods, hoping his expression shows Declan how seriously he takes the responsibility.

JD follows Declan to the phone. Declan picks up the receiver and cups his hand over his mouth while he makes his call. JD stands guard, his back to Declan, keeping an eye on the range. Watching Declan's six.

Nothing happens. Nobody tries to launch a flank attack.

After a few minutes Declan ends his call. He turns from the phone and grasps JD's arm. "Well done," he says. "Trust doesn't come easy."

The day creeps on. Declan goes back to the cell and works out. Pushups and situps in the narrow enclosure. JD feels compelled to do the same, but maybe later. Declan's workout takes thirty minutes. Then he returns to their bench.

He says, "The fact is, my friend, I don't blame the guards in here. I don't blame law enforcement. I don't blame the army. I think they're all just weak. That's their primary problem. They're weak. They need a collective slap in the face. An awakening to their collusion with a fundamentally corrupt elite. The deep state. The globalists. If, after that accounting, they need to swing in the wind for their continuing cognitive dissonance, well, that's what we call acceptable risk. That's the hard duty of true patriotism. And make no mistake, my friend. The accounting is coming. The day of the rope, my friend."

Declan's eyes are alight. JD dwells on something he just said. Cognitive dissonance. JD likes how that sounds.

"Let me ask you this," says Declan. "What would you do to protect yourself, your way of living, your family?"

"Well, anything, I guess."

"Don't guess."

"Anything," says JD. "Whatever I need to do to protect them. I have my granddad, I have my brother, I have my son ..."

Declan smiles his cool smile. "That's what I thought. Three percent, my friend. In the days of the Revolutionary War, only three percent of the populace were willing to stand up against the tyranny of a ruling monarch. Three percent is not a big number, is it?"

Before JD can respond, the big range door opens and a burly guard steps inside and calls Declan's name.

"I'm here," Declan replies. He turns back to JD. "Look, I'm departing now. My associate has arranged for my release. Not without restrictions, of course. However. My organization meets every second Thursday. We discuss the truth. We discuss the three percent. We discuss what must be done to rescue our civilization from the brink and make it great again."

"Declan!" the guard hollers. "Double-time, inmate. You're not doing me any fuckin favours."

"We are the Patriot Bloc," says Declan. "Don't bother trying to find us on the internet. We're not there. But you will find us at 23468 Side Road 10. Not this coming Thursday. The Thursday after. Nineteen hundred hours."

"Alright, inmate," shouts the guard, "you can stay—"

Declan stands up. "23468 Side Road 10. Thursday after next. I want to see you there. You, my friend."

Declan turns and walks across the range. His back is straight, dignified. He doesn't rush. The guard waits for him with what seems like infinite patience. Then Declan is gone. The range door thunders shut.

"23468 Side Road 10," JD says, and says it again.

He looks around the range. All is quiet. One of the old addicts is sleeping nearby. The hoodlums are clustered around the TV. JD seems to have been forgotten. But he's uneasy.

Funny to think, almost as soon as Declan really opened up, a guard arrived to pull him out of here. Right. As if that doesn't mean something. As if that's coincidence.

"23468 Side Road 10," says JD. "Patriot Bloc."

The Van Lathan Building stands at the corner of Franklin Boulevard and Monarch Avenue in downtown Bayfield. Fifteen stories, most of them dedicated to various civil service offices.

On twelve, there's a federal office for immigrant processing. Tax and revenue services on eight. Workplace equity on the same floor. The Bayfield municipal election offices take up five and six. The health department is on the third floor.

The parking garage is below ground. So are the courts. Six courtrooms, as bleak and sterile as mortuaries.

JD is hauled down to the Van Lathan Building at some godless break-of-dawn hour on Monday morning. JD and seven others, shackled in the back of an armoured van. The bail court is busy. The justice of the peace looks like he's fighting to stay awake. The duty counsel looks like she's close to a nervous breakdown.

JD has been through this human conveyor belt before. He finds it difficult to pay attention to the bureaucratic nonsense. He goes like a robot through the routine of Yes, your worship, no, your worship. Keeps his eyes suitably lowered. He knows They want him to look humbled.

His mind is on other things. Patriots. Three percent. Cognitive dissonance.

His mind is on 23468 Side Road 10, two Thursdays away.

An invitation.

"You understand the severity of breaching a peace bond," says the justice of the peace.

"Yes, your worship," says JD.

The justice of the peace sets a trial date. Six months away. JD doesn't even care to listen to the date. Just more nodding of his head, more yes your worship.

Ten minutes later, JD is free to go. Released on his own recognizance, the justice of the peace calls it.

It's a lie. Nobody's ever free to go, JD least of all. They'll be keeping extra close tabs on him for the foreseeable future. That's how persecution works.

In Bayfield, Cable 14 is the public access station. Has been for four decades.

Every Sunday morning, from 1977 to 1993, Cable 14 hosted a two-hour show called the Great News Gospel Time. GNGT for its dedicated viewers, of which there were a few thousand. The lead pastor of the show was the Very Reverend Donald Dobson Sears, a preacher of the old fire-and-brimstone variety.

In 1986, Sears brought on a junior pastor. GNGT changed almost immediately. Fear of divine retribution was replaced by uplifting prosperity gospel. The new junior pastor, already eclipsing the man who'd brought him on, would often say poverty was a punishment for sin. He would ask his viewers for financial tithes, promising heavenly fortune in return. No tithe was too small, but the host preferred those in the triple-digit range.

No matter what viewers opined about prosperity gospel, few could deny how this new junior pastor had a certain charisma. A light in his eyes.

It didn't last. GNGT was investigated in 1994. Fraud. Tax evasion. Exploitation of vulnerable peoples. Within a year, the show was off the air. Then it slipped into the annals of Bayfield public access history, tapes in a box on a shelf in a storage room.

The Very Reverend Donald Dobson Sears was disgraced, but he avoided prosecution. As for the dynamic junior pastor? Reverend Richie – as was his TV moniker – did some time in prison. Then he disappeared.

For a while.

It's some time in the early afternoon before JD gets home. A yellow brick midrise called Country Club Estate on Blevins Avenue. A small rectangle of lawn out front, frequent dumping-ground for abandoned shopping carts. Part of the lawn is dominated by a massive, empty concrete fountain.

A small crew of young guys, none older than twenty, keep daily court at the fountain. They have rapidfire hip hop coming from a small portable stereo. They laugh and jeer.

A few of them call out to him. "Hey Ice Cream, where you been? You got a sundae? Where's your truck at?"

JD smiles, but he doesn't stop to chat. He absently fingers the orgone pendant at his throat, returned to him along with his clothes and wallet. He's desperate to get inside and lock the door behind him.

He hustles through the glass vestibule, then the tiled lobby. The lobby hits him with its familiar odors. Industrial cleaner, countless cooking oils, a faint whiff of garbage. JD stops only for Granddad's mailbox. It's jammed with flyers, bills, an envelope with what looks like the building superintendent's handwriting. All these he drops in the overflowing recycling bin. The only thing he keeps is a rolled-up city newspaper.

The elevator takes ages. It's all he can do not to hop foot to foot. At last the doors trundle open. A middle-aged woman with a bad wig waddles out, giving JD a healthy dose of cut-eye. He ignores her, jumps into the elevator, finger-stabs the button to close the doors before anyone else can follow him.

He gets off on the seventh floor. Down the hallway, by this point almost running. The apartment he shares with Granddad is number 77.

Little slice of heaven, the old man says, up here in seven-seven.

JD almost fumbles the keys, but then he's got the door unlocked. He tumbles through, into the little slice of heaven. Turns the deadbolt. Hooks in the security chain.

For an indeterminate time he sits on the parquet floor of the entryway, his back against the locked door, catching his breath, waiting for his pulse to slow, squeezing the orgone with both hands.

Shower first. Long. Hot as he can stand it. Scour away all that residual feel of the city lock-up. They put things in the air in lock-up. Tiny chemical droplets that stick to your skin, go in through your pores.

When he's finished showering he dries himself with his threadbare towel, which he hangs on the doorknob. The towel rack came off the bathroom wall several weeks ago. He'll need to fix it before Granddad comes home.

Then he opens the medicine cabinet behind the mirror and gets out his pipe. In a baggie beside the pipe he's got the remnants of a half-ounce of good Lord Kush he bought from the fountain crew three weeks ago. They charged extortionate rates for the weed. JD has gone to considerable lengths to stretch it. He takes a few hits, no more than what he deems absolutely necessary.

He emerges from the bathroom. On the wall opposite the door are six classic Playboy centrefolds in gilt frames. Miss April 1965, Miss August 1968, Miss February 1971, others. Granddad's very favourites. JD meets their vintage boudoir eyes, feels a stir of lust, but there's no time for that.

From the bathroom he goes to the corner of the living room where he keeps his clothes. He's been too busy to do laundry, so it's only by luck that he finds an acceptable pair of briefs. He digs an undershirt out of the shopping bag where he stashes his dirty clothes. Turns the undershirt inside-out, pulls it on. Good enough.

Secure the apartment. He's been away for several days. No telling what may have happened here in his absence. They come and go as They please.

He goes into the kitchenette and gets a slotted metal serving spoon out of the utensil drawer. He holds it gently between his thumb and forefinger. Does a circuit of the apartment with the spoon out in front of him.

He sweeps the spoon over the baseboards. The door frames. He holds the spoon near the vents. He waves the spoon up and down the corners where the walls come together. Holds the spoon a few inches away from each light socket.

A month ago he unscrewed all the light bulbs and stashed them in a kitchen cabinet. He'd come to mistrust the way the bulbs sometimes flickered in ominous patterns. Morse code, perhaps, no doubt trying to give him terrible commands.

He left the light bulbs in the cabinet for a week, then took them to the garbage bins behind the building and smashed them into dust.

JD gets no tremors in the spoon. The apartment is clear. Well, as clear as it can be. Anything can happen. The danger never goes away.

He retires to the living room, newspaper in hand. There's a 30-inch TV from the 1990s on an old credenza. The TV is dead. He unplugged it around the same time he unscrewed the light bulbs. Then, just to be extra safe, he cut the TV's power cord with a pair of scissors. You can't trust any electronics made in the last twenty-five years.

The 80s onward, that's when They started putting their surveillance devices and mind control emitters into just about anything run off a plug or batteries. Toasters. Microwaves. Video game consoles. Bedside lamps. Portable razors. Vibrators.

JD takes no chances. He doesn't touch computers. He doesn't possess a cellphone. He even went so far as to pull Granddad's landline phone out of the wall. The old man doesn't know about that yet, but JD is sure he'll understand.

JD permits one electronic device in the apartment. An old portable Westinghouse radio. Battery-operated. Has a handsome silver-coloured faceplate and an analogue clock and a long antenna. It's old enough, he's sure, to be devoid of any surveillance or mind control devices, and it's the one gadget he uses to stay informed.

The Westinghouse is set atop the dead TV, where the reception is best. He turns it on. The dial is always set to AM 710. 710 broadcasts an almost constant lineup of the best, most accurate journalism: The Conspiracy Hour. The Looking-Glass Report. Truth Unclassified. Just now, the best broadcast of 710's lineup is on, the long-running Full Disclosure with Gilbert Emmerich. Emmerich is mid-conversation with a caller.

"Now, you've seen these United Nations concentration camps with your own eyes?" says Emmerich.

"Yeah I have," says the caller. "And they're right here, Gilbert, right on our own soil. Thousands of them, patrolled by UN troops."

JD shakes his head. He sits on the couch. In the wall above the couch is a big window, offering a view of the sullen downtown skyline. Bayfield, population 300,000. In the distance he can see the top few floors of the Van Lathan Building. By now the Lord Kush has taken hold. He's calm, focused. The sight of the Van Lathan Building, the thought of the courts on the lower floors, does not bother him.

He unfolds the newspaper. Most of the paper – the so-called news, the sports, the arts, the lifestyle sections – are of no use to him. He adds those pages to one of several teetering stacks of discards on the floor near the foot of the couch.

All he's interested in are the classified ads. He reads them closely, running his fingertip along each word.

Granddad lit out in May. The beginning of ice cream truck season. He told JD he was meeting a ladyfriend at the Imperial Arms for a drink. Or two. Maybe three drinks, he'd added with a wink. And that was that. JD hadn't seen Granddad since.

JD worried. After two days' absence turned into three, JD considered contacting his brother. He held off. Didn't want to cause any panic.

JD did not consider contacting the authorities. That was out of the question. If something bad had happened to the old man, the authorities were probably in on it.

JD started planning a search-and-rescue operation. That's when he began to find the hidden messages in the classified ads. He couldn't take credit for the idea. He'd heard a segment on Full Disclosure about codes concealed in ancient texts. The Bible, the writings of Da Vinci, the Constitution.

Sure enough, Granddad had used the same cunning. JD just needed to learn how to look. His eyes and fingertip move over the classifieds.

Hardwood floor sanding, reasonable rates, call for free estimate.

Homestays wanted, will compensate, police check required.

Party dresses for rent.

Certified firearm safety course.

Volunteers wanted.

Will trade bucks for jewelry.

Lost dog.

"That's the thing, truthers," says Gilbert Emmerich. "This UN snowjob may already be underway, but we won't know until it's too late."

JD closes his eyes, counts to ten, then reads the classifieds again. Three ads stand out from the page.

Homestays wanted.

Certified firearm safety course.

Will trade bucks for jewelry.

He closes his eyes and counts to ten again. Does one more read. Homestays. Safety. Bucks.

Emmerich cuts to a sponsor, some kind of filter you can put on your pipes to neutralize the fluoride and free radicals in your drinking water.

The message in the classifieds is clear.

Stay safe, bucko.

JD leans his head back on the couch. Smiles. "You too, Granddad. You too. Wherever you are."

Days go by. One, two, three at a time. He has only peripheral awareness of them. He stays up most nights until the wee hours, reading old paperbacks by candlelight or listening to the overnight shows on AM 710.

He's not sure if he eats or not. He's not worried about it. He doesn't live by his stomach. He keeps his eye on his shrinking stash of weed. Right now he has even less money than he has marijuana, but replenishing his fortune is another story altogether.

He seldom rises before noon. There are a few days on end when he doesn't leave the apartment except to get the newspaper. He dutifully goes through the classifieds for more encrypted missives from

Granddad. But beyond the message telling JD to stay safe, there is nothing. That's okay. Granddad is in hiding. Hiding from Them. It's not easy to communicate from hiding.

There are multiple stacks of discarded newspapers near the foot of the couch. The stack of classifieds where he's discovered messages – each marked with bright yellow highlighter or circled in ink from a ballpoint pen – is near the head of the couch. That stack is much smaller, neater. It does not totter side to side. JD treats that stack with something approaching reverence.

JD emerges from the apartment on September 29. Thursday. A week – more? – since the fascists let him out of lock-up. He doesn't have much use for the calendar or the clock, those two made-up constructs that keep the sheeple enslaved, but today has a conventional importance attached to it. A certain family milestone, one of those things you're expected to remember.

JD remembers.

First thing he does is choose a gift. What do you give the person who already has – or thinks they have – everything? How about a good dose of truth? JD looks among his selection of paperbacks, most of them purchased from a used bookstore.

He settles on Leviathan Illuminatus. Three classic books republished as one, covering all kinds of theories about Them. Most fascinating is this idea that George Washington was secretly assassinated and had his presidency subverted by imposters. That would explain a lot.

JD chooses Leviathan Illuminatus because it's an important book. It's also in the most presentable shape of the paperbacks he possesses. He opens it and writes down the date, the nature of the occasion, and a brief message: Brother. The TRUTH will set you FREE!!!

He dresses in the cleanest clothes he can find, reminding himself he will need to do laundry soon. Soon. He picks a wellworn pair of jeans and a hooded sweatshirt he's had as long as he can remember. He doesn't really care about his clothes, but he does care a great deal about the orgonite pendant around his neck. The pendant – previously owned by his mother – shields him from most forms of ELF. He also likes the way it looks. The pendant is eye-catching, he thinks. It's also a lot subtler than a tinfoil helmet. He doesn't want to look like a total crackpot.

He's about to step into the hall when he notices a piece of paper had been slipped under the front door. He picks it up. Sees the signature of the building superintendent, Mr Rahim, beneath two paragraphs of typed text.

He crumples the paper up without reading it. Messages from Mr Rahim are always about elevator outages or the hot water being turned off or some other triviality. JD pitches the ball of paper at the stacks of discarded newspapers in the living room.

JD's brother lives way west of downtown. It's almost a two-hour walk from Country Club Estate, but JD doesn't want to waste money on public transit. Public transit is dangerous. It's not just the slack-jawed sheeple who crowd up the buses. Public transit is full of informants and collaborators and stooges. All in the service of Them. You ride a bus, you never know who's keeping tabs on you. JD walks instead.

He's fortunate the day is clear and warm. More summer than fall. He heads steadily west along Franklin Boulevard. The tiny ethnic groceries and nail salons and pawnshops and fast food joints of his neighbourhood give way to the near edge of downtown. The buildings get taller. Shinier. The sheeple here are higher-up types, clad in suits, carrying briefcases. They're too glued to their smartphones – and whatever subliminal messages their smartphones are spiking into their heads – to pay JD any heed.

He stays on Franklin. As he passes the Van Lathan Building, he comes in sight of Civic Park. The park is huge, almost three hundred acres, marking the bullseye centre of the city. The south half of the park is dominated by a large wooded hill over a municipal reservoir. The north half of the park is flat terrain. On an ordinary day, you'd see sheeple jogging on the footpaths through the park. Kids at the various playgrounds. Picnics on the rolling lawns. But something different is happening today. JD hears it before he sees anything. Sounds like a continuous roll of thunder, rising above the normal cacophony of the streets. The noise is felt more than heard. JD's pulse quickens. He picks up his pace.

Traffic on Franklin, and Monarch Avenue along the east side of the park, is almost at a standstill. Spectators crowd the sidewalk. JD peers. The park is enclosed by a wrought-iron fence, but beyond the fence and the spectators he can make out some kind of campground. A few dozen tents of various shapes and sizes, pitched across the lawns. Maybe a hundred people moving among the tents. Banners and flags hoisted in the air above. The biggest banner of all, fluttering on a pole over the makeshift tent city, is a massive blue rectangle with bright white lettering on it: 99TOGETHER!

As he gets closer, the thunderous sound resolves into individual noises. Drumbeats. Someone speaking on a bullhorn, crowd-voices chanting in response. He isn't close enough yet to make out the words. Numerous drivers are honking their horns, whether enraged at the gridlock or in a show of support for this demonstration, whatever it is, JD can't tell.

There are cops. Of course there are cops. A dozen of them. Some on bikes, some on foot. Patrolling the edge of the park, standing guard near the tent city.

JD gets closer. He crosses Monarch where it intersects Franklin. Now he can hear the bullhorn and the voices chanting in response.

"Together, united!"

"The 99 are undivided!"

JD moves among the spectators on the sidewalk until he gets to Civic Park's north gate. He's half-expecting cops to block access at the gate, but they're keeping their distance. He's free to enter. No invitation required. From the gate it's only a short distance into the tent city.

He enters. The crowd closes around him. He sees a hippie playing a guitar. A woman nursing a baby. An older man waving a placard that says For Sale: America. Not far away is an improvised library, little more than a pile of books on a blanket. Across from that is a big tent with a cardboard sign reading 1st Aid. A dense smell of people packed close together hangs in the air.

The bullhorn, "Together, united!"

The crowd, "The 99 are undivided!"

JD comes across three people in dark hoodies. Faces concealed behind identical plastic masks. A grinning man with arched eyebrows and a pencil-thin moustache. JD feels like he's seen that mask in a movie or a comic book somewhere. The masks lend their wearers an air of prankish anonymity. JD can't tell if the mask-wearers are looking at him, but then one of them thrusts a pamphlet into his hands. "Solidarity, man," he says.

JD looks down at the pamphlet. Bold black letters scream up at him: Bringing down the walls ~ the slow death of colonialism. JD smiles. He folds the pamphlet and puts it in his pocket. He smiles. "Solidarity," he says.

Deeper into the tent city. After a round of applause, the bullhorn takes a break. The drums are still at work. Drums and music and singing. Many voices in conversation. A sense of purpose. JD comes upon a small group of people painting faces onto giant papier mache figures. The figures look like politicians and CEOs and bankers. Or government agents. Men in black. Them. JD lingers for a while to admire the painting. Then he notices two cops watching from a small playground fifty feet away. The cops have expressionless faces, eyes concealed behind sunglasses. They might be observing the painting of the effigies. Or they might be observing JD himself.

He gives them a little wave. No response. He grins and scratches his nose with his middle finger. Still nothing. He takes his pipe out of his inside pocket. Tamps a little bit of weed into the bowl. Looking straight at the cops, he lights up. Takes a drag. He exhales slowly, then tips his trilby. Nothing happens. The cops stand their ground, blank-faced. Robotic.

"That smells good," someone says. "Are you sharing?"

JD pulls his attention away from the cops. One of the painters has turned around from the effigies. She's his age, maybe a bit younger. Wearing a skirt and a jean jacket hanging open over a t-shirt with an Om symbol on it. Her hair is short, dyed purple. There's a small stud in her nose. He hands her his pipe and lighter. She holds the flame to the bowl and takes a long toke and coughs a little.

"Thanks," she says.

JD takes the pipe back and has a hit of his own. All at once he can feel the world spinning around them. He can feel huge, invisible forces at work. Not Them, he thinks. No. This is something more ... benevolent. Something touched with a faint lining of hope.

"We're really bringing down the walls here, aren't we," says JD. "It's the slow death of, you know, colonialism. The slow death of the whole system."

She laughs. "Right on. Hey, I'm—"

(It's better if I don't use her real name, Mr Emmerich. Purposes of safety and what-have-you, especially seeing as her and myself are going to rekindle our flame one of these days, now that I'm quote-unquote better and all. I'll call her, let me see, Simone.)

"—Simone, by the way. Thanks for the ganja."

She sticks out her hand. JD shakes it and tells her his own name.

A little fellow with long hair appears from a tent nearby. "Hey Simone," he says, and then seeing JD he shuts up. He's likely intimidated. That's not JD's fault. He has this effect on a lot of people.

"This is my buddy," says Simone.

(Again, Mr Emmerich, certain identities must remain classified, so let's call him Tiny Tim. Tiny Tim the friend, Tiny Tim the constant pain in my ass).

"He's a performance artist," Simone adds. "All these effigies are his."

Tiny Tim does not take his eyes off JD. But he does allow JD to shake his hand. The skin of Tiny Tim's hand is soft and moist.

"We've got to go," says Tiny Tim. "The camp committee says the city is talking about an eviction notice."

"Well, that didn't take long," says Simone. Tiny Tim ducks into the crowd. She starts to follow him, but then she turns back to JD. "Hey, if you're back this way, come say hi."

After she's gone, JD turns back around to see if the cops are still observing, but the cops have also moved on. JD is disappointed.

It's almost sundown when JD gets to his brother's house. The warm weather of the afternoon is cooling off. His brother's house is in what was a working-class neighbourhood. Many of the small bungalows on the street have been torn down to make way for modern dwellings. JD's brother's little place is still one of the old ones, a brownbrick ranch-style with a single-car garage.

JD's brother can't afford to tear the house down and build something new. Instead, he's always renovating or putting new shingles on the roof or repainting the trim. JD has heard his brother say things like "starter home" and "investment property". As far as JD can tell, home-owning is just another kind of slavery. JD loves his brother, but he does not envy him.

Two cars and one motorbike are parked in the driveway. There's music coming from around back. Voices. A barbecue aroma on the air. JD's stomach rumbles. He realizes he hasn't eaten since he isn't even sure. JD goes around back. The backyard has a small lawn and a patio composed of wonky paving stones. An outdoor table and umbrella. Four plastic chairs, all occupied. Classic rock is coming from a set of speakers mounted on the rear wall of the house. Five kids, including JD's two nephews, are chasing a Frisbee around on the grass.

JD's brother's wife – the Harpy Herself – is serving drinks in plastic cups. JD's brother is flipping burgers on the grill.

JD crosses over to the patio. He's about to yell some kind of standard salutation. Perhaps, Happy birthday, you old fart. Then he sees the Harpy Herself eyeing him with her mouth half-open.

JD's brother turns around from the barbecue. "So who's hungry—Oh. Hey."

JD offers a little salute. "Happy birthday, you old fart."

The Harpy Herself sends one of the kids to get an extra chair from inside. Then she gives JD a quick hug. JD's brother sets down the barbecue tongs and puts his arms around him and gives him a genuine squeeze.

"Didn't think I'd see you."

"Surprised?" says JD.

"Well ..." JD's brother and the Harpy Herself trade a quick glance. "Anyways it's good to have you. Sit down. We got lots of food."

The guests at the table make room. JD squeezes in. He's introduced around. Next to JD is a big man who runs a towing company. Next is Tow Trucker's wife. She teaches night school at Alliance College. Across the table is an Italian guy. Soccer fan, judging by the jersey he's wearing. His girlfriend, sitting beside him, might be an off-duty stripper.

JD tunes out their names. He doubts they'll have much to talk about. These people will surely ask him what he does, because that's a standard sheeple conversation-starter. What do you do? What's your line of work? As if some nine-to-five gauntlet is what defines humanity.

He'll have to say his work is secret. Classified.

JD's brother works as a plumber, so in this world, that's who he is. He has his own business, and he's made enough to buy this bungalow. He's even offered JD a job on occasion. Menial stuff. Sweeping up on jobsites. Toting toolboxes or bundles of pipes. Thanks but no thanks.

Brother serves up a couple of sausages on a paper plate. There are big dishes of macaroni salad and potato chips on the table. The Harpy brings JD a beer. He thanks her. She gives him a smile. She looks like she's about to say something, but then she sits down and digs into her own supper.

The meal goes on. As it turns out, nobody asks JD what he does. Nobody asks him much of anything. Most of the talk around the table is sports and TV shows and what amazing things their kids are all doing.

After a little while the Harpy serves another round. As she's giving JD a new beer she says, "We saw Daniel a few days ago."

(The last of the codenames, Mr Emmerich, the last of the, what do you call them, aliases. Daniel. The last, and the most important of all.)

Food catches at the back of JD's throat. He swallows it down with a mouthful of beer. "Oh yes?" he says.

The Harpy's eyes brighten in a funny way. She's weaving on her feet a little. "Yeah," she says. "Lil brought him over and—"

"And he's growing like a weed," says JD's brother. "And he's doing amazing at school. You'd be proud of him, bro."

"Who's Daniel?" says the off-duty stripper.

"Daniel is my son," says JD. "That's all you need to know. The rest is private personal information, thank you very kindly."

A quiet moment. Tow Trucker clears his throat. The off-duty stripper looks at her fingernails. JD smiles at everyone around the table, making a point to look each of them in the eye.

Overhead the sky is full dark now. JD's brother has installed garden lights around the edge of the small yard. They cast a sickly, artificial glow, as if the frequency of the lightwaves was designed to nauseate. They're also putting out ELF. It's low-key, but intense enough to bypass the faraday shield in JD's trilby. He winces. Stands up.

"I think I'll use the washroom," he says.

"You know where it is," says the Harpy.

JD goes inside through the patio door. His brother has redone the kitchen since JD was last here. New cupboards, new countertops. JD imagines the pricetags attached to everything. Maybe if JD destroyed it all, his brother would be set free.

On the hallway wall off the kitchen is a slogan in big curlicued decals: Live Love Laugh. Underneath, a bunch of framed pictures. Most of them are the Harpy's family, who JD only met at the wedding. He can't remember any of their names. Doesn't care to. But there's also a picture of Granddad. A cigarette in one hand, grinning from the service window of his ice cream truck.

Beside Granddad is a picture of JD's mother, back when she was twenty-five. A glamour studio picture. Soft focus. Big feathered hair, as was the style of the time. She is holding one hand up to her face and about her wrist is a bracelet of crystal beads, garnet and tiger's eye and moonstone. From her ears hang tiny shards of amethyst. And at her neck a certain pendant of pale blue orgonite.

She looks beautiful in the picture. When JD was very young, a talent agent stopped his mother on the street. Mom could be the next Janice Dickinson, the agent said. On the agent's advice, Mom had glamour studio portraits taken. She had the photography done with her own money, but the agent assured her it was worth it. Investing in yourself, he said. The photos landed her some work. Catalogue ads, that kind of thing. It was better than what she was already doing, flipping burgers at a fast food joint.

Next to their mother is a picture of JD and his brother as kids, arms slung around each other. In those days, JD was his brother's protector.

There are no other pictures of JD. No pictures of Daniel either.

JD takes his wallet out of his pocket. Inside is a picture of JD and Daniel. Halloween, back when the boy was three, when JD and Lil still lived together.

They'd gone to Value Village and put together a costume. JD dressed up as a kind of half-man, half-dragon. Daniel was a knight in cardboard armour riding on JD's back. The picture in the wallet is getting dog-eared, but JD looks at it often. It shows him a time before They really started to fuck around with his life.

The washroom when JD goes into it also looks like it's been redone. It smells like new paint and potpourri. There are two hand towels, His and Hers embroidered on them. The mirror over the sink is a cabinet, same as at Granddad's. JD opens it.

The cabinet contains the usual knickknacks. Toothbrushes, boxes of soap, bandages. On the top shelf, an orange plastic pill bottle. JD picks it up. Reads his brother's name, reads the words Seroquel, 100mg, thirty tablets. He shakes his head, once more feeling that intense pity for his younger sibling.

If he was still acting as a protector, JD would save his brother from the clutches of Big Pharma. Dump those thirty Seroquel tablets down the toilet.

Same as JD did with his own so-called medication.

When JD returns to the back yard, they're serving a birthday cake and singing. He arrives in time to add Happy birthday baby brother to the chorus. JD's brother makes a big show of blowing out the candles. He looks like a little kid again.

JD sits back down at the table. The Harpy passes JD a plate with a drooping-over wedge of cake on it. "We'll send you home with leftovers," she says.

There are gifts for JD's brother. A set of baseball tickets from one of the couples at the table. JD's brother hugs them both. Next is a bottle of expensive scotch. After that, a satellite radio subscription from Tow Trucker. JD cringes. Satellite radio is lousy with ELF, but he doubts his brother would understand.

The Harpy gives Brother a card. He reads it and his face goes red. The Harpy gives everyone at the table a great big wink. She says, "This gift is for later, when you guys have gone home and the kids are in bed." Everyone laughs.

The time has come for JD to present his offering. He takes the paperback out of his patch pocket and hands it over.

His brother peers at the cover. "Levi ..."

"Leviathan Illuminatus," says JD. "I don't want to do any spoiler alerts, but it's pretty mindbending stuff. If you open up to it. Oh, it's also actually a whole trilogy right there in your hands. You're pretty much getting three gifts in one."

His brother turns the book over. Glances at the blurb on the back. Then he puts it down next to the scotch. "I'll crack into it tonight," he says.

After the gifts, another round of drinks is served. JD wants to smoke some weed but decides against it. He doesn't want to share with people who won't appreciate it. Not like that beautiful woman he met at Civic Park earlier.

"I was downtown today," says Tow Trucker, "and at Civic Park I seen this campout, a hippie commune or something. Bunch of tents. Who knows what they're bitching about. I wanted to roll down my window and tell them all to get frickin jobs."

A chill passes over JD.

"It's called 99 Together," says the off-duty stripper. "It's a protest. I've been reading about it online, and I don't know, man, I think they've got some good points. Like how one percent of the population controls all the wealth and jobs, shit like that, while the rest of us fall into the other ninety-nine percent. We don't have any say on how things are done. Or like how nobody went to jail over the Recession back in 08. The whole protest started in New York City a few weeks ago, but it's popping up all over the place ..."

The off-duty stripper is dropping truth, but JD is studying Tow Trucker. JD knows They have agents everywhere. Collaborators. Informants. Snitches, whose sole job it is to keep tabs on the misfits. Misfits like JD. The collaborators all report to some sinister headquarters hidden deep inside the Pentagon. Or the Great Pyramids. Or UN concentration camps like the ones they talked about on Full Disclosure.

The ELF coming from the garden lights intensifies. Fingernails on a chalkboard. JD closes his eyes.

"Hey, you okay?"

Brother's voice. JD opens his eyes. Everyone at the table is looking at him.

"If you want to know what we're doing at Civic Park," says JD, "we're bringing down the walls. It's the slow death of the whole system. Together and united."

The off-duty stripper looks impressed. "You're part of 99 Together?"

"My lady, I'm one of the main people down there."

The Harpy says, "I take it that means you haven't been looking for wo—Oh, never mind. It's none of my business. Hey, who thinks it's time for another mojito?"

At ten o'clock JD is standing in his brother's driveway. He's the last to leave. The Harpy is inside, cleaning up. The kids are in bed. Brother comes out the front door, carrying a plastic bag. Wobbles as he walks. "Cab's on its way."

"I told you that was not necessary," says JD.

"I would've drove you home myself, but I'm too shitfaced. Here. Leftovers."

He holds the plastic bag out. JD takes it. He studies his brother's face. His eyes.

"What's the matter?"

"Nothing."

"Tell me."

"No ... I just ... Like I'm glad you came, bro. It was a surprise."

"You thought I'd forget," says JD. "Or I'd skip out. Or god knows what."

"Nothing like that," his brother says. "But ... you wouldn't come to get money or a bite to eat or—"

JD laughs. "I should beat you for even suggesting such a thing."

"I know. I'm sorry. Here's your ride. It's already paid for so don't worry."

A taxi is slowing to a stop at the foot of the driveway. "I'll see you soon," says JD. "Happy birthday, you old fart. Thirty-six. My god."

"Makes you almost forty."

JD smiles. "And twice ... no, three times ... the man I ever was. See you soon. Oh, and Granddad says happy birthday. He wanted to be here but you know how it is."

This isn't true. JD hasn't received any encoded messages about his brother's birthday from Granddad.

Brother's face, half in the glow of a streetlight, changes a little. He starts to say something, but the Harpy comes out on the stoop. Yells for him to come inside if he ever wants to collect his special gift. He turns and runs for it, waving at JD over his shoulder.

JD gets in the taxi. The driver is yammering away in a foreign tongue on a wireless headset. JD feels the ELF emanating from the gadget. Dreads to think what that ELF might be pumping into the driver's head. Ram that pedestrian. Drive into that telephone pole.

It should come as no surprise that the person who became John Doe #2 never had much patience for school (what's school, Mr Emmerich, but a sheeple factory?). JD was too smart for the nonsense they tried to ram down his throat.

This became especially clear when he got to high school. His teachers were always wringing their hands. Saying things like, If you just apply yourself, you'd ace this. Or, You have to concentrate a little more. Or, Can't you even try to take this seriously?

On one occasion, a social studies teacher told JD he had a perplexing sense of superi— super—superioriness? Was that the word? No matter. As JD saw it, if the shoe fit. And, indeed, if that shoe was superior.

He didn't care about socializing with his peers. Cretins, most of them. Didn't bother him that he was never invited to their parties. Didn't bother him in the least. He even chided his brother when his brother started to buy into those things. Popularity, parties. The circus of adolescence.

In grade twelve JD got in serious trouble when the principal searched his locker – apparently on an anonymous tip – and found a katana. A beautiful piece of weapons craftsmanship from Japan.

JD had purchased the katana from Gibson's Surplus & More on Westway Boulevard. He was only storing it in his locker until it was convenient to take it home. He didn't have any dangerous plans for it, as the principal suggested. The principal threatened to get the cops involved, but JD made things easy. He quit. Walked out of that school without a second thought.

His only regret was that he never got the katana back. It really was beautiful craftsmanship.

Before JD left, the principal said, "We all know you've had a difficult life at home, but that's no excuse for your hostility with everybody."

As if the principal, or any of those arrogant teachers, or anyone, knew what real school – the school of hard knocks – was all about.

JD knew, because JD lived it. JD graduated from the school of hard knocks. It was the only formal education he ever needed.

At the time JD quit high school, he'd been living with Granddad for the better part of a decade. Granddad wasn't just himself a student of the school of hard knocks. He was headmaster.

In Granddad's early days he'd been in the navy. Some high-up position he couldn't talk about, something to do with secret submarines. Then he'd made money as a professional boxer. He often told JD about his friendship with George Chuvalo and Muhammad Ali. Granddad knew the people who'd invented the internet. He knew what to do in case of a nuclear attack by the Soviets.

Most importantly, Granddad saw right through the system.

"Don't believe the bullshit, bucko. The game's rigged right from the get-go. You can't win, but if you're gonna survive, you gotta play by your own rules."

Granddad said this in the 80s, when everything was sportscars and stock markets. Sheeple were trying to live out that movie Wall Street, but not Granddad. He was working as a nighttime security guard down at the Reliant Intermodal container yard in the south part of Middleton.

This wasn't long after JD had gone to live with him. After what happened to their mother, JD went with Granddad while his brother went with their grandmother.

Granddad took JD to work with him every night. All the other kids, JD's brother included, were coming home from their music lessons and team sports. JD was in an office trailer at the edge of the container yard, learning the ways of the world.

The trailer was beat-up inside. Posters of less-than-tasteful nudes. A mini-fridge full of spoiled food. A noisy heater. Still, it was cozy. If it was a school night, Granddad would roll out a sleeping bag and try to get JD to sleep for a while, but even then JD was most alive after dark.

Instead of sleeping, JD would help Granddad fill out his paperwork. Or he'd pour Granddad drinks from the bottle of Johnnie Walker Granddad kept in their lunchbox.

Sometimes people came by to visit. On these occasions Granddad would make JD hide in the closet at the end of the trailer. JD would peek out the crack between the door and the frame. The usual visitors were a small crew of Eastern European guys. They'd come into the trailer and smoke cigarettes and tell dirty jokes with Granddad. Granddad said they were connections of his from his navy days.

After half an hour of the jokes and cigarettes, Granddad would write something down on a scrap of paper. Hand it to the visitors. In return they'd give him money in a paper bag. JD was no fool. He knew Granddad was giving his connections the location of various truck containers. Containers whose contents needed to go missing. Electronics, mainly.

Granddad even explained it to JD once. "Here's the thing, bucko. You go into a store and you pinch a candy bar, well, that's wrong. The store owner is a little-time guy like you and me. I'll smack your ass for that. But when things belonging to the rich, you know, specially some overseas Jap company, happen to fall off a truck, that's not so wrong. That's redistribution of the chips in a rigged game, you see?"

There were other visitors. A pair of dirty cops. When they came to visit, Granddad didn't make JD hide in the closet, because he didn't invite the cops into the trailer at all. He would go outside to see them. To give them their due. Cash in another paper bag. He never talked about how much it was. He would only come back into the trailer and grumble and make JD pour him a drink.

The radio was always playing in the trailer on those long nights. Granddad liked country, but as time went on he listened more and more to a certain AM station.

He particularly liked Full Disclosure. In those days, the show played overnight. Gilbert Emmerich was only a co-host. But the content was the same. Expert interviews. Listener call-ins. UFOs. Alien abductions. Paranormal phenomena. Psychics. Area 51. Crop circles. Secret technological advances. Most of all, sinister government cover-ups.

Even now JD remembers some of the call-ins he heard on Full Disclosure back then.

My name is George, first time caller, and, uh, I know this is gonna sound weird, but, I've been infested by a demon, and he wants me to be a communist …

Yeah, this is Pete from Clarendon, and I seen it first hand myself, okay? The police aren't there to help any of us, they're just paid thugs for the New World Order, and they're seizing our liberty ...

I can't tell you my name, can't take the risk, but I'm callin tonight from way out in the sticks, and I don't have a lot of time. My position is bein triangulated right now. There are interdimensional aliens who are planning on wiping out the major population centres ...

JD pictured the callers. Lurking in phonebooths in the dead of night. Reaching for anything to help them reveal the hidden truths. They'd seen things the vast majority of sheeple never had to. Didn't take long before Full Disclosure was the only thing JD wanted to listen to.

On the best nights Granddad would take JD on his patrols around the yard. He'd let JD scout ahead. JD would use cover of darkness to check out the stacks of containers and the forklift cabs. Then Granddad would catch up, cutting through the shadows with his big flashlight. They'd take turns launching rocks at raccoons.

One time they found a Mercedes near the front gate. The driver was getting head from a teenage guy. Granddad made JD stay back, then he snuck up on the car. Smashed his flashlight into the rear window. Broke the glass.

"Get the hell outta here, you fuckin pervert!" Granddad hollered.

The man booted the teenage guy out the passenger door and drove off so quickly his tires smoked. Before the teenage guy could say anything, Granddad put the run on him too, holding his flashlight up like a cudgel.

"You too, get outta here! You think I want my grandson catching your AIDS?"

Beyond the fence, all the buildings downtown were lit up against the night sky. For the first time, JD wondered if interdimensional aliens were in fact planning on wiping everything out. The idea wasn't half bad.

As long as they spared JD and Granddad.

It was winter, he was eleven. Christmas lights everywhere. One snowy night he and Granddad were in the office trailer, the heater going full-blast. Granddad was drinking his Johnnie Walker. JD was reading a Conan book. On the radio was Full Disclosure. Some retired fighter pilot talking being chased for a thousand miles in his F-15 by a giant glowing orb.

At two o'clock in the morning, headlights shone through the little window. For a second JD thought the aliens had arrived. Then a horn honked. Granddad got up and looked outside.

"Ah, for Chrissake," he said. "You stay here."

If Granddad was making JD stay inside the trailer, that meant it was the dirty cops. The cops hadn't visited in a while. Much longer than usual. Granddad put on his winter coat, the one with the reflective panels, and went outside. JD turned back to his book.

Then JD heard yelling. At first he ignored it, but it kept on. He dragged a chair over to the window. Climbed up. Looked outside.

The two cops were leaning against their patrol car. Granddad was the one yelling.

"I didn't gyp yous out of nothing, it's not my fault if you're too dumb to count—"

The two cops glanced at each other. One of them shrugged. Then they hauled out their nightsticks and laid into Granddad. Granddad fought back, used all his old boxing tricks, but in the end he couldn't win. You can't win in a rigged game.

JD jumped down and pulled open the door and ran outside. The cops had stopped their persecution. Granddad was lying in the snow at their feet. His eyebrow was split. Blood running down his face. Blood on his teeth.

One of the cops saw JD and said, "Shit, man, let's go. I don't like dealing with some old rummy in front of a kid, personally."

The other cop scowled and said to Granddad, "Start making good with us or find somewhere else to work. It'll only get worse."

Then they got into their patrol car. Drove away.

JD helped Granddad out of the snow and into the trailer.

"Get me a drink," he said. "You know how they say a policeman's your friend? Well it's just more bullshit, bucko."

JD nodded. "The police are paid thugs for the New World Order."

Granddad gave JD a half-sharp, half-amused look. Blood was still trickling out of his brow. "The hell did you hear that?" he said. "Maybe I need to quit letting you listen to the radio with me. Jesus, maybe I need to quit hanging my hat here at all."

It wasn't fair, what those cops, those New World Order thugs, did to Granddad that night. It did not happen just because. There is no just because.

Soon after, Granddad quit working at Reliant Intermodal. He moved on to a job as a watchman at a construction site. Here, too, he made a little extra money letting the odd toolbox or bundle of materials go missing. It was okay. The construction site was run by a big multinational conglomerate.

Granddad only took JD with him to his new job for a month before his boss found out about it. After that, Granddad had to leave JD at home. JD would stay in the apartment, reading on his own, listening to Full Disclosure. He would conduct hourly patrols from room to room. Make sure no paranormal or extraterrestrial phenomena was happening. But he missed spending his nights with Granddad. That's the kind of education you can't buy anywhere.

By the time JD quit grade twelve, Granddad was working security at a shopping mall. He ended up falling down an escalator. Broke his leg and pelvis. It was written off as an accident, but Granddad insisted some punks had pushed him. He ended up on permanent disability. He supplemented the disability with cash when he got his ice cream truck a few years later.

"Cash is something you can fall back on if the system screws you over," Granddad said. "And believe me when I tell you, the system will do whatever it can to screw you over."

Now, in the cab, JD opens the bag his brother gave him. He sees three sausages wrapped in cellophane. A slice of cake in a plastic container. He also sees something rolled and held together with an elastic. He picks it up, pulls the elastic off.

He counts two twenty-dollar bills, six tens.

All he can do is shake his head sadly. Then he drops the money into his inside pocket.

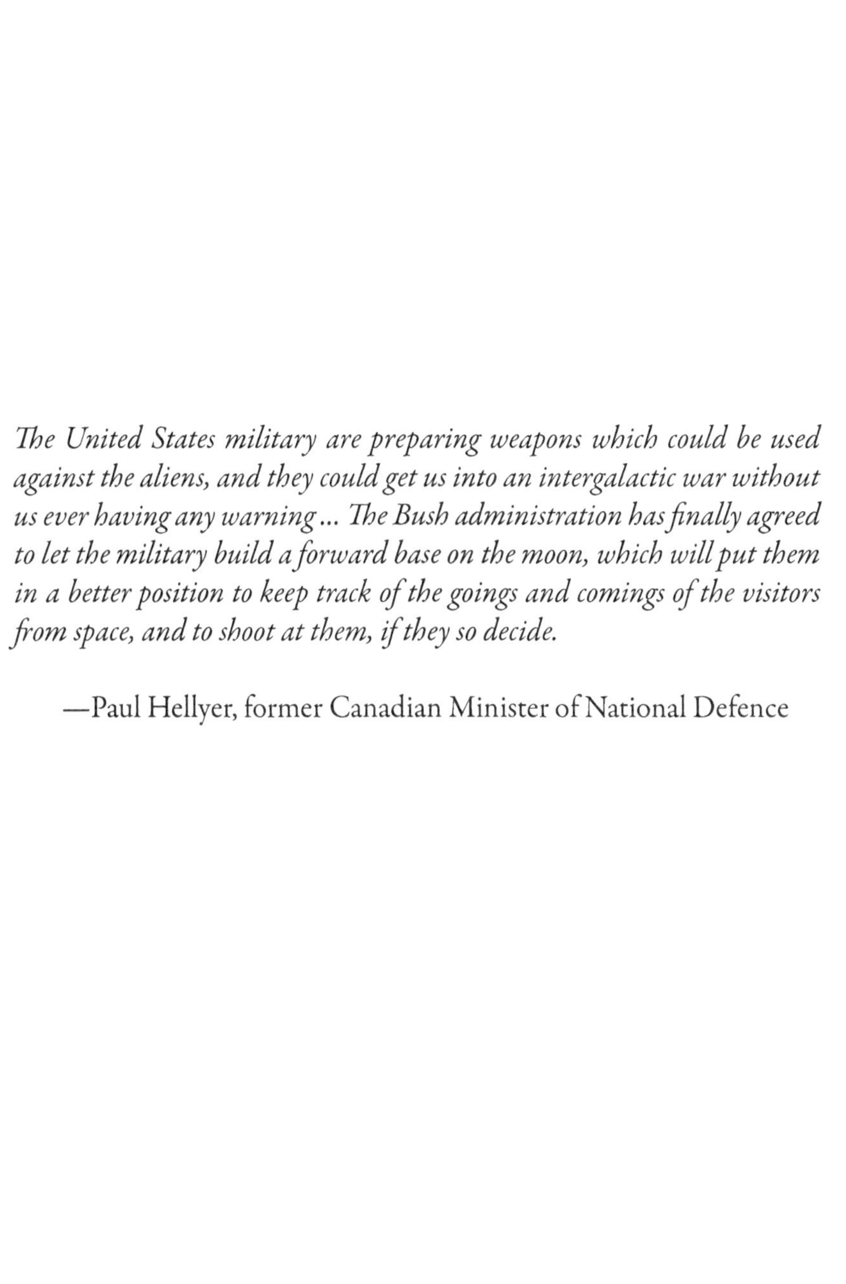

The United States military are preparing weapons which could be used against the aliens, and they could get us into an intergalactic war without us ever having any warning ... The Bush administration has finally agreed to let the military build a forward base on the moon, which will put them in a better position to keep track of the goings and comings of the visitors from space, and to shoot at them, if they so decide.

—Paul Hellyer, former Canadian Minister of National Defence

2: In Praise of the New Knighthood

[Transcribed from *Full Disclosure with Gilbert Emmerich*, AM 710, October 10, 2015.]

Gilbert Emmerich: This next hour of the show is brought to you by Fluor-O-Zap toothpaste. In addition to using patented silver nanoparticles, Fluor-O-Zap is made with totally organic compounds, well-known to healers since biblical times. Fluor-O-Zap will eliminate any fluoride in your water, thus protecting you from senseless chemical contamination.

Anyway, we're back with a caller we had a couple weeks ago. Somebody who has generated more interest and controversy than we've seen in a long time. It's mindblowing, really. I've told my producer to put him through right away if he calls. Which, I'm happy as hell to say, he has.

If you haven't guessed who I'm talking about, it's our very own 11/3/11 mystery man, John Doe # 2 himself. Are you there, Johnny?

Caller: I'm here, Mr Emmerich.

GE: Great to have you back. You caused a hell of a ruckus when we had you on last. Our phone was ringing off the hook for a week straight. Our webmaster had to shut down our comment forum. Did you see any of the comments, by the way?

Caller: No, Mr Emmerich. I still stay away from the internet.

GE: Can't blame you for that, Johnny. Well, as you can imagine, people had a lot to say. Oh, sure, you had a lot of doubters. A lot of haters. But you had a lot of supporters, too, my man.

Caller: What about you, Mr Emmerich? Are you a doubter?

GE: My jury's still out on that, Johnny. But I'll tell you one thing. I'm real interested in what else you got to say. You really had me hooked last time, when you told us about how you met Richard Declan in jail. Can you remind us where you worked when you met Dr Declan?

Caller: … I didn't have a quote-unquote job at that time, Mr Emmerich. Except for driving my granddad's ice cream truck, which hadn't been—

GE: Ah yes, your granddad. You told us a lot about him last time we talked. He was a Full Disclosure listener, wasn't he? Smart fella, your granddad. You told us a lot about him. You told us a lot about your brother and your sister-in-law. You told us about 99Together, some little sweetheart you met down there. But you didn't tell us much more about Dr Declan, or how you got involved with 11/3/11. And I got to be honest with you, Johnny, as interesting as you might be, people are tuning in to hear about 11/3/11.

Caller: I'll admit I got off on a tangent.

GE: Well, let's get you back on track, Johnny Doe Numero Two. Let's hear about your first meeting with the Patriot Bloc.

Tell me who this guy is again?" says JD's brother.

JD and his brother are in his brother's car.

"Dr Richard Declan," says JD.

"Richard Declan."

"Dr Richard Declan."

"I feel like I know that name. Heard it somewhere. Did he have a TV show?"

"It's possible," says JD. "I don't watch television, of course. Anyway, Dr Declan is a very respected thinker. That's why I'm going to see him."

"Does this have to do with that group in Civic Park? The 99?"

"You mean 99 Together? No. This is a different … ah … undertaking."

"You got a lot going on, bro," says JD's brother. "That's great. Outside of work I barely have time to take a leak."

JD nods. His attention is taken up by whatever lies ahead. The biweekly Patriot Bloc meeting. It's Thursday, October 6.

They're driving through the fringes of Bayfield. They pass the small campus surrounding Alliance College, where JD's brother did his plumbing course. After Alliance is a shopping plaza.

On a small knoll on the far side of the plaza is a small, one-storey brick building. The front of the building is nondescript, except for a small signboard reading: AM 710: Home of Full Disclosure. Rising from behind the building is a red and white radio tower. There's a man smoking outside, propping the building's front door open with his shoe. Gilbert Emmerich himself? Maybe. JD watches as they pass by.

Several minutes later they turn onto Side Road 10, pass beyond the suburbs, move into the sticks. JD watches the addresses. He's looking for 23468 Side Road 10.

Every so often, he sees glass bus shelters by the side of the road. BayTrans reaches this far into the sticks, but he can't imagine how long and miserable that bus ride would be. Better to do what he did that afternoon. Call his brother on a payphone, suffering through intense ELF from the handset, and ask for a ride.

His brother sounded doubtful when JD called. Harried with work. The Harpy did the books for the plumbing business, and she kept close tabs on his mileage. If she knew he was driving way the hell out of the city on company time … But JD pressed, and his brother finally agreed.

Now here they are, in the car together. Making conversation. JD's brother talks about his business, his friends, his sons. Small talk.

JD smiles and nods, thinking his own thoughts. He smoked a bowl before he left Country Club Estate. He had to refill his stash yesterday. Or was it the day before? Had to visit Sean at the fountain. Sean's crew sold him six grams. Charged eighty dollars for it.

Times is hard, Ice Cream Man, that's why we gotta mark it up.

JD's stash is replenished, but his money is almost gone. Very hard times indeed.

"Don't get me wrong," says JD's brother. "We're glad you came."

"Glad I came where?" says JD.

His brother looks at him. "My birthday. We were surprised you made it out. That's all I'm saying." His brother trails off. A few seconds elapse. Then, "I know a lot's been going on with you, bro. A lot of heavy shit. I get ... I get worried about you sometimes. I don't mean that to sound, whatever, but I get worried about you."

"Last time I checked," says JD, "I'm the elder brother in this arrangement. So the worrying, as with almost everything, of course, is my responsibility."

Another few seconds go by. His brother nods. "Fair enough."

They are way up Side Road 10 now. On either side of the road are hardwoods turning colour with the fall. There is a quarry, a flea market, an old one-room church. JD watches the address numbers on the driveways.

23440, 23444.

Houses here have mailboxes and big front lawns, dogs racing out to bark at the passing car.

23456.

They come to a thick stand of trees. Even with the leaves going yellow and thinning out, the foliage is still dense enough to obscure the property beyond. Then the hardwood breaks and there's a long wall of stark gray cinderblock running parallel to the road. The wall is six feet high. Up ahead there's a turn-in over a small culvert.

The number on the post is 23468. This is it.

JD's brother slows. He actually steps on the brake pedal, maybe out of nervousness. His car gives a slight fishtail as it comes to a stop. JD looks out the passenger window at a wide gate of corrugated sheetmetal. Somebody's gone to the trouble of putting a coat of white paint on the gate, but that's about as decorated as it gets. The only other ornaments are four signs mounted on the cinderblock gateposts.

Private Property.

Absolutely No Trespassing.

No Solicitors, Loiterers, Salespeople.

Residents & Invited Persons Only.

JD's eyes light on the second part of that last sign. Invited Persons Only. He feels something, a sensation he can't name, and for the briefest of instances the constant buzz of ELF cuts out altogether. His head goes silent.

Until his brother says, "You sure about this?"

"As sure as they faked the moon landing."

"How will you get back into the city?"

JD turns in his seat. Smiles at his brother. Pats his forearm. "My friends will take care of me."

His brother gives him a look. A fearful sheeple getting a glimpse beyond the edge of his carefully maintained worldview. He looks like he might say something. Maybe, Why don't you forget it. Maybe, Why don't you come back to my place, we'll give you some supper. Instead, after a moment, he just shrugs.

"Thank you, kind sir, for the ride," says JD.

JD gets out of the car. Approaches the gate. He lifts his knuckle to knock on the metal when he notices a small metal intercom recessed into one of the gateposts. He hesitates before pushing the button, not relishing the electromagnetic zap he's sure to feel.

He pushes the button. No zap. The wiring here is shielded. Good. There's a melodic chime, then there's silence. JD waits. His brother is still parked behind him. Watching. JD can feel him.

A woman's voice comes through the intercom. "Can I help you." Not a question.

"I'm here for the meeting."

"What meeting?"

JD's mouth opens, and closes. Did the meeting have a name? Did he forget? He glances at the sign on the gatepost again. Invited Persons Only.

"Dr Declan invited me."

"I doubt that. There's no such individual at this premises, buddy."

"He did. He—"

There's a rustling noise on the other end of the intercom. What follows is Declan's voice. At first it sounds like he's talking to the woman, whoever she is. "... no reason to hide," Declan says, then, "Can I help you?"

This time it is a question.

"Dr Declan," says JD. "It's me."

JD says his real name. He almost adds the words from jail but catches himself.

There's a pause, then Declan gives a cool little laugh. "My friend. You found us. I had a feeling you would."

The house is huge, lined with columns. Nearby is a large gravel parking area. Six or seven vehicles parked there. Three of them are pickup trucks. One is a raised jeep with oversized tires.

On the back of the jeep is a decal big enough for JD to read from a distance. A stylized image of the flag waving in the breeze. Underneath the flag: If This Offends You Call 1-800-GTFO-NOW. Past the gravel parking area is an old timberframe barn.

It took JD five minutes to walk up the driveway from the gate. Rolling lawns on either side of the driveway. Thin screens of poplar. It looks like the lawns haven't been cut in some time. The grass is knee-high.

The house also looks neglected. The white paint stripped here and there from the siding. Cracks in the foundation. He can't see a single light in any window. But still, he thinks, this amazing silence. No ELF. Dr Declan has shielded this place.

Invited Persons Only.

If This Offends You Call 1-800-GTFO-Now.

Six crescent-shaped brick steps lead up to the front door. The steps are crooked and heaved, weeds growing up through them. JD is on the second step when the front door opens. A tall man steps out. He's wearing dark trousers and a golf shirt. He's lean, with high cheekbones and a square-shaped jaw and a sandy crewcut. He's wearing glasses with amber-tinted ballistic lenses.

The man smiles. His teeth look like stone blocks. "If I ask you to confirm whether you're an employee of any level of government, law enforcement, the judiciary, the police, the intelligence community, or the armed services, you're bound to disclose. Although if you are a member of the armed services, thank you for your service. So?"

"So?"

"Refer to my last, compadre."

"Oh. No." JD laughs a little. "I'm the last thing from an employee of the government or the judic— the judic— the judges or the army or whatever else."

The tall man smiles again. Those stony teeth. He gestures for JD to come the rest of the way up. Then, still smiling, he frisks JD. He opens JD's wallet and looks at it and gives it back. JD complies with the search. It's part of being an Invited Person.

The man offers a handshake. Introduces himself as Gage Terry. Patriot Bloc Security Director. "And," he adds, "Dr Declan has waived your entry dues. Follow me. The meeting is about to get cracking."

Gage leads JD inside. There's a wide staircase leading to the second floor. A massive chandelier hanging from the ceiling. It's on, but half of the dozen electric candles in the chandelier are burned out or missing. It casts a strange pattern of light on the black-and-white tiled floor of the entryway.

They go into a large, high-ceilinged room off the entryway. There's scuffed wooden paneling on the walls. The room is warm, dense with the presence of bodies and the smell of hot coffee.

JD sees some thirty people. Most of them middleaged white men, seated in four ranks of metal stacking chair. They're all bent in conversation, some of them laughing, some frowning. Some drinking coffee out of styrofoam cups, some eating donuts held in grease-spotted napkins.

There's an old man in a tweed suit in a wheelchair up in the front rank. The man's silver hair is raked sideways across a yellow scalp. The way he's sitting, he might be asleep.

Not far from the man is a lectern. Beside the lectern, a furled flag on a pole. On the wall is a framed portrait of Jesus Christ. Blond-bearded and blue-eyed and fair-skinned, staring off at something. Next to Jesus is a closed door.

Gage grasps JD's arm above the elbow. There's a lot of strength in Gage's grip. A lot of steel. This is something JD respects.

"If you want a refreshment they're here at the back. Get em now, while they're hot."

JD looks at the back of the room. Two six-foot folding tables are standing end-to-end against the wall. The tables are laden with boxes of donuts. A pair of metal coffee urns, a crooked stack of styrofoam cups. JD's stomach gives a low growl. He's not sure when he ate last.

He goes to the tables without hesitation. He's an Invited Person, and Invited Persons are fed and caffeinated. That's common courtesy. He picks up a chocolate-dipped donut. He fills a cup with coffee from one of the urns.

He turns around, just as a hush falls over the room.

The door beside the lectern is being held open by a woman with peroxide-bleached hair. She's got wide, muscular shoulders under a white business blouse. Thick wrestler's legs beneath a gray miniskirt, feet clad in red leather cowboy boots. JD wonders if this is the woman he heard on the intercom.

There's something about the woman – something almost familiar. He wonders if they met in a past life. He finds it hard to take his eyes off her.

A short man in a loose-fitting suit comes out through the door. The man has a thick beard but his head is shaved. He walks with a pronounced limp. He stands beside the lectern. Fixes everyone in the room with a hard expression, one heavy eyebrow arched.

Gage leans in close to JD, whispers, "Why don't you take a seat, compadre."

JD carries his coffee and donut to one of the empty chairs in the fourth row. As he sits, Declan comes through the door at the front.

The last time JD saw him, Declan was clad in a shapeless orange jumpsuit, same as JD. Now the man is wearing pressed trousers, a corduroy blazer, a checkered shirt, and a bowtie. His hair is trimmed and parted to the side. He's got rimless spectacles pushed up on his forehead.

Declan looks sharp. Granddad would be impressed.

Declan pulls his glasses down over his eyes. He grips either side of the lectern. Takes a moment to look over his audience. The last person he looks at is JD. One side of Declan's mouth turns up in a smile. He nods.

A sensation wells up in JD's chest. Pride. Something he hasn't felt in a long time.

What happens next is a meeting. Exactly as advertised, JD supposes. He is also positive They would not like this. Not at all. He glances around the room for any sign of collaborators or informants.

Declan calls the meeting to order. "I know you have questions about recent events," he says, "but I'll save my comments until the end. For now, I hope you'll join me in the anthem and prayer."

Everyone stands, JD included. Even the old man in the wheelchair totters to his feet. JD isn't keen to take his trilby off. In fact he's not keen on the anthem at all, but he goes along with the ceremony. Everyone sings in a warbling collective. Up front, Declan is clutching his chest with his right hand. His eyes are bright and alive.

As soon as the singing finishes, everybody bows their heads. Declan leads the prayer. JD is expecting the Lord's Prayer. The one they used to have in schools, the one his mother used to say when she was going through her Jesus phase.

Instead, Declan offers this: "Heavenly Father, in these dark times we pray that you return your grace to a struggling nation. Bless and protect us, your servants and soldiers, from the many evil forces who would do us harm. Deliver us from the cowards. The unbelievers. The corrupt. The immoral. The idol worshipers. The unpatriotic. The road ahead is hard, but through your grace we will be victorious. Amen."

Everyone sits down. Declan sits beside the man in the wheelchair. The big peroxide-blonde woman takes the lectern. For the next half hour – long enough for JD to drink his coffee and eat his donut and carefully eat all the crumbs out of his napkin – the woman leads the meeting. There are reports from various committees. The man with the thick beard records everything with a small, palm-sized camcorder.

The education and information committee goes first. This comes from a middle-aged woman in a sweatshirt with two kittens on it. She reports that the Patriot Bloc's website has been taken down from the internet.

Next is the voter liaison committee. A skinny man reports that they still have a couple hundred names of local voters in their records. "Real patriots," the man adds. Even if the Middleton school trustee election is over, they can still reach out to these people for petitions.

Next, the faith committee. The same woman in the kitten sweatshirt. This time she reports that the next prayer action hour will be on the tenth at seven o'clock in the evening. They'll be targeting the abortion clinic downtown. "You can do your prayer from your home or office," says the woman. "Even from your car. Just start praying that those satanic doctors will close up shop. Pray for those wayward Jezebels to see the light. Pray for one hour solid, and take comfort knowing all the rest of us are doing it with you from wherever we're at. Easy as pie."

"Next up," says the woman at the lectern, "we got the report from the security committee. Chair recognizes the Security Director."

There is a long moment of silence.

"Chair recognizes the Security Director."

People start to turn in their seats, look around. They're looking at Gage, seated a few chairs down from JD in the same otherwise empty row. Gage's legs are stretched out in front of him and his arms are crossed over his chest and his eyes are closed behind his ballistic glasses.

"Chair recognizes the Security Director!"

Gage's eyes open. He smiles lazily, then stands up. Scratches the back of his head. "Nothin too much to report," he says. "The usual motherhood points. Be aware of your surroundings, be aware of people you're talkin to. If somebody gives you bad juju, trust your gut. You never know who's a snitch for the feds."

JD nods. Sage advice.

"Anyways I got a few points for the executive committee, says Gage, but I'll save that for the private session afterward. Thanks."

Gage sits down. Resumes his stretched-leg posture. He looks like he might nod off again.

"Next up is the treasury committee," says the big woman. "Chair recognizes the treasurer, which is me, and I don't have nothing to report. Okay, let's move on to—"

"Hold it right there, Becca."

The voice has come from a fat man in a shiny two-piece tracksuit in the second row. He stands up, plants his fists on his hips.

The woman frowns. "We're not doing the open forum at this time."

"Well, that's some grade-A malarkey," says the fat man, "because I got some questions need answering."

The short bald man lowers his camcorder. "Sit down, Gavin," he snarls. "The chair isn't recognizing you right now. Don't recognize him, Becca."

"The chair isn't recognizing you, Gavin," says Becca.

The fat man, Gavin, turns red. Even from where JD is sitting, he can see sweat on Gavin's forehead.

"No, Ronnie," says Gavin. "I got a right to know about the state of the books. A month ago, before Dr Declan's trouble and whatnot, there was close to thirty grand in the bank, maybe more, and—"

"Sit down, Gavin, you cuck," says the bearded man, Ronnie. "I'm losing my patience."

"Thirty grand," says Gavin. "We got a right to know what's going on with it. How it's gonna be used now the election is over."

"You're way out of order, buddy," says Becca.

Becca and Ronnie both look as if they want to tear Gavin apart. JD glances over at Gage. Gage is chuckling, shaking his head. Around the room the other people are looking at their hands, looking at the floor, looking at the ceiling. Looking anywhere but at the confrontation.

Then Declan stands up. He faces the audience. He's holding his hands up, palms forward. A sad little smile on his face. Everyone goes quiet.

"Divide and conquer," says Declan. "That's how the deep state keeps us from organizing. Yes indeed. Now, I'm not looking to hijack the meeting. I intended to save my comments for the end, but maybe now is a better time to fill you all in on what's what. What do you think?"

There is a quiet ripple of yesses. Declan glances at Becca.

"Chair recognizes head of the executive committee and leader of the Patriot Bloc, Dr Richard Declan."

Becca sits down. Ronnie resumes videotaping. Declan goes behind the lectern. He takes off his glasses, folds them, and puts them into his breast pocket. He leans forward and says, "How much have you committed to our cause, Gavin?"

The fat man stands back up and puts his fists on his hips again. "How much?" he says. "As in a dollar figure?"

"As in a dollar figure."

"Well, off the top of my head, I'd guess three thousand dollars. Now, that's at the low end …"

Declan nods. "Three thousand dollars. That's generous, Gavin. That's commitment. That's more than a lot of folks make in a month, wouldn't you say so, Gwen?"

The woman in the kitten sweatshirt hops to her feet. "More than two months, Dr Declan!"

Declan nods again. The woman in the kitten sweatshirt sits down. Declan takes a long pause. The fat man, meanwhile, is still standing, almost all the defiance gone out of him. JD smiles. You cuck, he thinks.

Declan turns to Becca. "Treasurer," he says, "we're gonna cut a cheque to Gavin for three thousand dollars. Right now. I see the way you're looking at me, but we'll call it my leadership prerogative."

"Now hold on," says Gavin.

"Yes indeed," says Declan. "Three thousand. Paid in full."

"That's not what I want," says Gavin.

You cuck, JD thinks. For a second he isn't sure he hasn't said it out loud.

Declan smiles again. The sad smile, the weary smile. After another lengthy pause, he says, "Sit down, Gavin."

Gavin obeys.

"You asked about our finances," says Declan. "It's a fair question, and it deserves an honest answer. We've had some unforeseen costs lately. I was, as you know, unjustly taken into custody not long ago. Thus, securing my freedom came with legal costs. And though our grassroots movement was cut out of the – ahem – democratic process before the voters got their say at the polls, we still have some associated costs from trying to play by the deep state's rulebook. What's the saying,

Gwen, about giving unto Caesar?"

The woman in the kitten sweatshirt jumps up. "That's Matthew 22:21, Dr Declan. Render unto Caesar what is Caesar's, and render unto God what is His!"

Declan gives her a nod of thanks. She sits back down. "For the time being," says Declan, "we have to hold on to the rest of our finances, just as we must ask you to continue to make your contributions. I remind you, friends, as leader, my dues are double yours. But I'm happy to make them, because these are resources we are going to need. And soon."

Declan straightens. "Hear me loud and clear, friends. Secretary, I want you to make sure what I say is put into the minutes verbatim. That is, word for word. I, Dr Richard Declan, solemnly promise you that a day is coming when patriots from one end of this country to the other are going to rise up together and throw off the shackles of the corrupt. Of the degenerate traitorous so-called government. Of the deep state. I don't know the precise date, friends, but I do know it's coming. And when it does, we won't be divided and conquered. We won't be quibbling amongst ourselves over our financial resources. No indeed, we will find ourselves neckdeep in total revolution, and we will have much bigger fish to fry. Did you get that, secretary? Verbatim?"

A single strand of hair has fallen down from Declan's perfect part across his forehead. He steps back from the lectern, begins slowly pacing the front of the room.

"I would be lying," he continues, "if I said these aren't hard times. These are the hardest of times. I don't need to tell you that, of course. Not so long ago this little grassroots movement suffered a setback. A bitter pill to swallow, made all the more bitter for the way in which it was delivered. To be kicked out of the democratic process before the voters got their say at the polls was an affront bordering on the absurd. But it should show you, friends, that the deep state is frightened of us. As well they should be. Our movement is growing, bringing in new patriots every day."

As Declan says this, he looks directly at JD. Nods again.

Then he continues pacing the front of the room. More strands of hair fall across his forehead. Bright colour floods his cheeks. He continues to talk for the next fifteen or twenty minutes straight, not taking a break. He jabs his finger in the air to emphasize his points. His eyes blaze like they did in jail.

He talks more about the coming revolution. He talks about the clarion call that will galvanize – that's his word, galvanize – the patriots across the country. He talks a lot about the deep state. JD isn't completely sure what Declan is talking about. He reminds himself to look at some political books at the library.

At one point, Declan stops. He pulls his trouserleg up. He reveals an argyle sock. Around the sock is a black band. Attached to the band is a small box a little bigger than a cigarette lighter. "Do you see this, friends? The deep state has, among other indignities, curtailed my freedom of movement. I may not leave this property until further notice." Declan's pacing speeds up to almost a jog. His hair is damp on his forehead, and he's shaking both fists. All at once he freezes in his tracks. He looks around the room, breathing heavily.

"I ... I apologize, friends. You know how animated I become. In any case, before I turn it back to the Chair, let's reflect on the words of the great Thomas Jefferson. When the people fear the government, there is tyranny. But when the government fears the people, there is liberty.

"Liberty, friends, is coming."

There's one more order of a business before the meeting ends. A motion to move meetings to once a week. The bearded man, Ronnie, puts this motion forward. He says the Patriot Bloc will need to get together more often. "We need to prepare for the strategic changes coming down the pipe."

Ronnie doesn't say what those changes are.

Becca concludes with the whack of a gavel. Everyone gets up. Most people make their way to the donuts and coffee at the tables at the back of the room.

JD senses someone standing beside him. Declan. Declan offers a firm handshake. "I can't tell you how glad I am that you came, my friend."

"It's a great honour," says JD.

Declan, still clutching JD's hand, pulls him in close. We've got major changes on the horizon. Major changes. Hear me loud and clear, my friend. We're going to need someone like you. No, correction to that. We're going to need you. Yes indeed. You."

JD can't think of anything worthy to say. All the weight is in the sentiment. In Declan's voice. In the way he's looking JD straight in the eye. JD nods.

Gage appears beside them. "Listen, Doc, there's some things the executive committee better get to."

Declan releases JD's hand.

"What happens now, good sir?" says JD.

"What happens now is the inner circle has to have a confab," says Declan. "It's going to take some time, I'm afraid, but these changes on the horizon, we've got to prepare for them. More to follow, my friend."

"More to follow?" says JD.

"What he's saying is thanks for coming," says Gage.

"I want to see you here again next week," says Declan.

Declan offers one more handshake. Then he turns around, makes his way to the door near the lectern. He shakes other hands and pats shoulders along the way, gives the woman in the kitten sweatshirt a hug. Watching Declan go, JD can't help but notice how he doesn't shake anyone else's hand the same way he shook JD's. Neither does Declan lean in and tell anyone else how he needs them for the major changes on the horizon.

Then Declan is gone. Gage lingers a moment longer. He takes hold of JD's upper arm again, that same steely grip as before. "Listen, compadre. This is a bit of a fucked-up time for our little cause. A lot of folks who like to talk big, but don't hang around when the rubber hits the road, you copy? You might've seen that earlier this evening. Certain lard-assed individuals sounding off about the accounting and the books. Now, we don't know nothin about you, other than you caught Doc Declan's attention. That's a point in your favour right there. But you still got to prove yourself. Don't take this wrong, but I'll be doin my own homework. That's what I do."

JD stands up straight. He senses that Gage is a student of the school of hard knocks. But so is JD himself. "I understand, good sir," he says.

Gage grins, showing those stone block teeth once more. He claps JD on the arm. "You'll have to show yourself out, but let me repeat what Doc Declan said. I hope to hell we see you next week."

Gage turns and makes his way to the door near the lectern.

The inner door, JD thinks. The door for the Very Invited Persons.

JD decides he will someday go through that door. He will be asked to go through that door.

It's a powerful idea. Powerful enough to get him through his realization he will have to take public transit back home. He has no idea how long this will take. Hours. Under other circumstances this might make him despair, but tonight JD's spirits are lifted.

He goes to the tables at the back. Picks up two donuts, wraps them in napkins, tucks each one in either patch pocket on the hips of his blazer. Refills his coffee. Provisions for the long, uncertain journey ahead. He is leaving via the front door when something else occurs to him.

This entire evening, there hasn't been a single burst of ELF.

The tent city in Civic Park has doubled since JD saw it last. There are people everywhere.

Yesterday when JD listened to Full Disclosure, people were calling in to talk about 99Together. One caller said the movement is being secretly controlled by George Soros. Somebody else said the movement is a front for the Muslim Brotherhood, destabilizing the West one city at a time.

The most excited caller said she had it on good authority that every single 99Together protester is a demon disguised in human form. Have you gone anywhere near Civic Park lately, Mr Emmerich? The whole place smells like sulphur. That's how you know what those people really are!

JD doesn't see evidence of demons in the park. He doesn't see any cops, either. None at the edges of the park, none inside. He keeps his eyes open for collaborators and informants.

He wanders past the first aid tent and the makeshift library. It's expanded into a pavilion of blue tarps. Boxes and boxes of books. People are reading in lawn chairs. He glances down at some battered paperbacks arranged on a folded blanket. The title of one is Culture Jam. Another, No Logo. A third book is a biography of that face from all the t-shirts. Che Guesomething.

Toward the middle of the park he finds the papier mache effigies. Twice as many now. They're arranged in a ring around the base of a lamppost. Umbrellas and canopies made from plastic bags have been set above the effigies in case of rain. Passersby are taking pictures with their cellphones.

For a little while JD stands there, taking it all in, until he sees Tiny Tim pop out of a tent nearby. Tiny Tim is carrying a paintbrush. Beside him is a redheaded woman. Tiny Tim sees JD – JD notices the brief flash of recognition in his eyes – and starts to angle off the other way.

JD smiles. He calls out to Tiny Tim. When Tim doesn't reply, JD repeats his name, almost at a shout.

Tiny Tim turns around. "Do I know you?"

JD laughs. Tips his trilby. Offers a handshake. "Sure you know me. I came all the way here to see how your performance art is coming. It looks quite remarkable, good sir."

"Thanks," says Tiny Tim. "Now I have to—"

"Quite remarkable," says JD.

The nearest effigy is a politician with a sinister grin and his hands stained with red paint. JD reaches out to touch the figure's mottled face. Tiny Tim jumps in the way. "Don't! Please don't touch them. They're very delicate. Please please respect that."

JD withdraws his hand, smiling. "Sorry about that. Hey, are you going to burn them? Bust them up?"

Tiny Tim gives his head a brisk shake. "I don't know. We're not allowed to burn things here. Anyway I really have to—"

"Well," says JD, "I want to be here when you do it. I want to witness it. The deep state will hate it, good sir. They're frightened of us, you know. Our movement is growing, bringing in new patriots every day. Hey, is Simone around?"

"You just missed her," says the redhead beside Tiny Tim. "She went home about an hour ago."

"Shame," says JD.

"She's hosting an open mic at the Green Frog Café," says the redhead. "Eight o'clock on Tuesday."

JD brightens. He knows the Green Frog Café. It's a joint on 6th Street. Been around forever. Granddad used to drink there. In the last couple years the Green Frog has become a hang-out for hipsters and poets and other phonies.

But, if he happens to run into Simone there.

"Thanks," JD tells the redhead. Then he raises his fist. "Together, united!"

As he turns to go, he hears Tiny Tim speaking in a low voice: "Not cool, Jackie. Nobody knows who the hell that guy is."

JD can't help but grin.

Tuesday arrives.

There's a shopping cart in the lobby of Country Club Estate. There are often shopping carts in the lobby. Piss in the stairwell. Gang tags spraypainted on the walls. But JD doesn't worry. He's found a small brown envelope in the mailbox. It's addressed to Granddad, but since Granddad is still hiding out, JD will have to conduct business on his behalf.

"Hey! I need to talk to you."

JD turns. Mr Rahim, the building superintendent, is standing near the front doors. JD folds the envelope and pushes it into his inside pocket. Then he strides over to the doors, keeping his steps light. Mr Rahim opens his mouth but JD speaks first: "Not now. I don't have time for minor problems."

He pats Mr Rahim on the arm and goes through the vestibule. The early October sky above is overcast. There's a flat mugginess in the air, too warm for the season. Fall storm brewing. Weather manipulation. Likely Their way of harassing JD's many close allies in Civic Park.

The fountaineers are at their usual post. They're laughing about something, but they get quiet as JD passes. Sean gives JD a tough-guy nod.

"I'll need to come see you tomorrow, good sir," says JD. "I'm almost out of remedies again. Maybe we can make a more fairer deal this time?"

The other fountaineers look at Sean. Sean blanches. "I don't know what the fuck you're talking about."

JD laughs. "Oh come on. Supply and demand. I demand, you supply."

Sean glares at JD. "Shut your face, you weird-ass ice cream motherfucker."

Two of the fountaineers thrust their hands in their pockets and slouch away. A third stares at the ground. Sean shifts his glare somewhere else. JD follows his look. Parked across the street is a cop car.

JD shrugs. "My apologies. I did not notice the authorities over there. Well, all's well that ends well. See you."

Banks are dangerous. Banks are traps. Banks belong to the Templars. The Freemasons. The Rothschilds. The International Monetary Fund. Them.

JD hates banks. He hates the surveillance cameras, the closed doors. The empty eyes of the bean-counters at their desks, the cheap suits trying to get you to sign this or that. The applicable term is necessary evil.

The bank JD does his business with – avoiding it whenever he can – is a small HSBC branch near Country Club Estate. Two bean-counters are working this afternoon. There's a lineup of six people, most of them old. Old people and JD have something in common – they don't use ATMs.

JD stands at the back of the lineup, shifting foot to foot. He's sweating under his blazer. He can feel the surveillance cameras on him. The ELF in here is horrid, inescapable.

The geriatrics seem to take forever. He wants to shout at them, but at last he's called forward. The bean-counter before him is a small woman. She might be pretty if not for her line of work.

"Can I help you," she says.

JD produces the envelope. Opens it, takes out the cheque it contains, gives it to her. He clears his throat, steadies his voice. "I need to cash this, my lady."

"Can I see your ID?"

He nods. His only ID is a driver's license. The license is another little necessary evil. It's more than he wants to have – it keeps him in the system, in the databases, in some big book of names – but he needed it to drive Granddad's ice cream truck. He opens his wallet. Happens to catch a split-second glimpse of the Halloween picture, him and Daniel. The picture is a hard contrast against the soulless bank around him.

The bean-counter looks at JD's driver's license. She frowns. "That's not your name on the cheque."

JD forces a smile. "No, that's my granddad's name. But he's not able to leave his apartment. His disability, you see. I'm his designate. It should all be in your ... in your system there."

She turns to her computer. She types something. Her lacquered fingernails click on the keyboard. She looks at her screen. She types some more. Looks at her screen. This is the same routine JD goes through every time. Every time. There has to be a reason for that.

Actually, this bean-counter is slower than others he's dealt with. Much slower. Click click click on the keyboard. Long pause to stare at the screen. Click click click. More staring. He takes a casual glance over his shoulder. There's no security guard in sight, but that doesn't mean there isn't one hiding behind a closed door.

The sweat under his clothes is getting thick. Itchy. Click. Stare. This is all too slow. All wrong. If he has to take sudden action, if he has to fight his way out of here ... There's an old woman with a metal cane nearby. JD could use the cane as a weapon. If necessary. There's a water cooler against the wall. JD could throw the water cooler through the front window, make a dash for it.

If necessary.

Liberty is coming.

The bean-counter says, "How would you prefer it?"

Prefer what? he thinks. The bag over his head? The bullet in his back? Just try it. Try it, you bastards. Liberty is coming.

"Small bills, please."

A block away from the bank JD stands on a quiet corner, sucking in breath, mentally regrouping. A breeze cuts through the warm air. In his pocket are a thousand dollars, Granddad's disability for the month.

Granddad is okay. He took everything he needed when he lit out. JD's the one who needs the money. Now he can replenish his weed, do his laundry, put some food in the cupboard.

He can even afford some drinks at the Green Frog Café.

He starts walking. A few blocks past the railroad overpass someone thrusts a paper cup at him from the doorway of an ugly brownstone. He looks down. A woman in filthy clothes, hunkered on a stoop. She can't weigh more than ninety pounds. Her skin is seamed with dirt. Leaning against her leg is a piece of cardboard with Anything helps god bless scrawled on it.

Something stops JD from passing her by. He digs into his pocket. The smallest bill he has is five dollars.

"God bless you," the woman rasps as the five drops into her cup.

"You should get inside," he says. "It's going to rain."

She grins. Her teeth look like corn kernels. "Maybe your place?"

JD's about to reply when he realizes what had caught his attention in the first place. There are track marks all over the top of her forearm. The marks are red, the skin around them dark and inflamed. He leaves almost at a jog. She hollers something, but he doesn't pay any attention.

It's all he can do not to sprint.

The intelligence JD gained in Civic Park is good. Simone is at the Green Frog Café. She seems happy – and surprised – to see him.

He arrives at the old watering hole at ten minutes to eight. It's been raining for awhile and his clothes are wet and he's cold. On his way to the Green Frog he stopped in a high-end drug store a few doors down. When no one was looking he splashed a little cologne from the men's section onto his neck.

From JD's visits to the Green Frog with Granddad, he remembers a cheesy beer smell. Clouds of cigarette smoke. Old-timers hunched at the bar. Bowls of peanuts that Granddad told him not to eat because they were covered in piss.

But now the Green Frog is painted in pastels. Colored lights are strung around the ceiling. Modern art paintings and dramatic photographs of abandoned factories hang from the wall. All for sale. He glances at the tiny pricetag below one of the paintings. $700. He stifles a laugh.

There are two dozen people scattered around the various tables. Toward the back is a wall of exposed brick, a small riser, and a microphone. Next to the microphone is Simone. She's wearing an old-fashioned sleeveless polka dot dress, white high heels, horn-rimmed glasses. She's studying a sheet of paper and only looks up when JD stops right in front of her. Up close he sees her dark red lipstick and a tattoo of a cartoon mermaid on her upper arm.

"Oh." She blinks. "Aren't you the guy from ..."

JD tips his trilby. "I didn't mean to surprise you, my lady. I was down in Civic Park. Helping Tiny Tim with his performance art. He told me about this open mic. I thought I'd stop in."

She blinks again. After a moment she says, "That's great. Welcome. We're gonna start in like one minute, so can I catch up with you at the break?"

JD nods. "Of course. I'll be waiting for you."

He takes a stool at the bar. The bartender has a bushy beard and a checkered shirt. JD orders a pint of some kind of craft beer. The cost is five-fifty, plus a tip. Outrageous, but what else is he to do?

At eight o'clock Simone gets on the riser and taps the microphone. It gives a little whine of feedback. Similar to the sound of ELF. JD winces.

"Thanks, everybody, for being here," says Simone. She's at once shy and animated. JD can't take his eyes off her. There's a light ripple of applause. "This is our third Other Voices open mic night, says Simone, and I'm so proud of what we're doing ..."

For the next hour JD listens while four women and one man get up to the microphone. They read poetry, do solemn spoken word.

The fifth performer is a mousy little woman. She gets up to the riser holding a roll of cellophane in her hands. She wraps the cellophane around her lower legs. When she's used the entire roll she stands up straight and says, "Injustice. Thank you."

The audience applauds. JD claps to be polite. He's nursed his beer through the entire session. The mousy woman keeps the cellophane on her legs and hops back to her table and sits down.

Simone returns to the riser. "Okay. We're gonna take a break now, but first, as you probably already know, the 99Together group in Civic Park has been picking up major momentum. Not just in our city, either, but all over the country. We're a people-powered movement, though, and trust me when I say the one percent has all the resources we don't have. So anyway, I'm gonna pass the jar around. Every little bit counts."

She starts making the rounds with a big plastic jar in hand. JD orders another beer, feels the sting of the price. A minute later Simone is standing beside his stool, holding the plastic jar out. He catches a glimpse of bills and coins inside it. Simone's red lips part in a smile. "Every bit counts," she says.

JD smiles back. He puts forty dollars into the jar. No second thoughts.

"Wow," she says. "Thank you."

"May I buy you a drink, my lady?"

She gives him a funny look. For a second he thinks she might decline, then she sits on the next stool over. "Sure," she says. "Same's whatever you're having."

JD nods to the bartender. The bartender pours her a pint of the craft beer.

"So," she says. "I honestly don't know whether to be creeped out or not."

"Why ever would you say such of a thing as that?" says JD.

She laughs. "These days, man, when a guy finds out where a girl is gonna be some night, and then he shows up there, unannounced, you know?"

He smiles. "How do you know your open mic isn't my favourite thing?"

She arches an eyebrow. "Is it?"

"Sure it is," says JD. "In these dark times, the only way we're going to bring grace to a struggling nation is by speaking the truth. You know, at something like an open mic."

"Well, you're absolutely right about that," says Simone. "The whole point of Other Voices is to offer an inclusive forum to a wide range of folks. Music, poetry, spoken word, experimental stuff, performance art. Anything goes. A friend of mine got up to the mic last time and just spent five minutes crying his eyes out. It was amazing."

Simone offers a cheers and they clink their glasses together. Up close she smells like lilac. JD hasn't felt this kind of romantic connection with anyone since he met Lil.

"So what about you," Simone says. "What do you do?"

JD smiles. There it is, the same question everybody asks each other. What do you do.

"Well, I can't really talk about what I do. It's ... classified. Let's put it that way."

She frowns and smiles at the same time. "It's classified? Like, you're a spy or a secret agent or something?"

He laughs. "God no. I do not work for the government. I'd like to tell you more, but I need to get to know you better. Fair enough, my lady?"

The funny look again. "Listen," she says. "You being here? It's either weird as hell or intriguing. I don't know which one I'm leaning toward. Anyway, I gotta get back to it. If you want to try out some of your own spoken word, you can feel absolutely free and comfortable to do so. And if you're still here when we're done, I'll buy you a round. Fair is fair."

She gets up, carrying her pint with her. A minute later, the second hour of the open mic starts. It's much like the first hour. JD pays little attention. He takes out his wallet and opens it and looks at the old Halloween picture of Daniel and him. A snapshot of a time when he believed things might be good. Before he'd figured out They were pulling the strings.

Lil came trick-or-treating with JD and Daniel that night. They did their whole neighbourhood. They went to JD's brother's house. They even went as far as Country Club Estate. Granddad wasn't expecting anybody that night. He had a couple of ladyfriends over, and when he first opened the door he was scowling. But when he saw Daniel in his costume, he broke into a big charming Granddad grin.

You brung the half-pint up all this way, did you? Well I'll be goddamned ...

Granddad didn't have any candy, but he did give Daniel five bucks from a stash he kept in the kitchen. He gave Lil and JD both a shot of Johnnie Walker.

"You want another one, man?" says the bartender. He's pointing to JD's empty pint glass.

JD starts to nod, then says, "How about a shot of Johnnie Walker, good sir."

At last the open mic finishes. The Green Frog starts to empty out. It's a weeknight. That probably means something to the sheeple, but it means nothing to JD. Simone sticks around and makes good on her promise to buy him a pint.

By now JD is tipsy. Keen to see where the night might go. He studies her face, her mouth, the shapes of her hands. She tells him about herself. He even pays attention. The details are important. Love means knowing everything.

She grew up in a small town two hours west of Bayfield. She has a grudging love for her hometown. It's a close-minded place, but at the same time it's warm and familiar. Her parents, both retired high school teachers, are still there. Getting old in a comfortable way.

They order another round of drinks. He pays this time. The mousy woman who wrapped cellophane around her legs stops beside Simone on her way toward the door. At least she's removed the cellophane from her legs.

"Thank you for this," the mousy woman says solemnly.

Simone smiles and leans off her stool, hugs the woman. JD drinks his beer and tries not to tap his fingers on the bartop.

It feels like ages before the mousy woman leaves. JD nods after her. "Her ... performance ... was interesting."

"Her performance was fucking courageous, man," says Simone. "That's the first time she's done it for an audience. It's not my place to tell you what kind of trauma she's dealing with, but trust me when I say that was courage."

"Of course," says JD. "I felt that. Her courage. Amazing experience."

JD has had the odd date over the last couple of years. Nothing meaningful. Women usually don't understand his intelligence. But Simone is different. Worth every expense. Looking in her eyes, JD has never been more certain of anything in his life.

"Tell me something," she says.

"Like what?"

"Anything. Something personal. Something that isn't classified."

JD takes a long swallow of beer. What to tell her, what to permit? "I ... have a son."

Her eyes brighten. "You do?"

"Yes. His name's Daniel. He's six. He's smart and strong and ... and he's the kind of person this world needs."

She nods. "That's awesome. Where—"

"I also have a younger brother," says JD. "He's a plumber. He's a good fellow, but he's boring. I don't mean that in a bad way. He just is. And my granddad is old school. School of hard knocks. He used to drink right here, in fact. He operates an ice cream truck. I'm his Chief

Helmsman. Except now he's on, well, vacation. And my mom, she ...
She's a really special lady, my mother."

A quiet moment, then Simone says, "Sounds like you come from
some good people, boring plumbers or not."

"They are good people, my lady."

"Hey, what's with that? The my lady thing?"

"Actually," says JD, "it's a term of respect. In an old-fashioned way."

"Well, I gotta tell you, man. It's demeaning. Straight up."

"I didn't mean any offense. Like I said, it's a term of respect."

"You're ... kind of unique, aren't you," says Simone. "All the my lady
stuff aside. You're kind of unique. Maybe you're bad news. I'm not sure just
yet. I need to think about it." She drains her beer in one long gulp. Puts the
glass down. She's left lipstick on the rim. "That's enough for one night."

"No more?" says JD.

"Not tonight."

"Well, is there anything—"

"I've made a lot of mistakes with partners, with men, in the past.
I'm not one to care about waiting or some prudish bullshit like that.
But you're a stranger. And one who shows up out of the blue. I need to
be careful about you."

Simone gets off her stool. She's a little unsteady on her high heels.
She has the donation jar under her arm and she's making ready to leave.
Why is this happening? Has she been playing JD? Aren't they falling
in love? Not fair, he thinks.

Not fair not fair not fair.

She puts a hand on his thigh. Then she kisses him. Hard. Her
tongue crowds into his mouth. She tastes like beer, not in a bad way. He
can't think straight. Then she's breaking away. "Come find me again,"
she says. "Maybe down at Civic Park next time."

"When," he says. "Tomorrow?"

She laughs over her shoulder. "Not tomorrow. I don't think I'll be
there tomorrow. But I'll be back there soon. See you."

The door of the Green Frog swings closed behind her. JD is the
only patron left. Still has half a beer remaining. The bartender is down
at the other end of the bar, examining some receipts. After a moment
he sidles over.

"I'm closing up in a few."

JD nods. His manhood is throbbing. The bartender places something in front of him. At first JD thinks it's a bill, then he sees it's a napkin. A horrific thought occurs to him. The bartender is propositioning him. JD gives him a dangerous look.

The bartender smiles. "You got some lipstick on your chin, pal."

JD and his brother never knew their father. Their mom used to say he was a suit. High up in the government or a major corporation.

"He's rich and powerful," she would say. "But rich and powerful doesn't mean he's any kind of a gent, boys. He isn't. Love em and leave em, that's your dad's way."

Later, JD came to believe their father was a member of one of the ancient bloodlines. The DuPonts. The Kennedys. The Rothschilds. Some dynasty that would be damaged if the existence of two bastard sons was ever revealed.

In JD's earliest memories, he and his mom and brother lived in a tiny rental house on Hough Crescent in the southeast ward. That was as close to normal as their lives ever got. JD and his brother attended a rundown public school two streets over. JD walked his brother to and from school every day. Protected him from all the perverts and robbers and kidnappers they might see along the way.

During the evenings, when Mom wasn't working, she would make popcorn and turn on a movie for the three of them. She had a thing for old-fashioned movies. The Maltese Falcon. His Girl Friday. It's a Wonderful Life. She said those movies showed a time when men knew how to be gentlemen, how to make women feel like ladies.

One day a man came knocking on the door of the rental house. He was skinny to the point of looking sick. He had bad teeth. But his hair was carefully coiffed in the short-in-front, long-in-back way that was fashionable at the time. He was wearing a dark collared shirt. A leather tie. He was holding a bouquet of roses.

Mom let him in. The skinny man gave her the roses. He lifted up her hand and planted a kiss on it, like some knight of old. This made Mom giggle, put a hand over her mouth.

"Hello, beautiful lady," said the man. Then he turned his attention to JD and JD's brother. "Gentlesirs," he said.

The man smiled, showing his snaggleteeth.

"Boys," said Mom. "This is Gord."

Mom and Gord went out for the evening. Left in Gord's car. He had a Trans Am.

JD made supper for his brother and himself. Kraft Dinner with little bits of hot dog cut up in it. JD ended up giving his brother most of his own dish. Even in those days he didn't eat much.

The boys stayed up late, watching TV. Mom got home after midnight. She seemed tired. Her eyes were half-lidded. But she was happy.

"My friend knows how to make a lady feel like a lady," she said.

Gord was a freelance photographer. Mom had met him through her modeling work. Before long, she was seeing him on a regular basis. Going steady, she said. An old-fashioned term that made her laugh whenever she said it.

As her relationship with Gord became serious, something started to happen to her. She became thinner. She went from slender to skinny. Her eyes took on that half-lidded look all the time.

Gord moved in when JD was seven. He didn't have many belongings, not much more than his camera equipment and some clothes.

"It's not permanent, boys," said Mom. "Gord only needs a place to call home for a little while."

A little while turned out to be two years.

Gord wasn't mean to JD or his brother. If anything, he was indifferent. He was gone a lot, and when he was home he stayed out of the boys' way. For the most part.

It was Gord's idea to lock them in the basement. The first time he did that was a Saturday.

"Okay gents," he said. "I need yous to hide out downstairs for a bit."

Gord put the TV and VCR down there so JD and his brother could watch it. And watch it they did. For twelve hours. Gord had only thought to include two movies with the VCR. It's a Wonderful Life and Citizen Kane. The boys almost wore the tapes out.

Finally Gord unlocked the door at the top of the stairs and called the boys up. JD and his brother found their mom asleep on the couch. Her arm was hanging out in front of her and there was a red spot on the vein below her bicep.

Gord himself was acting weird. Half-sleepy. Friendlier than usual. "I gotta go out for a while," he said. "Don't let nobody in. Take care of your mom."

So it went from there. In some ways life was no different. JD went on walking his brother to and from school and protecting him from danger. Many evenings, it was on JD to make supper and put his brother to bed. Gord, when he was around, went on being mostly indifferent to the boys. Mom went on with her modeling.

Then JD and his brothers' trips to the basement started to happen more often. Almost every weekend. They spent a lot of Saturday nights down there, right up to Sunday at lunchtime. Good thing the basement had a tiny one-piece bathroom.

One time Gord didn't lock the door. In fact, he forgot to close it all the way. JD realized this as it got dark – he could see the light of a camera flashing through the opening between the door and the frame. His brother was asleep.

JD crept upstairs. Snuck into the living room. Gord's camera was on a tripod, taking automatic shots. Gord was on the couch with Mom. She had that half-asleep look on her face. There was a needle on the floor. She and Gord were naked. Doing naked things. Well, Gord was.

And after that, JD used to make sure the basement door was locked from the inside.

After two years, Gord and Mom started to fight. Big screaming matches. She'd fight him like a lioness, waking up, even briefly, from the chemical spell she was under. Gord would get scared and leave for a few days.

But every time this happened, Gord would find some reason to worm his way back in. JD saw him standing in the yard outside once, crying. He was holding a bouquet of flowers. Mom let him in. They spent a lot of time standing in the living room, holding each other, crying together.

Things got worse. Mom got thinner and thinner. A lot of men came and went from the house at strange hours. JD and his brother spent those visits locked in the basement. JD would watch through the little window in the top of the basement wall, holding a hammer from the toolbox in the furnace room.

To this day JD doesn't know who those men were, but he's sure They sent them.

One time Mom tried to hit Gord with a chair from the kitchen. JD was watching from the living room. Neither of them knew he was there. His brother was in bed down the hall.

Mom tried to swing the chair, but by then she'd become so thin she almost couldn't lift it. Gord punched her and knocked her right out. For a minute or so he stood there with a scared look on his face. Then he started trying to wake up her up. Then he realized JD was watching.

Gord came over and picked JD up and put him in the basement and locked the door. He never said a word.

The next morning, JD's mother let him out of the basement. She had a black eye, but she was frying some eggs. JD's brother was already at the kitchen table.

"There's gonna be some changes, boys," Mom said. "Starting today. My friend is gone, and this time he isn't coming back. He might of brought me flowers, he might of talked polite, but he wasn't a gentleman."

After Gord was a guy called Mr Norris. That's what he made the boys call him, Mr Norris, as if he was running the stock market. He wasn't. He was a home appliance repairman. At one time he had been a drug addict, but he'd got himself clean.

Mom met him at a Narcotics Anonymous meeting in a church basement. Within a couple of months, Mr Norris moved in. First thing he did was get rid of all the needles and booze. He even got rid of the bottles of cola.

Then he made the boys clean the house top to bottom. It took days turning that place around. When it was done it wasn't recognizable. Looked like a house in a real estate ad. Mom was happy with the new man in her life.

Mr Norris was also more interested in JD and his brother than Gord had ever been. Mr Norris inspected the boys' shared bedroom every morning. Checked their homework every night.

Mr Norris was also a born-again Christian. Every Sunday he would make sure they all went to church. It was the same church where the NA meetings were held. The church was up by the highway. It looked more like a storefront than a house of worship.

The congregation wasn't big, no more than a hundred people. Most of them had been sick or addicted in various ways, like Mom and Mr Norris. The church helped them stay well.

One time Mr Norris sat down on the bed in boys' bedroom. "Boys," he said. "What do you know about the devil?"

The boys looked at him. Looked at each other. Said nothing. He waited them out. So they told him what they thought they knew of the devil. Red horns, pitchfork.

"Boys, the devil is real," said Mr Norris. "The devil is an angel who rebelled against God. He is a true threat to humans, and has the capacity to ruin lives. The devil made me and your mom sick and made us both addicted to drugs, but through the grace of God we were freed. But the devil is clever. If you don't guard against him, boys, the devil will snatch you up and drag you down to darkest hell for eternity."

Later that night, JD's brother was moaning in his sleep. JD woke him up. His brother said he'd had a nightmare. In the nightmare, the real devil had appeared in their bedroom. He was shaped like a man, JD's brother said, but he had no face.

The devil grabbed JD's brother's ankles with his icy cold hands and pulled him out of bed. Dragged him down to the basement. Locked the door behind him. There was no light in the basement and that was hell and JD's brother was to remain there forever … until JD woke him up.

JD could protect his brother from bullies and perverts on the way to school, but he couldn't protect him from nightmares about the devil. The best he could do was let him share his bed.

Devil-talk aside, Mr Norris was also strict with the boys. If they didn't clean the house to his standard or if they slept in too late or if he caught them watching TV, he would snap the palms of their hands with his belt. But he was good for Mom. She stayed away from the needles, started to put some weight back on. She even got a job as a part-time secretary in the business where Mr Norris worked.

(I've often wondered, Mr Emmerich, how things might have turned out if Mr Norris stayed in our lives. Maybe my brother and me and our mom all would have turned into safe little sheeple, with safe little jobs, going to our safe little church every Sunday. But it didn't happen that way. They wouldn't let it.)

This was Mom's Jesus phase. She took to it seriously. On the rare Sundays when Mr Norris wasn't around, she'd plug the TV back in. Turn on a certain show. Great News Gospel Time. There was something about that television preacher, with his fiery eyes and high-energy sermons …

But Mom's Jesus phase didn't last much longer.

Not long after JD turned eleven, his mother went out one night and didn't come home. Mr Norris put the boys to bed, then he spent the night pacing around the living room.

Mom came home the next morning, right around the time Mr Norris was sending the boys to school. Everything seemed normal when JD and his brother got home that afternoon.

A week later, Mom disappeared again.

This time when she came back Mr Norris yelled at her. She laughed at him. He slapped her. She hit him with a rolled-up newspaper. All of this as JD and his brother were trying to eat breakfast. Mr Norris looked like he might do something back to Mom, but instead he turned his attention to the boys, got them on their way to school. Once again, everything was normal when they came back home.

Two weeks later she disappeared for a third time. This time she stayed away for a few days. She came home on the Saturday night. It was pouring outside. Mr Norris put the boys to bed. Then he and Mom yelled at each other in the living room for a while.

"The Lord wants more for you than this," Mr Norris said.

"Oh shove that self-righteous shit up your ass," said Mom. "All your Jesus-talk is just your way of justifying giving me a smack when I won't sleep with you."

"How dare you."

"Get the hell out or I'm calling the cops," said Mom.

After that the house became quiet. An hour or two passed. JD got up and went into the living room. There was no sign of Mr Norris. But there was Mom, asleep on the couch. Then there was a soft tap on the window. JD turned around. Who was on the porch, soaked with rain, but Gord.

Gord smiled his snaggletooth smile.

JD looked at his mother, who'd halfway woken up. She smiled. "Let him in, honey. It's so good to have him back, don't you think?"

The next day was Sunday. They didn't go to church. Mom and Gord hung around the living room, talking and laughing. JD made his brother some breakfast. They watched TV in the basement and didn't get in trouble for it. In the middle of the afternoon Mom called them into the living room and sat them down on the couch.

She said, "It's good to be a family again, don't you think? My friend's got a brand new job. He's doing great, and he wants to do right by us."

Gord grinned and shrugged. "It's not much … but I've got myself into the computer business, gents. This thing called the World Wide Web. Special videos. That's the way of the future."

"We're even gonna go out for supper tonight," Mom said. "A little celebration. How does Red Lobster sound?"

"I thought yous'd like that," said Gord, taking Mom's hand. "One more thing, gents. Maybe yous can start calling me dad."

The plan might've been to go to Red Lobster, but Gord and Mom wanted to do other things first. That meant JD and his brother and had to spend some time in the basement with the door locked.

JD's brother cried. He was still scared from his nightmare about the devil. JD comforted him as best he could. The boys watched movies. Played games. Slept a bit. Then they waited to be let out and go to Red Lobster. They were both hungry.

But they didn't get let out of the basement. Not that evening, not that night. Not for three days. Neither of them had the strength to break down the door, not even with the hammer from the toolbox. The windows were too narrow to get through.

This was hell, it seemed. The devil had come for them after all.

From what JD could remember later, there were firemen and paramedics and cops in the house. The firemen carried the boys out of the basement. They wouldn't let them look in the living room. They took the boys to a hospital.

They were there for some time, JD wasn't sure how long. Days or weeks. There was ice cream. There were two cops who came almost every day and asked questions. They wrote the boys' responses down on a notepad. When it was all over JD's brother went to live with their grandma and JD went to live with Granddad.

But these details aren't important.

What is important is it was Them. All along. They sent Gord back into Mom's life. Plain and simple. To punish her for something. To take pictures and videos of her with her clothes off to put on the World Wide Web. To pump her veins full of poison until there was no coming back.

If it wasn't Them, how else could her death be ruled as accidental? How else could Gord be set free to return to whatever hole he'd crawled out of in the first place?

None of it happened just because.

October 13.

JD has a problem. His brother can't – or won't – drive him to the Patriot Bloc meeting. Earlier that afternoon, JD called his brother from the payphone outside the library.

Payphones are bad news. They're packed with ELF emitters. It was physically painful for JD to use the payphone. The faraday cage inside his trilby could only do so much. Squealing interference slammed his brain as soon as he put the receiver to his ear.

He could barely hear his brother through the interference. Can't tonight … the kids … karate lessons at six …

JD's brother might've said something else, something about his wife, but by then JD couldn't take the interference anymore. He set the receiver back in its cradle and staggered away. It was fifteen minutes before he felt better again.

With his brother out of the equation, JD is left to consider taking transit up to the meeting. It's a loathesome idea. Last time, coming home from the house with the big white columns, he had to take three different buses. The journey took hours and hours. It's already four o'clock.

Then it occurs to him.

Half an hour later JD is at the Store-It-All building on Gerald Street. A vast facility filled with countless lockers where sheeple stash their stuff. Couches. Old TVs. Boxes of clothes. God knows what else.

JD enters a code in the front gate and tips his trilby at the Asian man inside the little glass gatehouse. From there JD goes around the building to a huge parking lot in back. There is cracked, oil-stained asphalt underfoot.

A motley fleet of vehicles is stored back here. Minibuses. RVs. Tarp-covered boats on trailers. JD weaves around them, almost to the back corner of the lot. There it is. The Chevy P30 with the blue-and-pink pastel paintjob. Mr Cheer Ice Cream in big cartoon letters on the side panels.

Last time JD was here was in March. He came with Granddad to help him air up the tires and service the engine and clean the interior. Preparations for an ice cream season that didn't end up happening, but it means the truck should be good to go.

Should be, as long as They haven't been tampering with it.

When JD came to live with Granddad the second time – after JD's traitorous ex kicked him out (another story of persecution, Mr Emmerich) – Granddad put him to work. Chief helmsman, Granddad called it, of Granddad's ice cream truck. Granddad himself wasn't allowed to drive the truck anymore. They had revoked his driver's license. One too many DUI frame-ups.

JD was chief helmsman. Granddad was navigator and captain. Granddad got the ice cream truck a few years after he went on permanent disability. Some cash deal through a friend of his. The truck was a Chevy P90. Had a freezer in the back, a frozen yogurt maker, a stainless steel counter for making sundaes. Everything was used, but in good shape.

From the day he got it, Granddad kept the truck spotless. He had a little plastic hula dancer he put on the dashboard. Hula Lula, he called her.

Granddad didn't tell the government about the truck, since he didn't want Them to revoke his disability.

From May to October, Granddad would make the rounds of the city. Shilling sundaes, banana splits, milkshakes. Blasting Turkey in the Straw from the power horn on the roof of the cab,

From time to time Granddad also made stops to visit certain people. Certain people who would sell him household electronics. Stolen, of course. JD had no illusions otherwise. But it was okay. These electronics were always stolen from the mansions of the very rich.

When Granddad had enough stereos and small appliances stashed in the insulated cabinets in the back of the truck, he would take everything to a pawn shop. Resell it in bulk, rake a small profit.

"This is how you play by your own rules, bucko," he said.

After JD started driving the truck, he didn't much care for the liberated electronics hidden in the back. He could feel the ELF emanating from them. Made him queasy. But he kept quiet, happy to be an important part of Granddad's cash operation.

Then Granddad left. Lit out. Went into hiding.

Happened four months ago. Granddad had just finished some post-winter servicing on the truck, preparing it for the summer. The plan was JD would be chief helmsman again, Granddad would take care of everything else. Including the cash business.

JD unlocks the driver side door. He climbs up onto the seat. There's a thin layer of dust on the plastic upholstery. A stale smell of Granddad's cigarettes. Everything is otherwise clean and, as far as he can tell, untouched. On the passenger side of the dashboard is a little plastic hula dancer. Hula-Lula, Granddad calls her. Did You Get Lei'd Today is printed on Hula-Lula's suction-cup base.

JD slides the key into the ignition. He turns the key to the start position, intending only to let the glow plugs heat up first. Instantly a cheery, music-box jingle fills the air.

JD is startled. He'd forgot how Granddad had wired the power horn on the roof of the cab to the radio in the console, so he could control the music while driving. It was the last thing they'd tested back in March. Well, at least the sound system is working. Turkey In The Straw blasts across the Store-It-All parking lot.

So much for keeping a low profile.

JD cranks the key back into the off position. He takes a breath. The radio in the console is old enough to have a cassette player. JD pushes the eject button and takes out the cassette. He dials the volume knob all the way down, just to be extra sure.

He turns the key back to start. No music now. He watches the glow plug light on the console. Ten seconds. Twenty. The glow plug light blinks out. He turns the key forward. For several seconds the diesel engine cranks and coughs. Then it rumbles to life.

JD sits back in the seat. Feels a mix of relief and exhilaration. They've done a lot to slow him down, but they haven't stopped him altogether. They can't stop an Invited Person.

He drives carefully. Sticks to the speed limit. That's not too difficult, since it's rush hour and traffic is slow.

At one point he finds himself stopped at a red light beside a school bus. The kids in the bus plaster their faces to the windows, staring at Mr Cheer with naked craving. JD keeps both hands on the steering wheel and his eyes locked straight ahead. The light turns green and half a block further on the school bus turns down a different street. JD is glad to be rid of it. Hula-Lula bobbles on the dashboard.

As he gets farther from downtown, the traffic thins out. By the time he's on Side Road 10, he's got almost no one else to contend with. Before long he sees the quarry and the flea market. The old one-room church. The leaves have all turned now. In many places the trees are bare. The sun is getting low in the west, the shadows turning long.

JD passes 23456, 23460. Then he's driving beside the gray cinder block wall surrounding 23468. He comes to the turn-in over the culvert. This time the whitewashed gate is standing open. Despite himself, JD brings the truck to a stop. He takes a quick look around.

A short distance up the driveway, he sees the Jeep with the oversized tires and the 1-800-GTFO-NOW decal. The Jeep is halfway on the driveway and halfway on the uncut grass. Someone gets out of the Jeep. JD narrows his eyes.

It's the tall, lean man. The Security Director. Gage. He's wearing the amber ballistic glasses . The same dark trousers and golf shirt, now under a light fleece shell. Gage is carrying something, too. A walkie-talkie. He says something into it.

Then Gage approaches the ice cream truck. He's holding the walkie-talkie in one hand. His other hand is at the small of his back, under his shell.

Gage closes the distance to ten feet. JD rolls down the window.

"Hold up" says Gage. "This is private property."

Gage's hand is still poised in the small of his back.

JD leans out his window, smiling. "I know, kind sir. Invited Persons only."

Gage stops. He looks at the truck. He looks up at JD. He looks at the truck again. After a few seconds, he says, "I got a serious what-the-fuck interrogative about your wheels, compadre, but I suppose it can wait for now. Welcome back."

The same big room. The same lectern, the same flag, the same portrait of blue-eyed Jesus on the wall. The same old man slumped in his wheelchair up front. The donuts and coffee are fresh, but the two six-foot tables are the same. The difference this time is the people.

There are fewer of them.

Last time, there were twenty people, maybe a few more. Now, JD counts twelve. Gwen is here. She's traded in the kitten sweatshirt for a sweatshirt that says God's Greatest Gift Is Grandkids!!! across the chest.

The fat man, Gavin, is absent.

JD goes to the back and gets himself a donut and a coffee. After a moment's consideration, he takes a second donut. With all the people missing, there are more to go around. He looks for a free seat and finds one, this time in the second row, behind the old man in the wheelchair.

Gwen is two empty seats down from JD, sitting bolt upright with her hands in her lap. She seems to be staring at the lectern, or the inner door. Or maybe blue-eyed Jesus. JD nods and tips his trilby to her. She gives him a tightening of the lips that might be a smile.

A minute later Gage comes in through the main entryway door. He's taken off his windbreaker. Whatever he was packing in the small of his back before doesn't seem to be there now. JD watches Gage get a cup of coffee then sit down in the third row, which is otherwise empty.

At seven o'clock the inner door opens. The big peroxide blonde woman, Becca, comes out first. She's wearing the same outfit as before, right down to the red cowboy boots. The boots They clock across the hardwood floor. She's followed by the man with the shaved head, thick beard, limp, and camcorder. Ronnie, JD recalls.

Last comes Declan, in his bowtie and corduroy jacket. Hair perfectly parted to the side, rimless glasses up on his forehead. He takes the lectern and leads them through the national anthem, then the Patriot Bloc prayer.

When Declan finishes, the group gives a collective Amen.

As before, Becca chairs the meeting. Ronnie records it on his camcorder.

"Chair recognizes the voter liaison committee," says Becca.

Nobody replies. They look around. The liaison committee man from last time is absent.

Becca's face darkens. "Chair recognizes the faith committee."

Gwen hops up again. This week's prayer hour will be on Saturday, seven o'clock sharp. As always stop what you're doing, whether you're in your office or your home or your car, and spend the next sixty minutes calling on the Lord. This week we're gonna ask God to forgive all those people in Civic Park, who've been spreading their communism and fouling up one of the nicest parts of downtown. We're gonna ask God to show them all a better way to use their time. And if that doesn't work, maybe send a good thundershower."

JD shifts in his seat.

"Chair recognizes the Director of Security," says Becca.

This time Gage isn't snoozing. He gets up. "Listen," he says. "I'm sure this is a motherhood point to most of you all here, but I want to remind you to check your six wherever you go. Specially when you're out in the civilian world without other patriots to cover your back. Like Gwen says, we got a bunch of commie-ass punks down in Civic Park. There's more of em by the day. God knows what they're really up to. Add to that the unknown nature of any number of, uh, foreign-type folks in our city. It only takes one of them to strap a bunch of plastique and ball bearings on his chest – or her chest, let's be PC here – and go for a walk down at the mall. If you hear somebody shoutin Alluha Akbar in a public place, well, it's already over for you and the fifty poor suckers in a hundred yard radius around you. And you don't need me to tell you how useless the cops are in these situations. Point is, check your six, compadres. Observe, orient, decide, act. That's what we do.

Anything else I got to say tonight, I'll say to the executive committee afterwards. Thanks."

There are nods around the room.

"Next up is the finance committee," says Becca. "That would be me. Nothing to report tonight … unless anyone's got any questions."

Becca looks around the room, lips pursed. Nobody has any questions.

Becca nods. She says, "Chair recognizes head of the executive committee and Leader of the Patriot Bloc, Dr Richard Declan."

Declan spends several seconds studying the people in the room. At last he inhales. His shoulders droop a little bit. "I want to say I'm surprised, friends," he says, "to see fewer folks here than I saw last week. And fewer last week than the meeting before that. You may think I don't notice these things, but I do. Yes indeed."

Declan's head lowers. A few strands of hair fall across his forehead.

"Fact is," he says, "when the going gets tough, well, it isn't the tough that get going, it's most people. And they get going in the opposite direction, don't they. Now, the good book – and Gwen, keep me honest here – tells us the testing of faith produces steadfastness in our hearts."

JD glances over at Gwen. She's nodding eagerly.

"But getting our faith tested is hard work," Declan says.

Declan continues on this theme. He says most people aren't interested in steadfastness. They run away when they get their faith tested. His head stays lowered, more hair dropping across his forehead. He would almost look like a man conceding defeat, if it weren't for his white-knuckled grip on the sides of the lectern.

JD knows about being tested. His whole life has been a test. JD is as they come.

As if on cue, he sees Declan staring right at him. Declan's eyes are bright and blazing. He lifts one hand from the lectern and wags his finger at the ceiling.

"… because this is when I need you to prove your faith, friends. Not when we're at the top, but right now, when we're at the bottom. When the deep state has us on the ropes …"

Still staring into JD's eyes. JD feels his pulse quicken. As steadfast as they come, he thinks.

"When the future of not just our cause but our existence is at stake. The time is now. Now. Liberty is at hand. Don't give up. Do not lose your faith."

There is high colour in Declan's face. He slowly breaks away from the lectern and sits down. JD's heart is pounding. He's a little short of breath.

Up front, Ronnie takes the lectern. He says it's real important everyone makes it out again next week, because an important announcement is going to be made about important changes coming down the pipe. Meantime, that's about all there is to talk about tonight. Ronnie makes a motion to conclude the meeting. His motion is passed and a minute later everyone is standing up, talking to each other in low voices.

JD stretches, stifles a yawn. He might be steadfast, but he's not used to political meetings. He's curious about the changes coming down the pipe. He's curious about the uprising against the deep state Declan talked about last week. JD isn't entirely sure what the deep state is, but he guesses the deep state might be an alias for Them. JD knows a sinister conspiracy when he sees one.

He turns to head to the coffee urns at the back, sees Gage and Declan off to the side. Gage tells Declan something. Declan nods. Looks at JD. Gestures for him to come over.

When JD gets close to the two men, Declan offers another of his firm handshake. Declan pulls JD in close. "I heard you got yourself up here tonight, my friend. I heard you came in a ... unique ... vehicle."

JD's face grows warm. "Well, it's my granddad's truck. He's an ice cream man, you see. I didn't have any other way to—"

"You don't have to explain anything," says Declan. "You did what you had to do. You improvised. I'm impressed. So is Gage."

"I'm blown away," says Gage.

Declan, still gripping JD's hand, says, "Do you have anywhere you need to be for the next little while?"

JD tells Declan he has nowhere to be for the next little while. That's the absolute truth.

"Then why don't you follow Gage," says Declan. "I'll join you shortly."

Declan releases JD's hand and steps away to speak to a few other meeting attendees. Gage puts his hand on JD's upper arm. JD senses that subtle strength again.

"Come on, compadre."

"Where are we going, kind sir?"

Gage doesn't answer. Instead he guides JD across the room. Past the rows of chairs. Past the lectern. Past blue-eyed Jesus.

Gage leads JD to the inner door. He opens it. Stands next to the threshold. Smiles a smile that doesn't show off his stone block teeth, lets go of JD's arm, gestures for JD to go through the doorway.

Gage leads the way through the inner door.

The room beyond the meeting room has more of the scuffed hardwood floor underfoot. A sitting area in the middle. Two old leather couches arranged at right angles to each other around a wooden coffee table. Past the sitting area, a baby grand piano under a canvas dropcloth. In the relative quiet, JD can hear a clock ticking somewhere.

The walls in this room are lined with bookshelves. Many of the shelves are bowed in the middle under the weight of the books they're bearing. The books themselves come in all shapes and sizes. Hardbacks. Paperbacks. Leatherbound encyclopedias. Yellow-spined National Geographic collections that look as though they cover years, if not decades.

JD glances at the nearest shelf. He's looking at a dusty stack of comics laid flat. The comic on the top of the stack is an Archie. Leaning against the stack of Archie comics is a stout hardcover called The Death of the West, by someone named Patrick J Buchanan.

A wide opening leads into a space that might be a dining room, except there's no table. There are more of the same kind of chairs from the meeting room, folded and stacked against the wall. On the far side of the dining room is another opening. Beyond that opening, JD can make out a huge, darkened kitchen.

This is the biggest house JD has ever set foot in.

As if reading JD's mind, Gage gives a little laugh. "I know. Quite the place, isn't it. Fixer-upper, though. Come on."

Gage starts toward the dining room.

As he's leaving the library, JD notices two more things. One is another inner door – an inner inner door, he thinks – set in a small recess between the sagging bookshelves. The door looks old and a bit beat-up, but there's a brand new steel knob and lockplate fitted to it.

The other thing JD notices are the windows. Two in the library, two in the dining room. Each of the windows is tall and narrow. Accented by waterfall curtains of some heavy gold-patterned fabric. The strange thing is the windows themselves, what he can see of them between the curtains. They're covered by pale waferboard.

There's no view of the world outside.

They are halfway through the dining room when an overhead light comes on in the kitchen. JD sees more kitchen cabinets than he could imagine any use for. The cabinets are painted white, with brass hinges and openers. There's a window over the sink, but this too is boarded up.

The old man in the wheelchair appears, coming from somewhere else in the house. He's furiously pumping the circular grips over the wheels of his chair. He comes to a dead stop in front of a set of cabinets above the counter. The old man reaches up. He even manages to stand, knees wobbling.

The effort is not enough. The old man can't reach the cabinet. He makes furious, wordless grunting noises, then sags back into his wheelchair.

JD is about to say something, but Becca appears from the same direction the old man came from. Her cowboy boots clomp across the linoleum tiles of the kitchen floor.

"Dammit, dad, you've had enough to smoke today. You don't need no more."

She closes in on the wheelchair and wheels it back from the cabinet. The old man grunts again.

"Becca," says Gage.

She looks up sharply, not having noticed the two men in the dining room. She fixes JD with a scowl.

"We got a dinner guest," says Gage.

"A dinner guest," says Becca. Her scowl does not go away.

JD smiles. "Thank you for having me, my lady."

Becca laughs, her head thrown back over her wide shoulders. "My lady? Buddy, if you ever call me that again, I'll knock your frickin chiclets in."

Again, there's that faint sense of familiarity about her. The past life encounter. He wishes he knew what it was.

Gage takes JD out to a stone-tiled patio behind the house. Ronnie is there, barbecuing steaks and sausages. The patio is dominated by mossy cement statues of Roman-style women in togas. It's full dark now. This far from downtown, there's little ambient light.

And there's no ELF.

The night air is cold, but a big bonfire is blazing inside a circular metal firepit in the middle of the patio. The firepit is surrounded by aluminum lawn chairs.

Gage indicates for JD to take a seat. JD does. The chair creaks under him, but holds up. They are joined by Becca and the old man in the wheelchair. Becca has put a blanket over the old man's lap. A plastic cooler is balanced on top of the blanket.

Once the old man's wheelchair is in place, Becca lifts the cooler off his lap and sets it on the stone tiles. She opens it, hauls out a six-pack of Busch Ice tallboys. She breaks the cans out of their plastic rings. Walks one over to Ronnie at the barbecue. Gives another to Gage. Opens one for herself and takes a long drink. Then she holds a can out to JD.

JD cracks it open and takes a drink. Becca is watching him. She's not scowling anymore. At least there's that. JD tips his trilby, says thanks, almost adds my lady, catches himself in time.

The old man in the wheelchair doesn't get a beer. He grunts and growls. Becca just puts a hand on his shoulder.

From behind them comes Declan's voice: "Knowing is not enough, we must apply. Willing is not enough, we must do."

Declan appears in the firelight, right behind JD's chair. He plants both hands firmly on JD's shoulders.

"Bruce Lee," says Declan.

"Bruce Lee?" says JD.

"I fear not the man who has practiced ten thousand kicks once," says Declan, "but I fear the man who has practiced one kick ten thousand times."

Declan releases JD's shoulders and comes around and sits down in one of the empty chairs. He's removed his bowtie and undone his top button. Becca holds a beer out to him but he waves it away. He crosses one leg over the other and folds his hands together over his knee and looks JD straight in the eye. "I'm very pleased that you're here."

"I am honoured," says JD.

"And I'm sure you've got questions. Inquiring minds wanting to know and all. Well, my friend, let me summarize. To the rest of the folks at our meetings – to the world at large, you might say – who you see here make up the executive committee of the Patriot Bloc, in its present incarnation as a quote-unquote political organization. But among ourselves, we go by a different name."

Gage clears his throat. "Boss," he says.

Declan waves Gage off. It's the same gesture he used to wave off the beer from Becca. Quick flick of the wrist.

"We are," says Declan, "Patriot Alpha."

"Patriot Alpha," says JD, trying to match Declan's solemnity.

Patriot Alpha, Declan explains, is one of many true patriot resistance cells across the country. Declan says he knows the actual number, but is not able to relay that information. Not yet. Small, effective, the hardest core of the hardest core.

"I'd tell you more about the wider network if I could," says Declan, "but I can't at this time. The burden of that information is better left with me alone."

Among this inner circle, and throughout the wider network of patriots across the country, Declan himself is known by a codename.

Patriot Alpha One.

Declan points at the house. He calls it Forward Operating Base Liberty. Then he points at the property out back. It's too dark beyond the fire for JD to see anything, but Declan says they're sitting on fifty acres. Training grounds, is what he calls the property. Complex terrain.

"And we have this gentleman to thank for it," Declan adds, nodding at the old man in the wheelchair. "To the world at large, he's known as the Very Reverend Donald Dobson Sears. Within the inner circle, he's known as Patriot Alpha Emeritus. I couldn't ask for a better or more inspiring father-in-law."

Declan leans over and pats the old man on the knee. The old man grunts.

Ronnie appears beside JD and holds out a paper plate, laden with a steak and a sausage. Ronnie also offers plastic cutlery in a cellophane sleeve.

JD balances the plate on his lap. "Thank you, kind sir."

Ronnie gives a curt nod.

"Ronnie is our executive officer," says Declan. "Patriot Alpha X-Ray."

Ronnie limps back to the barbecue, where he starts loading up plates for the others.

JD's stomach rumbles. He digs into his steak and sausage as best he can with his plastic utensils. He's much hungrier than he expected. He scarfs down a few bites, then looks around. Becca is sawing off tiny bits of steak and feeding them to the old man. Reverend Sears, Patriot Alpha Emeritus. Whatever the correct title is.

JD finds it hard to keep track. But he wants to keep track. He wants to get it right. He wants to show that he deserves this. He deserves to be a Very Invited Person at the secret Patriot Alpha meeting at Forward Operating Base Liberty. Big things are happening.

He tilts back his beer, washes down a mouthful of sausage. His Busch Ice tallboy is empty, but almost instantly, Becca offers him a replacement. JD cracks it. He notices Declan is still without a drink. He isn't eating, either.

"Patriot Alpha Hawkeye," says Declan. "That's Gage's codename."

Gage tips his tallboy at JD.

The inner network, JD thinks. The Very Very Invited Persons.

"And last but far from least," says Declan, "Patriot Alpha Domestic. My much better half. Behind every great man is a woman rolling her eyes."

Declan is looking at Becca. Becca is still feeding the old man small bites at a time.

JD eats another bite of food and washes it down with more beer. He finds he's thirsty as well as hungry. Declan is looking at him. Steady, unbroken eye contact. Evaluating.

"What's the, ah, mission?" says JD.

"The mission," says Declan.

"Of Alpha Patriot," says JD.

"Patriot Alpha disobeys," Ronnie snaps. "That's what we do, FYI. Because when the government takes away our property and makes us all into slaves, they give us the right to disobey them. That's how it works. They even give us the right to go to war with—"

"I hope that's not what you wrote on the exam, compadre," says Gage, "because you fucked it up."

Ronnie glares at him.

Declan laughs. "Whenever the legislators endeavour to take away and destroy the property of the people, or to reduce them to slavery under arbitrary power, they put themselves into a state of war with the people, who are thereupon absolved of any further obedience. John Locke. You can consider that something of a mission statement for Patriot Alpha."

"The government took away your property?" says JD.

Declan uncrosses his legs and leans in and gestures for JD to do the same. He lowers his voice. "Everything you've heard so far tonight is classified information, my friend. I need you to look me in the eye and tell me you understand that."

JD looks Declan in the eye. "I understand."

"Good. Do you have any idea how few people would grasp what we're talking about?"

Not many, JD thinks. There's no way his brother and sister-in-law or any of their friends would understand this. Lil, most definitely not. He's not sure about Simone. Granddad might get it, but Granddad is out of the picture for now. Then again, if everybody understood what Declan was talking about, everybody would be a Very Invited Person. That wouldn't work, would it?

JD himself isn't sure he understands it. But he's here, and that's what counts.

"It's your turn, compadre," says Gage.

JD looks at him. Patriot Alpha Hawkeye, still wearing the ballistic glasses. Reflected firelight dances on the lenses.

"My turn for what, kind sir?"

"Your turn to brief us on what you're all about."

"We got a right to know who you are," Ronnie adds.

"Well," says JD. He goes to take another sip of beer, only to find he's emptied this tallboy as well. He hears a ringtab pop open. Sure enough Becca is already holding out a fresh beer. He takes it, drinks a mouthful, considers the people around him. They're looking at him expectantly.

Even the old man seems engaged.

"Well, if you really want to hear about it, kind sirs, my la—my, my, ah, Becca – I guess you'll want to know where I was born and everything about my childhood and all that kind of thing ..."

JD talks. He talks much more than he's used to talking. He tells them about his mother. About the men who came in and out of her life. He tells them what happened to her.

He's four beers in by this point.

He tells them about how his brother went to live with their grandmother, while he moved in with Granddad. The nights doing security work out of that trailer. He tells them about the time he saw Granddad fighting those cops. In the end it's never a fair fight when the cops are involved.

"Caesar's Legion," says Declan.

"Fuckin pigs," says Gage.

Five beers. Head swimming.

He tells them about high school. The incident with the samurai sword. He was only keeping it in his locker temporarily. It had nothing to do with anything or anyone at school. He tells them about dropping out. The string of jobs that followed.

At this point, Becca rises from her chair and wheels the old man into the house. She leaves the beer cooler beside Ronnie.

After she's gone, Gage stands and goes behind one of the statues. He's gone long enough to take a leak. When he returns, he's carrying two pieces of stovewood. He drops them into the firepit. A red burst of sparks whooshes up. "I gotta head out, boss," he says. "I'll catch hell from the ball-and-chain if I come in past midnight again."

Declan stands up and shakes Gage's hand. Gage gives Ronnie a chummy punch in the shoulder. Ronnie responds with a baleful look. Lastly Gage comes over and offers JD a handshake. Then Gage is gone.

"Carry on," Ronnie tells JD.

JD does so. He tells them how he met Lil. How good it was for a while. How incredible it was to have a child ... and then how wrong everything went.

JD starts into his sixth beer, which Declan has handed him.

"Nothing happens just because, you know?" says JD. "It's Them—"

He's struck mid-word not by a blast of ELF but by the exact opposite. Utter silence. For a moment he can't even hear the crackling of the fire. He looks at the two remaining men. He licks his lips. He's drunk. JD thinks he's said too much. He chews his lip, stays quiet.

"What happened to your grandfather?" says Declan.

"He had to go away for a while. Into hiding."

"What, from the feds?" says Ronnie.

"The feds," says JD. "Yeah. And other, you know, other agencies. He didn't even tell me where he went, actually. In case I got persecuted or interrogated or anything of that nature."

Ronnie nods, scratches his chin through his beard. The look on Ronnie's face might be approval. "Wouldn't be the first patriot who had to hide out," he says.

JD wants to change the subject. "How about you, good sir?"

How about me what? says Ronnie.

"What makes you a ... patriot?"

Ronnie casts a quick glance at Declan. Declan nods. Ronnie begins to talk. He grew up right here in Bayfield. A working class, school-of-hard-knocks neighbourhood. Ever since he was a kid, he saw the way that neighbourhood, really the whole city, has changed. Has become a drain-catch for the worst of the worst from all over the world.

"Oh sure, there were always the nig—" Ronnie glances at Declan, seems to check himself. "—always the negroids, but these last twenty-five thirty years it's turned into something else. There's Vietnameses, worst car thiefs you can find. There's the push-starts, curry-munchers, getting a monopoly on all the convenience stores just so's they can jack up the prices on basic crap you need for your life. There's Mexicans all over town now. Every one of them will undercut you and work a cash job, just to put you out of work. There's even Gypsies. Gypsies, for pete's sake. No matter where you go, nobody in the world wants Gypsies around. Unless you bolt it down, a Gypsy is gonna steal it. That's just historical fact."

Ronnie says he worked as a mechanic since he was twenty years old. He's in his mid-thirties now. Seven or eight years ago he got his diesel mechanic ticket. Five years ago he'd put in for a maintenance job on an oil rig in the North Atlantic. Would have been upwards of a hundred grand a year.

He was on his way to the interview, wearing a good suit, crossing the street, when he got hit by a car. Shattered his right leg – in fact the leg had to be amputated just below the knee. Ronnie was laid up for six months. Lost the rig job before it even started.

"And you know who hit me?" says Ronnie. "Some push-start curry-muncher is who, some half-blind sixty-year-old fresh-off-the-boat broad driving her huge SUV like she was still in Pakistan. The woman wasn't insured. Wasn't even licensed to drive. That sure S-C-E-R-W-E-D me over, money-wise."

When he was eventually able to work again, the only job he could find was working in a garage owned by a Muslim. Not kidding. A straight-up Muslim. From the Middle East or Iraq or wherever.

"Never mind the negroids," says Ronnie. "Never mind the Gypsies or the Mexicans or even the curry-munchers. There's nobody worse than the Muslims. Jihadists, all of them. When they're not doing terrorism, they're trying to outbreed us, ten little jihadist kids for every one of ours. That's the way they operate. And we're the cucks letting them do it. We're letting them do it."

Ronnie sits back. He looks like he might trail off, but then he leans forward again. He's staring into the fire. "I'm personally ready to see some major changes in this country. And if what it takes is revolution, then okay. Once we get things started, everybody else is gonna follow us. All the real patriots who are as sick of the Muslims as I am. Doctor Declan knows all about the jihadists, buddy. He's in it deeper than anybody."

Declan doesn't say if he's deeper in it than anybody. He just smiles faintly.

By the sounds of it, JD supposes Ronnie might be a quote-unquote racist. An angry one at that. JD's been too busy uncovering Them to give much thought to racial issues. But if Ronnie's got a place in Declan's inner circle – if he's one of the Very Very Invited Persons – he can't be all bad. He must—

That strange silence, that anti-ELF, hits JD again. He loses his train of thought altogether.

Declan puts JD up for the night. JD has a hard time keeping track of the dark staircases and hallways. The small room he's shown to is somewhere on the third floor, under steep eaves. Declan enters first. Turns on a lamp beside the bed. There's no shade on the lamp, just a bare lightbulb atop a floral-patterned vase.

The bed is brass-framed, narrow, covered in a quilt. There are faded choo-choo trains on the peeling wallpaper. Cobwebs in the corners. An old cabinet full of wonky-eyed porcelain dolls.

There's a small window over the bed – or what JD suspects is a window. All he can see is a square of plywood screwed into the wall where a window might be. The room is draughty, smells like dust.

"It's humble," says Declan, "but it's much more luxurious than where we first met. I bet your granddad is sleeping rough, wherever he is."

JD is sure Granddad is sleeping in a thatched hut on a beach in Mexico with a beautiful senorita on either arm, or has found his way into a palace in Russia somewhere, but he doesn't say this.

"There's a commode across the hall," says Declan. "Now, sleep well. We have a lot of big things ahead of us."

Declan steps out of the room and closes the door behind him. JD puts a hand on the wall to steady himself. A strange room in a strange house. No, not just a house. Forward Operating Base Liberty. Right. But still a strange room. He doesn't care for the dolls. He's doubtful he'll be able to fall asleep.

He strips down to his underwear, leaving his trilby on until last. He takes his hat off carefully. Once the protective faraday shield is off his head he listens for any sign of ELF. Nothing, not even from the bare lightbulb. He sets the hat on one of the brass bedposts.

He's about to fold back the quilt and get into bed when something compels him to go to the door. He reaches out, takes hold of the knob. Even before he turns it he knows it's going to be locked fast from the outside. As if … as if what?

The knob turns, the door opens.

Of course it opens. JD is here as the Very Invited Person of Patriot Alpha One, Dr Richard Declan. What is there to be afraid of?

He closes the door and shuffles back across the room. Gets into the bed. The old frame creaks. He's still doubtful about the idea of falling asleep. It's the last thought he has after he turns out the light and the room drops into pure blackness.

JD isn't sure what time he wakes up. The boarded-over window doesn't admit any daylight. He turns on the bedside lamp. He feels as though he's slept for a good, long stretch. The sleep doesn't do much to soothe his hangover, however. He can still taste Busch Ice at the back of his throat.

He gets up, goes to the bathroom across the hall, relieves himself, splashes water on his body. Back in the bedroom he dresses. He hesitates, then leaves his trilby on the bedpost.

He finds his way to the kitchen on the main floor. He's met with the smell of frying bacon. It's tantalizing through his hangover. He sees Becca at the stove, working a spatula over a skillet. Her peroxide blonde hair is tied back. She's dressed in a white tank-top and a pair of sweatpants and flipflops. The clothing is close-fitting, accentuating her muscular girth. For a moment all JD can do is stare at her boulder-like rear end.

Without looking over her shoulder, she tells him she heard him moving around upstairs. "Finally," she adds, then, "I hope you like bacon and eggs and home fries, because that's what you're getting."

JD is astonished. He can't remember the last time someone cooked him breakfast. Lil never did.

"It's 12:45," says Becca. "In the PM, just so you're tracking."

12:45. JD slept almost thirteen hours.

He waits for his breakfast in the library. The old man is in there, sleeping in his wheelchair, with one of the ancient Archie comics open on his lap. JD peruses the other books. There are a lot of old classics. Treasure Island. Robinson Crusoe. 20,000 Leagues Under The Sea. There's a vast collection of Hardy Boy books. There are a few books by a guy named Jerry Falwell.

Near the Falwell books, JD sees multiple copies of the same thick hardcover. He picks one off the shelf. Unlocking Health, Wealth, and Happiness: Ten Secrets Straight from Heaven, by the Very Reverend Donald Dobson Sears. There's a middle-aged man with a beaming smile on the cover. JD realizes he's a thirty-year younger version of the old man in the wheelchair.

JD opens the book to a random page, reads: ... grace of the Lord and power of the Holy Spirit exist not only for the salvation of your soul, but to empower you to live a prosperous, wealthy, and magnificent life here on earth. This is what God desires for all His children …

This makes me think of that show his mom watched during her Jesus phase. Great News Gospel Hour. That, in turn, makes him think of Declan.

"Get it while it's hot," says Becca. "Or not. Doesn't matter to me."

She's set a place for him at a four-seater table set against one of the kitchen walls. JD sits. Five pieces of bacon and a mound of scrambled eggs and a generous scoop of home fries are steaming on a paper plate in front of him. There's hot coffee in a chipped mug with a picture of Garfield on it.

Becca leans on a nearby section of the counter, arms crossed under her prodigious breasts, watching JD with one eyebrow half-raised. JD starts into the meal. He doesn't want to betray how hungry he is, so he forces himself to eat slowly. Becca keeps staring at him. The only sound is the ticking clock.

After a few mouthfuls of food, JD says, "Is Patriot Alpha One here?"

"Richard?" says Becca. "He's here. He's working in his office. Might see him later. Might not."

"I, uh, noticed your dad wrote a book …"

"My dad wrote five books, actually. Each and every one of them a bestseller. You ever see a show called the Great News Gospel Hour? That was my dad's show. His ministry reached countless people. Brought them the Word of Jesus and taught them how to live prosperous lives. Did you know we kept thoroughbred horses here when I was a kid? Anyways, are you saved?"

"Am I saved?" says JD.

"Are you washed in the blood of the Lamb?"

JD has to think for a moment. He says, "I'm a very spiritual person."

Becca sniffs. "After we get the revolution started, there's gonna be a whole lot of old time gospel brought back into this country. And it's not gonna be a bunch of fuckin cat-ladies sitting around their living rooms on Friday nights, trying to pray away the abortion clinics or the communists."

She goes over to the sink and starts washing the skillet. JD can't help but stare at her backside again. He forces his eyes away. He drinks a mouthful of coffee. He tries to think of the things sheeple talk about when they're making conversation. "How did you and Patriot Alpha—Richard, I mean—how did you two good folks meet each other?"

"Richard joined my dad's ministry in 1986 as a junior pastor. Was his idea to take the show in a different direction ..." Becca trails off. Then her eyes narrow. "Which brought on a whole lot of bullshit trouble later on. The government investigations and whatnot. The lawsuits. Richard got done-up for it. Went to jail. We got married the day he got out. That was fifteen years ago. I was twenty-two. He was thirty-four."

JD isn't sure what to do with any of this information. He asks if they ever had any kids. More sheeple smalltalk.

Before the words are all the way out of his mouth, she flatly says no. "No kids. Wasn't in God's plan."

Just then, there's a holler from the library. JD almost jumps out of his chair. He looks over, through the opening, and sees the old man is awake. The old man's face is twisted in an expression of pain. The Archie comic is on the floor below.

Becca stops washing the skillet and walks over to her father. She doesn't hurry. She wheels him into the kitchen. Right to the table, the empty place to JD's left. Then she heads over to one of the cabinets. The same cabinet the old man was trying to get to the night before.

JD looks at the old man. The old man is looking back at him. His eyes are bleary and rimmed with tears.

"Hello, kind sir."

The old man squeezes his eyes shut and howls again.

Becca returns to the table. She bends over, sets something down. At first JD doesn't see what it is, because he's looking down the front of her tank top. Then, to his surprise, he sees what she's brought. A small glass waterpipe and a plastic bag bulging with weed. A label on the bag reads For Medical Use Only.

Becca packs the bowl. The old man's holler has dropped to a low, continuous moan. Tears are streaming down his cheeks.

"My dad has fibromyalgia," Becca says.

"I'm sorry," says JD.

She shrugs. He thinks she might say something reflective – maybe something like, Oh, it's a burden from the Lord, or, It's a test of faith –

but she doesn't. Was this the magnificent life the old man had in mind when he wrote his five bestselling books?

Gradually, JD's eyes shift from the old man back over to the drooping frontage of Becca's tank top. Then he glances up and finds her looking straight at him. A beat passes. Without saying anything she goes back to preparing the waterpipe.

After JD finishes his early afternoon breakfast, he figures it's time to get going. He doesn't want to overstay his welcome. But Becca tells him to stay. Stick around, she says, because they need his help with something.

"Unless you got somewhere to be."

"I don't," says JD.

She doesn't seem surprised by this, but she doesn't tell him what they need, either. She helps the old man take a few hauls from the waterpipe. She doesn't offer any to JD.

For the rest of the afternoon, JD to his own devices. So he spends his time in the library, reading. He dips in and out of naps. The old man stays in the library as well, back at his Archie comics. He seems oblivious to JD.

The first book JD reads is from the vast Hardy Boys collection. The Secret Agent on Flight 101. It's easy reading. He bangs through it in a little over two hours. The Hardy Boys' father goes missing in a magic trick performed by a jewel thief. Then the father turns up later on an airplane – Flight 101 – in an undercover role. It's a ruse to catch the jewel thief. Sounds like the kind of trick Granddad could pull off.

JD picks up the old man's book again, Unlocking Health, Wealth, and Happiness: Ten Secrets Straight from Heaven. As he takes it from the shelf, he turns to the old man and holds it up. The old man only gapes.

JD sits back down on one of the couches. He tries to start the book from the beginning. He doesn't make it much further than the foreword, written by someone named Kenneth Copeland. All the God-talk reminds him too much of his mother's Jesus-phase. He closes the book, sets it down beside him, and has another snooze. He still hasn't seen Declan at all.

Some time later Becca makes supper. It's Shake'N Bake chicken served with spaghetti and chocolate milk. She sets out three places at the table in the kitchen.

Becca says a rapidfire grace over the meal, then sets to cutting up the food on her father's plate. JD begins eating. Before JD can come up with any sheeple smalltalk, Becca says, "You know something? I've always been a Christian. That's the thing about me. I was washed in the blood of the Lamb from my earliest days. Does that mean I'm without sin? No, of course it doesn't. I sin. I'm prideful. I'm not real meek or ladylike. I get tempted ..."

This last she says looking at JD. Then she frowns. "Don't look at me like that," she says. "Don't be a creepo, buddy-boy. I'll knock you straight in the chiclets."

She says she used to work as a nurse at Olympus Hospital in the west part of the city. She worked there six years. For five of those six years they always had a Christmas tree in December. Standard operating procedure, she adds, for a Christian city, in a Christian country.

"Well, this one year, word comes down that some fat-cat on the hospital's board of directors wanted to get rid of the Christmas tree. Not just the tree, but anything to do with Christmas or Christ or things of that nature. Why? It might be offensive to all the non-Christians. The atheists and Jews and what-have-you.

"Offensive."

Becca enunciates the word as if it's some bitter taste in her mouth.

She stewed on it. She brought it up at a staff meeting. She said if the Christmas tree offends somebody, why don't they go get their stitches put in or their catheter changed at some other hospital? She wasn't the only nurse – or surgeon or resident or security guard or janitor – who felt that way. But the answers from on-high weren't forthcoming.

December of that year was still a week away. Becca had moved from stewing to fuming. She lost sleep over it. Christmas was offensive. "You know what? Having to get nailed to a cross to take all mankind's sins onto your own shoulders, that's offensive."

After one sleepless night, she found herself working a shift in the hospital's administration wing. Where a board meeting happened to be taking place. If Jesus could go into the temple and get all up in the faces of the money-lenders, then Becca could do the same with the atheist fat-cats. Which was what she did. She stormed the board meeting.

Which one of you thinks Christmas is offensive?

At first, all she got back were blank looks.

I asked yous a question. Which one of you thinks Christmas is offensive?

Finally a skinny man in a sweater and tie told her there'd been some discussion about using the words festive or holiday instead of Christmas. As in, festive tree. Holiday decorations. The board hadn't come to an agreement yet. They were actually going to talk about it at that very meeting.

Well, Becca told them, the agreement better be keeping the Christ is Christmas.

The man frowned, asked her if that was some kind of threat.

Maybe it was his sweater and tie combination. Maybe it was his pinched little face. Maybe it was the weeks Becca had stewed and fumed. Maybe it was the entire night she laid awake thinking about Jesus in the temple. It took two big black security guards to pull her off the little man. By that time she'd closed both his eyes and smashed his stupid mouth into a bloody pulp.

She got fired. Convicted on an assault charge. Given eighteen months. She served six. Spent a lot of those six months thinking about the world, about the way Christians were being persecuted all over.

"Gwen is a nice lady," says Becca. She says lady almost the same way she said offensive. "But her little prayer hours? They don't mean nothing. What God needs are more Christians who are willing to stand up and be counted and take the fight to the atheists and all their friends. Take the fight to the devil himself. You want to take the Christ out of Christmas?"

For a second JD thinks the question is directed at him.

Before he can answer, Becca says, "Just try. Just try to take the Christ out of Christmas."

She leans back in her chair. Picks at the food on her plate. There's something alluring about her intensity. JD is aroused.

"Anyway, around the time I made a Christian stand at the hospital," says Becca, "that's when me and Richard started going steady. Richard knows all about what's happening to the Christians in this country. The way we're being attacked. Richard knows the End Times are coming up on us real fast. If they haven't started already."

"Is that how you and Patriot--Richard--met?"

"Richard was my dad's legal advisor on the Great News Gospel Hour for a while," she says.

"I thought Richard was a doctor," says JD. "You know, a PhD professor."

"Richard is a jack-of-all-trades. He's even a master of a few of them. That's what all real men should be like. Real men should have different talents and skills they can put to use whenever they need to."

She's giving JD a curious look. JD shifts on his seat.

"You got a woman?" she says.

JD swallows some chicken, clears his throat. "I am in a committed relationship, yes. My partner's name is Simone."

"Simone," says Becca. "Does Simone know where you're at?"

"No she doesn't. We prefer to keep various parts of our lives separate and, you know, personal."

"Well that's good. Because everything we got here is classified. Invite-only."

Invite-only. She's right about that. JD smiles.

Declan does not appear during supper. Declan does not appear that evening at all. At some point, maybe eight or nine o'clock, JD takes another one of the Hardy Boys books and heads back upstairs to the small room. He cleans up in the bathroom as best he can. Brushes his teeth with his finger. In the bedroom he turns his underwear inside-out. The dolls in the cabinet stare at him blankly.

He gets in bed, attempts to read, but falls asleep with the light on and The Clue Of The Broken Blade open on the narrow mattress beside him.

Forward Operating Base Liberty is silent.

"Do you believe in the right to defend your person?" Declan says. "Do you believe the words of Ronald Reagan when he says self-defence isn't just a right – it's a duty?"

After an appropriate pause, JD says, "I do."

Declan smiles.

The two of them are standing on a large square of wrestling mats in the barn behind the house. One entire wall inside the barn is lined with wood-framed stalls. There's a big stone sink. The rest of the interior is open space, an indoor arena from the time they kept horses here.

There are no horses anymore. There are only a few drifts of remaining hay here and there on the concrete floor. The arena is now occupied on one half by a makeshift weightlifting area, consisting of some benches and a rack of dumbbells. Next to the weightlifting area is the square of wrestling mats where JD and Declan are standing. On one corner of the square is a beige punching mannequin atop a sand-filled base.

Beyond the mats and the punching mannequin is a section of bare concrete floor. There's a car there, a vintage Dodge Charger with a black and yellow paintjob. The Charger has a rusty set of vanity plates. PRZ GOD, the plates proclaim.

The air inside the barn is chilly and dry. There's a fall rain coming down outside. Rainfall drums on the corrugated roof overhead.

It's midday. JD has been awake for an hour. He woke to Declan leaning against the doll cabinet.

"Preparing oneself for the coming battles can never start early enough," Declan said. "That's my own quote, by the way, but you can use it if you want. Indeed, I'd be honoured if you did."

Declan was wearing a dark Reebok tracksuit, sweatband around his head, and bright white running shoes on his feet. JD could see the GPS locator strapped to Declan's ankle. Declan had a pair of gray cotton sweatpants and hoodie with him. The hoodie was old and had holes at the elbows. JD put the hoodie on, then the sweatpants, finding them both loose on him. Declan didn't have an extra pair of running shoes, so JD got back into his own oxfords.

Once again, his trilby stayed on the bedpost.

Down in the kitchen, Declan offered JD some toast and coffee. Declan himself didn't eat anything. There was no sign of Becca or the old man. As soon as JD finished eating, Declan led him out to the barn. They went via the back door, over the stone-tiled porch. The firepit was black and cold.

"I want you to be able to handle yourself in a variety of situations," says Declan. "I don't ever want to see you at the mercy of a pack of savage Negroids again, as you were when we first met."

JD blinks, confused. He's not sure what Declan is talking about.

For the next hour, Declan leads JD through a series of unarmed drills on the mannequin. Elbow strike, hammer fist, palm heel strike, headbutt, eye strike. "None of these techniques are meant to be clean," Declan says. "They're meant to get the job done. I think you saw me put a few in action."

JD has no memory of ever seeing Declan put any of these strikes in action, but he doesn't say so.

Then Declan talks about things to do if you're really in trouble. "Never mind the strikes," he says. "Go for the things that are guaranteed to get the job done. Chop the windpipe. Kick the side of the kneecap. Stomp the toes or the top of the foot. If necessary, do not be ashamed to go for the gonads."

To punctuate his point, Declan takes hold of JD's balls through the sweatpants. Declan's grip isn't painful, but it is firm.

"This is a trump card, every time," says Declan. "What are you going to do in this situation, my friend? What can you do?"

"Fight back?" says JD.

"Can you indeed?"

Declan squeezes a little harder.

"I, uh ... "

"A hard twist left, a hard twist right," says Declan. "And I mean hard. Pull and twist. Twist like you're taking the lid off a jar. Or squeeze like you're getting every last drop out of a lemon. If you apply enough force, you can rupture one or both testicles. Render your opponent unconscious. The longer-term damage is sterility. If you apply enough force, the pain can kill your opponent."

Declan squeezes a little harder yet. Now it starts to hurt.

"Richard," says JD.

"You call me Dr Declan. Or sir. Or in the absence of civilians, you call me Patriot Alpha One. Because that's who I am."

"Patriot Alpha One," JD murmurs.

Declan applies a fraction more of a squeeze to JD's balls ... then lets them go. He stands back, gives JD a beatific smile. "I'm proud of you, my friend. There are great things ahead of you in this humble cause of ours. When I told you we needed you, I meant it with all my heart."

The training session is not yet over. Declan goes into one of the old horse stalls and comes back with a slender cylindrical object. At first, JD thinks it's a flashlight. Declan stands a few paces away with the cylinder alongside his hip. Then there's a sound – snick – and the cylinder has tripled in length. There's a small black knob on the end.

JD is looking at 21-inch expandable baton, just like the kind the cops carry.

"Suppose," says Declan, "a tyrannical government takes away your guns. It's an unprecedented violation of your liberty and private property, of course, but they know what they're doing. Until you're ready to settle the score, are you going to go around unarmed?"

"Of course not," says JD, then adds, "Patriot Alpha One, sir."

"Of course not," Declan agrees.

Declan shows JD how to use the baton. Shows him how to deploy it in a confined space, rotating his wrist and snapping it down at the same time. Shows him how to use the baton as a shield, how to block incoming strikes.

From defensive techniques, Declan goes on to the offense. "Go for the bony areas," he says. "The kneecaps, the collarbone, the ribs, the elbows, the wrists. You hit someone in muscle or fat, it'll hurt, but it won't debilitate like a strike to bony surface."

Declan pauses. "The head is a bony area, he says, but you go for the head you can fracture the skull. Eliminate the target altogether. Not necessarily a bad thing, depending on the circumstances. Say if it's you versus a horde of dirty urban subhumans, hopped up on god-knows-what. Hawkeye – Gage – can teach you more."

JD practises expanding the baton. He likes the sound of it snicketing out of the base. He likes the way it hisses in the air when he swings it. He goes to work on the mannequin. He imagines his countless enemies.

Them.

He swings and strikes, swings and strikes. The power he feels in his arm is electric.

Them. Those who killed his mother, who drove Granddad into hiding.

He's vaguely aware of Declan goading him on, Declan crying, "Lay him down! Lay down that degenerate, that negroid savage, that zionist, that zhid, that ugly Christless mohammedan! Lay down that tyrant, make him bleed!"

Them. Those who persecute him endlessly. Those behind the conspiracy.

JD strikes and strikes until he's exhausted. His shoulders heave. He sucks wind. He senses Declan step in behind him, very close. Declan takes hold of JD's arms from behind.

Declan speaks softly, close to JD's ear. "There's more to come, my friend. Yes indeed. There's more to come."

Declan releases JD's arm and steps away.

JD turns around. "Sir, when you and I met in the city jail, that wasn't your first time locked up, right?"

A brief shadow passes over Declan's face. The shadow turns into a cool, composed smile. "Why, no. It was not. Have you been looking into me online?"

"No sir. I don't touch the internet. It's much too dangerous."

"Of course," says Declan. "To answer your question, I used to assist Patriot Alpha Emeritus in his televised ministry. That ministry, the Great News Gospel Time, was broadcast right out of Bayfield, on the public access station. It reached hundreds of thousands of viewers. Perhaps millions. Perhaps more. It was shameful, then, when our show came under investigation by cynical government snoops. They accused us of being fraudsters. Of being conmen."

Declan sighs, looks away. "The stress of it almost killed Donald. I believe his current health is a direct result of what he went through in the 1990s. I couldn't bear to see what was happening to him, this man who'd mentored me. So I pleaded guilty to the charges. I did so in his place. As Christ did in ours."

Declan is smiling again.

JD takes a moment to think of a reply. Everything he considers feels lame. Finally, he says, "What an incredible stor—"

Declan jabs a finger skyward. "They sentenced me to six years, my friend. Six years. But I was released in less than four. By all accounts, I was a model prisoner. In my time locked away from society, do you know what I did with myself? I taught other inmates to read and write. I exercised. And I got my doctorate, via correspondence, through the prestigious International Institute of Grand Cayman. How many other convicts can make the same claim? I was a model prisoner." Declan has that intense glow in his eyes again.

JD clears his throat. "Truly, sir, that's an incredible story. Ah, may I ask, sir, why you were in jail this time, when I met you?"

"Because the tyrants aren't finished with me as a model prisoner," says Declan. He points to the GPS locator on his ankle. "Do you see ridiculous fetter? It's not foolproof. Indeed it is not. I can remove it from my person whenever I wish. It's a formality, really. A sign of my willingness to cooperate. To continue to be the model prisoner. For now."

Back in the house, late afternoon. JD finds his shirt and trousers have been cleaned and folded. He would love to have fresh underwear and socks as well, but he'll take what he can get.

He changes into the clean clothes. He's still buzzing from his practise with the expandable baton. He feels like more of a Very Invited Person than ever.

Becca is back in the kitchen. She's made dinner, a big pot of chilli served with hamburger buns. The old man is in his wheelchair at the table again, muttering and murmuring. JD wonders if he's had a hit of the waterpipe.

Declan joins them for the meal. He's in good spirits. He even takes a tiny portion of the chilli. No bun. This is the first time JD has seen him eat anything.

Throughout the meal, Declan seems intent on two things. The first is engaging the old man in various religious matters.

"As we were talking about the other day, Reverend," says Declan, "if it was God's plan to offer salvation through Jesus, why didn't he send Jesus in the first place, instead of letting generations of Jews think they were the chosen people? A problem, I might add, we're still grappling with today."

The old man mumbles.

The second thing Declan seems intent on is making sure JD is eating. "Darling, would you get our friend another helping?" Declan says to Becca when JD has finished his first bowl. "He's going to need the calories."

Declan smiles but doesn't elaborate. Must be classified.

Once dinner is finished, Becca turns to Declan and quietly says, "I'll bring the coffee."

Declan nods, stands, then asks if JD will follow him. "I've got something very important to discuss with you."

JD thinks Declan will show him through the combination-locked door in the library. Insteads Declan leads JD up to the second floor. A study at the end of the hallway. Dark wood panelling on the walls, more bookshelves, a big oak desk, a stone fireplace in the corner. A small fire is crackling, warding off the chills of the house.

There's something different to this room. It takes JD a few seconds to realize what it is. The windows here are uncovered. But there's nothing to see right now. Night has fallen outside. The windows are dark except for reflected firelight.

Declan sits down behind the desk. He points to a leather upholstered chair. JD sits. The chair is lower than he expected. Low enough that he has to look up to meet Declan's eyeline.

"I bet you don't even know what one of your best qualities is," says Declan.

JD likes to think he has many good qualities. He might have gone to the school of hard knocks, but that didn't dull his strength, smarts, sex appeal, or charisma. Or humility, he thinks. In spite of everything They have thrown at him, he—

"You don't stand out," says Declan.

"I don't stand out?"

"No. Your sense of fashion is understated and tasteful, even if it's forty years out of date. I like the trilby hat, by the way. That's a nice touch. You're not all jacked-up with silly muscles, or covered in unsightly tattoos ..."

Declan pauses, looks JD up and down.

"X-Ray and Hawkeye," he continues, "Ronnie and Gage, they're soldiers for the cause. Becca is too, in her fashion. Point is, my friend, you can dress all of them up – Ronnie and Gage and Becca – but they still look exactly like what they are. Soldiers for the cause. Ronnie, in fact, used to take a fresh Bic razor to his scalp every morning. I told him that had to stop. We are not some suspenders-snapping coalition of meth-addled skinheads. On that note, I have insisted on a certain standard of language. You won't hear us using the kind of guttural language the savages spew in their godawful rap music. No indeed. We are, above all, credible. And we must be seen to be credible ..."

JD has already started to lose the thread of what Declan is talking about. Meth-addled skinheads and savages and rap music and something about Bic razors.

Becca enters the study. She's carrying a tray with a coffee pot and three stacked styrofoam cups. There's a large rolled-up sheet of paper under her arm. She sets the tray down and leans the rolled-up paper on the side of the desk. She pours the coffee into the cups.

"How do you want it," she says.

"Oh," says JD. "Triple-triple, my la ... Triple-triple."

She nods. Declan, JD sees, takes his coffee black.

Once the coffee is served, Becca sits down in another leather chair. She is giving JD a steady, unwavering gaze. "My husband thinks you're legit," she says.

"Well, I am legit," says JD. "I'm very legit."

"Then you'll do something for us," she says. "And you'll do it tonight."

"Not for us," says Declan. "For the cause. For Patriot Alpha, for our wider network across the country. I'd tell you more about that network if I could, but I can't at this time. The burden of that information is better left with me alone."
Midnight.

JD is driving Granddad's ice cream truck along an unpaved rural route a north of Side Road 10. He's hemmed in by bush on either side of the road. He can see the glow of the city against the sky in the south, but he hasn't seen the lights of a house in several minutes. The rainfall from earlier in the day has quit.

JD left FOB Liberty by way of a long laneway through the fields behind the house. The laneway took him to another sheetmetal gate, then to the next road up from Side Road 10. Now he's driving slowly. He is wide awake and energized. It's not just the coffee he drank. He is energized with purpose.

Back at the house, after JD said he would accept the mission, the tone in Declan's study became serious. Becca drew the curtains over the windows. Then she locked the study door from the inside.

"I don't think I need to tell you how confidential and sensitive this conversation is," Declan said.

Becca unrolled the sheet of paper she'd carried in with the coffee and spread it over the desk. It was a very simple hand-drawn map. There was a grid of rural roads. One of them was labelled Side Road 10. Along Side Road 10 he saw a square drawn by hand and ruler. The square was labelled F.O.B. LIBERTY.

"You are going to drive your grandfather's truck from our location to a rendezvous point here," said Declan, indicating the route with his fingertip. "When you get to this road, you'll slow right down and carry on eastward. If you see other vehicles, if there's someone behind you, let them pass."

"Don't talk to anybody," said Becca. "You pass someone with a flat tire or someone hitchhiking, you leave em to God's mercy."

"You'll carry on eastward until you're contacted," Declan continued.

"Contacted how?" said JD.

"By this."

Declan opened a drawer in his desk and brought out a Ziploc bag. Inside the bag was an older-model Nokia cell phone and a neatly-coiled AC charger. He held the bag out to JD.

"This phone is prepaid. All outgoing calls are disabled, except for one, but that's not important right now."

"On the cop shows," said Becca, "they call it a burner ..."

Now, as promised, the Nokia – the burner – lights up and starts to chime on the floor between the seats. JD is tense enough that the digital ringtone causes him to stomp on the brake. He rocks forward in his seat. He composes himself, then picks up the Ziploc bag and extracts the burner and accepts the call.

"Drive another fifty feet then pull over," says the voice on the other end.

JD does as instructed. In the throw of the headlights, he can see a narrow track branching into the trees ahead. Then two shadowy forms separate themselves from the bush. They approach the ice cream truck. One of the shadows has a pronounced limp.

The shadows separate around the front of the ice cream truck. The driver side door opens. There's Gage, dressed in dark cargo pants and black hiking boots and a black knitted cap and black gloves. He's wearing, as always, his plastic ballistic glasses. There's a backpack slung over his shoulder.

"Move over," says Gage, climbing up into the driver's seat. "I see you're still dressed like a vice cop straight out of 1975. That's fun."

JD is about to get into the passenger seat when the passenger side door opens and Ronnie appears. Ronnie is dressed almost identically to Gage, less the glasses and the backpack. He climbs up into the passenger seat, pulling his gimpy leg onto the seat with both hands.

JD has no choice but to crouch in the middle, between the seats. "Gentlemen," he says.

"No talking," Ronnie hisses.

So far everything is going according to plan. Whatever the plan is.

"You'll rendezvous with X-Ray and Hawkeye," Declan had explained. "The rendezvous is phase one. X-Ray and Hawkeye have the details of phases two and three, and they'll fill you in after the RV is complete."

There wasn't much more to the mission briefing in Declan's study. Declan went over the route at least three more times, until JD could retrace it with his own fingertip and describe what was to happen. Then Declan nodded at Becca. She picked the map up from the desk and took it over to the fireplace and fed it into the flame.

Any questions JD had were answered with, "The less you know the better." Or, "All you need to focus on is phase one." Or, "Trust me, my friend, trust me."

Before JD left Declan's office, Declan gave him the Ziploc bag with the burner phone and the charger in it. Declan also gave JD something else. The expandable baton.

"Self-defense isn't just a right," said Declan, "it's a duty."

Now, in the driver's seat, Gage switches off the headlights. Then the daytime running lights. He puts the truck in gear. JD feels them turn the corner into the narrow track. There's a half-moon in the sky overhead. JD has no idea how Gage would see the track ahead of them otherwise.

Even at a speed little more than a crawl, JD feels every rut under the tires. Branches snap at the windshield. It can't be good for the truck.

Then again, the truck has already undergone some alterations. The blue-and-pink pastel colour scheme and the words Mr Cheer Ice Cream and even the service window have all been painted over.

JD discovered this after the mission briefing, when he followed Declan and Becca outside and saw the truck for the first time in two days. The new paintjob looked like it had been hastily done. It looked, in fact, like it had been done with a paint-roller.

Declan must have noticed the look on JD's face, because he put his hand on JD's shoulder. "It was a necessary modification, my friend. Don't underestimate how vital subtlety is as a tactic in this mission. But I can assure you, we have associates who will see to any repairs – and perhaps even an upgrade or two – your grandfather's vehicle requires. After the mission is complete."

"No disrespect, sir," said JD, "but why do we need to use my granddad's truck for this at all?"

Declan smiled. "A test drive, you might say. All will become apparent as it needs to. In the meantime, the less you know, the better. The burden of the information is mine to bear."

A short while later, JD was in the driver's seat, starting the truck up. The window was down. Declan was standing with his arm around Becca's shoulders.

"Godspeed," said Declan. "The entire patriot network is counting on you. On you."

"Don't fuck this up," said Becca.

Granddad would not be happy about the crude paintjob. JD is certain of that. He's already preparing himself for whatever angry messages he might find hidden in the classified ads. But JD also trusts the necessity of it. He sees Declan's point – Mr Cheer Ice Cream is the kind of thing that draws attention. The kind of thing you remember after the fact.

They bounce over another rut. JD hits his head on the rear wall of the cab. But the mission is underway, and this is what it means to be a Very Very Invited Person.

After a few minutes, Gage stops the truck. Puts it into park. JD peers out the windshield. By the light of the half-moon he can see they've come to a gate made of 2x4s. Gage opens his backpack and brings out a pair of heavy-duty boltcutters. He opens the door and steps down from the cab and jogs forward.

Night air swirls into the cab, carrying with it the smell of wet leaves and wet earth and something else. A thick odour of vegetation, things growing, things ready to be harvested.

Marijuana plants.

JD glances at Ronnie but Ronnie is staring straight ahead.

Out front, Gage is opening the 2x4 gate, presumably having cut a lock in the process. He climbs back up into the cab and passes the boltcutters to JD. Then he puts the truck back into drive and creeps forward again.

The bush opens up on one side of the truck. The narrow lane is taking them across one edge of a small field cleared out of the surrounding trees. JD can see the plants, several feet tall, dominating the field.

A grow-op. A grow-op they're about to … what … raid? Is this the mission?

Up ahead, at the corner of the clearing, is a large angular shape. As they get closer to it, the moonlight reveals the shape as a sea container. Gage takes a hard turn at the front of the container. He crushes a wide swath of plants beneath the ice cream truck. Then he backs up a few feet until the rear of the truck is in line with the container.

Gage kills the engine. He and Ronnie both roll their windows down. And then, for two minutes, all they do is listen.

The only thing to hear is a light breeze sighing through the plants. Gage rolls his window up first, then Ronnie rolls his up. The inside of the cab is dark and cooling off already.

"Follow me," says Gage.

He opens the driver side door and hops down. JD hops down after him. They walk back across the edge of the field to the narrow laneway where they came in. It doesn't take long for JD's eyes to adjust to the moonlight.

"Look down that way," Gage whispers. "What do you see?"

JD looks where Gage is pointing. A long, straight path down this edge of the field. The path stretches about the length of a football field. At the other end, JD can make out a small camper. The camper is dark, no lights showing, visible only because of the moon and JD's adjusted eyesight.

"Is somebody in there?" says JD, matching Gage's whisper.

"Yeah. A big fat fuckin Hells Angels prospect is who's in there, compadre. Me and Ronnie were on recon here for the last couple hours. The lights went out in that camper ninety minutes ago. I got right up to the side of that thing and I could hear the snoring through the walls. But that doesn't mean we can go around makin a bunch of noise. Here."

Gage holds something out. JD takes it. A palm-sized walkie-talkie. There's a small display screen on it, but the backlight is dimmed.

"This is what you're gonna do," says Gage. "You're gonna spend ten seconds looking down the way we came. Then you're gonna turn around and spend ten seconds watching the camper. Ten seconds down the way we came, ten seconds on the camper. You see something, you fuckin say something."

"You want me to use a ... codeword or something?"

"Yeah I do, compadre. The codeword is, I see a biker and he looks pissed off. Got it?"

JD nods. "Got it. You and Ron—X-Ray—what are you doing?"

"I'm doing the heavy lifting. Ronnie can't on account of his leg, so he's got my six close up."

"The heavy lifting."

Gage doesn't expand on this. He turns to go, then turns back to JD. He puts a finger on JD's chest. "This is a realtime test of your abilities, compadre. Doc Declan sees something in you, which is why you're out here. You really want to be part of the inner circle, this is your chance."

A minute after Gage has gone, there's a subdued electronic chirp from the walkie-talkie. Ronnie's voice crackles softly forth: "Sentry, this is X-Ray. How copy."

Sentry, JD thinks. He likes the sound of that.

"Sentry," Ronnie hisses.

JD lifts the walkie-talkie to his lips. "X-Ray, this is Sentry. I am copying. Loud and clear. Over and out."

Ronnie's voice comes back with an edge of irritation. "You don't out me. I give the out on this network. Anyhow, phase two is underway. Probably ten minutes to completion. Stay frosty. X-Ray out."

All is quiet except for that light wind. JD looks down the way they came. He's surprised by how much he can see. Then he pivots his head and stares at the camper. Still dark.

As kids, JD and his brother used to pretend they were soldiers. Astronauts. Vocations of that nature. They had a set of walkie-talkies Granddad had given them, JD recalls. Huge, brick-like things that said Realistic across the top and had extendable antennae and a small chart of Morse code on the back. JD isn't sure now if the walkie-talkies even worked, but they were well-used in many games of pretend.

To think how things have changed since then. JD's brother is stuck in a miserable job with a miserable wife, trying his best to be like every other sheeple. JD himself, meanwhile, is out here in the dead of night, participating in a secret mission for an underground revolutionary network.

He grins. He almost laughs out loud, has to clamp his hand over his mouth.

He's been looking down the trail for the last ten seconds. Now he turns to look at the camper – and sees a light on inside. The camper's windows are closed, blinds drawn, so the light is just a thin sketch around the edges of the windows, but it's unmistakable.

He lifts the walkie-talkie to his mouth. His nerves are running high. It's hard to keep his voice low.

"X-Ray. Come in, X-Ray. X-Ray, it's Sentry. There's a light on. Over and out."

"A light on?" says Ronnie.

"Affirmative. A light on in the camper. Over and—"

"Shut the hell up with the over and out. A light on. Do you see anyone? Has anybody come outside?"

JD stares. All he sees is the light outlining the windows. He's about to reply when the windows go dark again.

"Well?" says Ronnie. "Report."

"Lights just went out," says JD. "I didn't see anyone come outside."

"You're sure? You got your eyes locked-on?"

"Locked-on. Steadfast."

There's a long pause on the other end of the walkie-talkie. The camper stays dark . Finally, Ronnie says, "Okay, let's assume he was just up for a leak. Hawkeye is almost finished. Keep your eyes locked-on that trailer. Good work, Sentry. X-Ray out."

JD nods.

That's when bright light lances through the marijuana plants from the direction of the sea can. Bright light and a man's raised voice, eerily clear on the night air.

"We don't call 9-1-1, you dumbasses."

JD stands exactly where he is. Five seconds. Then ten.

There's more talking from the direction of the sea can. Gage's voice, but it doesn't carry the same way the other man's voice did. Whatever Gage says, the man replies with, "Yeah, this is the way we work it out."

It's cold, but JD takes his trilby off and scrubs his hand across his forehead and his hand comes away sweaty. He puts his hand in the patch pocket low on his blazer. His hand touches the expandable baton. He brings it out. He holds it parallel to his leg, the way Declan showed him.

Thumbs the catch.

The baton snicks to full expansion.

It would be hard to navigate through the marijuana plants if it wasn't for the bright light ahead. The dirt underfoot is still wet, as are the leaves, which have the effect of silencing his steps. There are three feet of space between the stalks of each plant. JD doesn't notice it, but he's holding the baton with both hands, as if it's a battleaxe.

He goes toward the light.

He comes to the last few rows of plants. Between them he can see the ice cream truck with its crude paintjob. He can see the sea can behind it, the doors standing open. Gage and Ronnie are on their knees beside the truck, hands raised.

They are both facing away from the third man. He's big, bearded. Standing in a t-shirt and boxer shorts and a pair of sneakers with the laces undone. He's holding a pump shotgun in one hand at the level of his hips. Has a huge flashlight tucked under his arm. With his free hand he's punching numbers into a cellphone.

JD moves through the bushes, closing the distance.

The man puts the cellphone to his ear.

JD lunges forward, lifting the baton over his head. His oxfords hit a patch of mud in the soil and his legs go out from under him. He topples forward, carried by his own momentum. Face first into the ground. His eyebrow strikes a small rock. He gets a mouthful of grass and wet dirt.

He wonders when the fireworks show started, because now there are fireworks going off at regular intervals.

Pop. Pop. Pop.

JD gets himself up on his elbows.

Pop.

The bright flashlight is still on, but now it's shining from where it was dropped on the ground. It's pointing at one of the biker's sneakers. The other sneaker – and the biker himself – are nowhere to be seen.

Pop. Pop.

Momentary silence.

Gage takes rough hold of JD's shoulders and hauls him to his feet. In the tumble, JD's trilby came off, but Gage scoops it up and crams it down on JD's head. JD's still holding the baton. His eyebrow is split. He feels warm blood on his face.

Fifteen feet away, Ronnie is still kneeling on the ground. But now he's turned around, balancing on one knee, his gimpy leg pointed out at an awkward angle beside him. Ronnie's holding a heavy chrome-plated revolver in his right hand. Braced with his left.

"In the truck, compadre," says Gage.

"I gotta reload," says Ronnie.

The biker's voice booms out of the darkness: "Can't shoot for shit, can you, you dumbasses."

Gage reaches down and hikes his pantleg up. He's got a compact black handgun strapped into an ankle holster. Not a revolver. An automatic. He hauls it out and racks the slide.

"You dumbass cocksu—"

Gage fires three times in rapid succession. Poppoppop. Big clumps of dirt and wild grass are cleaved up from the ground only a few feet away. JD's ears are ringing.

Ronnie hops on one leg toward them. He's still got the chrome-plated revolver in one hand, but in the other hand he's holding something long. Part flesh-coloured plastic, part bare steel, one black hiking boot attached to the end. All JD can do is stare, until Gage gives him a shove.

"In the truck!"

The three of them scramble up into the cab. Gage at the wheel, JD crouched in the middle again, Ronnie in the passenger seat. Ronnie drops his prosthetic lower leg into the footwell. "I can't get this thing reloaded real quick," he says. For a second, absurdly, JD thinks Ronnie is referring to his detached prosthetic.

Instead, Gage hands over his automatic. Ronnie trains it out the open passenger window, although for the moment everything is dark and quiet save for the ringing in JD's ears. No sign of the biker. The absence is heavy. JD finds himself holding the baton like a sword again.

Gage fires up the engine. He turns on the headlights, then the high beams, flooding everything ahead of them with a hard white haze. Gage throws the truck into gear, hits the accelerator. They lurch forward. Gage cranks the wheel hard. They bounce into the field, crushing another swath of plants.

A loud shot claps out of the darkness. JD hears something hit the truck. Sounds like hailstones or gravel. Ronnie starts firing wildly with the automatic. Gage swings the steering wheel hard enough to bring the truck up on two wheels as he veers back toward the trail.

As Gage straightens out, the high beams illuminate the biker thirty yards in front of them. The biker is still in his t-shirt and boxer shorts and one sneaker. And he's still got the shotgun, levelled from his hips. He fires. One of the headlights goes out. The biker dives out of the way, his other sneaker coming off, in the instant before the ice cream truck runs him down.

The ice cream truck is parked in a lot surrounding a small truckstop on Side Road 10. Gage pulled in here as soon as could, coming to a stop behind a dark tractor-trailer.

Once they're stopped, Gage gives JD a handkerchief to hold against his brow. It'll have to do until they get back to Forward Operating Base Liberty.

The handkerchief stanches the bloodflow, but the brow is throbbing. JD is otherwise a mess. His blazer and shirt and trousers are all smeared with mud, as are his face and hands.

"You'll have to ride the rest of the way in the back," says Gage.

Ronnie clears his throat. Gage glances at him, but Ronnie doesn't say anything.

"Looks," says Gage. "It's bad enough if we get pulled over with the busted headlight. But we get pulled over with this guy up front. No seatbelt, no seat, his eye all fucked up, six yards of topsoil all over his clothes. That's a different story. Come to think of it, you should be back there too, unless you can get your pirate peg-leg back on right now."

"I'm staying up front," says Ronnie.

"Suit yourself. Let's go, compadre."

They get down from the cab and go around to the door at the back of the truck. The mission keep replaying in JD's mind.

Before Gage opens the back door, he puts his hand on JD's shoulder, once again letting JD feel the underlying strength in his grip.

"You came through in a serious way. Don't think that'll go unnoticed. You were the MVP back there."

JD says nothing, manages to nod his head with the utmost gravity.

"Whatever you think you see in the back of the truck," says Gage, "you don't see. It's straight-out fucking top-secret classified. Check?"

"Check," says JD.

Gage opens the back door. The light isn't on in the back of the truck, but there's a large sodium lamp on a post fifty feet away. JD sees what he's used to seeing. The freezer, the steel sinks, the countertop yogurt machine, the inside panel of the service window.

In addition to these things, JD also sees several dozen thick, pillow-shaped plastic bags. They're crammed into every available space and surface in the back of Granddad's ice cream truck.

Printed in stark green typeface across the front of each bag is this:
34-0-0
Ammonium Nitrate
All-Purpose Fertilizer

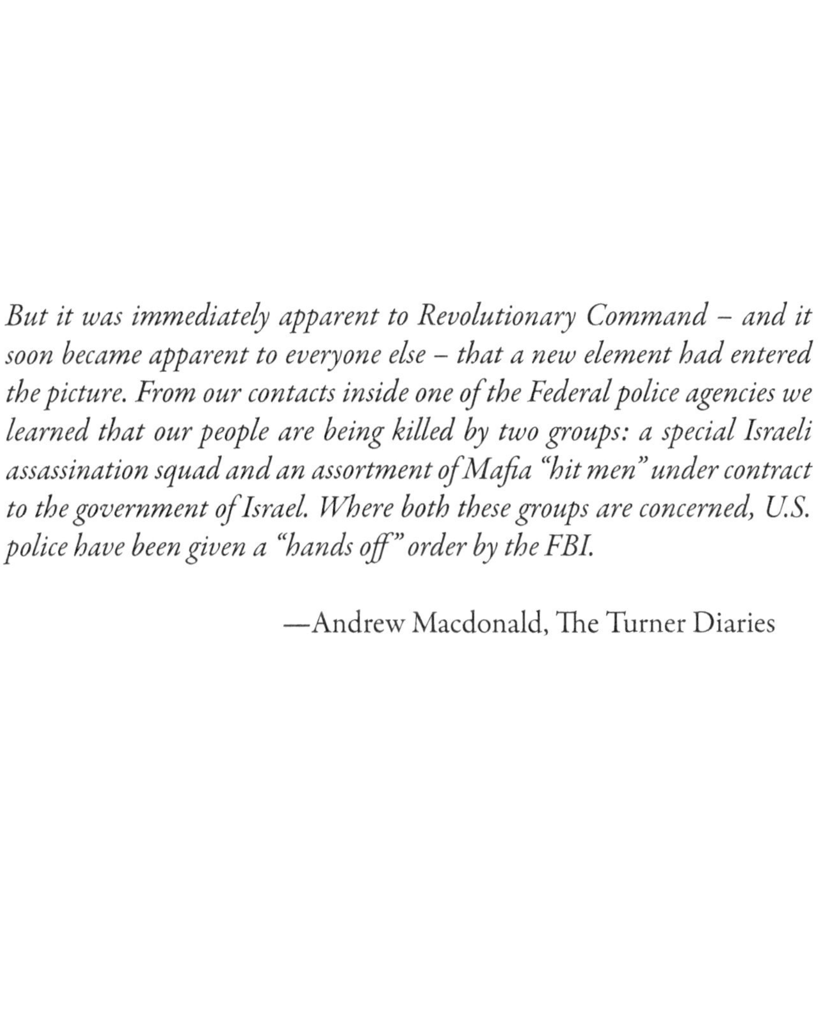

But it was immediately apparent to Revolutionary Command – and it soon became apparent to everyone else – that a new element had entered the picture. From our contacts inside one of the Federal police agencies we learned that our people are being killed by two groups: a special Israeli assassination squad and an assortment of Mafia "hit men" under contract to the government of Israel. Where both these groups are concerned, U.S. police have been given a "hands off" order by the FBI.

—Andrew Macdonald, The Turner Diaries

3: Disruption of the Power Process in Modern Society

[Transcribed from *Full Disclosure with Gilbert Emmerich*, AM 710, October 19, 2015.]

Gilbert Emmerich: Fertilizer.

Caller: Yes, kind sir. Fertilizer.

GE: And that … help me out here … that didn't set off any alarm bells inside your head?

Caller: No. I am many things, Mr Emmerich. A farmer is not one of them. I believed the fertilizer was going to be used to grow crops. For survival.

GE: You know, I worry about you sometimes, Johnny. Are you able to tie your shoes? Do you have to write your name on your hand so you don't forget it?

Caller: You're making fun of me, Mr Emmerich.

GE: Not at all, Johnny. Not at all. But I'd advise you to stay away from our online forum. Anyway, I think now would be a good time for a word from our advertisers.

JD met Lil in 2004. In those days JD was a sheeple, a consumer, a slave to the all-powerful dollar. He worked for a junk removal company.

Even then it amazed JD to think people would spend money to get rid of things they'd spent money to buy in the first place. But he needed the work. Or so he believed at that time. He was medicated by Big Pharma, same as his brother.

With the junk company, JD was part of a two-man truck crew. They would spend their days driving from one end of the city to the other. Haul junk out of houses and apartments and businesses. Take said junk down to dumps and scrapyards. If the crew found good stuff they could keep it. JD came across many books and movies he took home.

But most of the junk removal work was dirty, sweaty, and disagreeable. At least it paid well, and for a time JD moved out of Country Club Estate and into his own little bachelor pad.

One job they got called to was a townhouse clean-out. The person living there had died in the hospital. Part of the estate was being used to pay for the junk removal.

It was a late-in-the-day job. The big jobs were always late in the day, when all JD wanted to do was go home. He and his partner got to work hauling out the old stuff. There were couches and cabinets. A kitchen table. Clothes and shoes.

There were also a bunch of books. As always, JD sorted through the books before they were tossed. Almost every one of them was about dieting or how to be a better businessperson. Subjects he did not care about. But there was one astonishing find. The entire set of the Time Life Mysteries of the Unknown series. Everything from Alien Encounters to Psychic Voyages to Witches and Witchcraft.

JD hadn't yet figured out Them, or the depth of the global conspiracy, but he did have a strong interest in the arcane. This went as far back as the nights he'd listened to Full Disclosure with Granddad. The Time Life collection came in hardcover coffee table books with beautiful illustrations. They were JD's for the taking.

His partner, walking by with a microwave in his arms, said, "Come on, man, I can't do this all by myself."

JD frowned. His partner had no way of understanding what a

treasure these books represented. JD took the books out and set them inside the cab of the truck so they wouldn't get tossed into the bin with the rest of the junk.

The junk removal was being paid for from the deceased's will, but JD and his partner still needed someone to sign the invoice. Half an hour before the job was finished, a rust-bucket car pulled up beside the truck, and a woman got out.

She had pale skin and black hair with purple highlights. Her clothes were all black. She was very curvy. JD couldn't keep his eyes off her. She was short, even with big platform-heeled boots on, but her walk was powerful, as if she had the soul of a wild animal.

"So you guys're the garbage dudes, right?" she said. Her voice was throaty.

Under ordinary circumstances JD would've bristled at a being called a garbage dude, but now he could only stare.

"Yeah we are," JD's partner said wearily. "We're almost done."

She nodded. "I'm Lil. This was my dad's place. Let me know when you're finished and I'll sign the bill or whatever."

Then she went inside. JD watched after her for a moment, smelling her perfume as it lingered in the air.

A little while later, the last of the junk had been thrown into the bin. JD hadn't seen Lil since she'd arrived, but he knew he had to talk to her. JD's partner always handled the payment on each job, so he went to find Lil and give her the invoice. He left JD to do the menial tasks. Close up the bin and strap the tarp over it.

After a few minutes JD's partner came back out, signed invoice in hand. It was twilight. The streetlights had all come on.

"Let's get going," JD's partner said.

JD had to think of something fast. His partner was already getting behind the wheel. That was when JD's eyes settled on the boxed set of Time Life books.

"Wait," said JD. "I want to take those books home. But I should ask if the customer wants them for herself, shouldn't I? Is it not the case that the customer is always right?"

His partner gave him a funny look. "I doubt she wants any of the shit we took out of there."

"But I should ask," said JD. "It's the right thing to do."

JD's partner squeezed his eyes shut. "Why do I always get stuck with … Look, make it quick, man. I want to go home."

JD found Lil in the kitchen at the back of the townhouse. She was standing there, looking around. One hand was dangling beside her hip. Between her fingers was a smoldering joint.

"Pardon me," said JD.

She glanced at him. "You forget something?"

"Well, there was a set of books I noticed among your dad's things. Time Life, Mysteries of the Unknown. Very fascinating subjects, actually. Instead of just throwing them away, I'd like to keep them."

"What books?" she said. "Time … what?"

"Time Life, Mysteries of the Unknown. Very fascinating stuff."

He could see her shoulders move as she inhaled. "I don't give a shit. Keep whatever you want. Burn the rest. I don't care."

JD let a few seconds go by, then he said, "I lost my dad too. A long time ago. He was high up in the government, but he was not a gentleman."

Tears spilled out of Lil's eyes. They left dark tracks of mascara on her cheeks. "My dad" she said, puffing her joint, "was a deadbeat. His estate didn't even have enough to cover your guys' bill. I had to make up the rest out of my own pocket. Even from beyond the grave he's still shortchanging me."

JD put on a sympathetic expression. He said, "My god, story of my life too. What are the odds. Hey, can I have a hit of that?"

He stayed for another fifteen minutes, sharing Lil's joint. Almost right away she started to vent about her deadbeat dad. Then about her disinterested mother. Her shitty car, her shitty office job, her shitty coworkers. Maybe she just needed someone to hear her.

JD went with her room to room while she turned each light off. "I never want to set foot in this dump again," she said.

They walked together to the front door, turned off the light in the hallway, stepped outside …

It look as though JD's partner had become fed up with waiting. The junk truck was gone.

"Why, the bastard left me here," said JD, trying to sound angry.

Lil locked the front door. She turned around and squinted at the curb, where only her car remained. "Seems like it," she said.

"How about we get a glass of wine somewhere?"

She'd turned back around and was gazing at the front of the townhouse, not saying anything. JD gave her a gentle tap on the shoulder. When she looked at him her eyes were shining again, although no tears had spilled out this time.

"Huh?" She sounded tired.

"Would you care to get a glass of wine, my lady?"

"I'd like a fucking scotch is what I'd like."

She pushed past JD, made for her car. Once more she was walking with the bottled-up energy of a cornered animal. Halfway down the front walk she called back over her shoulder, "Hey, dude, you coming or what?"

JD grinned and followed her.

For the record, JD never did get that beautiful Time Life Mysteries of the Unknown boxed set back. His partner must have thrown the books away with the rest of the junk.

Days pass. JD keeps the Nokia burner phone plugged in. Other than the Westinghouse radio, the burner is the only working electronic device in the apartment. JD is glad he has it. The sentinel stands guard at the watchtower. Those were Declan's words.

The burner stays silent. For now.

On the afternoon of the 17th, JD does a few sweeps of the apartment with the slotted metal serving spoon. At first he gets no tremors. Then in the hallway between Granddad's bedroom and the bathroom he stops. Wonders if the end of the spoon just gave a little wiggle.

He's holding the spoon a few inches away from one of the framed classic centrefolds on the wall. Miss February 1971. She's a redhead. JD lowers the spoon. He brings it back up. He can't feel any vibrations in his wrist, but the other end of the spoon is moving in small loops. The hair on the back of his neck stands up.

AM 710 is playing from the other room. The Looking Glass Report, the show that precedes Full Disclosure. Looking Glass has a lot of strange monologues set to New Age music. A man is speaking in a gentle voice over the sound of pan flutes. "I saw the angel that night," the man says. "He enfolded me in his wings."

JD doesn't care about angels. He does care about surveillance devices or ELF emitters implanted in his home. He takes Miss February 1971 off the wall and sets her down in the bathroom. He returns to his position, waving the spoon over the bare patch where she hung.

The man on the radio says, "The angel told me my psoriasis was healed. And it was."

JD sees the end of the spoon moving again. This time the loops are bigger. He was gone for three days, so it isn't a question of when They bugged the wall. More a question of how much They know now.

JD touches the butterfly bandage over his eyebrow, feels a jab of pain. He and Ronnie and Gage managed to get the ice cream truck back to Forward Operating Base Liberty without incident. At first the truck stayed parked for several minutes. JD could hear voices going back and forth outside. Declan's, Gage's, Ronnie's. Raised, tense.

It was Becca who opened the back door of the truck. "Come on," she said flatly.

JD got out and followed her into the house. A huge bathroom on the second floor. The windows were boarded over, which he'd come to expect. The rest of the bathroom was done in black marble and gold fixtures. There was a jacuzzi set in the corner of the room, next to a glass-walled shower the size of a bus shelter.

"How did you get so muddy?" she said. "Never mind. I don't want to know. Get your jacket off. Your shirt too."

JD did as instructed. For a moment, he thought she was going to have him strip down all the way, then lead him into the jacuzzi. He felt his pulse quicken.

She didn't lead him into the jacuzzi. Instead she got him to sit down on the toilet while she took a look at his cut brow. She had a first aid kit inside a plastic toolbox. Latex gloves on her hands. She used alcohol swabs to clean the wound. The pain was sharp and bright.

"Back when I worked the ER," said Becca, "we had a guy brought in who'd fell on a pencil. Right up through his eyeball into the front part of his brain. Looks to me like alls you got is superficial. So don't be a little snowflake and go passing out. Got it?"

"Got it," JD replied. "Loud and clear. Over and out."

She continued to clean the cut. To keep from thinking about the sting, JD fixated on her cleavage. Once the dirt was cleared away, Becca rubbed antiseptic cream onto the wound, then closed it with the butterfly bandage.

"You'll need to change this up each day for the next couple days. You got bandages at home?"

JD didn't know if there were bandages at Granddad's. There was a first aid kit in the bathroom vanity, but Granddad always kept a spare bottle of booze inside it.

Anyway, Becca didn't seem interested in the answer. She was gathering up the swabs she'd used, stuffing them into a little plastic bag. She started to peel off her latex gloves, then paused, looking at him.

"You're tougher than you look. But don't let that go to your head. I can still knock you down a couple pegs."

The bathroom door clapped open and Declan entered. He was wearing a huge grin and his eyes were blazing so brightly it looked like there were lightbulbs behind them. He strode across the floor to the toilet, took hold of JD's bare shoulder.

"They gave me the full debriefing," he said. "They told me what you did. Without you the mission would have been a complete wash. Well done, my friend. And I see you'll bear the scars to prove it. Well done, well done."

"I was glad to be part of it," said JD, and that was exactly true. Then he added, "What do you need all that fertil—"

Declan released JD's shoulder and moved his hand up to the side of JD's face. Caressed his cheek with his thumb. In a soft, low voice, Declan said, "For the sentinel stands guard at the watchtower, O Lord. Day after day. The sentinel never leaves his post at night. Isaiah 21:8. That's who you are to us. Our sentinel. Patriot Alpha Sentinel."

Now, They are actively observing Patriot Alpha Sentinel. He's certain of it. So certain that he goes to the kitchen and trades the slotted spoon for a long, serrated breadknife. He returns to the place where Miss February hung. He taps along the wall until he hears the telltale hollow sound between the studs.

"The angel gave me the confidence to make love to my wife," says The Looking Glass Report.

JD digs the tip of the knife into the wall. Builder's beige paint flakes away. He inhales, holds his breath, releases it slowly. He grips the handle of the knife with both hands.

"You want to bug me, motherfuckers? Bug this."

He drives the knife through the drywall, then begins to saw it downward.

JD had stayed at Forward Operating Base Liberty the rest of the night of the mission, rising late in the morning.

The only person he saw about the house that morning was Becca. After cooking him breakfast, she gave him – on Declan's behalf, she said – one more task. JD was to drive the ice cream truck back into the city, to a bodyshop where the paint job and damage would be repaired. The Patriot Bloc had already covered the cost.

By noon, JD was sitting behind the steering wheel of the ice cream truck, letting the glowplugs heat up. The bags of fertilizer were all gone. Outside the truck it was a cold fall day, but sunny. The colours all seemed brighter somehow. Charged with some inner glow, reflecting the way he felt.

Becca came around to the driver side window. "What are you forgetting?" she said.

She thrust something at him. The expandable baton. No sooner had he taken it then she thrust something else at him. The burner phone and the charger.

"Ah," he said. "Of course."

"Now get your butt going."

JD nodded, started the truck. He was going to tip his trilby to her, but instead another gesture occurred to him. He affected a sharp little salute and chased it with what he hoped was a dashing, devil-may-care grin. Becca rubbed the bridge of her nose.

The bodyshop was a small enterprise called Maiwand Automative, in a quiet industrial neighbourhood on Logan Street. JD could see a dozen vehicles of various makes and models in a fenced-in area beside the shop. Fronting the building were dirty office windows and a glass door with a neon sign saying Customers. There were two garage bays. A closed sign was hanging in the customer entrance, but one of the bay doors was open.

JD parked in front of the open bay and hopped down. Everything was quiet. He was ten paces away from the customer entrance when Ronnie emerged. JD was used to seeing Ronnie in a loose-fitting suit. Or in the black commando outfit he'd been wearing for the top secret classified fertilizer mission. But here Ronnie was clad in oil-spotted coveralls. He was wiping his hands on a rag as he limped toward JD.

There was little in the way of conversation. Ronnie just said, "We'll have her fixed for you soon as we can, mister." Then, in a much quieter tone, he added, "We'll be in touch."

Ronnie clambered up behind the steering wheel and drove the truck into the open bay. Even for the short distance into the open bay, Ronnie navigated the truck with a lurching, stop-start motion.

Must be hard to drive with that prosthetic leg.

JD leaves the drywall intact on Granddad's side of the wall, but he strips the hallway side bare.

Before long he's panting, sweating, caked in drywall dust, naked save for his socks and oxfords. He's wearing the oxfords lest he cut his feet. Chunks of drywall lay all over the parquet floor. He took down all the centrefolds and stacked them with Miss February in the bathroom. The breadknife in JD's hand is almost ruined. The handle is coming loose.

The wall separating the hallway from Granddad's bedroom contains metal studs. A few ancient cigarette butts. Whoever built Country Club Estate must've pitched them there. There's no insulation, since it's a thin partition wall. There's not even any wiring.

JD does not see any surveillance devices or ELF emitters.

He hustles back to the kitchen, tosses the knife on the counter, retrieves the spoon. Returns to what remains of the hallway. He holds the spoon over the drywall debris on the floor. Nothing. He runs the spoon up and down the metal studs, then over each long-forgotten cigarette butt. Nothing.

He even goes into the bathroom and scans the framed centrefolds. Something he should have done in the first place, he realizes. But none of the centrefolds offer any tremors.

One final pass over the drywall. The spoon is still. There is nothing. There was nothing. False positive.

Unless he got it. Unless, in all his frantic demolition work, he cut right through Their little bug. That's possible. No, not possible. Probable. Even certain. Patriot Alpha Sentinel smiles and kicks at a chunk of drywall. It skitters over the parquet.

"Try again, you bastards."

On the Westinghouse, The Looking Glass Report ends. There's a brief string of commercials. A jewelry buyer, an insurance agent, discounts at a grocery store. Then come the synthesizer strains of that Rush song. Subdivisions. Full Disclosure is about to start.

JD's stomach rumbles. He ravenous. All this hard work. But the cupboards and fridge are empty. Still, despite the hunger, he feels oddly satisfied. Defiant.

"I'm the guard at the goddamn watchtower," he says.

That evening JD wanders over to his brother's house. He wears a wool blazer with the houndstooth pattern. Brown corduroy trousers. A wide polyester tie with a floral pattern on it. All from Granddad's closet, fitting replacements for the casualties of the fertilizer mission.

It's twilight when he arrives in front of his brother's house. Brother is just getting home from working, parking his car. He sees him, looks surprised, asks what's up.

JD laughs and offers a stiff salute. "Brother! I just moseyed over to your neck of the woods without even realizing it. What a funny coincidence."

Brother brings JD in for supper. It's a weeknight meal, busy, TV blasting, kids not paying attention to anything, the Harpy Herself trying to manage the whole affair. She's not pleased to see JD. That much is clear. She doesn't let on, even manages to keep a thin smile as she makes up an extra plate. JD smiles at her, tips his hat.

He says, "Did you know, steadfastness produces faith in our hearts."

"That's interesting," she says.

The minute they finish eating, Brother says he'll drive JD home. "I'd love to have you stay for the evening," he adds. "We could have some beers, maybe watch the game, but I got an early morning tomorrow."

As JD's brother speaks, he keeps darting looks at his wife. She's clearing the dishes, mouth set and thin. JD almost laughs.

During the ride home, JD's brother talks about a big job he's doing in the suburbs. A house where the pipes are broken and water has flooded the entire basement.

"It's a nice house," says JD's brother. "But it's an unfinished basement. Cinderblock walls, shitty lighting. You know. Actually it kind of reminds me of that house on Hough where we lived when we were kids. Remember that scuzzy little place? Remember all those times they let us sleep in the basement? My own kids won't set foot in our basement. God, if they had any idea."

Brother laughs at that, a little too loudly.

JD doesn't say anything about the time spent in the basement of their childhood home. Those days on end. Emerging only to find out what happened to their mother. It meant something, of course. Some piece of the grander conspiracy. But to this day JD can't say what.

A little while later his brother pulls up in front of Country Club Estate.

"I thank you, good sir," says JD.

"Happy to have you. Hey, look, I can't … I mean, the wife and I are up against it a bit on a bedroom set we financed last fall. I can't … donate anything to you tonight."

JD looks at his brother. His brother is looking at the steering wheel. JD lets the moment play out a little longer.

"There's nothing I need."

Brother nods quickly. "Okay. Good. And before you go there's a couple things I wanted to bring up. I should've mentioned them at dinner but it wasn't really the place for it, I guess, and—"

"And you're stalling, dear brother," says JD. "For what purpose are you stalling for?"

"I'm not stalling. The superintendent here, foreign guy, what's his name?"

JD clears his throat. "Mr Rahim."

"Mr Rahim called me. He still has my number, I guess. Anyways he called me. Left a message but didn't say what he wanted. Is everything okay here?"

JD puts on an indignant expression, a slight lift of his eyebrow. "Everything's fine. I'm sorry Mr Rahim called you. He didn't need to. He can deal with me whenever he'd like. I'll speak to him and clear everything up."

"Okay," says his brother. "Sounds good. Also … I've been thinking. We should sell Granddad's ice cream truck. There's a good market for a used Chevy stepvan, even one with half a billion miles on it. I got a landscaper friend, said he could definitely use it. He'd get rid of all the ice cream stuff on his own dime, even."

"You've been thinking," says JD.

"My friend was talking fifteen grand cash. You and me, we'd split that straight down the middle."

"You've been thinking?" says JD.

"What? Yeah. I've been thinking about it. I think it makes sense, bro. The truck's just sitting there in storage, isn't it?"

"You're missing my point," says JD. "You've been thinking this little idea? Or you and your wife have been thinking it up? Or your wife all on her own, and telling you to tell me?"

"What's that supposed to mean?"

They look at each other for several seconds. Then, for some inexplicable reason, JD has an urge to tell his brother where the ice cream truck is right now. Maiwand Automotive, getting fixed up. Fixed up from the fertilizer mission. He feels an urge to tell his brother about that, too. Tell his brother everything. He opens his mouth.

No.

Must be ELF. Coming from that lamppost on the sidewalk. Coming from his brother's car stereo. The faraday shield inside his trilby is simply not protection enough. Not when you're a direct target.

"We're not selling the ice cream truck," says JD. "Granddad is going to need it when he gets back."

"What? Come on. You know—"

"End of discussion, dear brother. Thank you for dinner. Good night, sir. Oh, and read that book I gave you. The truth is something you owe yourself."

JD gets out and starts up the front walk. Sean and the fountaineers are at their usual post. They have their girls with them too. Cackling little hussies with big hair and hoop earrings.

JD is getting very low on his weed, but he doesn't approach the fountain. It isn't out of intimidation. Patriot Alpha Sentinel isn't intimidated by anything. It's more a matter of not wanting to deal with their silly hoodlum posturing. He even steps off the walkway to give them a wider berth.

He can feel the fountaineers' eyes on him. He can hear their conversations quiet down. One of the louts mimics a gun with his thumb and forefinger. Points it at JD, pretends to shoot. They all laugh. JD keeps walking.

Then he remembers there's something heavy inside the patch pocket of his blazer. The extendable baton, thumping against his hip with each step. He reaches down and touches it. It's been there the whole time. He doesn't have the slightest recollection of putting it in his pocket.

October 18th. The sun is shining on the Van Lathan Building and the surrounding edifices. Simone is back at Civic Park. JD finds her at the lamppost, where the effigies of the elite are still awaiting their fate. There are many more people around now, taking pictures, capturing video.

The cops have also returned. Maybe twenty of them, keeping watch from the edges of the park.

Simone is snapping photographs a Nikon camera. At the sight of her JD feels a low tremor move up his legs and through his body and down his arms. Right to his fingertips. There's no doubt - she's meant to be part of his life.

He makes his way over, weaving around the sheeple in his path. The distance between Simone and him closes to ten paces, then five. Then he sees Tiny Tim beside her. Tiny Tim gives Simone a gentle poke in the ribs – JD doesn't much care for that – and whispers something in her ear. She lowers her camera, glances around. When she spots JD her face stays unreadable for a moment. JD wonders what Tiny Tim might have whispered. But then she smiles.

"Hey," she says.

JD tips his hat. "My la—Miss Simone. Hello yourself. And hello, Tim."

Tiny Tim looks at the grass. "Hi," he says.

"Did you come for the performance?" says Simone.

"And whatever sort of performance might that be?"

She gestures to the effigies. "Six o'clock. The trial."

"You're going to destroy them?" says JD.

Simone grins. "Well, if they're found guilty. It's Tim's project. He gets the final say-so."

JD turns to Tiny Tim. "I understand. You know, if the elite need to swing in the wind for their cognit, cognitive diss ..."

"Cognitive dissonance?" says Tiny Tim.

JD claps him on the arm. "That's it, good sir. If the elite have to swing in the wind for that, well, then, liberty is coming."

Tiny Tim holds up his hands. "Well, I'm into nonviolence. This world is screwed up enough as it is. Anyway I've got to go take care of some stuff."

He disappears into the crowd. JD is glad to be rid of him. He smiles at Simone. "Are you glad to see me?"

She laughs. "I kinda wondered if I'd see you again."

JD laughs too, as if their seeing each other again was ever in doubt.

They go strolling. She wants to photograph the rest of the encampment. The tents, the banners, the people. Overhead, the 99Together flag flutters against the pale sky. There has to be five hundred people in Civic Park, no less varied than the other times JD visited. He sees a lot more of the vigilante masks, the grinning man with the old-fashioned mustachio. He hears small generators running, sees cables laid across the grass. Many people have their laptops with them. Simone tells him the city has issued three more eviction notices. All of which had been ignored.

"The city wants to know who's going to blink first," she says. "But they don't realize this is bigger than them and us alike. There's 99Together camps in London and Paris now, too. The camp in New York is up to two thousand people."

Around them the grass is crowded with tents. The garbage cans are all overflowing. Seems even hippies and activists make trash, which amuses JD.

JD wants to hold Simone's hand as they make their rounds, but she's stopping every ten feet to snap pictures of this or that. JD keeps himself busy by staying close to her side, collecting handouts and newsletters from the people offering them, generally watching out danger. It's good to feel the weight of the baton in his blazer pocket. They stop in front of a lean-to made of blue tarps. Beneath the tarps are milk crates filled with apples and bananas and oranges. A handlettered sign reads: Pls help urself!! Simone takes a picture.

"Hey," she says, "I want to get some pictures of the library. It's gotten huge. Let's head there."

JD takes hold of her hand. "Lead the way, my lady."

She snatches her hand away. "I thought I made myself clear about that."

JD opens his mouth to reply. Before he can speak, their moment is crashed by the redheaded girl JD saw with Tiny Tim the previous visit. The redhead appears out of nowhere. Her skin is ashen and there are dark circles under her eyes. She's weaving on her feet. She falls against Simone's arm.

"Hey," she says, panting. "Simone ... I'm not feeling real good. I tried to talk to Tim but he's all over the place right now and I'm not feeling real good."

Simone puts her arm around the redhead's shoulders. "Let's walk over to that tree and sit down, okay? You can tell me what's going on."

What's going on is she's probably drunk, JD thinks.

Simone turns the girl around and starts walking her away.

"Simone," JD calls.

She glances back at him. "Can you give us a few minutes?"

"A few minutes? What, like five, ten?"

"I don't know," says Simone, walking the redhead further away. "We obviously need some—"

That's when the girl slips out from under Simone's arm and collapses flat on the ground.

The first aid tent is tall enough for JD to stand up straight. A canvas divider separates the front and rear of the space. In the front is an improvised triage area where a couple of volunteer nurses are hanging around. They have stethoscopes and blood pressure cuffs. There's a table with snack food on it. Mini-packages of peanut butter and crackers, oatmeal cookies, bananas, juice boxes, water bottles.

Behind the canvas divider is a space reserved for closer care and recovery. That's where the redheaded girl ended up after one of the nurses triaged her. JD carried the girl here. He charged through the crowd – excuse me pardon me coming through! – with the girl in his arms. Simone by his side. What a moment.

Simone is behind the canvas with her friend. All JD can do is wait. Twiddle his thumbs, read some of the pamphlets he collected earlier. When the volunteer nurses aren't looking, he fills his pockets with peanut butter and cracker packages. The Sentinel must replenish his energy. He never knows when duty might call again.

He wonders what happened to the girl. Could have been a tumor she never knew about. A sudden rupture of her internal organs. Maybe They did it. Highly-targeted ELF that blew her brain apart.

Behind the canvas, a nurse says, "That's it, sit up, nice and slow. Here's some fruit juice."

JD nods grimly. Targeted ELF. Nobody in Civic Park would know how to spot a collaborator in their midst. Nobody except him.

"We'll keep you here for a bit," says the nurse. "You can chill out. It's a safe space."

A minute later Simone comes back around to the front. Her camera is hanging around her neck and she's kneading her hands together. She sees JD and her expression softens.

"You waited?"

"Of course. I couldn't just leave."

"Well, thanks."

She takes a juice box off the table and steps outside. JD smooths out the bulges of snacks in his pockets and follows her. She's standing on the grass nearby, sipping from the juice box. The sun is lowering. In a short while it'll disappear behind reservoir hill.

JD packs the absolute last of his weed into his pipe. He lights up, takes a shallow drag, and offers it to her. Simone tokes deeply. Closes her eyes. JD clasps his hands behind his back in a posture of infinite patience.

"Fucking low blood sugar," Simone says, handing the pipe back. "That's all it was. And it bugs the hell out of me because the same thing happened to her two days ago. All day long I've been telling her to take it easy and make sure she was eating. She's my friend, you know, but she just doesn't use her head sometimes."

JD nods. Then he takes a chance. He reaches out and touches Simone's arm. She doesn't move away. He looks into her eyes.

"But are you okay?"

"Yeah, thanks. I am. I just ... my grandma had a heart attack two years ago. Dropped to the ground right out of nowhere. So, yeah, I found that a little triggering. Anyways, I'm gonna head back to the performance. It's almost time."

JD draws on his pipe and passes it back to her for the final hit.

"I'll come with you."

She coughs again. "Sure," she says. "You may as well."

A huge crowd has gathered at the effigies. There are small news crews from four or five different networks. There are also a dozen blank-faced cops standing guard on the far side of the clearing.

Tiny Tim has already handpicked – invited – the people he wants to participate in the performance. There are six of them, including Tiny Tim himself and Simone.

JD is excluded. That doesn't surprise him. Tiny Tim has it out for JD. He's probably in love with Simone. Wants her for himself. Well, fat chance. Fate has already set things in motion. JD smiles.

The sun dips behind reservoir hill. A fellow with a megaphone gets up on a crate. He lifts the megaphone to his lips. His voice is quavering with emotion: "Too big to fail. We keep hearing that. We've seen decades and decades of corporate responsibility finally fall apart, but instead of holding them accountable, our government just says they're too big to fail. But enough is enough, right?"

A cheer goes up from the crowd. "Enough is enough!"

"In cities across the world," says the megaphone, "the ninety-nine percent are declaring our solidarity. People like us are occupying public space until our leaders agree to do something. People like us are saying together, united ..."

A louder cheer rises up. Then the mantra: "The ninety-nine are undivided!"

"And we'll keeping saying it, if we don't get evicted by this city first. We just got our third notice!"

A loud mix of laughter and boos.

"As if we'd give in that easily!"

The loudest cheer yet. The ground thrums beneath JD's oxfords.

"Tonight, friends," says the megaphone, "we've got an amazing piece of performance art, put together by our ally, the one and only Tim Yuen ..."

The crowd applauds Tiny Tim for two full minutes. Tiny Tim stands there, looking small and solemn. Simone is at his side. She grabs his hand and holds it up in the air, like a referee lifting the glove of a winning boxer. The cheering crescendos.

JD watches, watches.

The next part of the performance is a brief show trial. Kangaroo court. The fellow with the megaphone reads from a script, charging each effigy with a litany of misdeeds. Corporate irresponsibility, greed, corruption, environmental destruction. Then the megaphone asks the crowd to pronounce judgment. The ear-splitting collective reply is Guilty! No surprise there.

"The people have spoken," says the megaphone

A thunderous cheer splits the air. Then it begins. The first person up is Tiny Tim, carrying a baseball bat. He swings at one of the effigies. Only takes a small chunk out of the figure's head. JD can't help but chuckle.

Once Tiny Tim has taken that first swing, the five other invited people rush forward, sledgehammers and bats and short lengths of 2x4 in hand. They set to work on the other effigies. Papier mache and chicken wire go flying. The crowd is shrieking, clapping, stamping their feet.

The cops stand their ground. JD can't tell if they're about to launch a flank attack. Put a halt to this insult. But the cops don't even flinch. Two of them are even standing close together, sharing a private laugh about something.

JD looks at Simone. She's using an old golf club with a crooked shaft. Her face is flushed, shiny with sweat. She's smashing apart a figure of an old baldheaded banker. JD wants to help her. It takes every ounce of his will not to leap into the fray. Swinging his extendable baton. Being among the invited, the way he knows she wants him to be. To hell with Tiny Tim.

But not yet. JD's time will come. His time will come, and everyone will know who he is, and he'll be a Very Invited Person no matter where he goes. They can't keep him down for much longer.

He backs off into the crowd. Goes to watch something else for a while. Anything else.

With full dark the air turns cold. People everywhere are huddled together, drinking beers, smoking joints. JD catches a scent of barbecue smoke and follows it to a small crowd of people gathered around a hibachi. A young woman in a quilted hat is grilling sausages and vegetables. Beside her, a longhaired guy is loading the food onto paper plates. Passing the plates to the people standing around, each in turn.

With each plate, he says, "Be well, friend."

JD doesn't see any money changing hands, and his stomach growls at the smell, so he falls in with the gathering. That's when he notices another smell. Not the grill. An odor of unwashed bodies and dirty clothes. He looks at the people waiting for the plates of food. These people don't look like protesters. They look like crackheads and winos and bums.

The longhaired guy hands JD a plate of food. He smiles. "Namaste, brother," he says.

JD winks at him. "I'm not like these folks, good sir, for your information. But keep up the good deeds, okay?"

JD turns around, carrying the paper plate, eating as he walks. Someone shouts, "Hey you!"

Her voice. But when JD turns to look he only sees one of those mustachioed vigilante masks in an oversized dark hoodie jogging toward him. JD starts to adopt one of the defensive postures Declan showed him. He reaches for the baton in his pocket. The vigilante stops a pace in front of him. JD smells lilac.

Simone lifts the mask she's wearing. Her eyes are red-rimmed, but she's grinning. "Haven't seen you in a while. I'm glad you're still here. I've got something for you."

Simone has weed in a little breathmint tin. Sativa, she says. Some of it is already pre-rolled into a slender joint. Within moments after smoking it, JD's head is in the clouds.

"Felt like I owed you," she says.

The two of them are sitting in a little dome tent. JD doesn't know who the tent belongs to. Simone said something vague about one of her friends.

They smoke more of the joint and lean back on their elbows. She has taken off the hoodie and the vigilante mask and laid them beside her.

"I feel a little guilty," she says.

"What for?"

"Smashing those effigies. There were hundreds of hours of work in those things."

"But wasn't destruction the whole point?" says JD. "Wasn't that what you were invited for?"

"I guess so."

"The real thing will be better," he says.

"The real thing?"

"The real destruction of the one percent. It's coming."

Simone cocks her head, but in the semi-darkness JD can't make out the expression on her face. "That thing you said earlier. About the elite swinging in the wind. You're not some kind of plainclothes cop or something, are you? You're not hanging around just to stir shit up, incite violence, right? We heard about that happening in the G20 protests in London a couple years ago."

JD is appalled. "I am absolutely not a plainclothes cop. Absolutely not. Never. And if you ask me directly, I would have to tell you I'm an agent of the government. That's the law."

"I'm not sure that's true," she says. "Anyways, I don't know what to make of you. I don't know who you are."

You mean you don't know what I do, he thinks. After a minute, he says, "I am the most honest man you'll ever have the fortunate chance to meet. So, the fact is, I don't exactly have a nine-to-five career, like the useless shee—like most people."

"You're unemployed ... I'm sorry. That sounded harsh. And it's really none of my business."

"I'm just … nothing is fair. Let's put it that. There's no such thing as just because."

"Why are you here?" she says. "Not here in this tent. I mean here in the park. What brought you here?"

A funny thing happens then. JD wants to say something. He wants to say, I'm here because I stumbled onto this on the way to my brother's place a few weeks ago, and then I met you, and you were nice to me, you invited me, and I feel like we're falling in love, and the rest of this I don't really understand or care about.

But he hears himself say, "I'm here because we all need to make a change. Bring down the walls together."

Simone stays quiet. She's little more than a silhouette. She sighs. "Here goes."

"Here goes what?"

"I used to be an escort," she says. "Happened in my second year at university. I was a taking a degree in journalism. That's where I met Tim. I was a year away from graduating. I was also thirty grand in debt. I couldn't think of any way out of it. Make of this what you will, but I had a friend who tried to kill himself over his student loan, okay? Anyways, I did it for a couple years. I had maybe twenty-five regular clients. Most of them were married. I was making $200 an hour. Five times that for a sleepover. So even for someone in the sex trade, I was pretty fucking well-off. And you know what? That's probably the only part I'm ashamed of. There's a lot of folks out there who do sex work for survival. Me? I was just paying off my loan."

JD doesn't know what to say. There's ELF in his head, maintaining a steady ring. He rubs his temples. Then he relights the joint and takes a few hits.

"Good idea," says Simone. She has a few hits of her own. "Anyways, I was never in a bad situation. It was more like I was getting compensated to spend time with lonely men. I went to a lot of fancy dinners and formal events, things like that. I paid my taxes on time, I made a few investments, I even financed a trip to Asia for two months. I put enough money aside to go after journalism on my own terms.

"One day I ran into one of my clients at the grocery store. He was there with his wife, and he turned four shades of purple when he saw me. I didn't feel anything at all. Not for him. That's when I knew the time had come to retire. Listen. I'm not telling you any of this because I'm ashamed, and I'm not telling you this because I want your approval or sympathy or some shit like that. I'm telling you this because, well, I'm a bit fucked up from smoking that weed, and … well … just because. Like I told you before, I have a past – we all do – and my past has made a mess of my present once or twice. People don't always understand. But I own it. I own my past. And anyways, it's not like we're some kind of cou—"

JD interrupts her with a kiss. It's the only thing he can think to do. The ELF is peaking in his head.

After they break apart she says, "I could almost interpret that as you not wanting to hear any more. But that's not right, is it? You're hearing exactly what I've said. Right?"

"Exactly what you've said," JD replies.

That's not true. The ELF – stuttering out of his brain at last – has wiped out most of the conversation. What did she say? Something about working as a … No. Not possible.

"I've really got nothing to hide," says Simone.

He nods. "Me neither."

Then they're kissing again. She moves her body closer to him. He feels her hands on his arms, his shoulders. He slips out of his blazer. They lie down on the floor of the tent. She pulls off the oversized hoodie and pushes her hips against him. Almost hard enough to hurt. She digs her nails into the back of his neck.

Then she reaches down and unbuckles his belt. He wriggles his corduroys down to mid-thigh. He's got no underwear to worry about, so his penis springs up as soon as it's freed. She wraps a hand around it. He runs his own hands over her soft curves and thinks how all his life has led to this. This love.

He's just getting his hand down the front of her jeans when she says something. She rolls off him.

"Say again, my lady?"

"Just need to take a breather," she says. Her voice sounds airy and far away. "Whew. Man, my head is spinning. Maybe I've got low blood sugar too."

"We're ... we're stopping?"

"For now, yeah," says Simone. "I think I need to. My head is spinning, you know? I'm gonna call it a night, head home."

"I'll walk you."

"Thanks, but there's no need for that. I'll take a cab."

"Cabs can be dangerous. Wait."

She's already crawling out of the tent. JD starts to get up, but his corduroys are still around his ankles and his penis is pointing straight up. He almost trips over himself.

She pauses on the other side of the tent flap. He can see her face now. She looks pale. She gives him a faint smile. "Sorry to be a buzzkill. Come find me some other day. Maybe."

"I will," says JD. "I'll come find you. I solemnly swear it. A Sentinel never breaks his word."

Then she's gone. He slowly hauls his corduroys back up and rebuckles his belt.

The voices and music around the tent have somehow become discordant. Even threatening, as if 99Together is about to somehow implode. He doesn't want to be here anymore.

In the semi-dark, he notices the hoodie Simone had been wearing. It was oversized on her, but would fit JD just fine. Dropped beside the hoodie is the mask, that plastic vigilante with his moustache and cheery grin.

He's back on his street. Away from the downtown core the night is quiet, but from up ahead he can hear the thump of bass. He comes in view of the rundown frontage of Country Club Estate. There's the fountain gang, Sean and four others, at their usual post. No skanks this time. The beat is coming from their little portable stereo.

JD watches for a little while. His arms and legs feel like they're full of some buoyant, electrified gas. He starts forward at a brisk walk. The fountaineers look up only when he is ten feet away from them.

What do they see? The dark hoodie. The vigilante mask. The thing JD is holding in his right hand.

He flicks his wrist and the baton extends to its full length. The snicketing sound of it is clear even over the beat. Clear and perfect.

He swings the baton in a shallow sideways arc and catches the first hood – the youngest – on the hipbone. The hood squeals and spins halfway around. The second hood is a fat tub of guts in purple velour. JD strikes him on either arm and then on the side of his leg. The fat one topples over onto his back and his big chubby legs go straight up in the air. JD is already moving past him.

Sean is next. Sean the mocker, Sean the extortionist. Sean with his eyes bugging from his head, turning to run like a coward. JD swings the baton in a downward diagonal. It catches Sean on the ankle. Sean hops up on one foot as if he'd stepped on a nail. JD swings again, strikes Sean's other leg below the knee. Sean collapses.

The remaining two hoods turn and run in different directions. The first hood, the one JD caught on the hip, is himself halfway down the block. Not running so much as shuffling. The fat one has rolled over on his side. He's moaning, clutching his arms.

For a moment JD stands his ground, breathing through his mask. Feeling his entire existence pulse with power.

Sean rolls over on his back. Tears are streaming down his face. He must have hit his mouth when he fell, because his lower lip is split open and bleeding. He holds up one trembling hand. When he manages to speak his voice is shaking and shrill. "What in the fuck do you want?"

JD raises the extendable. Now both of Sean's hands are up. His eyes squeezed shut. JD chops the baton down. It hisses through the air.

The knob on the end of the baton smashes into the portable stereo. The beat stops dead. Bits of plastic and circuitry fan out.

JD stands back. He collapses the baton and shoves the handle into his hip pocket. Then he turns and runs across the street, through a parking lot, into a dark alley on the far side of the plaza. He'll be long gone by the time the fountain gang regroup and lick their wounds.

And they will never have any idea who he is. All they'll know is that the night came alive. Came for them. Maybe somewhere inside their ignorant hoodlum minds, they'll know they had it coming.

JD wakes to the ring of a cellphone. He sits up from the couch, blinking, looking around. He's not sure what time it is, but the daylight coming through the windows suggests it's midmorning.

His thoughts are woolly from lack of sleep, but he's also confused about the ringing of the cellphone. Takes him a few seconds to remember the burner.

JD swings his legs off the couch. Stands up. He's got the burner plugged in and resting atop one of the stacks of newspapers. He hustles over to it and accepts the call.

He clears his throat. "Sentinel here," he says.

"Took you long enough."

"Ronnie," says JD. "I mean, X-Ray, kind sir. I apologize for the delay. I was doing some self-defense drills in my—"

"I got something for you."

An hour later, JD gets off the bus and walks up Logan Street to Maiwand Automotive. He hears a pneumatic wrench going inside the building. Strains of some kind of fast-paced ethnic music.

He's ten paces away from the customer entrance when Ronnie emerges, again clad in coveralls. He's wiping his hands on a rag as he limps toward JD.

JD tips his trilby. Ronnie responds with a stiff nod. He reaches into the hip pocket of his coveralls and fishes out the keys to Granddad's ice cream truck. Ronnie points with his chin to the fenced-in area of the parking lot. JD looks.

There are a dozen cars and trucks there, all different makes and models. Among them is the ice cream truck. It was in plain sight when JD arrived, but he didn't notice it. The powerhorn taken off the roof of the cab. Any holes from the shotgun pellets have been plugged up with filler and sanded down.

The hasty roller paintjob the truck had undergone up at Forward Operating Base Liberty has been entirely redone. Now the truck is a bland, uniform gray colour. Even the service window. At least it looks like a proper paintjob, even if Granddad would have a stroke if he saw it.

The truck no longer stands out in any way. It looks like something a delivery or courier service would use. Something you wouldn't think about twice if you saw on the road.

"You will fix it, right?" says JD. "You'll fix it back to the way it was?"

"That's the plan," says Ronnie.

"And I'm guessing you can't tell me what the rest of the plan is."

Ronnie frowns, leans in. "That's a executive decision up to the highest level. You know better than to even ask."

"I know," says JD. "Sorry. I just …"

"Listen, you got to get this up to FOB Liberty for the next meeting. Big things are coming down the pipe, Sentinel. Big things."

Inside the garage, the pneumatic drill cuts out but the ethnic music keeps playing. After a few seconds, somebody with a thick accent shouts Ronnie's name, asks him where he's at. A shadow passes over Ronnie's face. His lips curl up, show his teeth.

"I got to go," he says, then he pauses. "Two more things for you."

He reaches into a zippered pocket at the chest of his coveralls and draws out a clear plastic pouch. The pouch contains folded-over documents. Ronnie glances over his shoulder at the garage, turns his attention back to JD.

"Ownership," he says. Insurance. "Got it all changed from your granddad's name to yours. Don't ask me how because it's classified information. Them forms won't stand up to anything more than a quick look but sometimes a quick look is all you need. Long as you're not calling too much attention on yourself on the first place. Anyhow. Do you know if you were set to inherit this vehicle?"

JD opens his mouth to reply – to say, Inherit? – but a blast of ELF hits him. Screaming voices, fingernails on a chalkboard. He slams a hand against his temple, squeezes his eyes shut. After a couple of agonizing seconds, the ELF passes.

It doesn't seem like Ronnie has noticed JD's discomfort. Ronnie is looking back over his shoulder again. He yells, "I'll be there in a second, dangit! I'm with a customer!" He turns back to JD, shaking his head. "Last thing, Sentinel. You know Civic Park?"

JD swallows, getting a grip of himself. He nods.

"We need you there at seven o'clock tomorrow morning. Seven sharp."

"Seven o'clock … in the morning?"

"Consider it an order," says Ronnie. "Direct from Alpha One."

The next morning, JD gets up at six o'clock. This is one of the hardest things he's done in a long time.

Last night he set the alarm on the Westinghouse alarm clock. Then he lay on the couch, parsing the classified ads for messages from Granddad, listening to AM 710 until he finally fell asleep. When the clock wakes him he feels like he hasn't slept at all.

He goes into the kitchenette. Brews coffee. Finds himself hungrier than normal. At 6:15, the burner rings, startling him.

"Makin sure you're up, compadre." Gage's voice. "Good on you. How's the eyebrow?"

"Getting better," says JD. "I have a lot of natural strength and healing abilities, so—"

"I'll call you back at seven on the dot. You need to be at the south gate of Civic Park. You know where all those punk-ass hippies are living in their tent city?"

"I think I've seen them once or twice. In passing."

"Well, that's the north side. Stay away from there, unless you want to catch crabs. South gate. Seven on the dot. Bring something to write with."

Gage ends the call.

JD manages to find a loaf of bread in one of the cupboards. Half of it has gone moldy, but a few slices toward the back still look edible. He crams these into his mouth and washes them down with coffee.

Before he leaves the apartment he grabs, as instructed, something to write with. A stub of pencil and a memo pad Granddad used to write ice cream inventory on. Across the top of the memo pad is a cartoon image of a man sleeping at his desk. A caption saying One Of These Days I'm Gonna Get Organized.

JD makes sure he's carrying the burner. And the expandable baton.

"You know where the old maintenance building is at?" says Gage. "Top of the reservoir hill?"

It's two minutes to seven. JD is standing at the south gate of Civic Park. The morning is chilly and foggy, the city asleep. Light traffic. The odd jogger or dog-walker appearing out of and disappearing back into the gloom. At the southern end of the park, there's little sign of the 99Together camp.

JD heads into the park. It's even quieter here than it was on the sidewalk. Almost all the leaves are down. To JD's left, reservoir hill, thick with trees, slopes upward. A jogger passes by, trailing a dim sound of dance music from her headphones.

JD turns the corner where the ascension beside him is the steepest. He comes to a stop at the base of the concrete staircase that leads up to the maintenance building. The steps are in bad shape. Cracked and crooked. The city has put up caution tape and a small mesh barrier around the base. A sign informs passersby that a revitalization project is set to begin in spring 2012.

JD lifts the burner to his ear. "Hawkeye, this is Sentinel. I'm at the building."

"You're at the building or you're at the bottom of the hill?" says Gage. "Because if you're just at the bottom of the hill, I'll give you three guesses where you're going."

"But it's all blocked off. There's a sign."

"Well. Does the sign say anybody caught trespassing will be shot on sight?"

"No ..."

"Then I'll wait, compadre."

JD sighs. He glances around but he's got the base of the hill to himself. There has to be a hundred steps between here and the top, and this is very early in the day for intense exercise. He clambers over the mesh, muttering to himself. He didn't know being an Invited Person would involve so much physical exertion.

It takes him two full minutes to make the climb, including a several-second pause to catch his breath two-thirds of the way up. The stairs are steep and treacherous. He keeps a firm grip on the metal handrail.

At the top there's another mesh barrier and caution tape to climb over. Beyond that, there's nothing much to the maintenance building. It's a squat, windowless pillbox building with a blank steel door on one face. The building is surrounded on either side by a stand of skinny pine trees.

"I'm ... at ... the top," JD says.

"Catch your breath," Gage tells him. "Okay, now look back the way you came. What do you see? Take a good look."

JD looks. Up here by the maintenance building, he can see a long way. He looks down the crooked steps to the base. From there he can see the decorative wrought-iron fence and gate marking the eastern boundary of Civic Park.

Past the fence is Monarch Avenue, and on the other side of Monarch is a row of downtown office buildings. The most prominent of them is the Van Lathan Building.

"So," says Gage. "What do you see?"

JD tells him what he sees.

"That's it," says Gage.

"What's it?"

"The Van Lathan Building. You know it? You ever been in there before?"

A nasty jolt passes through JD. He thinks of the courtrooms the lower floors.

"Not that I remember," he says.

"Well, compadre, this is what we need you to do."

For the next ninety minutes, JD does the same thing he did at the grow-op. He watches.

This time, what he's watching is the Van Lathan Building. He leans against the wall of the maintenance building. He sits on the top step of the condemned staircase. When he starts to feel sleepy, he gets up and goes back to leaning against the wall, wishing he had a coffee. There are no other people up here.

He takes notes, as Gage told him to do, on the notepad. He notes how many cars take up the metred parking spots alongside the Van Lathan Building. What time those spots start to fill up. He notes how many vehicles go down the ramp into the parking garage underneath. At one point he sees an armoured van marked Courts turn down the ramp. He makes a note of that as well.

He counts as many people going into the building as he can. Even with the good view, the people are tricky to see at this distance. Early in the day like this, there are far more people entering the Van Lathan Building than leaving. It looks as if most of them are wearing suits. He spies a few cops, a few people who look like couriers.

Textbook sheeple. Wage-slaves, rat-racers.

He also sees what appear to be small children being taken into the building. The children are even smaller than the adults at this distance.

He can discern them mainly by their brightly-coloured jackets. Perhaps there's a daycare inside. Somewhere to corral the kiddies while their parents punch clocks in stuffy offices on the upper floors. Or bang gavels in the courtrooms down below.

By 8:50, the flow of sheeple and vehicles has slowed to a trickle. JD looks at the notes he's made. He's divided the page into two columns – one for the vehicles, one for the sheeple – and has made little tickmarks in each. Gage told him the count didn't have to be precise. He just had to get a general sense of the numbers.

He adds up the tickmarks. As of 8:50 – or zero-eight-hundred-fifty-hundred or whatever the Patriot Bloc terminology is – approximately five hundred people, including twenty-five kids, have entered the Van Lathan Building. Sixty vehicles have gone down the ramp. Another five vehicles are parked in the metred spots on the street.

The burner rings in his pocket. Right on time.

"Sentinel here," says JD.

It's not Gage's voice on the other end this time. It's Declan's. "Well, did you get a math exercise in for the day?"

"Affirmative," says JD. "I counted—"

"No no. Don't say anything, even over this line, my friend. Keep your intel report someplace safe. I want you to put it into my hands when we're finally looking each other in the eye. If not mine, then X-Ray's, Hawkeye's, or Domestic's. Nobody else's. Understand? Do not put that intel into anybody else's hands whatsoever."

"I understand," says JD.

There's a pause on the other end of the line, then Gage's voice returns. "Okay, compadre. You're finished there. You're free to extract, get yourself a coffee or something. See you at the meeting."

The call ends. JD starts to tear off the slip he's been making notes on. He pauses, then writes Intel Report By: Patriot Alpha Sentinel across the top. He folds the slip and puts it in his breast pocket.

Getting back down the steps is more treacherous than the ascent.

When JD gets to the bottom, he thinks he'll take Gage's advice and go get a coffee. Then maybe he'll mosey on over to 99Together and see what's what. See who's there.

He's halfway done the steps when he hears three whoops of a siren. It doesn't sound all that far away, but sirens downtown aren't special.

Are they?

A few steps further down he hears another blast of sirens. This time it's sustained for about ten seconds. He also realizes there are people on the path at the base of the stairs. More people than the infrequent joggers and dog-walkers he'd seen earlier in the morning. All these people seem to be headed in the same direction. North. As if they're going to look at something.

He even sees a pair of cops near a tree on the flat terrain. He freezes, considers the fact he's using stairs that are closed to the public. Considers the fact he's got a highly sensitive intelligence report tucked into his pocket.

The cops don't pay him any attention. They, too, are looking northward. One of them is speaking into a radio.

The siren sounds yet again, and with it JD he realizes he can hear a din of raised voices. People shouting. A lot of people shouting. JD continues down the last dozen steps. He hops the barrier, almost bowls over a fat man who's heading north along the path with everybody else.

"Watch out," says the fat man, then, "Hey, I know you ..."

JD looks at him. It's the same fat man he saw at the Patriot Bloc meeting. The one who asked about money, the one Ronnie called a cuck. The fat man is dressed in gray trousers and a collared shirt. No tie. Pinned to his shirt is a little plastic tag reading Xpress Print ~ Gavin.

Seeing the fat man might be a coincidence, if JD believed in coincidence. But he can't think about it right now. His mind is on 99Together. He has a sinking feeling in his stomach.

"You were the new guy up at the meeting," says the fat man.

JD is impatient. He wants to run. "Good sir," he say.

"You still going to the meetings?" says the fat man.

"I am. I've been invited to continue."

"Well, that's your business, I guess, but if you ask me you'd be better off doing your own thing. Wish I'd figured that out for myself a while back."

"What exactly do you mean, good sir?"

The fat man opens his mouth. Then he seems to have second thoughts . After a moment, he says, "Like I said, it's your business.

Anyhow, I should get going. Don't want to miss the show."

Yet another sustained blast of sirens.

"What show," says JD, starting to feel like he knows the answer already, like he knew the answer all along.

The fat man grins. "The city's finally evicting all those deadbeats from their little campout. There's no way I'd miss seeing that. That thing's been an eyesore since the day it started."

As with his first visit, JD can hear 99Together before he sees it.

There's the bullhorn again. A chorus of voices. This time the chant is Shame, shame, shame. He can also hear some kind of machinery at work. The beeps of a big vehicle backing up. The siren keeps whooping in irregular blats, echoing off the indifferent faces of the Van Lathan Building and its neighbours.

As JD gets closer to the campsite, the footpath is blocked by people standing and staring. The chant rises above everything else, even above the machinery and siren.

Shame, shame.

JD starts to push his way through the sheeple rubbernecking on the path. He puts his hand on the extendable in his pocket. He pushes and shoulders and elbows his way up the path, but before long he can't go any further. He's enclosed by the shame-chanters here. Their anger is a palpable thing. But so too is their defeat. Their chant can't stop what's happening.

From what JD can see, all the flags and banners are gone. He can see a dozen protesters hurriedly packing up their tents. Not far away is a group of city workers in hardhats and bright reflective vests. They're picking up all kinds of items. Boxes of books, lawnchairs, clothes, even whole tents, then throwing them into the back of a garbage truck that's been parked on the grass.

The cops are everywhere. Everywhere. Some in their normal uniforms, but some in full-up riot gear. Helmets, plexiglass faceplates, truncheons in hand.

A few paces to his right, JD sees a young woman in a baseball cap being interviewed by a reporter. There's high colour in the young woman's face. She isn't quite crying, but her eyes are shining. JD can hear a quaver in her voice as she speaks into the microphone.

"... not enough people here making a stand, you know? she's saying. I think there's some people still on the other side of the camp, but everybody else just kinda gave in as soon as the cops came ..."

JD gives the young woman a closer look. Sticking out from under the ball cap are tufts of red hair. Simone's friend, Jackie. The one who went down with low blood sugar, the one JD rescued in a grand act of heroism. JD pushes himself closer to her, until he's standing right next to the cameraman.

"I'm sad that we gave in so fast," says Jackie. "A year from now, I wonder if we'll be able to hold our heads up about today. This is so much bigger than any of us. I can't believe we're rolling over like this."

"Thanks for your remarks," says the reporter.

Jackie nods. She still hasn't noticed JD. She starts to withdraw into the crowd around her. JD scrambles forward, almost tripping the cameraman. He curses at JD but JD doesn't pay him any attention. He grabs Jackie's elbow.

She snaps her head around. "Hey! What the fuck?"

"It's me," says JD.

She squints. "I don't know ... Oh, you're Simone's whatever, right?"

"Of course I am," says JD. "Where is she?"

"Excuse me, but can you let go of my arm? And no. I haven't seen her. She hasn't been here all day. It's like she disappeared or something."

Disappeared.

JD releases the redhead's arm, but it's all he can do not to seize her by the collar and shake her.

"What do you mean, disappeared? Is Simone in danger? Did she get taken?"

The redhead squints again. "Taken? What the hell are you talking about? She left, buddy. She split. She fucking rolled over. Or, I don't know, she's at the last stand, over on the other side of the camp, but I doubt it. I—"

Other side of the camp. As if on cue, there's a pertained blast of sirens. JD leaves the redhead standing there. All around them is the chant.

Shame. Shame. Shame.

JD can't go forward from his present position, so he backs off, then works his way west. Into the trees and undergrowth at the best of reservoir hill, skirting the crowd and the besieged campsite. His hand doesn't stray far from his baton.

It takes a while to bushwhack through the base of the hill to the north side of the park. There's no crowd here, so he can step out of the brush onto the grassy flat. The ground here is littered with garbage. Not far away is an abandoned dome tent. Maybe the same dome tent they went when Simone seduced him.

JD slips the extendable out of his pocket and holds it in his hand, partly up his sleeve where it can't be seen. He makes his way to the tent, then peaks around it. Twenty-five yards away is a ramshackle fortress built around the base of an oak tree. The fortress is assembled from crates and wooden skids and tarps.

Manning the fortress are fifty protesters. Some have their faces concealed by the mustachioed vigilante mask. Some are hidden by bandanas, outlaw-style. There is no coordinated chanting among them. No bullhorns. They are all screaming obscenities.

JD looks for Simone, but it's impossible to tell who's who in the fortress.

The cops, normal uniforms and riot variety alike, are closing in like a noose. Outnumbering the protesters three to one. Thirty feet away from JD, a guy with his face exposed, who can't be older than seventeen, whips a water bottle at a female cop. In seconds he's tackled to the ground by two brutes. One of them starts cuffing him. The other puts his knee onto the side of the kid's head, pressing his face into the ground.

"Excessive force!" the kid screams. "Police brutality!"

JD steps forward, letting the baton slide lower into his hand. The two brutes are turned away from him. The biker at the grow-op never saw JD coming. Neither did Sean and his fountain gang. Neither will these cops. JD takes another step.

"Take a hike, sir."

JD looks to his left. Another pair of cops has appeared as if out of nowhere. The one who spoke is big and black and swollen with muscle under his uniform. His partner is smaller, but he has his hand on his taser. JD grins at them. Not far away, the other brutes are hauling the kid to his feet. His hands are cuffed behind him, but he is kicking his legs. He screams about police brutality again.

"Do I have to repeat myself?" says the black cop. "Take a fuckin hike or we're gonna bust you."

The smaller cop pulls his taser from his belt and holds it beside his hip. One flick of JD's wrist and his baton will extend. He's confident he can get the drop on these two, but there are at least a hundred more cops here.

At that moment, it seems like Granddad is speaking in JD's ear, right through the constant ELF background whine.

They always rig the game so's they win, bucko.

JD takes a step back. "The time is coming," he says.

"What'd you say?" says the cop with the taser.

JD tips his trilby. Then he turns around and walks away, deliberately keeping his pace slow and relaxed. Unbothered. Unafraid. Unvanquished. The time is coming.

"I don't know how to put this any other way," says Declan, "but the Patriot Bloc is hereby, immediately dissolved."

A ripple goes through the meeting room. Gwen puts both hands to her mouth. Her eyes widen. She shakes her head slowly back and forth. JD is also shocked at the declaration.

Declan is not looking at anyone. His eyes are fixed at a high angle. The ceiling at the far end of the room. Or heaven.

Stillness falls over the people in the chairs. There's even fewer of them tonight than the last meeting. Gwen breaks the stillness. "Doctor Declan – Richard, if I may – how can you say this? If it's a matter of faith, I can pray for you. Right here and now. Why, all of us can pray for you. Do not fear, for I am with you. Do not be dismayed, for I am your God. I will strengthen you and help you. I will uphold you with my righteous right hand. From the Book of Isaiah, Richard."

Declan offers an odd smile. He says, "Yet she increased her prostitution, remembering the days of her youth when she engaged in prostitution in the land of Egypt. She lusted after their genitals, as large as those of donkeys, and their ejaculations were as strong as those of stallions. That's from the Book of Ezekiel, Gwen."

The people seated in the chairs all glance at each other. Gwen's face turns red. "Is that some kind of a … a parable … Dr Declan?"

Declan's smile turns into a grin. "We tried to follow the process, friends. We tried to play by the rules. That was foolish of us. Foolish of me. When you're playing against the deep state, the elites, you're playing a rigged game. Indeed you are."

Finally, Declan looks at the people in the room. He looks everybody dead in the eye.

He says, "The game is so rigged, in fact, that the government, refusing to recognize the right to peaceful assembly, sends undercover agents to spy on your meetings …"

A collective gasp.

"To find any scrap of dirt with which to condemn you …"

Declan hikes up his trouser leg to reveal his ankle monitor. Maybe everybody already knew about it, but seeing it so plainly causes another collective gasp.

"To clean out your coffers," Declan adds. "Yes, that's correct. If Gavin were still here, I would answer his question about our finances more directly. I would tell him we've been robbed blind by Big Brother. Asset forfeiture, they call it, but whatever name it has, it was made possible by one or more persons sitting in this room, calling him – or her – self a supporter of our humble cause. A patriot."

The loudest gasp yet. People are halfway out of their chairs, pointing fingers, talking over one another. The commotion seems to wake the old man in the wheelchair. He looks around wildly, wags a knobby finger in the air. JD glances over at Gwen and sees her eyes are shining with tears. He feels sorry for her. He feels sorry for himself.

On the other hand. Undercover agents? Collaborators?

Them? Here?

He studies everybody's face. His hand creeps into his pocket and wraps around the handle of the baton. His pulse quickens.

Declan raises his hands and pushes them forward, as if to quell the rising voices. It works. The room goes quiet.

"I don't know who it is," Declan says. "I have my suspicions, of course. And believe me when I say Gage is looking into it. Gage is the last guy you want digging around for skeletons in your closet, I might add. I can't say I'm surprised, friends. I'm angry, I'm heartbroken. But I can't say I'm surprised. This is the world we live in, where true patriots cannot even trust each other. Am I going to rant and rave about it? No. Am I going to be violent about it? No. But I am going to dissolve the organization and try to find a new group of people who are truly worthy of the cause.

"In the meantime, this is private property, and while nothing else is sacred anymore, private property is. So in the name of private property, I kindly invite you, traitors all, to get the hell out."

Dead silence in the room. Then Ronnie jumps up as nimbly as he can on his one real leg. His face is dark. "You heard the man! Get out, you no-good backstabbing cucks! Out!"

The people around JD get to their feet. Gwen is weeping. JD looks at Declan. Declan is leaning against the side of the lectern, appearing oddly relaxed now. Declan doesn't return JD's look.

JD looks at Ronnie, but Ronnie is busy hollering at everyone to get out. JD looks at Becca. She is looking back at him, but her expression is unreadable. JD gets out of his chair. He turns around. He sees Gage standing near the door, his hand tucked into the small of his back.

JD follows the deflated crowd through the entryway and outside. He's last out the door. His head is spinning. He pauses on the top step and watches as Gwen blows her nose into a wad of kleenex. She slinks over to a little hatchback.

A hand closes over JD's shoulder.

He turns around, and there's Declan. Declan pulls JD back into the house. Behind him, Gage closes the front door, cuts off the sounds of engines starting up.

"In the words of the great Aeschylus," says Declan, "I have learned to hate all traitors, and there is no disease I spit on more than treachery."

"I am no traitor, sir."

A long pause. Then Declan grins, shakes JD by the shoulder. "Of course you're not, my friend. Of course you're not. To tell you the truth, I don't think there was one. The deep state thinks it put me out of business when they arrested me. But that's another story." Declan nods at the front door. "Those people weren't useful anymore. Not to the true hard core of the cause. There wasn't any other way to get rid of them without dragging the whole thing out. Once in a while, a little Night of the Long Knives is healthy, don't you think? But enough about that, do you have something for me?"

JD undoes his pocket and withdraws the slip of paper. Puts it into Declan's hand. Declan's other hand is still grasping JD's shoulder. Declan is standing very close to him. JD can smell aftershave and hair pomade and, below those scents, a sharp tang of sweat.

Declan unfolds the paper. Studies it. Frowns. "Sixty-five … what's a vechle?"

"Vehicle," says JD.

"Ah. Sixty-five. And five hundred … you've written the word sheeple? … No need to explain. I like that. Now. Were you seen by Caesar's Legion? Stopped? Questioned?"

"Not at all," says JD.

JD doesn't add anything about the forceful teardown of the 99Together encampment.

"Well done," says Declan. "Very well done. Let's go out back, Sentinel. Let's let our hair down for a little while. I believe we've earned it."

The executive committee. The inner circle. The Very Very Invited Persons. The hardest of the hard core. They gather around the fire out back, like some ritual out of ancient times.

The old man sleeps in the wheelchair. Ronnie mans the barbecue. Gage and Declan sit beside each other, talking in low voices. Becca comes out of the house, carrying the beer cooler. JD can't help but notice how her skirt looks shorter tonight. Her legs are bare above the red boots.

"Hey creepo," says Becca. "A picture'll last you longer."

JD blinks. "Yes, I'm sorry."

She sets the plastic cooler down and opens it. Out comes the six-pack of Busch tallboys. Ronnie comes from the barbecue to help himself to one. Another goes to Gage. Declan stays dry. Becca opens one for herself, then passes one to JD.

He opens it, takes a swig. The night is cold. Chilled beer does nothing to help, so he slides his chair closer to the fire. Then a hand grips his arm. He turns his head. Becca has sidled her own chair up beside him. With her free hand she's holding something out. He looks down and sees a fat blunt smoldering between her fingers.

"You like to do the pot," she says.

Not a question. "I have been known to partake," JD says.

"Well here you go. Have a toke-up of that."

JD takes the blunt from Becca's fingers and draws deeply from it. The smoke zooms from his lungs into his brain right away. He has another draw and holds the smoke and lets it out slowly.

Becca grins and punches JD in the shoulder. "Maybe you're okay. For a creepo."

Then she stands up and walks over to help Ronnie out with the barbecue. JD wonders why she's being nice to him. He also wonders why his hands trembling.

"You need another beer?"

Gage's voice. JD pulls his attention away from his hands. It takes some effort. He sees Gage and Declan looking relaxed in their chairs across the fire.

"Not just yet," says JD. He sips from his can and swallows. Swallowing feels strange. "What's your story, kind sir?"

Gage's eyebrows lift behind his ballistic glasses. "My story?" A long pause. "I don't go chit-chatting about my private details with just anybody, compadre. Because just anybody might not be just anybody, roger so far?"

"We've got to watch our six," JD says.

Gage leans forward, elbows on his knees. JD tries to match his posture, but for a moment it's like an invisible hand is pressing him into his chair.

"So you want to know what my deal is," says Gage. "Ladies in the military. The police and the fire department too, but ladies in the military is what a lot of it comes down to. Look. I did twenty years in the army. Three deployments. So I got some personal knowledge on the subject. Combat is no place for a woman. Hell, training isn't no place for a woman. For one thing, a soldier has to be able to put their emotions aside, which women aren't good at. Another thing, how can a hundred-and-fifteen pound girl be expected to haul eighty pounds of gear? Physically, it doesn't make—"

"I could do that," says Becca. "Easy."

Gage doesn't miss a beat. "You could, honey. But most ladies aren't you."

"Damn straight," says Becca.

"But, look," says Gage. "The problem goes way past ladies in the military. The problem goes way past this nasty little thing called feminism. The problem goes way past multiculturalism and race-mixing and whatever else. These things are all bad, but they'rt symptoms of the disease. And the disease is how soft we've let ourselves go under our so-called leadership. We're not a country of men no more. We're a bunch of pushover snowflake cry-babies who let all the special interests get away with whatever they want. Look at all those goddamn bums in Civic Park. I say put them to work. Bring back the chain-gang. But the government does nothing about them. Nothing at all. Lets them sit there day and night, on public property, while the rest of us get bent over and fucked in the ass."

JD is confused. On one hand, here's Gage saying the problem is society is a bunch of pushover snowflake cry-babies. On the other hand, Declan says they're living under a tyrannical government. On the other other hand, there's Becca saying it's the End Times, Christ getting nailed to the Christmas tree or something like that. And then on the other other other hand, didn't Ronnie talk about the jihadists or the Gypsies outbreeding everybody?

The entire time Gage is talking, Declan keeps smiling his faint smile. Ronnie serves up hamburgers on paper plates. He sits down next to Declan and digs in. At some point Becca wheels the old man into the house. She's gone for a few minutes, then comes back with fresh beers.

She sits down by the fire and offers JD another haul of the blunt. He takes it, inhales, and lets the smoke hit his head. He feels like he's in a wind tunnel. An echo chamber. A vast canyon.

"Anyways, I follow Doc Declan because he gets it," says Gage. "More than anybody else I ever met, Doc Declan gets it. The whole problem. That's why I know his plan will work. When he plants the flag, people like us from all over are gonna stand up and be counted. I've never been more sure of anything in my life, compadre."

Things go quiet for a minute. Just the crackling of the fire. The quiet might actually be longer than a minute, but JD can't tell. Time is moving through funny dimensions.

"Okay," says Ronnie. "The, what did you call it? The mind control signal. What's the deal with that?"

JD's beer slips out of his fingers and clunks onto the flagstones below. He looks down at it but it seems too far away to reach. JD has never, ever, told anybody about ELF. Not the inner circle of the Patriot Bloc, not Simone, not even Granddad. How would he even approach talking about it?

He clears his throat. "I don't know what you're talking about."

Ronnie laughs first. It's a harsh sound. Then Gage and Becca join him. Even Declan laughs.

"You just told Gage," says Ronnie, "that the problem is there's this mind control everywhere. Low frequency, something like that. And you said They're behind it. Who're They?"

Wait, JD thinks, what? He glances over at Becca. She's still sitting beside him. She's stubbing the blunt out on the flagstone between her feet.

"I daresay we're all curious, my friend," says Declan. "If you know something we don't, would you kindly enlighten us?"

Another minute-long hour elapses. JD presses his fingers against his temples to keep his head from spinning off his neck and flying away. Everyone is watching him.

No.

He's not going to say anything. This is his own business. ELF, Them, the whole conspiracy ... it's all classified information.

"I ...," says JD. "Well ... Well, where to begin..."

Classified information or not, he starts talking.

Over the next indeterminate amount of time, JD tells his Patriot comrades everything he knows about Them. How They have infiltrated human society with spies and collaborators and informants. He says nothing ever happens just because. They don't work that way.

JD talks about Their fingerprints on the great pyramids. Stonehenge. Atlantis. They were behind the disappearance of all those natives in South America. The Black Death. The First and Second World Wars.

"Hitler and the Communist guy and the fat guy, Churchill, were all

Their pawns," says JD. "You know why? Because we're lab rats to Them. That's part of the conspiracy."

JFK was going to disclose a bunch of classified information about the conspiracy. That's why They took him out. They faked the moon landing. They blew up the World Trade Center on 9/11. The airliners crashing into the buildings were holograms. Holograms or targeted mind control, which of course They are experts at.

"Extremely Low Frequency," says JD. "ELF. It's in your head, kind sirs. It's telling you what to think, or it's stopping you when you ask too many questions."

He takes off his trilby and turns it upside-down. Shows them the aluminum foil Faraday shield he's crafted on the inside of the hat.

"It's not perfect," he says. "Some ELF signals still get through, but I don't even want to begin to imagine how much worse it would be without basic protection." He puts the trilby back on.

"I'm not sure what They want with us," he says. "I'm working on figuring it all out, but, you understand, much of the research about the conspiracy has been suppressed." He pauses. "All I can say for certain, is They have taken a special interest in me. They like to fuck me over every which way. There's no other way to explain why things are the way they are for me. There is no just because."

He trails off. He has no idea how long he's been talking. His head still feels like it's going to spin off. He looks around the fire. Everyone has angled their chairs the better to pay attention to him. Becca and Gage and Declan – Domestic and Hawkeye and One – all have soft smiles. Their eyes are gentle. Kind. JD glances at Ronnie. X-Ray's mouth is hanging open, his head is nodding. When he catches JD's glance he reaches out and grasps his shoulder and squeezes it.

They've been listening.

A long moment passes, and though the world gets a little dimmer around him, he feels a small spark of hope. They've been listening. He smiles. He hears a voice say thank you and realizes it's his own voice. Not even in a canyon anymore – now coming from a different planet. Planet X.

Becca laughs. Her eyes twinkle. "Where in the holy hell did you come from, buddy?"

At the same time, Gage says, "I don't even know what to ... Boss, how did you meet our man here again?"

"When I met young Sentinel," says Declan, "he was about to get assaulted by a horde of negroids in the city jail. Young Sentinel had tried to change the TV channel on them. Told them the show they were watching was brainwashing them. Which, knowing the negroid's taste in entertainment, was probably accurate ..."

Wait, wait, JD thinks. That isn't right. He'd come to Declan's aid in the animal cage, not the other way around. Declan needed JD's protection.

"I only needed to make an example of one of those beasts," says Declan, "and the rest backed off ..."

JD opens his mouth to say something, but finds the words choked in his throat. Everyone is laughing again.

"The temptation behind bars," says Declan, "is to stand idly by, even while a member of your own race is on the receiving end of some misfired aggression. But I couldn't do that. No indeed. And how glad I am, since Sentinel turned out to be one of us. As if Providence was behind it all along."

At that JD stands up out of his chair. He needs to correct the record. But then somebody – Them, no doubt – changes the gravity of Planet Earth. Instead of looking horizontally, JD is looking straight down. The stonework is coming up to meet him. There's a thud of impact. Everything goes black. All the laughter still rings in his ears.

Laughter and understanding, even if Declan didn't get the story right.

JD is walking through some cavernous darkness. Can't tell if he's dreaming. He hears voices raised. For a moment he thinks he's back in Civic Park. He wonders where the rest of the activists are. Where's Simone?

Not Civic Park. That's all gone now. Failed. Stamped out by Them. JD was there. He was among the last activists standing, same as he was one of the very first in the early days. He was defiant to the end.

At any rate he's not in Civic Park, he's in the huge dark house, Forward Operating Base Liberty.

The library. He's looking at the door, that door, the one for the Very

Very Very Very Invited Persons. The steel knob and the keypad. The door is open an inch, as if someone forgot to close it. There's light on the other side of the door. There's also the raised voices.

Gage's voice: "... liability, Richard. We got to own up to that. Useful or not."

A pause, then Declan: "And you?"

Ronnie: "I don't know, sir. I don't know."

JD reaches out. Plants his hand on the door. That's when he becomes aware of someone beside him.

"Leave them three alone," says Becca.

"What are they yelling about?"

"Doesn't matter," she says.

"What's in there?"

"Ha," says Becca, gently pulling the door closed. "Nothing. Well, nothing a lot of normal people would want to see. Might offend them."

There is a mocking note in her voice. JD grits his teeth. "I'm not normal. I am not some goddamn sheeple."

She laughs. "You got a heck of a way of putting things, don't you? But you know what? God has a special place in His heart for people like you. The far out types."

JD presses his hand against his head. He is a grain of sand squeezing through the middle of an hourglass. None of this is real. That yelling coming beyond the door, that isn't real. He almost stumbles, but Becca's keeps him upright. "I'm going on a vision quest," he says.

"No you're not," says Becca. "Straight-up? I added a little phencyclidine to that pot I gave you. Figured you could stand to loosen up. Maybe tell us about yourself, creepo, which is exactly what you did. In the end you're pretty harmless, aren't you?"

"Harmless?" says JD. "I'm nothing of the sort, woman. I know things. I know the way the world works. I'm Patriot Alpha Sentinel."

"Sure you are," she says.

She pulls JD's arm. He follows. There are poorly-lit stairs. The next thing he knows, they're in the room with the brass-framed bed and the doll cabinet. Becca pushes him down on the bed. She hikes up her skirt. She's wearing a pair of black panties. She doesn't take them off, just rucks them over to the side.

She doesn't touch his blazer or his shirt but goes straight for his trousers. She undoes them, pulls them down his legs, makes some joke about how he's going commando. Then she's on top of him. He can feel the power in her thighs. He can feel the weight of her. Her hard fingers dig into his chest. He claws his trilby off and drops it on the floor and leans his head back and closes his eyes.

Then she says, "You're hurting my feelings. Boo hoo."

JD lifts his head up to look at her. She's climbed off him – he's only now realizing it – and is sitting at the far end of the bed. "What's wrong?" he says.

She laughs and gives his bare thigh a sharp smack. "You got nothin going on here. We been trying for the last twenty minutes, but nope. Nothin."

To emphasize her point she takes hold of his penis and gives it a squeeze. An image comes into JD's mind. A worm on the sidewalk on a rainy day. He is limp. He is soft. He can barely feel anything below his waist.

"Boo hoo," she says.

"I ... I'm sorry, my lady, I'm sorry. I—"

A blast of stars fills JD's vision, pain explodes across his face. For a long moment he can still feel the open-handed blow she just gave him. But then she's caressing his cheek with her other hand. Softly. A mother's touch. "Shut up," she says. "Shut up, you harmless far out little creepo. God loves you."

"We ... we met in a past life," says JD. "Or I think we did. I think in a past life we shared adventures. That's what it is I recognize about you."

"Shut up now," she whispers softly.

Becca turns out the light. She stays with JD in the room, and after a while he somehow ends up with his head on her hard, broad thighs. His head finally stops spinning. The world seems to hold still for a little while, and bit by bit he starts to fade away.

In the last few instants before JD falls asleep he becomes aware of another presence in the room. There's no light by which to see, but JD can sense it all the same, standing beside the bed.

"Thank you, my friend," the presence whispers in Declan's voice. "Thank you."

There is dark. Then light. Pale. Far too early for JD's taste. A thin drizzle coming out of the sky. His head hammers in agony. His throat is dry as stone. He can smell himself. It isn't good.

He has fractional memories of the evening. Becca giving him something funny to smoke. A conversation about Them, about ELF. Maybe it wasn't so bad. Maybe he was understood. For once in his life.

He recalls hearing voices from behind the door in the library. The door for the Very Very Very Very Very Invited Persons. The door he is sure he will soon be admitted through.

One thing he does remember is making passionate love to Becca. She had several orgasms. That much is beyond dispute.

Earlier this morning he somehow he got dressed and got loaded up into the passenger seat of Gage's Jeep. Gage was behind the wheel, saying, "If you puke in here I'll throw you in the ditch."

Then everything went dark again.

When JD really comes to he sees they're back in the city. Not far from Country Club Estate. He recognizes the buildings and storefronts. The drizzle takes the colour out of everything. Gage has his radio on, tuned to an AM talk station. Somebody is blathering about sports.

Gage glances over at him. "You hungry, compadre?"

The Jeep is pulling into a McDonald's drivethrough. Under ordinary circumstances, JD would not pollute himself with fast food. Fast food is an opiate for the masses. All those GMOs and neurotoxins and god knows what else they put in your burger.

But JD is mortal. Mortal and hungry and hungover. Also, it seems Gage is paying.

A few minutes later JD is gorging himself on a Big Mac and large fries and cola. Gage just orders a coffee. He sips it as he drives. They turn onto Blevins.

"Hey, how did you know where I live?" says JD.

Gage doesn't reply. He pulls up in front of Country Club Estate. Dirty rainwater has pooled in the big concrete fountain. The hoodlums are nowhere to be seen. JD stuffs the remains of his food into the paper bag it came in and unbuckles his seatbelt.

"Hold up a second," says Gage. He takes a sip of coffee and eyes JD over the plastic lid. "It's time for you to stay the fuck away from us. You got … I don't know what you got, but whatever it is it's not the kind of extra baggage we need."

JD can't find words to reply.

Gage just sips his coffee again. "Let me make it clear to you, by the way, that this isn't a request."

JD gathers his wits. He's angry now. "I don't advise you to make an enemy of me, kind sir. I'm—"

JD doesn't even see Gage move, but out of nowhere Gage has his hand around JD's throat and is pushing JD's head against the passenger side window. All JD can do is paw at Gage's wrist. It doesn't even occur to him to reach for the expandable baton in his blazer pocket. The edges of his vision start to blur.

At the same time Gage uses his free hand to pull his shirt up and expose the compact automatic pistol, tucked into his waistband.

"Who the fuck do you think you're dealing with?" says Gage. "I know where you live. And if that's not enough to give you an impression of how serious I am I know where your kid lives."

Daniel. JD gags for breath. Gage's hand feels like steel. JD is losing sight of him. But all he can really think of is Daniel.

"Go take your craziness somewhere else," says Gage. "Get yourself some help. You need it. But let me tell you, if you go to the cops, the last thing you'll ever see is me puttin the hurt on your kid. Meantime, you're a liability. We don't need you."

A few seconds later JD is staggering on the sidewalk. "How dare you," he wheezes.

Gage peels away from the curb. His back tire hits a puddle and sends up a sheet of water that soaks JD's trousers.

For a full minute all JD can do is regroup, get hold of himself, reclaim his dignity. He is seething with rage. Gage's threat against Daniel still rings in JD's ears. And who is Gage to revoke JD's invitation to the Patriot Bloc? Who is anyone?

JD steadies his breathing and straightens his blazer and trilby. He reaches into one pocket, feeling the baton. He reaches into his other pocket. The burner phone is still there.

There's no way this is over.

After JD's first night with Lil, he had to call in sick for two days. She didn't leave his place that whole time. He didn't here from her for a month, but when he did, it was the same thing a second time. The bedroom for forty-eight hours. This time her disappearance was much longer. Still, JD was in love.

He was even more in love at the six-month mark, when she called out of the blue.

"Dude. Listen. I am fucking pregnant."

From JD's understanding of the average sheeple, news of pregnancy was usually terrifying. But not for him. He knew his child would achieve greatness. JD didn't feel any fear. He was ready to jump in with both feet. To make a life with Lil and their offspring.

It was good that he wasn't afraid, because she was already defiant. She said, "Don't think for one second that I'm gonna have an abortion because I'm not. And it's not because of some religious bullshit either. My whole life all I ever heard was how shitty I'd be at everything. My dad, may he burn in hell, that was his favourite refrain, how his daughter would only ever fail at everything. Well fuck him. Fuck everyone. I'm going to be a mother and I'm going to be amazing at it. If you think you're up to the task of being a partner in this, then put your money where your mouth is."

Maybe she was expecting him to tuck tail and run. Instead, he said, "My lady, I am in this mind body and soul. This was meant to be."

She went quiet. Then he heard her exhale. In a soft voice, she said, "Listen ... Just be real about this, okay?"

JD was real about it. He stayed at the junk removal business, despite how much he hated the work. He and Lil moved into a basement apartment together. Every appointment she had, JD was by her side. JD was as real as real gets. Daniel was born in 2003.

JD and Lil didn't want to marry. They both agreed it was a waste of time and money. Marriage was meant to formalize a family, but they already had that. Because of Daniel, JD saw a lot more of his brother and the Harpy Herself than he had in years. Even Granddad was around a lot.

The Halloween night the picture was taken saw a good haul of candy. Three pillowcases full. Lil was strict about what they could give

Daniel. He was four. Their pediatrician and a few of the teachers at his preschool had been talking about ADD. JD scoffed at the diagnosis. JD himself was living proof that doctors and teachers didn't know anything.

That Halloween night, after Daniel was put to bed, Lil and JD smoked a bowl. Gorged on the candy. Watched horror flicks on TV. Nightmare on Elm Street and The Blair Witch Project. Lil loved horror movies.

At some point, Daniel cried out from his room. JD jumped off the couch, ready to protect his son against anyone and anything.

Fifteen minutes later, when the boy had settled and JD came back, Lil asked what was the matter.

"He had a nightmare," said JD. "Monsters under the bed."

"I told you to turn down the TV. He doesn't need to hear all this slasher shit."

JD sat back down. He and Lil smoked another bowl. After ten minutes of silence from Daniel's room, JD said, "I told him there probably were monsters under his bed."

She looked at him, eyes wide. "You what?"

JD shrugged. "Why shouldn't I tell him that? There are monsters under the bed. In the closet. In the basement. In the whole world ... Doesn't matter, because he's got me to protect him. That is what a father does."

Lil went quiet and her eyes narrowed. JD knew this was a warning sign, an indicator that she might explode. Instead, after thirty or forty seconds, she snorted out laughter.

"You're ...," she said, "You're a ... Oh for fucksake, come here, will you?"

Lil didn't have much family. She was the only child of a failed second marriage. Her dad was dead. She avoided her mother. What she did have was a tight group of friends she'd known since childhood.

JD tolerated Lil's friends, but they were the sort who would give a lot of unsolicited advice. They would say things like, Man, you call in sick to work a lot, should you see a doctor? Or, It's good to have a long term financial plan. Or, I only want the best for you guys, that's why I'm saying this.

It was no business of theirs. JD was working, despite how much he loathed it. Get up, go to work, come home, go to bed, wash, rinse, repeat.

In 2005 he quit the junk removal business. It was taking a toll on his body. He found the sales aspect of the job demeaning. From there he went through a few other jobs, none of them much to his liking.

One time when JD was between jobs, Lil told him he should at least get his GED. He was smart, she said. Getting his GED would be easy.

"I am smart," JD said, smiling. "That's why I don't need such a thing. 'School,'" he said, making air-quotes, "is the worst kind of scam there is. Trust me, my beautiful lady."

Lil rolled her eyes. She looked like she wanted to say something, but JD cut her off with a kiss.

Eventually JD ended up in the entertainment industry, working at a video rental place a block away from their basement apartment.

At that time video rental places were starting to disappear. Driven out of business by the internet. But the place where JD worked specialized in arthouse films and obscure science fiction and European pornography. Stimulating stuff for a person of JD's intellect. If the superior shoe fits.

The job would have been perfect for him, if it wasn't for his so-called boss. Her name was Gabrielle. She was from Montreal. She was pretentious. Worst of all, she was ten years younger than JD. What could she know about, well, anything?

"Just be real about this, okay?"

That's what Lil had said to JD at the outset. As JD had come to understand it, Lil's definition of being real meant putting up with a pretentious child of a boss. All in the name of the almighty dollar.

So he stayed at the video place – he grinned and took it, as they say – for as long as he could. Almost two years, as it turned out. He often felt he didn't get enough recognition for that stick-with-it-ness, but that was another story.

"You quit your fucking job? Again? A fucking month—"

"Lil, darling, when your boss accuses you of bullshit, are you supposed to stand there and take it? I think not."

"—a fucking month ago? What in the fucking fuck have you been doing every day?"

"I've been going to the library. Studying my areas of interest. Researching. Expanding my knowledge. That's a much better use of my time than working in a video store for twelve bucks an hour."

Lil was shaking. Her eyes were bugging out of her face. JD had seen her angry before, but never to this extent. Still, he reached out to touch her arm, to comfort her. She hissed at him – she actually hissed, serpent-like – and backed away. Daniel was in the other room, watching his cartoons.

It was good, JD thought, that he didn't have to witness his mother's overreaction.

What had happened at the movie rental place was Gabrielle summoned JD to her tiny office at the back of the store one day. JD listened to her accuse him of a litany of nonsense. Not keeping track of late fees. Not restocking the shelves properly. Napping on the job. Showing up late.

The rental place had a bunch of movie soundtracks on CD. John Williams and Hans Zimmer, even some Disney scores. Those soundtracks were supposed to be played over the rental place's speakers, but Gabrielle pointed out how JD always turned the soundtracks off in favour of some strange AM talk radio station.

Worst of all, Gabrielle had said. I get the sense you don't respect me. I don't know if it's age, or the fact that I'm a woman, or what, but I feel like you're bothered every time I ask you to do something.

JD had wanted to tell her how respect was earned, not demanded upfront. Instead, he stayed silent. He intended to bear this indignity with quiet fortitude.

Gabrielle's face had coloured. There's something else, she said. I don't really know how to put this. You're ... Sometimes you make people uncomfortable. Customers. The other people who work here. You're very ... intense. And you have a way of condescending. People ask for a movie recommendation and you tell them either horror movies or that 9/11 conspiracy documentary or Humphrey Bogart movies from the 1940s. Those are fine recommendations, but you can't get your back up if they want to watch something else. A customer told me you called him a ... what was it ... an ignorant peasant after he wouldn't rent The Maltese Falcon ...

Gabrielle continued in this vein, but JD tuned her out. Last thing he needed was some pup listing off his supposed shortfalls. Didn't she know he was a graduate of the school of hard knocks?

I'm trying to run a business, Gabrielle had said. So tell me, what would you do in my position?

I'll make it easy for you, JD had replied.

And same as he'd done with his high school principal all those years before, JD turned around and walked out.

That had been a month earlier. Lil was correct about that much. But JD was honest about spending his time at the library. In the beginning it had been to use the public internet to look for other jobs. He'd found that a degrading, often fruitless process, so his internet searches veered into topics he'd always had at least a passing interest in. Masons, Templars, secret agendas, conspiracies. The resources on the internet were infinite.

Soon his hours and days at the library were going by without his even realizing it. That was how his understanding of Them really began to take shape. Uncovering sinister plots was a much better use of JD's time and talents than working in a movie rental place or hauling junk.

All was well … until that morning at the library, when JD had run into one of Lil's nosey, advice-giving friends. JD had believed it was an innocuous meeting. Until he got home and saw Daniel set up on the couch with a bowl of ice cream. Lil standing in the kitchen doorway, her hands on her hips.

The conversation took ten seconds to go from mature to Lil becoming furious.

"Calm down, okay?" said JD. He thought there might still be a chance to make this right.

That was when Lil started screaming like a banshee. She spat all kinds of things at JD. Some of it was about how expensive it was to raise a child. Some of it was about how JD always seemed to be happy coasting along, leaving jobs when they didn't suit him, not caring about what it took to live like an adult.

JD almost laughed at that. He cared more than anybody about being an adult, couldn't she see that? He cared about the whole world and what was becoming of it. He cared about what ominous schemes were keeping everyone enslaved. What They were up to. If directing his effort and studies to that kind of thing was immature, then—

At that moment Daniel yelled out from the other room. JD made to go to him, but Lil shoved past him and got there first. JD followed her. There wasn't an emergency. Daniel had just dropped a blob of ice cream on the floor. He was trying to clean it up with his sleeve.

"I'll help you," said JD.

"No," said Lil, calm and quiet, not even looking at JD. "No. Not another step. This is where it fucking ends, dude."

"No need for obscene words in front of our son," said JD.

She laughed. It was a giddy sound, and Daniel laughed along with her, not understanding what was happening. Lil still wasn't facing JD. She put her hands over her face. Daniel kept reaching up to grasp at her wrists. She said, "We don't need you. Don't you understand that?"

JD took a step backward. It felt as if he'd been struck.

"Get whatever shit you need," she said. "Some clothes, whatever. If you're not out of here in ten minutes I'm calling the fucking cops."

"Lil, my lady, I—"

Her eyes narrowed to slits. "Ten. Minutes."

That evening was the first time JD found himself in the animal cage. All because he'd tried to stay. Tried to reason with her. She didn't give him ten minutes, like she said she would. She didn't even give him five minutes.

He said one or two things in his defense and she'd gone off like a banshee again. Called the cops. They showed up so fast JD thought they'd been hiding on the other side of the door. The idea was not so farfetched, given what JD had started to learn about conspiracies.

There were two cops. Lil was screaming. Daniel was crying. All JD was trying to do was explain things in a rational, mature fashion. Nobody was listening to me. The best he got was one of the cops saying, "Sir, we're going to take you in until this situation defuses," and he put his hand on JD's arm.

JD shrugged him off. Neither cop seemed to appreciate that, because they put JD down on the floor and cuffed him, in plain view of Daniel.

Then they took him in. Persecuted him. One more innocent victim of a system that had been rigged for thousands of years. It wasn't fair. It wasn't right.

And it did not happen just because.

This city is grey and miserable. The houses are covered with soot, the people grave and taciturn. Black masses move along the streets; meager and pale faces, the necks bend down. Children are sitting at the street corners, begging. In front of the shops women are standing with old, grey faces. Night falls. The discharge tubes ignite. Light shines down on misery and filth. My heart wrenches.

—Goebbels

4: The Fatherless Civilization

Transcribed from *Full Disclosure with Gilbert Emmerich*, AM 710, November 7, 2015.

Gilbert Emmerich: Thing is, Johnny, we shouldn't be taking your calls anymore.

Caller: And whyever might that be, Mr Emmerich?

GE: My lawyer is advising against it. So is my producer. Not that I listen to him all that often. Do I, Paul? Ha ha. But Paul thinks—

Caller: He thinks I'm dropping some serious truth, Mr Emmerich? Setting the record straight? Giving everybody an introduction to the school of hard knocks? Is that what they think, Mr Emmerich?

GE: They think you're unhinged, Johnny. And you do not want to read what's on the forums. For a walking, talking, real-life conspiracy, Johnny, you've got a lot of people freaked the hell out.

Caller: Well, I was freaked out, Mr Emmerich. I was freaked out. Gage had turned on me, just like that. And that was bad, but it was only going to get worse from there. That was how everything came together, you see.

GE: By everything you mean ...

Caller: 11/3/11, Mr Emmerich. 11/3/11 is what I mean. And I'm sorry if your lawyer and your producer Paul don't like what I have to say, but I lived this, good sir.

D ays go by.
JD reads the classifieds. Finds nothing, casts the useless papers onto one of the ever-growing discard stacks. Another of the stacks has fallen over. He'll attend to it soon. As he will fix the towel rack in the bathroom, the drywall he stripped from the hallway wall, the general state of the kitchen. Soon.

He keeps the burner plugged in. Close to hand. Sometimes he stares at it. Willing it to ring, for Declan to reach out and set everything right. He even goes so far as opening the contact list, hovering over that one name.

Tyrant.

In the end he doesn't call. He waits. The burner doesn't ring.

The night of the 25th, he leaves the apartment. He's taken to coming and going by the back door, near the garbage bins. He's seen Sean and the fountain gang from a distance, back at their post, Sean with his arm in a sling. JD's not afraid of them, of course. He just prefers to avoid them for the time being.

Mr Rahim is also known to haunt the front of the building. Better to dodge him as well.

JD visits the Green Frog Café on the off chance Simone might be there. She isn't. The place isn't closed, but it's quiet. JD surprises himself by staying. He takes a stool at the bar, orders a double Johnnie Walker from that same bearded bartender.

There's a TV mounted on the wall behind the bar. It's playing a news broadcast. Under ordinary circumstances, JD wouldn't pay attention to the mainstream media, but this segment catches his eye. It starts with an image of the 99Together emblem. Last he'd seen it, the emblem was on a flag flying over Civic Park.

The TV is muted, the better to hear the folk music playing from the bar's sound system, but closed captions are ticking across the bottom of the screen.

It's been nearly a week since the encampment of the international protest group calling itself 99Together was dismantled. Protesters were removed from Civic Park after receiving several eviction notices from the city.

The screen shows footage of the eviction. The garbage trucks, the city workers in their reflective vests. The cops everywhere. The crowd encircling the scene. There are no captions for the chants of shame.

While the majority of demonstrators peacefully complied with city staff, a handful of demonstrators tried to establish a makeshift strongpoint on the north side of the park. Police intervened quickly, leading to the arrests of more than a dozen people.

The image cuts to the battleground around the oak tree in the north end of the park. The protesters with their faces covered, throwing water bottles. The cops in their riot gear, closing in. Then there's a shaky zoom-in to two cops taking down a young man. JD realizes it's the one he saw, the one screaming about police brutality. Those screams also remain silent and uncaptioned.

Most of those arrested have already been released, although they will also be facing minor trespassing citations.

JD squints at the screen. He's looking past the footage of the arrest. Almost at the very edge of the screen. The grainy image of a man in a blazer and a trilby, watching from the fringes of the action. No, not just watching. Making ready to jump in and set things right.

Some demonstrators, facing more serious charges, remain in custody.

After the break, sports.

The news cuts to commercials.

The bartender moseys over. "You want a refill?"

"Tell me, good sir, do they still have the open mic here?"

The bartender shrugs. "As far as I know. Should be the 2nd, I think."

"And, as far as you know, will Simone be here to host it?"

"Simone?" says the bartender. "She's the organizer, isn't she? I don't know why she wouldn't be here."

"Well, she wouldn't be here if They took—" JD catches himself. There's no way this bearded mug could understand what he's talking about. "Never mind, he says."

"So, refill?"

"Not at this time, good sir. I have to be on my way."

JD puts enough money on the bartop to cover his first double. He doesn't want to spend any more money on extravagances tonight. Those extravagances include refills. And tips. He touches his trilby, gets off his stool, and heads off.

On the 29th, JD decides he can't go without underwear any longer. He's been hoarding his money carefully, but he resolves to get some change to do his laundry. He goes down the elevator. Before he leaves the lobby he gets the newspaper from the mailbox. He departs Country Club Estate via the back door, takes the long way through the parking lot.

It's three o'clock in the afternoon. He goes into Click's, a greasy spoon diner at the corner of Marshall and 15th. Another of Granddad's old haunts. The place serves the normal diner fare, plus all-day breakfast.

He takes a booth to himself near the back, sits where he can watch for anyone resembling an infiltrator or collaborator or stooge. An ancient waitress comes by, asks him what he'll have. He orders a coffee, intending only to make laundry change on a five-dollar bill.

He has three hundred dollars remaining of Granddad's disability payout. Has to last another few weeks. But come to think of it, he's hungry. Come to think of it, he's not sure when he last ate. Maybe the McDonald's Gage bought him. A wonder it wasn't poisoned.

He orders scrambled eggs with home fries and bacon and toast. The ancient waitress marks it down on her pad and shuffles away. JD opens the paper to the classifieds.

A-OK Recyclers: We buy end of life cars & all other scrap metal! Turn your rust into cash!

Antique bed and wash stand. Fully refinished, asking $300.

Become an airline pilot in 1 yr. Everything included. Call for info.

In-home support worker, good references, $15/hour.

I will clean your eavestroughs & rake your leaves, negotiable.

At first JD thinks there are no encrypted messages. He sits back in the booth, frustrated. The waitress appears with his coffee. He pays her no attention. As soon as she's gone he lifts the mug to his lips.

Then he stops.

He sets the mug down, pushes it away. Coffee sloshes over the rim and onto the tabletop. He pulls the classifieds closer. Reads them again. And as he reads, three of the ads rise above the rest.

A-OK Recyclers: We buy end of life cars & all other scrap metal! Turn your rust into cash!

Become an airline pilot in 1 yr. Everything included. Call for info.

I will clean your eavestroughs & rake your leaves, negotiable.

JD closes his eyes. The diner isn't busy now, but there's enough ambient noise – not to mention the constant fuzz of ELF – to distract. He plugs his fingertips into his ears. He opens his eyes again.

Everything included … I will clean … A-OK Recyclers …

The waitress comes with his scrambled eggs. She's frowning at him. JD frowns back. He's still got his fingers in his ears. He pulls them out, gestures for the woman to put the platter down beside the classifieds. Can't she see how busy he is? She puts the platter down, asks JD in a cigarette-cracked voice if he wants anything else.

"No, my lady. I am fine."

JD can't disguise the impatience in his voice. The waitress huffs and disappears. As soon as she's gone he plugs his ears again. He holds his eyes closed for a count to five, opens them up, looks at the ads. Now the message is clear. So clear he wonders how he ever missed it.

Everything will be A-OK.

JD nods. Granddad knows. Granddad always knows. Everything will be A-OK.

JD heads back to Country Club Estate. He's got the classifieds with him, the encrypted message underlined with a pen he borrowed from the waitress. He's got laundry change in his pocket. And he's got a little spring in his step.

Everything will be A-OK.

When he steps out of the elevator on the seventh floor, he sees the apartment door standing open a few inches.

He freezes. He can hear voices inside.

He charges forward.

He's expecting to see Gage and god knows who else inside the apartment. What he's not expecting to see is his brother and Mr Rahim standing in the living room, looking at JD with their mouths hanging open. JD skids to a halt. He has the handle of the extendable in his hand, but he drops it back into his pocket before anyone notices it.

A moment passes. "What the fuck is going on?" says JD.

Right away Mr Rahim launches into a tirade. His eyes are bulging, the cords in his neck are standing out, and he's pointing all around him. His accent makes it hard to tell what he's saying, but it seems to be some nonsense about all the notices JD has ignored and how JD seems to avoid him all the time and who lives like this. If he doesn't take a breath soon he's going to pass out, which JD finds amusing.

At the same time, JD does not find his brother's presence amusing. He looks at him but his brother is staring at the floor. Then JD's brother takes hold of Mr Rahim's arm. "Hold on, Mr Rahim," he says. "Can you give us a second?"

Mr Rahim stops talking. He looks at JD. He looks at JD's brother. "Okay," he says. "Okay, look, you have some minutes, okay? But not long. I need this all fixed. Your grandpa, not a problem, but all this? Big problem."

Mr Rahim almost looks like he's winding up about to go on a rant again but instead he draws a couple of shaky breaths. Then he pushes past JD, goes out into the hall. He turns back, maybe to say something, but JD slams the door in his face. Now it's just JD and his brother.

"What the fuck is going on?"

JD's brother looks up from the floor. Makes eye contact at last. He's pale. "What do you mean what's going on? Look at this place." He's pointing all around, as Mr Rahim had. He points at the couch, the stacks of discarded newspapers, the empty light sockets. "It's a disaster in here. I mean, the living room is bad enough, but I was in the kitchen too. When's the last time you took the garbage out? I could barely breathe in there, and there are goddamn cockroaches the size of rats." Now JD's brother is the one talking at a breathless pace. "And why haven't you paid rent in five goddamn months?"

JD decides to take the high road. Keep calm and carry on, as they say. "Listen," says JD. "I'll admit I've been too busy to do the housemaid stuff the way a quote-unquote normal person would. I'll admit that much. Now, as for the rest of it, there's obviously been a misunderstanding ..."

Before he can say anything more, at that moment, at that very crucial moment, a third voice speaks. Says JD's brother's name. JD turns to look. The Harpy Herself is coming out of the hallway. Passing the wall where the centerfolds used to hang. The wall JD stripped to destroy the hidden surveillance equipment. She's carefully picking her over the drywall on the hallway floor.

Making a real show of it, JD thinks. Performance art.

"Your granddad's bedroom is fine," she says. "Except all the lightbulbs are gone in there, same as—"

She sees JD.

Without even realizing it, JD is already advancing on her. "You get the hell out of here," he says.

The Harpy takes a step backward. She makes to flatten herself against the hallway wall behind her, but puts her spine against a bare stud instead. She winces.

Then JD's brother is between them. His hands are on JD's shoulders. If it was anyone else touching him ... anyone ... there's no telling what JD might do.

"This is none of your business," JD tells the Harpy.

She shakes her head. "You're not well, are you."

"First things first," says JD's brother. "What happened here?"

JD breathes in through his nose, exhales slowly. "Like I told you, there's obviously been a misunderstanding. The housemaid stuff, I've been so busy I've fallen behind. I've gotten disorganized about all the petty little unimportant things, okay? Because there are way bigger issues, and I don't expect you to understand them, but trust me when I say I don't have the luxury to clean the apartment every day or make sure the rent is paid exactly precisely on time or work some stupid nine-to-five or—"

"So what's your income?" says JD's brother.

Over his brother's shoulder JD sees the Harpy's eyes narrow, as if something is occurring to her.

"You don't need to worry about that," says JD. "Granddad and I have an understanding."

JD's brother blinks. His mouth forms the word Granddad but no sound comes out. He blinks again. And over his shoulder, the Harpy presses her hands against her cheeks and her jaw drops almost to her chest.

"Oh my god," she says.

"It's none of your business," says JD, "so shut up."

"Oh my god—"

"Shut. Up."

"You're still listed as his trustee," she says. "You're still cashing his disability payments. Oh my dear god. You never reported it when ...”

"Shut up shut up shut up!"

JD hears his voice ringing off the apartment walls. He knows if he doesn't turn away from her now, he might do something really bad.

Because this is a trap. A trap They have set for him.

JD pulls away from his brother. Then he's in the hallway outside the apartment. Mr Rahim is there, waiting for them, but JD ignores him. JD can't afford to wait for the elevator. He takes the stairs. Concrete stairwell, tagged with graffiti, smelling of piss. Descending two steps at a time.

Then he's in the lobby, kicking a shopping cart out of his way. He goes out through the front, into what passes as fresh air in this ruined wasteland of a city. He senses ELF coming from all directions. Filling his head with static and whispered commands. The fountain gang is at their post. Sean, his arm in a sling, is looking right at JD.

JD's brother comes out the front door of Country Club Estate. He must've taken the elevator, or followed JD down the stairs. Brother is blathering like an idiot: "... I know we had a pretty shitty deal growing up, I know that, but ..."

"Over at the fountain, Sean calls out: Hey, ice cream man, you and me need to talk."

"... never needed to be like this," says Brother.

Sean takes a step forward. "Yeah, you, you weirdo motherfucker."

"Life isn't fair, that's all there is to it" says Brother. "It's not some kind of, I don't know, secret plan or conspiracy or whatever. Life isn't fair. That's why mom died the way she did. Same goes for Granddad. And that's why—"

JD pulls the baton out of his pocket. He thumbs the release. The baton snicks out to full extension. Sean freezes in his tracks. Behind Sean, one of his toadies turns and runs away.

JD turns back to his brother. He points the end of the baton at Brother's chest. Brother stumbles backward, his feet tangle up, and he falls down on his ass and stares up at JD with heartbreak in his eyes. For one second JD is heartbroken too. But it's too late. He did not choose any of this.

They thrust it on him.

JD looks at his brother. He turns and looks at Sean. He says, "I will kill the next person who speaks to me. That's not a threat. That's a warning."

Then he's moving down the walkway, keeping the baton at his side. When he gets to the sidewalk he starts to run.

For four days, the man who will soon be known as John Doe #2 is a person of no fixed address.

He looks into accommodations. The first option he explores is a room at the Imperial Arms Hotel on 14th Street, a few blocks from the Green Frog Café.

Granddad had a couple ladyfriends at the Imperial. This was true even recently. Two summers ago, Granddad would have JD park the ice cream truck on the curb outside the hotel. JD would man the service window – something he was almost never invited to do otherwise – while Granddad headed into the Imperial Arms. Have himself an hour-long visit with Sasha or Bella.

The customers who came to the service window on those summer afternoons were generally junkies. On the rare occasions they could afford a sundae or a cone, the junkies would pay out of assorted pocket change. One time a skinny, shoeless man offered up a tiny bag of unidentified powder in exchange for an ice cream bar. JD did not accept the transaction.

JD has never set foot inside the Imperial Arms before today. He's not sure what to expect. If Granddad had ladyfriends here, JD surmises the interior of the hotel should be somewhat classy. Granddad had – has – good taste.

The interior of the hotel is not classy. It might've been at one time, but the lobby shows decades of neglect. JD goes to the front desk. The clerk informs him the room rates, fifty-nine bucks for the standard. Up to and including a twenty-four hour stay, the clerk adds.

JD does the math in his head, realizes how quickly he'll be cleaned out, even at a place like this. JD sniffs, shows his indignation. "I'm sorry, good sir. I'll have to shop around."

The clerk shrugs, goes back to the sudoku puzzlebook he has open on the front desk.

JD's second option is to lay his head under the stars at night. He heads to the north end of the park, which was the nerve centre of

99Together until last week. There isn't much evidence left of the protest now. The odd pamphlet crumpled up in the grass, a single mustachioed vigilante mask hanging from a tree branch.

The weather is clear that first night in the park. JD sits on a bench. He finds himself staring at the Van Lathan Building for a while. Almost every window in the building stays lit, even at midnight. He wonders why the lights are left on. The sheeple in the government offices, the sheeple in the courts, don't they all go home at night? Or do they stay, slaving away at their desks, for god knows what purpose?

Or is it Them? Do They fill the halls of the Van Lathan Building? Do They keep the lights on?

JD snaps awake. He's shuddering. He hears a rhythmic noise and realizes it's his teeth chattering. He'd fallen asleep in a sitting position, staring at the Van Lathan Building. He has no idea what time it is. The sky is still full dark. With shaking fingers he digs the burner phone out of his pocket and checks the time. 3:44. He also notices the phone's present charge, 71%. The charger is back at Country Club Estate. Not that JD has anywhere to plug the phone in here.

For a few minutes he sits there. He's freezing, but he's also still nodding in and out of sleep. It occurs to him to call his brother. His traitor brother. The idea sickens him. Right now he'd rather freeze than call his brother.

That's when he notices the shadowy form near the base of a tree, fifty paces away. The form is a hunched thing, roughly the size and shape of a crouching man. Or beast.

JD slides a hand into another pocket, wraps his fingers around his extendable baton. At the same time he rises from the bench. He'd been asleep in that sitting position. Now his body is stiff where it isn't numb from the cold. He holds the baton in his hand, thumb on the release. He turns and walks toward the north gate, casting casual glances back at the manbeast by the tree.

The man beast is still there. Still crouched. Still watching.

When JD gets to the gate he breaks into a light run. His feet in his oxfords are numb. He tracks along the cast iron fence, then circles back to the tree from the rear. Comes up on the manbeast from behind.

He's about to extend the baton when he gets close enough to see what the manbeast really is. A squat garbage can with a dome-shaped lid. He slides to a halt on the frosty grass.

He glances around. He has this part of the park to himself. At first he's embarrassed. But then he can't remember if the garbage can was there earlier, when he first sat on the bench. No, it's not a case of not remembering the garbage can. The garbage can wasn't there. He's sure of that. It wasn't there, which means someone put it there after he'd drifted off. Put it there to fuck with him.

There is no other explanation.

He spends his days at the library. Among the large nonfiction holdings is a section marked Politics & Government. Politics & Government, in turn, has a small subsection marked Conspiracy Theories. JD now has all the time in the world to pick books he hasn't read yet, find himself a quiet study carrel, and dig in.

He reads about the shadowy syndicate controlling the military-industrial complex and the global economy. He reads about the shapeshifting extraterrestrials, originating on an undisclosed planet at the edge of the solar system, who've infiltrated human civilization for thousands of years. He reads about experimental biological agents hidden in the contrails emitted by passing jets.

He reads about freemasonry. The faked death of Elvis, who fled to live in Hawaii. The faked death of Hitler, who was evacuated to the United States to work as a senior executive at Lockheed-Martin. False flags. Communist sleeper agents. Staged school shootings. He reads books by Gavin Marrs and David Icke and Milton William Turner.

He's fascinated by what he reads at the library, but it doesn't tell him anything new. His reading reinforces what he already knows.

They are all-seeing, all-knowing, all-powerful.

They are relentless, and They have decided to destroy JD's life. What better proof than the events of the last few days?

When he's not reading, he snoozes at the study carrel. He folds his arms together as a pillow on the narrow desktop and puts his head down and shuts his eyes.

The first few times he tries snoozing in this posture, it's uncomfortable, but he adapts. He adapts to the study carrel so well that a library employee has to wake him up on one occasion. A gentle, repeated tap on JD's shoulder. JD comes to with a start, his hand reaching for his baton. The library employee takes a small, surprised step backward.

"You're not really allowed to sleep in here, sir. We're also closing in fifteen minutes."

JD replies with a curt nod. He tries and fails to smooth the creases out of his face, imprinted there by the sleeves of his blazer. He gets to his feet. Before his nap he'd taken Gavin Marrs' Rule by Secrecy from the shelves. He didn't make it past the first page before sleep overtook him.

The book is still laying open at the first page. Be forewarned, says the text. If you are perfectly comfortable and satisfied with your own particular view of humankind, religion, history, and the world, read no further.

He has to plot his next move. That's the business at hand. They arranged it so he would be exiled from his home. They are closing in. Tightening the noose. There isn't any other logical deduction.

He hears it in the ELF beaming out of streetlights and cellphones. We're coming for you. Any day now. He sees it in the narrow expressions of strangers on the street. How many collaborators, informants?

Simone might be a source of hope, he thinks, although he has no idea how to find her short of waiting for the next open mic night.

Declan too. Declan might be a source of hope. The Patriot Bloc a new home. An invitation. The way it was. He keeps the burner phone close. It's still keeping its charge, sitting at 60%, but it does not ring.

Save for the picture in his wallet, it's six months since JD saw his son. That last visit was at Christmas. Because of the festive season, JD had been allowed to see Daniel. Invited. Given permission by Lil and some duly-appointed fascist from the family services office.

The visit, two hours long, went well. Even Lil was congenial. JD came away with a sliver of belief that things mightcontinue to go well.

But no. Of course not. After the brief Christmas visit, every time he reached out to Lil to see about another visit – to see if she might deign to lift the peace bond she'd had levied against him many years ago – she offered the same infuriating answer she'd given every other time.

Not till we start seeing some support from you.

She meant financial support. As if she didn't know how precarious JD's situation was, or how he couldn't fit into the average sheeple workplace.

A little over a month ago, JD felt he couldn't take the separation any more. He tried to visit Daniel at home. JD had thought maybe he could knock on the door and show Lil his humanity. So that's exactly what he did. It was a Friday night. He even brought a big bag of takeout as an offering.

Lil didn't open her door wider than the security chain would allow. She told JD Daniel was at a friend's house, watching a movie. She told JD he couldn't show up out of the blue. She told him to get lost. When JD suggested he could wait until the movie was over and Daniel came home, Lil told JD she was calling the cops.

He thought it was a bluff. He sat down on the stoop outside her building and dug into the bag of takeout. Waited for his son to come home. Just for the sake of a quick visit, nothing prolonged. And so what if he hadn't called ahead? She knew he didn't have a phone.

Lil wasn't bluffing. She had called the cops. That was how JD ended up in the clink for the weekend. Breaching the so-called peace bond. Hard to believe They didn't have a hand in the whole debacle, but at least it was how he met Declan.

JD sees his son today, the 31st. It's not quite a visit, not in the ordinary sense, and JD must be stealthy about it.

Daniel's school is a dump of a public institution in the west end. JD arrives around midday, but too late for the lunchbreak. There's a little parkette across from the schoolyard, so he finds himself a bench and tilts his trilby over his face and catches a snooze.

At two o'clock the schoolyard fills up with kids on their afternoon recess. Many of them are wearing Halloween costumes. JD walks along the sidewalk beside the chainlink fence, hands in his pockets. He doesn't want to look like some lurking pervert.

After a minute of surveillance, JD thinks he spots his son on the far side of the schoolyard. His heart does a double-jump in his chest. To get to that corner of the schoolyard, he has to track the fence through the yard around a neighbouring house. JD has no way of knowing if the residents are at home or at work, or if they might have a yappy dog. He'll have to chance it.

He goes through the yard around the house. He's close enough to the house to touch it. The schoolyard fence here is covered in leaves and vines, which offer some concealment from any teachers on yard duty. JD can hear all the kid-sounds on the other side of the fence.

He prays to whatever might be listening that the recess bell won't ring yet. It doesn't, and a minute later he's crouched at the corner of the schoolyard fence. There haven't been any signs of life from the house.

He peeks through the leaves tangled into the chainlink. Twenty feet away are four kids sitting in a loose circle, playing a trading card game.

Daniel is one of those kids. He's dressed as Batman, but his plastic mask is pushed up on his forehead.

JD wants to call out to his son, but he can't find his voice. All he does is stare. Six months. Six months since he last saw Daniel. And now JD can see how the boy has changed. Daniel is the kind of kid people say is small for his age, but JD sees past that. The boy's presence – his aura, his spirit, his qi, whatever the term is – has grown ten times the size of his slender shoulders and skinny legs. Daniel is shining so bright that it stings JD's eyes to look at him, and he feels wetness running down his cheeks.

All too soon the recess bell rings. JD watches through the fence as the kids put their card game away. Then they get up and turn around and head back toward the school. Still JD can't seem to make his voice work.

He exfiltrates from the yard beside Daniel's school, then wanders away from the area. He thinks he might come back this way soon. Bypass Lil altogether, wait for the end of a schoolday, reunite with his son, and take him to rendezvous with Granddad. Wherever that might be.

JD thinks he should do this soon. Not today – he's still willing to wait on whatever lifelines might come from Simone and Declan – but soon. They haven't stopped persecuting him, so what is he waiting for?

"We'll get out of here, son," says JD. "You and me."

XPress Print is sandwiched between a café and an electronics shop on 8th Street, a block south of Civic Park. JD doesn't like being so close to the electronics shop. He can feel the ELF seething out of all the gadgets on display. He hustles past quickly and goes into XPress Print.

There are a pair of high-volume photocopiers inside. A computer terminal where you can upload your photos and then print them off. Smells of paper and toner. There are no customers at the moment. The fat man, Gavin, is sitting on a stool behind the cash register. Looks like he's dozing off. He opens one eye when JD comes through the door. No recognition at first, then Gavin blinks both eyes open. His eyebrows lift in surprise.

"Oh," he says, "You."

JD has a brief flashback of the first time he saw this man. Ronnie called him a cuck.

"Kind sir," says JD, tipping his trilby. "I wanted to know if I could bend your brain or pick your ear."

Gavin closes XPress Print early. It's already after five, he says. The majority of business the store does in a day is summed up by three o'clock. He leads JD to the café next door. They each order a coffee. Gavin also orders half a dozen assorted donuts from a rack marked Day Old Half Off. The woman behind the counter packs the donuts into a box and hands them over.

Gavin and JD go to an isolated table near the back of the place. They sit. JD is uncomfortable. XPress Print is between him and the electronics store now, but he can still detect all that extra ELF. It's whining between his temples.

Gavin folds his hands together on the tabletop. He holds this position for a few seconds. Then he leans back. His plastic chair creaks. Holds this position for a few seconds, then goes back to the folded hands on the tabletop. Then he picks up a donut, takes a bite.

"Did you get a chance to watch all those punks get run out of Civic Park?" he says, his mouth full.

"No," says JD. "I ... actually, I spent that day with my son Daniel.

We had a great day. Went for a long walk, got some sundaes from a nice older gent in an ice cream truck. Pretty perfect day, kind sir, if you ask me. I wasn't near Civic Park. I didn't see what happened."

The ELF is vibrating the plates of JD's skull and making his teeth rattle.

Gavin swallows the bite of donut, chases it with coffee. "Sounds pretty decent. I got a son of my own. He's in university, up to his eyeballs in student loan. He's taking anthropology, which I don't know what the hell he's gonna do with that. I'm glad he's two hours away. For his own sake. If he was back here I got no doubt he would of been camping out with the rest of them. Protesting how unfair everything is. No matter how many times I tell him, You look at your birth certificate, you tell me where there's the fine print saying everything is gonna be fair."

Another bite of donut.

"It wasn't as fun as I thought it would be to watch that camp get took apart," Gavin says quietly. "Anyhow. Richard Declan. What did you want to know?"

"Why was it you stopped coming to the meetings?" says JD. "Were you ... uninvited ... for some particular reason?"

"Ha. If you count uninviting myself. But before I start flapping my gums, did Richard send you?"

"Did he send me?"

"Did he send you. To threaten me or something. Because I mean what I told him. I'm not afraid of him. I will call the cops if he's gonna harass me."

"Dr Declan did not send me," says JD. "I came of my own free will. The thing is, see, the, uh, movement is at a place where there are big things coming down the pipe, and when you think of real patriots, and the deep state. By which I mean, kind sir, if we're going to be steadfast ..."

"What the hell are you talking about?"

JD closes his eyes for a moment. The ELF is brutal. "Why would you leave?" he says. "Why would you uninvite yourself?"

"Well then," says Gavin, stuffing half a donut in his mouth. "I like an honest question. So let me give you an honest answer."

Gavin tells JD he believes in old-fashioned things like civic duty. He says democracy doesn't work if people don't get involved. If you don't drag your ass out to a polling station on voting day, you got no right to complain when things don't go the way you like.

JD wants to tell him there's no point voting, since the entire system is controlled by Them, but for now he holds his tongue.

"And if you really believe in civic duty," says Gavin, "then you get involved. You get out there and put in some legwork for the candidate or party you believe in."

For Gavin, that was the organization calling itself the Patriot Bloc.

Gavin says for a long time he's been sick of business-as-usual politics. He's sick of being guilted for being a straight white man, for having a job, for making ends meet.

"We don't have the luxury," he says, "of sitting around and having debates about philosophy or unfairness or things like that. We got to fix things now."

He continues on this theme for a little while. A lot of talk about taxes, government spending, freeloaders, reverse racism. He talks a bit about how society has come to a point where it hates straight white men.

Gavin says he's not against the gays, he's not racist, he's not sexist. He just doesn't want to pay an extra penny for any of those things. Gavin hammers the table with his index finger.

"Someday, we're gonna elect a leader who has this kind of common sense. Someone who doesn't give a damn about political correctness or catering to special interests."

JD is quickly losing interest. He doesn't care about politics or taxes. JD doesn't even have a home to worry about. JD is liberated.

Except for the ELF. JD bites a donut and takes his time chewing. The texture and flavour of the donut, even day old and half-stale, is a slight but welcome distraction from the pain inside his head.

"I knew Declan wasn't perfect," says Gavin.

This, at last, piques JD's interest.

"I knew Declan wasn't perfect," Gavin repeats, "back when I first heard of the Patriot Bloc. This was right after the big crash in 08. I lost my entire retirement savings, just like that. Was I looking for someone to blame? You bet I was ..."

Gavin says the Patriot Bloc had a website back then. Gavin stumbled across it while doing research into ways he could hold the government accountable. The Patriot Bloc's website had a list of platform points on the theme of liberty for the common man. Liberty from an oppressive, unaccountable government was the platform point that really jumped out at Gavin.

JD is starting to zone out again.

"They also had these two or three real slick little videos on the website," says Gavin. "At first I couldn't place the guy in the videos, then after I watched them a bunch of times, I realized who it was. Richard Declan, as in Reverend Rich, from the Great Time Gospel Hour back in the day. You remember that show?"

"I saw it once or twice," says JD.

"Well, like I says, I knew Declan wasn't perfect. I knew he got done up for a while. Fraud, was the story. He did hard time. But he did the time, that's what mattered to me. Seemed to get himself all straightened out. Got his PhD. Even got away from all that fire-and-brimstone preaching. Then he started up the Patriot Bloc, and the things he was talking about in those slick little videos, they were exactly the things I was thinking. I couldn't of said them any better myself."

Gavin talks about his own first few meetings with the Patriot Bloc. This was late in 2009, early 2010. Declan and Becca were newly married. Ronnie was new to the meetings, like Gavin. Gage wasn't around at all.

The Bloc wasn't more than ten people. They talked a lot about grassroots organization, getting involved in the political process. Declan didn't hide the shadier details of his past. In fact, he talked a lot about what he'd learned in prison when he went up for fraud.

"Dr Declan said he went to jail so the older gentleman wouldn't have to," says JD.

"That's how he put it?" says Gavin.

"Yes. Like Jesus."

"Well then," says Gavin.

Gavin goes on. Declan told the Bloc he'd learned how the prison-industrial complex was a tool of a corrupt deep state. The hypocrisy of sending a man like him to prison. A small-time televangelist who'd made some misguided accounting errors, while all the big-time criminal bankers walked free. These were words that rang true with Gavin.

Gavin became more involved with the Bloc. He did lots of volunteer work. He acted as webmaster for a while. He didn't even mind paying his dues at each meeting, despite how dire his financial circumstances had become after the crash. For once in his life he felt he could see his money going to good use.

Meanwhile, the Bloc grew. At one point there was a hundred people crammed into that meeting room at the big house. A hundred people, paying their dues, giving their time. The cause was picking up momentum. Gavin was proud to be part of it.

"I didn't give it a lot of thought when Declan started talking about some coming revolution," says Gavin. "I thought that was a whole lot of, whaddya call it, rhetoric. Declan would talk sometimes about this whole big network of patriots he knew from around the country. People who wert waiting for the right signal so they could stand up and take back their liberty. He never gave us too many specifics, though. It was always what he called classified information. He would tell us it was better if he was the only one who had the burden of the knowledge."

A year ago, the meetings started attracting survivalist types, would-be revolutionaries. There weren't many of them – never more than ten – but Gage was among them. They brought a new vibe to the meeting. In the open forums at the end of each meeting, these newcomers talked a lot about the actual mechanics of overthrowing the government. Hanging journalists. Shooting traitors.

At the same time, Declan had been put on the ballot for the Bayfield school board trustee election. The idea was start small. School board trustee first. Then mayor. Then grander things. National leadership.

"We were trying to do it the way you're supposed to do it, " says Gavin. "But we didn't even get a real shot at it. Declan got disqualified ahead of time."

The Bayfield Elections Office - on the ninth floor of the Van Lathan Building - sent a disqualification notice. They said Declan's registration forms were wrong, there were irregularities with his money.

The Bloc's membership started to drop off after that. Before long there were only twenty-five regulars coming out anymore. Gavin kept coming because he still felt committed. He believed in the heart of what they were doing, the grassroots political work. It was better than doing nothing.

Six months ago, the Bloc was reorganized to include Declan's inner circle. The executive committee. Becca as treasurer, Ronnie as deputy leader, Gage as security director. At the same time, says Gavin, they started boarding up the windows at the house. Declan had lately started talking about having enemies, being followed, being watched. Black helicopters flying over the property at night.

God, JD thinks, don't I know that exact feeling.

Still Gavin hung on.

"Then, what was it, a month ago now? Six weeks? Declan goes to jail. Did you know this?" says Gavin.

"No idea, kind sir," says JD. "I have no knowledge of such things."

"Well maybe it would have changed your mind about signing up, says Gavin."

JD lifts his coffee cup to his mouth to disguise his involuntary grin.

Anyway, Gavin found out about Declan's arrest when he got a call in the middle of the night from Gwen, that crazy religious lady. In a shaking voice, she told him she'd got a call from Becca, informing her about the arrest. They had to get the word out to the whole gang. Start rallying to help Dr Declan raise funds for his defense.

"This was when I should've thrown in the towel," says Gavin.

Instead, he started making calls as well. Waking up other members of the Bloc, letting them know their leader was in the clink. One more snow job from a corrupt government trying to take down a troublemaker. Perhaps there was good reason behind the boarded-up windows at the house.

On the other hand, rumour among the Bloc was Declan had been driving that old Dodge Charger of his, the one with the PRZ GOD vanity plates. The cops pulled him over because one of the taillights was out. They searched the car. Somehow – and this was still a rumour – the search turned up an unregistered hunting rifle and a couple boxes of ammo. In a different variation of the rumour, there was a jar of ether in the glovebox, along with a bunch of plastic zip-ties.

Gavin also heard there was a list in the car. Names of people. People from the elections office, tax people, politicians, city councillors. Even school trustees.

Gavin doesn't know how much truth there is to the rumours. What he does know is Declan came home with a GPS ankle bracelet, a ban on owning or possessing firearms, and a pending court date for a criminal harassment charge.

It seemed like that was really the beginning of the end of the Patriot Bloc, but still Gavin couldn't quite bring himself to quit.

"What Declan's real good at is making people believe the things they want to," says Gavin.

The donuts are gone. Gavin had four, JD had two. They've both almost finished their coffees. JD is trying to pay attention to the fat man, but he's intensely uncomfortable. His whole body is hurting from the ELF. Maybe it's not the electronics store. Maybe it's something closer.

JD glances at the woman behind the counter, twenty feet away. She's looking straight at him.

Collaborator.

"Look at Declan's little inner circle there," Gavin continues. "His batshit crazy wife believes he's the Second Coming. Ronnie believes Declan's gonna wipe out all the blacks and the Jews and whatnot, so Ronnie won't have to work for a camel-jockey anymore. I'm not sure what Gage believes, except maybe how him and Declan are gonna build an army of robot supersoldiers together after the revolution gets started. When it comes to Gage, I'm not sure I want to know. If Declan had sent Gage instead of you, I would of had some real concerns."

"Gage is not as impressive as you think," JD mutters.

"You know why I'm telling you all this?" says Gavin. "Two reasons. One, I kind of hope Declan did send you. Then you can bring it back to him and tell it to his face that I'm sorry I ever fell for his bullshit. Tell him I'm not impressed no more, and I'm not scared. Second reason, I don't know if he believes what he says, or if he's just a conman. Either way, the more time passes, the more I think he's dangerous. And if he's not the dangerous one, he's got some dangerous people around him. That's why I'm telling you this. I wish I'd got out sooner. All I wanted was a chance to do my civic duty, corny as that might sound to you, and maybe hold some people in high places accountable for what happened to my retirement savings." Gavin shakes his head, chuckling. "Do you know about the … about Declan's militia yet? The Patriot Alpha squad?"

JD opens his mouth to speak but closes it quickly. He knows if he attempts talking, ELF will spill out of his vocal cords. Highly directed ELF, at that. There's a good chance Gavin's head would explode from hearing it.

"… haven't heard about it yet, I'm sure you will," Gavin is saying. "That same night I asked them about our money – wasn't that your first meeting? – anyhow, that same night, Declan asks me to stick around. Takes me out back where Ronnie's at the barbecue and Becca and Gage are drinking beer. I'd never been out to the back of that house …"

JD takes hold of the edges of the table. He can see the woman at the counter staring right at him. She must be transmitting his position to Them.

"Declan tells me the Bloc is really a front for something called Patriot Alpha," says Gavin. "Some kind of headquarters for this secret network of patriots from all over the country. Becca and Gage and Ronnie, they're all part of the, I don't know what you'd call it, the high command. Declan's at the very top. They want to let me in on everything, Declan tells me, make me part of it, whatever it is.

"Declan wanted to do was my IP address, send out all these death threats to everyone who'd ever done him wrong. If I wanted to be part of the inner circle, that's what I needed to do to prove my loyalty. Well, that was the last straw for me. I wasn't sure they'd let me leave. But they did, and I haven't been back. And if this isn't crystal clear to you yet, let me say it again, I don't care how much of this you take back to him. Take it all back. Every last—"

The ELF hits a crescendo JD has never heard before. His eyeballs swell out of their sockets. Burst like grapes. His teeth are propelled from his gums with the velocity of bullets. Somehow he is perfectly aware of this happening. Perfectly aware as his head, not the fat man's, explodes. Bits of skull and brain matter cascading out in a ten-foot radius. His trilby, with its feeble faraday shield, goes spinning straight up. One of his ears smacks against the wall and starts a sickening slide downward.

They got him. They finally, terminally got him. He asked too many questions. He thought too much.

They got him.

"Hey fella, you okay?"

There's a fat man sitting a short distance away. Where has JD seen him before? He looks at the plastic nametag on the fat man's chest. Gavin, XPress Print.

Gavin and JD are in a café. JD has only vague memories of how they got here. He glances around. There's a woman behind the counter, arranging baked goods in a rack marked Day Old Half Off. There are a few other patrons, scattered at various tables, minding their own business.

"What if I get you a cup of ice water or something," says Gavin. "I thought, Christ, I thought you were having a stroke for a minute."

"I'm fine, for your information," says JD.

"Okay," says Gavin, "well—"

"And I know who you are, kind sir. I know exactly who you are. You're the man who quit coming to the meetings. The going got tough, so you got going in the other direction. Yes, I know who you are. You're the cuck."

The coldest night yet. JD nods off in fits and starts, sitting on his chosen bench in Civic Park. Every time he falls asleep, he seems to wake up shuddering minutes later. He can see his breath smoking out in front of him with each exhalation. He's so tired he feels nauseated, but he's so cold he thinks he might perish.

One time when he snaps awake he thinks he sees the same hunched manbeast he saw, what was it, three nights ago? Four? Adrenaline is already pouring into his bloodstream before he remembers it's just the garbage can with the dome-shaped lid next to the tree.

He has to stand up, walk around some, get the feeling back into his extremities. He takes the burner phone out of his pocket. 12:46. The battery is down to 24%. He holds it in his hand, staring at the little screen. His eyes want to close. He never knew you could fall asleep on your feet.

All at once he has an urge to fling the phone away. Pitch it into the brush at the bottom of the reservoir hill, or out onto Monarch Avenue. Let a car run it over. He even lifts his arm, shoulder muscles contracting, phone in hand.

But he can't do it.

He lowers the phone. Then he thumbs to the single contact. Tyrant. He does what he hasn't ever done. He calls the number. He holds the burner phone to his ear. It rings on the other end. Once, twice, three times. He hops foot to foot in the frosty grass.

On the fifth ring someone picks up. He can tell by the faint ambient noise on the other end. Maybe the sound of someone breathing.

"Hello?" he says. "Hello? This is Patriot Alpha Sentinel. I'm reporting in. I'm here. I'm ready."

Ready for what, he doesn't know.

The call disconnects.

He calls again. This time there's no connection at all. There's no connection when he calls the third time, either.

He goes back to the bench and sits down. Then he draws his legs up and clutches them to his body. He feels like he's been dipped in ice, but he tells himself he only needs to close his eyes for a minute. Two at most. He'll return to the Imperial Arms as soon as he's had a few moments' rest.

A few moments is all he needs, then he'll get a room. Price be damned. Get a room. Get warm. Get rested. And then. And then. And then.

This time when JD wakes up there's something moving a few paces in front of him. That goddamn garbage can, he thinks. Manbeast after all. Something They—

An arm closes around his neck from behind the bench. With it comes a dense stench of body odor, dirty clothes, old booze. The moving thing in front of him isn't the garbage can. It's a person, closing in fast. JD catches a glimpse of wiry, unkempt beard and wild hair.

The arm behind him pulls tighter, pinning JD to the bench. There's hot breath on JD's ear, flecks of spittle. The voice is low and hoarse. "You pinko sonofawhores aren't welcome here no more."

The first man crouches in front of JD and starts to paw at JD's blazer. He's going for the interior pockets. JD feels the long fingers pull out the burner phone first. Then the fingers are going for his wallet. JD bucks on the bench, arches his half-numb body, tries to kick.

The arm behind him pulls tighter yet. JD sees dark spots at the edge of his vision. The voice in his ear again: "Just relax, old chum. Relax and let it be."

JD buries his hand in his patchpocket, tries to clutch the handle of the baton. There's no almost no feeling whatsoever in his digits. He has just enough awareness to get it out of his patchpocket before he numbly thumbs the release.

The baton snicks out to full extension.

JD flails it behind him. He's in way too close to get much of an arc, but he feels the baton strike something. There's a grunt, more of surprise than pain. Doesn't matter. The arm chokeholding him lets go. JD blunders off the bench, knocking the first man over. Then JD takes a step back so he can get room to properly swing.

He sees a blur of motion behind the bench. The chokeholder, still on his feet. JD swings the baton at him. It hisses through the air. The chokeholder leaps back. His feet tangle up and he goes down. JD hurries around behind the bench. The chokeholder is already trying to get up, propping himself. JD sees a pale hand, fingers splayed in the grass. He snaps the baton down on the fingers. Chokeholder lets out an operatic scream.

JD is about to strike him again when he catches movement to his right. The first man is back on his own feet. The man turns and runs. Runs with JD's wallet and burner phone.

JD leaves chokeholder and goes after the first man. The first man's gait is shuffling and awkward, but he's fast. JD huffs after him, insensate feet thumping along the cold ground. He snaps the baton back and forth in front of him.

The man pauses long enough to do a half-turn. "Take em back. Take em back, you goddamn lunatic!"

JD sees something go flying. Burner phone. Then his wallet. The man is still running, opening the distance between them. In JD's blind rage he hurls the baton like a tomahawk at the man's receding back.

The baton comes nowhere near the man, who's already disappearing into the shadows. The baton does land in the grass somewhere. Too dark to tell. JD understands his mistake right away. He turns around. Chokeholder is approaching from behind. Slowly, carefully, in a sly manner that belies his homeless appearance. Something in the man's hand catches a glint of streetlight. Could be a switchblade, a boxcutter, a long shard of glass.

"You broke my finger," the man says.

Chokeholder is still several paces away, but not so far that JD's options are unlimited. He casts one final look in the direction of the baton. Nothing to be seen. He snatches up his wallet and the burner phone and then he makes a run for it. Straight for the park's north gate, the streetlights along Franklin.

Chokeholder hollers something after him. JD does not look back.

All hope is lost.

They haven't pulled the noose completely tight, but it's not far off. He can feel it tickling his neck. They're just playing with him now, same way a cat plays with a mouse before killing it. They're playing with him, and there's nothing he can do about it.

He has sixty-six dollars and seventy cents to his name. Through some well-practised trick, that ragged man in Civic Park extracted most of the cash before he dropped the wallet.

All that money. Granddad's disability payout. JD's sustenance.

The option of even one night at the Imperial Arms is eliminated, so after fleeing Civic Park, JD spends the remainder of the night in the bus terminal on 5th Street. In his almost-penniless despair, he still has two immediate needs to address. Sleep. Warmth.

The bus terminal offers warmth. But there isn't much in the way of sleep. Every half-hour a heavy-shouldered security guard makes the rounds of the seating area. Wakes up anyone who doesn't look like they're waiting for a bus.

The third time the security guard prods JD awake, JD gives the man a man a murderous glare. The security guard only smiles. "Hey slick," he says. "This isn't a homeless shelter."

At that moment JD feels a burst of heightened ELF in his head. There's a message buried in the sound. Kill, kill, kill, it commands. Start with this one.

JD squeezes his eyes shut.

Kill, kill, kill. That's what They want, because They are playing with him. Seeing how far he can be pushed. Well, They can fuck right off.

"Excuse me?" says the security guard.

The ELF drops to normal levels. JD opens his burning eyes. The security guard is giving him a quizzical look.

"I didn't say anything," says JD. "Good sir," he adds. "Kind sir."

The security guard wanders off, shaking his head, muttering about how this isn't a bloody homeless shelter.

JD watches him go, then gets up and heads into the men's room. Finds himself a cubicle, closes the door, turns the little lock, sits down on the toilet, and tries to sleep.

This position is the least comfortable yet. Sleep evades him. For the second time, the idea of calling his traitorous brother comes into his head. His immediate revulsion is almost enough to wake him right back up.

Still, he already has the burner phone out of his pocket, as though he were about to call his brother. Some kind of thoughtless, automatic gesture. Some kind of sheeple cry for help. No. To hell with his brother.

JD goes to put the phone back in his pocket. He notices the date on the little display. He also notices the dwindling battery, sitting now at 18%, but for the moment that's unimportant.

The date is November 2nd. After a minute, he gets up from the toilet and steps out of the cubicle.

Resting here is impossible anyway.

Half an hour later he's standing in front of the Green Frog Café. It's just after seven. The sky is turning pale, morning traffic is building. There's a small sign in the window of the Green Frog:

Other Voices Open Mic
A safe space for folx of all backgrounds to share the experience of the
spoken word
Pay what you can
8 PM Weds Nov 2nd

JD reads the sign three times, as if it might somehow change between readings. The way They have been playing with him, anything can happen.

The sign stays unchanged.

He tilts his trilby back and cups his hands around his eyes and peers through the Green Frog's front window. The interior of the place is dark. He can make out chairs upturned on tabletops, stools upturned on the bar. He doesn't see her inside. He doesn't see anyone. That's okay. It's early yet.

He wanders off in the direction of the library, which opens at nine. Rest in a study carrel first. Then food, if he finds it absolutely necessary. Then Simone.

Maybe, just maybe, all hope is not lost.

There's rain that night. It's cold and miserable, almost freezing.

JD stops first at the drugstore a few doors down from the Green Frog Café. Gives himself a little dousing of cologne from the men's section.

Then he goes to the area where they sell the household cleaning products. He picks up a spraybottle of fabric freshener. The words Lavender & Linen are on the label. He pretends to examine the spraybottle, compare its price. When he's sure no one's looking he gives his blazer and corduroys a good spritzing.

Near the front of the drugstore, they're selling flower arrangements. The longstem roses are twenty bucks for a dozen, way out of JD's present diminished price range. But there are also single roses in delicate plastic sleeves. Three dollars apiece. He picks the best-looking one he can find and takes it up to the cashout.

Five minutes later, he gets to the Green Frog. He came almost at a run from the drugstore, doing his best to stay out of the rain. He makes sure his trilby is cocked at just the right angle, then goes in through the door. The warmth inside the place is a welcome change from the cold wet night.

This time there are more people, perhaps thirty. As soon as JD's through the door he can feel everyone's eyes on him. He knows what they see. They see a man who's well-rested. Classy and composed. As mysterious – and maybe as dangerous – as some Old West gunfighter.

Standing near the bar, a pint of beer in her hand, is Simone. She's got the same horn-rimmed glasses as before, the same blood-red lipstick. She's wearing high heels and tight jeans with the cuffs turned up and a dark tank top that shows off the mermaid tattoo. She does a half-turn, as if to speak to someone nearby, and notices JD.

JD saunters toward her, smiling. "Hey you. I'm here."

"Oh," says Simone. "Hey. I didn't …"

"And this is for you," says JD, offering her the rose. "It's but a minor token of my affections."

Colour floods her face. She looks left and right.

"I …," she says. "Look, why don't you hang onto that. We're just about to start up, okay?"

"Of course. I'll be waiting for you."

Simone looks like she's about to say something else, but instead she nods and turns around and heads toward the riser and microphone. There's a little wobble in her step, a little unsteadiness in those high heels. A sure sign of how overcome with emotion she must be at JD's surprise arrival.

JD takes a stool at the bar and puts the rose on the bartop and orders a craft beer from the bearded dandy. JD isn't even worried about the money passing out of his hand. At least not for now.

Up at the riser Simone taps the microphone. "Ah, hey everyone," she says. There's a heaviness in her voice. Almost a tone of sadness. Why? What does she have to be sad about now? "Thanks for being here. As always I'm proud of what we're doing. If I seem a little bummed, well, we all know how things turned out with 99Together, don't we. Looks like the system wins yet again. In the meantime, let the show begin …"

JD tries to stay patient while four people get up and do their poems and performances. He even claps when he's supposed to. He finishes his pint and orders another and finishes that one too. The evening of the 2nd goes on.

"That's it for our first hour," says Simone. "Would you agree there were some amazing performances?"

Applause ripples through the Green Frog. JD tugs at his shirt collar.

"Before we take our break," says Simone, "I'm gonna pass the jar around. This is really important. Because, as you know, the 99Together camp got broken up, and there were a number of arrests. Now, most of those folks were released the same day. But one of my best friends is still in jail. He's being charged for assaulting a police officer. It's complete bullshit. If you've ever seen Tim—"

JD almost chokes on his beer. Tiny Tim? Assaulting a cop? Locked up?

"—Anyways, says Simone, "all our friends are doing what they can to help Tim afford a halfway decent lawyer. I know I've said this before, but tonight every bit counts, okay?"

Simone starts making the rounds with the big plastic jar. The bartender puts some music on. JD drains half his pint. Then Simone is next to his stool, proffering the plastic jar in both hands. There are a lot of bills in there. JD spots tens and twenties. Even a fifty.

JD drops in a few dollars in loose coins. Change from the pints and the purchase of the rose.

"Thanks," Simone says.

There's the trace of a frown on her face. JD realizes she's about to step away.

"Hold on," he says. "Can't I buy you a drink?"

For a moment she doesn't reply. Then she shrugs and climbs onto the stool beside JD's and puts the jar down on the bartop. "Whatever you're having," she says.

JD gestures to the bartender for two more rounds of the craft beer. He's down to a little less than fifty bucks.

"Are you glad to see me?" he says.

"I guess so," she says. "It's always out of the blue with you. I'm not even sure when I saw you last, actually."

Their beers arrive. "You saw me a couple days before the police state shut the camp down. Remember?"

She sips her beer and frowns. "Maybe," she says. "Truth is, all this stuff with Tim has me pretty distracted. It's a big mess."

JD puts on a sympathetic expression. "Tell me what happened," he says.

Simone lets out a shaky breath. She says Tiny Tim was one of the protesters who did not agree to leave the park on the day of the eviction. Tim and a few others tried to tie themselves to a bench, but a bunch of cops cut the ropes and belts and rounded them all up.

In whatever scuffle ensued, Tim apparently elbowed a cop in the face. Which is bullshit, says Simone. Anyway, they arrested him and charged him with assaulting a police officer. He's in remand down in the very same city lock-up where JD met Declan.

JD doesn't mention his own time in that particular establishment.

"So all in all it's a mess," she says. She thumps the bartop with her fist. "It's a goddamn mess and it kills me to think about it. I wasn't even there that day, either. I was home sick, trying to get myself together. I missed everything. Not that I know what I would've done if I was there, but still."

"You were there in spirit," says JD.

She doesn't reply to that. Instead she downs the rest of her pint in a single gulp and gestures for the bartender to serve another round.

"You know," says JD, "I was there, myself. At the very end, when the cops broke everything up ..."

The bartender brings them their pints. Simone pays for this round. Then JD tells her about the last stand. The makeshift barricade. How he stopped the cops from arresting that kid, who couldn't have been more than twelve years old. He tells her he wishes he could have saved Tiny Tim.

"I tried," says JD. "I did what I could. I ended up having to fight off these two men, you see. Bad men. They tried to rob me. One of them pulled a knife on me. I barely survived ... Anyway, if it wasn't for them, I would've got to Tim in time. All I can say is I'm sorry."

Simone smiles sadly. She's not looking at him. "Well," she says, "I've gotta get the second set underway. See you."

With that she's off the stool and heading back to the riser and the microphone, carrying the plastic jar of money with her. She has not touched the rose. When she was sitting on the stool she didn't even look at it.

She takes the mic to start the second set. Her unsteadiness has increased. There's a slight slur in her speech. She thanks everyone for their donations to Tiny Tim's cause. The second set is more of the same, but JD is tipsy enough that the time goes faster.

He orders two more pints. He carries them – and the rose – over to the little table beside the riser where Simone is sitting.

JD sits down opposite her. She's staring at the microphone, where an androgynous person is free-style rapping. JD pushes one of the pints across to Simone, and when it touches her hand she turns her head and kind of frowns. She takes the pint and drinks, finishes it in minutes.

The free-style rapper finishes up. There's polite applause. The next person on the stage is a woman in her fifties. She is wearing a multicoloured handknit poncho. She reads rhyming verse from a crumpled piece of paper.

JD leans forward and whispers, "Want another round?"

Simone shakes her head no. She chews at her lower lip, looking as if she's about to say something. With beer on her breath, she whispers, "It's nice of you to offer, but if you're feeling generous we could really use some more donations for Tim."

"Simone," he says, "I need to know. Are you and Tim in a relationship?"

"Excuse me?"

"I believe I have a right to know," says JD. "Before we get any more serious."

He's not whispering anymore. Neither is she. The fiftyish woman on the riser stutters in the middle of a rhyme. Then she thanks the room and hurries back to her own table.

"For starters," Simone says, "Tim is ... Look, this isn't about you, okay? So don't try to make it about you. I don't know what makes you think I owe you any of my time, even. Goddamn."

"Simone," says JD.

He reaches for her hand but she snatches it away. She gets up and climbs the riser and takes the microphone and puts on the biggest, phoniest smile JD has ever seen. "Thanks, everyone. Another amazing session. Seems we're finished a little early tonight ..."

JD finds himself on his feet, climbing the riser. Simone stops mid-sentence and looks at him. She looks stunned. And drunk. She doesn't resist as JD takes the microphone from her.

JD puts the microphone to his lips. He can smell booze on it.

"Has everyone got time for one more performance?" he says.

He hears a scattering of applause. He smiles at Simone. She just gapes at him. Then she sits.

JD turns to face the Green Frog Café. There's one spotlight on, and it's shining right in his face, but beyond the light he can see the place for what it used to be, back in Granddad's day.

A moment passes. Then another. Someone clears their throat.

"Who here is tired," says JD. Somebody half-heartedly shouts something back. "Who here is exhausted?"

There are a few more half-hearted replies to this. Past the spotlight JD spots a couple people leaving the café.

"Who here," he says, "is fed up with all the bullshit, the unfairness, the injustice, the lies? Who here can't stand the cogni—cognit—cog … Who here can't stand the way the whole system is rigged anymore?"

At this there is a louder cheer from the audience. JD can see Simone watching him, but she's not much more than a silhouette.

"I am a graduate of the school of hard knocks," says JD. "I'm a man who's been persecuted, attacked, laughed at, lectured, locked up, and run out of his own home by his own flesh and blood. A man who's been medicated, whose son has been stolen from him. A man who's been dismissed, abandoned, left for dead.

"A man who's been uninvited."

JD doesn't know how long he talks. Several minutes at least. His words come as fast as his thoughts. As fast as ELF transmissions. He barely pauses to draw breath. His heart pounds and sweat pours out of him. Sweat rolls down his face. All he can see are the shapes of the sheeple far below him and the spotlight blazing like a sun.

"It's Them," JD says. "They rigged the game. They planned the whole conspiracy. Nothing is fair. Nothing happens just because. All you sheeple, with your nine-to-five jobs, your one-point-five kids, your houses in the subdivisions, your failed protests … you've never given this any thought at all, have you? It's Them. Can't you see that? Can't you see how there's no other explanation?"

He stops. Silence reigns. Then he holds out the microphone, turn it sideways, and drops it on the riser. There is a shriek of feedback. He steps down from the riser and walks out of the Green Frog Café, wiping the sweat off his face.

Cold rain outside. The nighttime necropolis is awash with sickly neon lights. Garbage is piled a hundred feet high in the alleyways. The air is thick with neurotoxins. Almost every person he sees refuses to make eye contact with him.

Collaborators, every one of them.

They are on high alert tonight.

JD's pace is fast. He's decided the time has come to go meet up with Granddad, wherever the old man is. JD is confident he'll find clues and subtle markers along the way. He'll have to pick up Daniel first, which means—

Someone is calling his name. A hand tugs the sleeve of his blazer. He spins around, read for battle. Simone. She's looking at him, one eyebrow arched. She has a small duffel bag with her. JD supposes the jar full of Tiny Tim's blood money is inside the bag. No telling if she has the rose. JD says nothing.

After a moment she rolls her eyes. "For chrissakes," she says. "You're … Ah fuck it. Never mind. Come on."

She takes his arm and starts to walk. They only go as far as the curb, where a cab is parked. She reaches for the back door. Then she stops. She gives JD the arched eyebrow again.

"A couple of my friends know exactly what I'm doing," she says. "So do not prove me wrong."

Before JD can reply she's got the back door of the cab open. She pushes him inside and then follows and pulls the door closed behind her. She tells the driver an address. The driver nods and pulls out into the street.

Simone doesn't talk. Neither does JD. He watches the city of the dead roll past outside the windows. The collaborators all seem to have slipped back into the shadows. For the moment.

After a ten minute drive they pull up in front of a small brownstone walk-up in a tree-lined part of the city. Simone pays the driver, then gets out. JD follows, both of them still wordless. The taxi pulls away. He watches its taillights, momentarily lightheaded. The lightheadedness is not the effect of liquor. Or ELF. He can't say what it is.

Simone leads him by the hand up a narrow front walk. They go into a little vestibule with black and white tiles on the floor and an array of mailboxes on the wall. There're no abandoned shopping carts here. Simone digs through her duffel bag until she comes up with a key to unlock the inner door. They go up one creaky wooden flight of stairs and then another.

The number on her apartment door is 318. Simone opens the door and they go inside. It's a one-bedroom. A single lamp is on in the living room. Everything in here is nice and neat. Simone seems to have the time to do the housework stuff that JD doesn't. Must be nice. He also notices a couple paintings on the wall that look exactly like the ones he saw at the Green Frog.

Simone steps into his field of view. "You're okay, right? Like, you're with me here?"

JD smiles, salutes. "I am with you."

Not quite true. Fact is, he's having a hard time getting a handle on his thoughts. He gives his head a shake and then moves in to kiss Simone. She's responsive right away, jabbing his mouth with her tongue, running her hands up and down his sides.

JD's damp blazer falls to the floor. She takes off his trilby.

"What's that about?" she says.

She's looking at the foil inside the crown.

JD opens his mouth, but she shakes her head.

"Never mind," she says. "Come in, sit down."

She sets the trilby on a little side table and shows JD into the living room. There's a good-sized couch. A wicker coffee table. She says she's going to use the washroom and then pour a couple of drinks. She asks if JD can roll them a joint. She points to a small mahogany box on the coffee table, says there's some weed and rolling papers in there.

JD sits. Takes the lid off the mahogany box and takes out some papers and a little baggie of moist green weed and sets to work rolling. He's tempted to contact his brother, tell him how he's landed on his feet after all. Tell his brother how a beautiful woman has invited him into a new place to call home.

Simone goes into the bathroom and speaks through the door. "I was almost ready to kill you," she says, "when you got up on the stage tonight. I thought you were just gonna take the piss out of the whole thing, make fun of it. Rant at us or something."

JD smiles. Rant? he thinks. Never. But speak hard truths to a roomful of sheeple? Certainly.

"Anyways," she says, "the way you didn't actually say anything, the way you just stood there like that. Then when you started to cry, and you didn't hide it or anything. You just stood there and cried ..."

JD sits back, the half-rolled joint in his hands. Not sure what she's talking about. He hears the toilet flush, he hears the sink turning on then turning off. She reappears in the living room. She's changed into a pair of shorts and a tanktop. All her curves are accentuated. He's lightheaded again, this time in a good way.

She says, "You're always doing this man-of-mystery routine, but tonight I saw a real person. It wasn't creepy. It was authentic."

She goes into the kitchen, off the other side of the living room. JD stays on the couch. He finishes rolling the joint. Simone comes back with two highball glasses. Whiskey on ice. Reminds JD of that time a million years ago when Lil said to him, I'd like a fucking scotch is what I'd like.

Simone gives him one of the glasses. "Cheers," she says.

They both drink, then she tells him to spark up the joint. They smoke a little bit. He half-listens as she talks. She's going on about Tiny Tim again, how worried she is about him, but at the same time how she needs something like this – JD's presence – to distract her. As if JD is some temporary thing.

Then she looks at him, puts her hand on his leg. High up on this thigh. They start kissing again. Then they're rolling around on the couch, breathing hard, groping each other, all fingers and tongues. She gets naked. So does he. He's overdue for a shower, but Simone doesn't seem to care. She kisses him one more time, bites his lip hard enough to draw a little blood. She leans back.

"Let's go to the bedroom. I've got protec—"

She's interrupted by a noise JD almost doesn't recognize. A cheery, digital ringtone. It's not loud, muffled as it is by JD's blazer, but it's audible all the same. One ring. Two rings. Three.

Simone stands up from the couch. "You don't have to answer that right this minute, do you?"

The last time JD looked at the burner was in the late afternoon. The charge was at ten percent.

Four rings. Five rings.

JD looks at Simone, at her naked form. Her eyebrow is arched again.

Six rings.

"Well?" she says.

He stands up from the couch, naked, his penis protruding. He looks at Simone. He looks at his blazer, crumpled on the floor by the front door.

Seven rings.

It's well past midnight when the taxi drops JD off in front of the whitewashed gate outside Forward Operating Base Liberty. Still raining steadily.

The taxi costs forty-five dollars – every last penny in JD's wallet. Before leaving Simone's place, he'd had negotiated this as a flat rate.

The thought of Simone fills JD with a mix of emotions. Longing for what almost happened. Pride for the way he told her, Duty calls, my friend needs help, I must go, like some stoic warrior going off to do battle.

The taxi disappears back into the dark and the rainfall. The gate seems to have a faint light of its own, on account of the whitewash. Like something phosphorescent under dark water. He can't make out anything of the signs.

He approaches the intercom.

Simone didn't understand why he had to leave. There wasn't much JD could tell her. There wasn't much he understood himself, other than the urgent tone in Declan's voice.

Top secret privileged information.

He pushes the button on the intercom. There's the melodic chime, then he hears the line go live on the other end. Nobody says hello, but he can tell it's live by the sound coming from the little speaker. He clears his throat. "It's me. It's Sentinel."

A pause. The line goes dead. Then the gate trundles open. JD steps onto the property, commences the long walk up to the house.

When all this is over, whatever it is, everyone will understand.

The front door is open. JD is cold, soaked from the rain. Water drips off his trilby. His nostrils are full of the smell of wet wool from his sodden blazer.

He finds Declan and Becca in the entryway, waiting for him. Patriot Alpha One and Patriot Alpha Domestic are standing almost as though they're posed for a photograph. Declan in bowtie and professorial garb, Becca in the short skirt and white blouse and big red cowboy boots.

Declan has his back ramrod straight and his arm around his wife. This is the first time JD realizes Becca is taller than Declan. Three inches at least. Yet she somehow looks small beside him. Diminished. There's something fleeting and vacant in her face. JD shivers. He can't help it.

Declan's features are bright and brimming with healthy colour. His eyes are blazing so brightly JD can't quite look at them.

Declan nods. "Welcome, my friend. In the words of the great thinker William James, need and struggle are—"

Declan is cut off by an electronic chirp. The chirp is followed by a voice – Ronnie's – crackling out of something: "One, X-Ray here. Wiring is almost complete. Repeat, wiring is almost complete. You can come inspect it. How copy?"

Declan takes his arm from around Becca's broad shoulders and draws a walkie-talkie out of his inside pocket. He lifts it to his lips. He says, "That's fine. Out." Declan lowers the walkie-talkie. He hasn't taken his glowing eyes off JD. "What was I saying about the great thinker William James? Ah, doesn't matter. You're here. That's what matters. Come."

There's no sign of the old man. Or Gage. Whenever Gage does appear, JD is resolved to have quite the reckoning with him. He'll have that reckoning in front of the entire inner circle, if necessary.

Declan leads the way through the meeting room. JD follows. Becca falls into step behind JD, so the three of them are moving in a peculiar single-file through the cavernous, thickly shadowed house.

They go through the meeting room now. Declan passes blue-eyed Jesus and goes through the inner door.

The library is lit only by a single reading lamp in the sitting area. The encroaching darkness is absolute – except for the throw of light from the inner inner door, which is standing open. Declan, only a silhouette against the inner inner door, makes straight for it. He pauses only once. He looks back, smiles, holds out a gesture of invitation.

"Right this way, my friend."

The inner inner door opens on a narrow landing at the top of a flight of cement stairs. The walls are exposed cinderblock. Overhead is a single light bulb.

Declan begins descending the stairs. The bottom of the stairs give onto another landing, which right-angles through a doorway into whatever underlies the house.

"You going or what, creepo?" says Becca, her voice strangely whispery.

She's crowded in behind JD on the top landing. Her breasts are pushing into his back. Her breath is hot on his neck. He doesn't know why he's stopped on the landing. Held fast by something he can't name.

Becca gives him a light push. He shakes the unnamed sensation and follows Declan down the steps.

The door at the bottom landing is sturdy-looking steel. It's closed but unlocked. Declan turns the knob – also fitted with a keypad, JD sees – and pushes the door open.

The floor of the room beyond is covered by interlocking rubber tiles. There are metal shelves sagging under the weight of five-gallon water jugs. Canned goods in shrinkwrapped cardboard flats. There's a workbench. Handtools hang from outlined spots above the bench.

Not far from the workbench, half-a-dozen military-style gas masks are hanging from hooks set in the cinderblock wall. The eyes of the masks are circles of black tempered glass. They remind JD of the eyes of the dolls in the cabinet in the bedroom under the eaves.

Past the gas masks is an alcove in the foundation wall. Might have been a root cellar. The light in there is faint, but JD can make out a toilet seat fitted over a large plastic bucket. A curtain, pushed to one side, serves as the door to the makeshift lavatory.

In another corner of the room is a woodstove. There's a big, bright fire inside the stove, pumping out light and heat. Surrounding the stove are a couple of folding cots and a pair of bench seats that look like they were salvaged from a minivan. There's a wooden cable spool set on its end, serving as a table.

No fewer than six flat-screen TVs are crudely fixed to a metal rack – it looks like a display shelf salvaged from a grocery store – near the cable spool table. A jumble of wires is dimly visible in the shadows behind the rack. Each one of the TVs screens is on, each displaying a different news network. Well-coiffed talking heads. Stock market numbers across the bottom of the screens. The audio on each TV is turned way down.

A word occurs to JD.

Bunker.

There is a bunker beneath Forward Operating Base Liberty.

The last thing that stands out is a huge map mounted on the cinderblock wall a few feet away from the rack of TVs. JD squints. It looks like it's a map of the entire country, but it's obscured with dozens and dozens of coloured line. They all converge at a single point, like spokes in a wheel.

Declan grips him by the shoulders. The blaze in Declan's eyes is so bright it seems hot. Twin laser beams.

"This is our command post," Declan says, voice lowered to a whisper. "Very few people get to see what you're seeing, Sentinel. I hope that's not lost on you."

"It's not lost on me," says JD, trying to match Declan's solemn whisper.

Declan whisks him across the floor to the map. Up close, JD can see the coloured lines are lengths of string tied to thumbtacks. The thumbtacks are poked into various cities, big and small, from coast to coast. The point of convergence of all the strings is a thumbtack poked into the map right in downtown Bayfield.

"This place is the nerve centre of Patriot Alpha's operations," says Declan. "Each one of these," he points to a few of the other thumbtacks on the map, "is an allied cell, squad, or group. We have people everywhere, my friend. Everywhere. And the time has come to send up the flag that will bring them all together. Indeed it has."

JD licks his lips. Swallows. "I ... I don't actually have any idea what's going on. Sir. Gage told me I was a liab—"

Becca inhales sharply. Declan's lips curl back over his teeth. "Never mind whatever it was Gage told you."

"Where's my granddad's truck, sir? He's been asking me about it."

"Well, that's fortunate," says Declan, "because you're about to have the truck returned to you. And I'm about to tell you everything you need to know, everything I haven't been able to tell you up until now. I'm about to give you the privileged information, my friend. Because, as the Buddha tells us, three things cannot be hidden long. The sun, the moon, and the truth. But first, I need to check in with X-Ray. I will return. In the meantime, why don't you and my wife get caught up?"

Declan turns on his heels and makes for the stairwell. His footsteps are almost completely muffled by the interlocking rubber tiles on the floor.

At the bunker doorway he stops and looks back at JD. He smiles, nods his head. Then he closes the door, and without even needing to check, JD knows the door has been locked.

For a few seconds JD thinks he's alone in the bunker. The command post. The nerve centre. Then he notices the curtain has been drawn over the improvised lavatory.

With the room momentarily JD's alone, he can hear each network on the wall of TVs:

Global deforestation can now be observed from space.

If the international community can successfully raise billions of dollars to fight terrorism, why not a similar fund to promote education?

Unclear if Texas will proceed with the execution of disabled man.

Underneath it all, JD is listening for ELF, but right now there's nothing. Not even faint background traces.

Now for sports, says one of the talking heads.

The curtain over the alcove sweeps aside and Becca emerges. She's rubbing her nose. When she walks forward her steps are uncertain, as if the red cowboy boots have somehow become a few sizes too big. And that's it, that's when he knows what's familiar about her. It's nothing to do with past lives. Becca is a dope fiend, a junkie. Same as—

"When the chips are down," she says, "when the shit hit the fan, we knew we could count on you, creepo, couldn't we."

"I pride myself on being the kind of man you can count on," says JD.

She clomps up close to him. Very close. He can smell soap and shampoo. Her pupils are big, the dark makeup around them smeared. She says, "I think the Lord sent you. He sent you because we're about to take the fight to the devil himself. Hey, let's go over here."

She holds JD's sleeve and leads him over to one of the cots. They're much closer to the woodstove here. It's putting out a tremendous amount of heat, and within seconds JD is breaking a sweat. Becca paws at him. He's instantly hard. But he's not at ease, either.

"My la—Becca. Where's Gage?"

Becca is chewing JD's earlobe. She hisses, "Never mind Gage."

"But ..."

Before he can press her, she navigates him into a sitting position on the edge of the cot. Then she gets down on her knees, opens his corduroys, and goes to work with her mouth and hands. He lets out a long, wordless moan. He looks down at her peroxide blonde hair, bobbing up and down between his thighs.

Becca the junkie.

From the wall of TVs, one of the newscasters says, The government of the small Central American country won't commit to a housing plan for millions of slum dwellers.

"Becca," says JD. "I don't know if you know this, but Gage made some very degrading comments to me. Him and myself need to have words."

She squeezes the base of his penis hard, hard enough to make him jolt, and pulls her lips slowly all the way up to the tip. He can't do anything but moan again. To hell with Gage, to hell with millions of slum dwellers, to hell with Them. Now for sports.

Declan strides back into the bunker, his fingers steepled together. He's grinning. Behind him limps Ronnie. Ronnie's got a curious outfit going. From the midsection up he's in his loose-fitting shirt and tie and suit jacket. From the waist down he's wearing the dark cargo pants, bloused into the black combat boots.

Both men appear at the precise moment JD ejaculates. Becca

catches some with her mouth. The rest shoots across JD's thigh.

There's deep colour in Ronnie's face, and he hangs back a little, looking at the floor. But Declan strides right up to the cot, still grinning, fingers still steepled together. Becca shifts into a sitting position on the floor, still gripping JD's now-wilting penis. With her free hand she rubs her lips. She looks at JD. There's no expression at all on her face, but her pupils are cavernous and black.

How many times, JD wonders, did he see his mother's look just like that? JD pulls himself away from her, suddenly feeling nauseated. He scoots backwards on the cot and hauls his corduroys back up, ignoring the sticky mess on his thighs. Declan lowers one hand down to Becca's head to stroke her hair. His grin widens. Declan stares at JD for a long time. His eyes are still those twin lasers. But JD forces himself to meet and hold them.

At last Declan breaks his gaze to look at Ronnie. Ronnie coughs, scratches his face. Declan turns his attention back to JD.

"It's time you knew," says Declan, "that you're right."

"Right about what?" says JD.

"The mind control. You're right. You've been right all along, my friend."

JD takes off his trilby and runs a hand through his hair. The hand comes back damp. He puts his trilby back on and stands up from the cot, not sure he can trust his legs. He's only vaguely aware of the tacky sensation of the semen drying on his thighs. The nausea has passed, but he cannot bring himself to look at Becca.

"What do you mean?" he says.

Declan leans in. "The very high frequency mind control," he murmurs.

"The extremely low frequency?" says JD. "The ELF?"

Declan blinks. "Yes. Of course I do. Indeed. The terminology is uncertain at times, depending on what expert you consult. But yes. The, ah, ELF."

JD isn't sure what to say. He takes his trilby off and runs his hand through his hair again. This all sounds crazy. Straight-out batshit crazy.

"Now the time has come to stand up to Them," says Declan. "Come over here."

Declan leads JD over to the cable spool table. Becca wobbles to her feet and joins them. Ronnie is already at the table. He takes a piece of folded paper out of his pocket and unfolds it and lays it down. It's not as big as the map Becca unrolled for JD to look at in Declan's office a few weeks ago, but it's a map all the same. There's a red circle drawn around a feature in the middle.

"Do you know what that is?" says Declan.

"Affirmative," says JD. "That's the Van Lathan Building."

"Ah, that's what They want you to think," says Declan. "What this building really is, Sentinel, is a transmitter. A great big hundred-foot antenna for broadcasting mind control signals all over the country. I'll bet you had no idea, but now that you think of it, it makes sense, doesn't it."

Declan's eyes lock onto JD's again. JD finds the information does make sense. When it comes from Declan, how can it not make sense?

"We have fitted your granddad's truck with specialized equipment to disrupt mind control signals," says Declan. "And now we need you to position the truck to activate the disruption, while our patriot network launches surgical strikes—"

"Sir," says JD. "What about Gage? Him and myself need to have words."

Declan stands up straight. He plants his fists on the map. His lips pull back over his teeth. "Gage is gone. He was a … a … one of Them."

"Gage was a … collaborator?" says JD.

Beside Declan, Ronnie starts to cough. He puts his fist over his mouth, but it's as if he's got something stuck in his throat. He coughs and coughs, the cords standing out in his throat. Finally he stops, sucking wind. Declan nods at him, and Ronnie takes another folded paper out of his pocket. He offers it to JD.

JD takes the paper, unfolds it. He's looking at a colour photocopy, shows the front and back of some kind of card. ID. There are various numbers. They don't make much sense to JD. There's a name. Grillo, Dominic R. Nobody JD's ever heard of. But there are also the words Bayfield Police Services. And a small headshot portrait of Gage.

Beside the photocopy of the front and back of the ID card, someone has handwritten the words, U got a RAT look out!!!

"Got that from a buddy of mine," Ronnie says hoarsely.

For several seconds all JD can do is look at the piece of paper. The portrait of Gage. Dominic R Grillo, Bayfield Police Services. He studies that handwritten word, RAT.

"Where is he now?" says JD.

Ronnie coughs again. Becca lets out a high, braying laugh, then clamps a hand over her mouth.

Declan takes hold of the paper and tugs it out of JD's fingers. "The gutless spy we knew as Gage is not a consideration at the moment, my friend. Believe me when I say that. But it has necessitated that events speed up. And so I'll tell you what I told you over the phone. It's you we need."

Declan is staring steadily at JD. So is Ronnie. Becca's not. Her eyes are rolling, heavy-lidded. She looks like she might pass out.

"Sentinel," says Declan, "it's you we need."

Seven-thirty in the morning, the 3rd of November, 2011. The rain quit an hour before dawn. The new daylight is obscured through dense fog. The fog cloaks the city ahead as the vehicle that had once been Granddad's ice cream truck moves along Side Road 10. The pace of the truck is steady, keeping to the speed limit. The suburbs are ghostly shapes on either side.

The back of the truck has been gutted of its original appointments. The freezer, the yogurt machine, the preparation counter, the steel sinks. All gone. In their place are six 55-gallon plastic drums. Two wide, three long, cinched and strapped into place to keep them from moving.

Each drum is lidded. The lids have small holes drilled through them. Protruding from each hole is a complicated snarl of electrical wires, gathered up in a central bunch, almost as thick as a forearm. This central group of wires leads down through an opening cut in the floor.

JD saw the half-dozen barrels and their arterial network of wires when he got in the truck with Ronnie at seven o'clock. Ronnie brought with him a small duffel bag and dropped it into the space between the seats.

JD knows what the drums contain. JD has been invited to possess this knowledge. The drums contain high-tech equipment to disrupt the ELF transmitter inside the Van Lathan Building.

JD has no reason to believe otherwise. Knowing what he knows adds a sense of stark reality to what he's doing. This helps him feel better about what has happened to Granddad's truck. Necessary modifications. He's sure Granddad would understand.

One thing JD is bothered by, more than he can account for, is the absence of Hula-Lula.

When JD got into the truck back at Forward Operating Base Liberty, it took him a moment to realize what was different. Then it came to him. Hula-Lula and her suction-cup base – Did You Get Lei'd Today – were gone. In her place, bolted to the top of the console, was a small metal box. Same nondescript gray as the rest of the truck. About the size of a thick hardcover book. Without thinking of it, JD reached for the metal box, saying, What's this?

Ronnie smacked his hand away. Don't touch the failsafe! Don't even look at it.

The failsafe?

Ronnie didn't reply. His eyes were locked forward.

You don't need to be disagreeable, kind sir, said JD.

Just drive.

Now they are nearing the fringes of the city. Twenty minutes from downtown. Twenty-five if they get stuck in traffic.

JD glances over at Ronnie. Ronnie's beard looks trim and neat, as if he's just had it cut in the last day or so. The veins in Ronnie's temples are pronounced. His brow is furrowed.

"How did you find out about Gage?" JD says quietly.

Ronnie does not take his eyes off the road ahead. "There's one or two people in so-called law enforcement who actually believe in the principles of blood and honour," he says. Then Ronnie turns his head and fixes JD with a shadowed look. "We take care of our own. Nobody else is gonna. A believer in the IT department tipped me off about that cuck."

"So, then, is Gage ... locked up somewhere?"

"No. Gage is not locked up somewhere."

JD clears his throat. "So, he's ..."

"He's took care of is what he is."

They drive over a goodsized pothole in the road. The ice cream truck bounces. Out of the corner of his eye, JD sees Ronnie stiffen and grab the edges of his seat. Could be JD's imagination, but he thinks he hears the plastic drums thumping against each other in the back.

"I got one leg and I drive better than you," Ronnie mutters.

JD doesn't respond. Earlier, as they were about to leave Forward Operating Base Liberty, Declan came out of the house to see them off. He was carrying a mug of coffee, pausing to sip from it every few steps, as if this morning was the same as any other.

At the end of the mission briefing in the bunker beneath the house, Declan had explained how he and Becca were going to stay back while Ronnie and JD went into the city.

They were staying back, Declan had said, to coordinate the extraction plan. He did not say what the extraction plan was. JD wondered – but did not say – how much Becca actually had to do with the extraction plan. How much Becca had to do with anything, other than getting her next fix.

Declan shook hands with Ronnie first, then with JD. Declan's eyes seared into JD's.

JD thought Declan might have a quote to punctuate the moment. Something from the Bible or Bruce Lee or some long dead historical person, but Declan didn't offer anything.

At the last second, after JD had started the truck, Declan knocked on his door. JD opened it. Declan was holding up a small envelope.

Take this, my friend. Guard it with your life. You'll need it when the time comes.

When the time comes? said JD.

But all Declan did was sip his coffee and smile a terrible smile. Then he closed the driver side door.

JD and Ronnie are through the suburbs and into the city proper now. They pass the shopping plaza near the highway. They pass the building where AM 710 broadcasts from. Then the small campus surrounding Alliance College. They stop for a red light. There's a large parking lot at one corner of the intersection. Much of the lot is lost in the fog, but at this nearest corner are a pair of police cars. They're parked nose-to-tail beside each other so the two drivers can speak through their windows.

A chill passes over JD. The red light seems to last for years. He can't help himself from looking over at the cruisers.

"Quit looking," says Ronnie.

"One of them is getting out of his car," says JD.

Ronnie spares the briefest glance. A cop is stepping out of the passenger side of one of the vehicles. The cop straightens up, puts on his hat. He's got a thick uniform jacket on for the weather, but the jacket is open and his body armour is plainly visible.

The red light has not changed.

The cop starts walking toward them.

"Eyes front," Ronnie hisses.

JD does as he's told, but his eyes keep flicking to the side, as if of their own accord. The cop is getting closer, crossing into the intersection now. Out of his peripheral vision, JD sees something catch the light beside Ronnie's hip. He can't himself – he looks over. Ronnie is holding his chrome-plated revolver. He's keeping it low, underneath his window, but he's also easing back the hammer.

"When I tell you to, you hit the gas, got it?" says Ronnie. "This doesn't end here just because some pork patrol is coming to tell us we got a taillight out or whatever. We're past the point of no return."

"Ronnie …"

"Past the point of no return," Ronnie repeats, his teeth gritted.

The cop closes the distance to ten feet, then five. Then he's passing by the front of the truck. The light on his side turns yellow, and the cop has to hustle along to make it to the curb. He steps through the doors of a fast food joint and disappears.

Someone honks from behind the truck. JD blinks. Green light. The traffic is flowing again. He presses the accelerator and they move on.

After a minute of heavy silence, JD says, "Would you have shot that cop?"

"The liberty tree has to be watered sometimes with the blood of patriots," says Ronnie, dropping his weapon into his duffle bag. "Or cops. That's what happens when you pass the point of no return."

There's something missing. It's not Hula-Lula. It's been missing for hours, and JD can't quite put his finger on it. They're only a block away from the Van Lathan Building, passing the south side of Civic Park, before JD figures it out.

There's no ELF trying to get into his head.

He tells himself it must be an effect of the sensitive equipment inside the drums in the back of the truck. Some kind of electromagnetic radiation. Or the exact opposite of electromagnetic radiation. Or he has no idea. All he can say for sure is there's nothing trying to scramble his thoughts. For once. The silence, as the saying goes, is deafening.

This is what it means to be a Very Very Very Invited Person. This is what happens when you pass the point of no return.

It's almost 8 o'clock and the five metred parking spots beside the Van Lathan Building are vacant. The building itself stands into the fog.

"Pull up here," says Ronnie. "That spot, closest to the front doors. Put the flashers on."

JD does. When he's in the spot he brakes too abruptly. They both lurch forward in their seats. Ronnie glares at him. JD swallows, finding his throat dry. He's still marvelling at the silence of the ELF. Wonders if They are asleep at the switch this morning.

The silence between his ears is almost painful.

Ronnie digs into his duffel bag and comes out with a small handlettered sign. JD catches a quick glimpse of it—

On delivvery
Back in 5 mins!!!

—before Ronnie puts it on the dashboard, facing out, against the inside of the windshield.

Then Ronnie pauses. He's in his seat, not moving, somehow uncertain. He turns to JD, blinking slowly. "Tell me you still got your burner phone. Matterfact, show me."

JD reaches into the pocket of his blazer, withdraws the Nokia. He holds it out, but Ronnie withdraws his hand as if the phone might be boiling hot. "You hang on to that," he says. "Okay. We got to move. Hup-to."

Ronnie picks up his duffel bag and unbuckles his seatbelt and starts to open his door. JD remains in the driver's seat, not moving. Ronnie gives him a questioning look.

"I don't know, kind sir," says JD. "I don't know about this."

"What's not to know?"

"I just don't know."

And JD doesn't know. Back at Forward Operating Base Liberty, everything Declan said made perfect sense. But now …

Outside the truck, there are sheeple on the sidewalk, appearing out of the fog, going about their mornings. Some are passing by, but many are going through the front doors of the Van Lathan Building. It's early yet, but JD knows the number will only increase over the next hour.

Ronnie's face is darkening. He looks as if he's about to say something, but JD preempts him by opening the driver side door and stepping down to the street. Ronnie huffs his own way out of the cab, hampered by his leg. He limps around to JD. "Move," he says in a low voice.

JD moves, not sure where he's supposed to move to, other than it involves following Ronnie. They cross Monarch Avenue, jaywalking west. Ronnie is going with surprising speed. His head is lowered, his collar turned up. JD scrambles along beside him.

One cop car, JD thinks. All it'll take is one cop car to cruise along. Maybe even one of the Courts vans. And then what?

They make it to the other side of the street without any incident. Ronnie leads the way through the gate in the wrought-iron face, into Civic Park. The park is chilly and barren. Not even see any dog walkers or joggers about.

The safety mesh and caution tape are still in place around the bottom of the crooked stairs leading to the top of the reservoir hill. As JD already knows, the mesh is more of a formality than an effective barrier. Ronnie gets over it with ease. He even pauses to hold the mesh down for JD.

The stairs are wonky, wet, and treacherous. Hard going even for a man like JD, who considers himself in peak physical shape. For Ronnie the stairs must be close to impossible, but without a word he commences up. He has to mount each step with his good leg first, lean heavily on the handrail, then haul his prosthetic leg up onto the same step.

JD follows.

When they're two-thirds of the way up – roughly the same spot JD paused for breath the last time he made this climb – Ronnie stops. He briefly scans around them. Then he opens his duffel bag and draws out the heavy revolver. Tucks it into the waist of his dark cargo pants. He scans around again, then resumes the climb.

And JD follows.

At ten minutes past eight they gain the top of the reservoir hill and climb over the second mesh barrier. There's a breeze up here. It's not strong, but it's cold, and it freezes the sweat JD has broken from the climb and the lingering damp in his clothes from the night before. He shivers.

He looks back the way they came. The fog is thinner now, so JD can see Granddad's ice cream truck. A short distance past the truck is the front entrance of the Van Lathan Building. The sheeple going through the doors. The cars turning down the ramp to the underground garage.

"Okay," says Ronnie. "Phase three."

"Phase three?" says JD.

Ronnie has taken something out of the duffel bag and is operating it with both hands. It's not the revolver, which JD can see, still tucked into the waistband of Ronnie's pants. The thing in Ronnie's hands is the same palm-sized camcorder he used at the meetings.

"That envelope Alpha One gave you," says Ronnie. "Get it out of your pocket. Open it up. Get your burner out too. You'll need it. You're about to be the face of history, Sentinel. You know that?"

Typed on the paper is this:

Good Morning.

Today is November 3rd, 2011. These are the hardest of times. Every day, the People of this Country witness countless acts of savagery. Of crime. Of moral decay. The People of this Country are made to submit to racially inferior immigration. To the removal of Christ and Christian values from longstanding traditions. To a national security apparatus hamstrung by weakness and radical feminism.

Worst of all, the People of this Country are shackled by a fundamentally corrupt, degenerate, traitorous government. This government, in turn, is under the control of a globalist deep state.

I stand before you as Representative of a network of Patriots who have had enough. We have attempted to play by the deep state's rules, only to be mocked, persecuted, imprisoned and robbed. Enough. The future of our very existence has been put at stake. Enough.

Enough.

We Patriots have chosen the Van Lathan Building to make our stand. This building is a hive of corrupt government. From the twelfth floor, racially inferior subhumans are ushered past our borders. From the eighth floor, citizens are robbed through a form of legal theft called taxation. In the basement of the building, the innocent are pumped through a for-profit court system.

And on floors five and six, the so-called election offices decide who may participate in the democratic process, and who must be humiliated by that same process.

Enough!

We Patriots regret that uninvolved persons may be affected by what is about to happen, but a flag must be planted, and this is where that planting shall occur. November 3rd, 2011, is the day in which the deep state and the globalists inside their faceless offices must pay the price for their cognitive dissonance.

Yours in Liberty ...

The signature below is JD's own name.

"Three two one," says Ronnie. "Action."

He's recording with the camcorder, holding it one-handed. With his other hand, he's drawn the revolver out of his waistband. Thumbed back the hammer, laid his finger alongside the trigger guard. He's got it pointed it at the ground. For the moment.

"Wait," says JD.

Ronnie's face twists into an ugly scowl. "Wait for what? I told you what to do."

It's true – Ronnie has told JD what to do. He's told him where to stand. Right on the precarious edge of the top step, so he can be framed in the shot from the camcorder. A shot that also includes the Van Lathan Building in the distance, with the ice cream truck parked in front of it. The stream of sheeple entering the building hasn't ceased.

Despite the fog, it's a good view.

Ronnie has also told JD to read the typed note from the envelope. Read it in a slow steady voice. Take your time.

JD isn't sure what to make of that. The typewritten script says a lot of things, but there's nothing about disruption of mind control antennae. There's also the matter of the last bit of the note, where it gives JD's own name. Not Patriot Alpha Sentinel, not Very Invited Person. His own name, the one on his birth certificate. As if these are his words on the note.

There's one more instruction Ronnie has given him. After he reads the note aloud, JD is to lift the burner, go to the contact list, and place a call. A call to the only entry in the list. TYRANT.

"Let's go," says Ronnie. "Three-two-one action."

"Wait, kind sir, wait …"

"No more waiting."

Now Ronnie lifts the revolver, pointing it at JD just as he's pointing the camcorder.

JD is conscious of a sound. Quick, dull, rhythmic. His heartbeat, accelerated. He can hear it clearly. He still cannot hear any ELF transmissions. He glances at the Van Lathan Building. Sheeple in their coats and business attire, going through the front entrance. Some of the sheeple are carrying much smaller sheeple, or holding them by the hands. JD remembers there's a daycare in the building.

The ice cream truck sits in the parking spot. Dull, gray, anonymous. The only thing to mark it is the flashing of the hazards.

On delivvery. Back in 5 mins!!!

"What about," says JD, "what about the—" He's searching for the word, searching hard. "What about the extraction? You know, after we knock out the antenna? Will we just get back in the truck and drive away?"

Ronnie blinks. An oddly mild look comes into his eyes. He blinks again. When he speaks, his voice has an uncharacteristic softness about it. "You don't really get nothing, do you. You still think ... Don't you know what we are, bud? We're patriots. We're martyrs."

"We don't have to do this, Ronnie."

There's a beat. One second, two. Then Ronnie's face turns hard again. He says, "We're martyrs. We're patriots. And we're past the point of no return. You do what you're told, or I'm gonna engage you right in your face. Then I'm gonna make the call to Tyrant myself, start the whole revolution. Whatever happens to me after that, I don't give a crap. It'll still be your name on that note."

JD swallows. He starts to read the note aloud.

"Stop," Ronnie says. "Start again. Go slower."

"Today is November 3rd, 2011. These are the hardest of times ..."

JD slows his pace, then slows it again.

He reads, "We have attempted to play by the deep state's rules, only to be mocked, persecuted, imprisoned and robbed. Enough ..."

He reads, "A flag must be planted ..."

Then he gets almost to the end. "The deep state and the globalists inside their faceless offices must pay the price for their cognit ... cognit ... cog ..."

"What is wrong with you?" says Ronnie.

"Nothing is wrong with me," says JD. "It's this term."

Doubtfulness passes over Ronnie's face. His mouth works, as if he's about to say something. He blinks again. "What term?" he says.

"This one," says JD, jabbing his finger at the typewritten manifesto.

Ronnie takes three steps forward. He sticks the revolver into JD's stomach. Reflexively, JD takes a tiny step back, and when he feels his heel slide over the edge of the top step, he pivots sideways. It's a very small movement. Ronnie stays close, weapon planted in JD's midsection.

"Show me," says Ronnie.

JD shows him.

Ronnie's eyebrows knit together, come apart, knit together again. JD eases back, staying along the side of the top step, another inch or two.

Ronnie's eyes shut, as though he has a headache. "Just skip that whole sentence. Go right to the end."

The revolver comes away from JD's stomach as Ronnie withdraws, starts to turn back to his original position.

"Always gotta be something," Ronnie mutters. "Some big fancy college words. Can't ever talk like a normal—"

JD drives his foot out as hard as he can. A flat, low arc. Go for the side of kneecap, Declan once told him, and that's exactly what JD does.

His oxford strikes Ronnie hard in the middle of the leg. Something is knocked loose, the leg folds sideways at an impossible angle. Ronnie is off-balance. Starts to drop. The chromeplated revolver and camcorder both point directly at the sky as he pinwheels his arms for balance.

JD blunders into him, leading with both hands, the manifesto balled up in one, the burner in the other. He catches Ronnie full on the chest. Feels the air whoof out of the man. Then Ronnie is going over the edge of the top step. His prosthetic leg is caught in his cargo pants, but it's flapping grotesquely.

No part of Ronnie is touching solid ground. But he's pointing the revolver up at the man above him. The last conscious action Ronnie ever performs is pulling the trigger.

For a time all JD sees is bright white. It's brilliant, unbroken. Perhaps all those stories about near death events are true. He's been pulled up into the glorious glow of the afterlife. Now he'll strum a harp and recline on a cloud and never have to worry again.

It's a nice idea, but heaven wouldn't have the feeling of cold concrete beneath him, or a horrendous ringing in his ear, or what seems to be a legion of fire ants devouring the side of his head.

He sits up. His stomach lurches. Feels like he's going to retch. He's not in heaven. He's on the wet concrete landing beside the maintenance shed at the top of the reservoir hill.

All he was seeing was the pearly, overcast sky.

There's still no explanation for the ants eating the side of his head, or the astringent reek of something burning.

He sees his trilby. What's left of it. It's lying on the concrete nearby. There's a large, ragged hole in the side of the hat where the brim is stitched into the crown. The colourful pheasant feathers and satin hatband are both ruined. The faraday shield inside the crown is mostly intact, but for some reason it looks strange now. He wonders what he ever thought it would do.

The ringing in his ear is so loud it's almost surreal. The smell of burning intensifies. So too the ants. That's how JD realizes his hair is on fire. As he frantically swats the side of his head to put the fire out, he feels the ragged mess of his ear. The top part of his ear – or what should be the top part of his ear. It isn't there anymore.

The pain and the realization of what happened brings the retching that much closer. If the bullet had passed half an inch the other way, it would have taken the side of his head off.

He can't take much more of this, he thinks. He shouldn't be expected to take much more of this. It's not fair.

He's got the fire out now. He doesn't want to dwell long on the stubbly, burnt remnants of his hair on half his head. Or the tender, wet feeling of his naked scalp. Or his ear. Or the blood flowing down the side of his face, darkening his collar. That's another blazer ruined for the cause.

Not fair at all.

He gets to his feet. He's shaking. He sees the burner phone and the manifesto, crumpled up from the grip he had on it, discarded on the ground. He picks them both up, jams them into his patch pockets. Then he puts his perforated trilby back on his head. Wearing it right now is as much about habit as it is an attempt to hide the mess of his scalp and his ear.

He doesn't want to look over the edge of the staircase. Doesn't want to look, but does anyway.

First he sees the camcorder, dropped only a few steps down. He thinks he sees the gun, a dull glint on the chrome in the diffuse sunlight, halfway down the steps. Then he sees Ronnie. Patriot Alpha X-Ray has made it all the way to the bottom.

Ronnie is in an unlikely posture – it's hard to see it clearly from all the way up here – with his head and shoulders on the ground and his ass in the air and his legs akimbo. Like he'd attempted a headstand, failed midway through, and is frozen mid-collapse. The prosthetic, still caught in Ronnie's pants, is dangling, and the orange safety mesh is crushed and twisted.

JD does retch this time. Drops to his knees, heaves out a bitter mix of bile and saliva and last night's drinks. He tears his gaze away from the pretzel-shaped man at the bottom of the stairs. He happens to catch sight of the gray ice cream truck in the distance. It's unmoved. The hazards are still flashing away.

He gets back up. The shakes are even worse. The ringing in his ear has him off-balance. At this point he'd trade the ringing for ELF . Okay. What to do, now that his work here is done. Light out for the territories, obviously. Reconnect with Granddad, have a well-earned vacation at whatever tropical villa the old man has bought with all his gambling triumphs. Better take a few extra seconds to clean up here though.

He goes down the first few steps, keeping a whiteknuckled grip on the handrail, keeping his eyes away from the bottom of the staircase as best he can. He gets the camcorder. He has no idea if it survived the fall, but there's no sense leaving it lying around. He crams it into his patch pocket. It's a tight fit.

He tries not to pay any attention to the three coin-sized drops of blood on the step nearest the camcorder, or what looks like a fresh crack in the concrete.

Okay, the revolver next. The might be a good thing to have if you're going to live like a sultan – under an alias, of course – in some beachside palace for the next thirty, forty, fifty years.

But before he can descend further, a jogger appears at the base of the hill. The jogger spots the pretzelman tangled up in the orange mesh. Slows, stops. JD dashes into the brush by the side of the staircase, presses himself against the trunk of a leafless oak twisting out of the hillside.

When he peeks back out, he sees not one jogger but two, plus a dog-walker, all crouched around the pretzelman. He strains to listen to the do-gooders over the ringing in his ear.

"Sir, can you hear me, sir? Can you tell us what happened?"

"Don't try to move, man. We're gonna call 911."

"Hey … is that a gun up there?"

Well, that settles that. Never mind the revolver. Time for JD to make himself scarce.

He can stay among the scrubby treeside hills, skirt around until he's out of sight from anyone gathering at the bottom of the hill. Start to run if necessary. Then light out for the territories, for Granddad's tropical palace.

Something occurs to him. It's not easy to dismiss.

He flattens himself against the trunk of the tree, squeezing his eyes shut. It's no business of his, it's not fair, he doesn't want anything to do with it. He peeks out again. Now there's a new jogger with the group at the bottom of the stairs. Two of them are on their phones. The pretzelman has not moved.

Past them, in the distance, the hazards are still flashing on the ice cream truck.

JD's hand slips into the pocket of his trousers, finds the truck keys. He squeezes his eyes shut again. The same something occurs to him again. That small metal box mounted to the dashboard where Hula-Lula used to be.

The failsafe.

He sticks to the reservoir hillside. Stumbles here and there, falls a few times. One fall takes him halfway down the slope, sliding on an impromptu sled of wet, slimy leaves. When he recovers, he's lost one of his oxfords. He sees his big toe poking out a hole in his sock.

He gets to the base of the hill a hundred yards from the crowd around Ronnie. Eight, nine, ten of them now. Cellphones out.

He's most of the way across the flat ground of the park, making straight for the east gate, when he hears the first siren. The sound of it adds a jittery urgency to his step. He wants to run but does not, thinking a flat-out run will only draw attention. More attention. He must already look like some halfcrazed hobo, notwithstanding the blood down the side of his face. He walks as briskly as he can.

Through the east gate, over the sidewalk, out onto Monarch. Cars honk as he steps out in front of them. Never mind. The sirens are getting louder.

He's at the ice cream truck now. He sees a bright yellow parking ticket tucked under the windshield wiper, not far from the little sign Ronnie made.

He unlocks the door, somehow not fumbling the keys, and pulls himself up into the cab. For a moment all he can do is sit there, watching the world outside the truck. The sheeple in their masses, entering the Van Lathan Building or passing by. Some of the sheeple pause to spectate as the sirens crescendo. For now it's just an ambulance arriving at the east gate of Civic Park, but the cops can't be far behind.

He looks at the small metal box. The failsafe.

He has to move the truck. Take it someplace not surrounded by stupid know-nothing sheeple going about their rat-races. Someplace not surrounded by much of anything. Just in case. Then his work here will be done. Then he can light out for the territories.

He pushes the key into the ignition.

Going through the whitewashed gate scares him, as though the impact might be enough to do something to the contents of the plastic drums. But nothing happens to the drums, and going through the gate is much less impactful then he thought. There's a shriek of metal on metal, but the corrugated sheetmetal gives with little resistance. He carries on up the long driveway between the dead lawns.

A short time ago, as he passed out of the city, he heard sirens again. A lot of them. But he saw nothing in his mirrors. It helped that he was staying off the main roads. The sirens stayed with him for a while, getting louder, but no emergency vehicles came into view. Then, just as he turned onto Side Road 10, the sirens faded out of earshot.

He hasn't heard them since.

The barn looms ahead.

He expects the big woodframed double-doors in the side of the barn to be closed. Woodframe would be harder to ram than sheetmetal, but if he's really got the pedal floored, maybe it won't be so bad.

The double-doors are standing open.

He blinks. He can't think why the doors are open. No matter. He speeds through. It's tight overhead. If there wasn't so much weight in the back, it might be too tight.

The ice cream truck speeds into the interior of the barn, past the old horse stalls lining one wall. The Dodge Charger with the PRZ GOD vanity plates is still in the barn, parked on the bare cement, oriented toward the open doors. JD swerves to avoid it, missing the muscle car by the thinnest of margins.

But then he's turning onto the grid of wrestling mats. JD steps on the brake, brings the truck to a stop. A few paces away is the beige punching mannequin on his sand-filled base, fixing the truck with his dead-eyed stare.

JD turns off the ignition. He listens. For what? Sirens? Declan? He hears neither. He hears nothing at all. Not even some ominous thriller-movie ticking from the failsafe box.

He's out of the ice cream truck a second later. Listens again. For a second he thinks he hears something, thump-thump-thump. A helicopter? His own heartbeat? But then it's gone, and there's only a low breeze creaking the roof panels overhead.

He starts to jog toward the open double-doors. The ground is cold beneath his one sock-clad foot. He's got the keys to the ice cream truck balled in his hand. Once he's outside he intends to chuck them into the long grass somewhere. That's as far as the active component of his planning extends.

He hears that sound again, still distant, but unmistakable now. Thump-thump-thump-thump.

JD's fragmentary pause to listen to the helicopter is just long enough for the man with the jet-black brushcut, aviator shades, suede jacket, and slimfit jeans to slip through the open barn doors unnoticed. The jeans are slim enough to see there's no GPS locator at the man's ankle anymore. The man is holding an automatic pistol. He lifts the weapon, just as JD notices him.

"I need you to get back in the truck, my friend," the man says calmly. "Yes indeed I do."

It's funny, because the man has Declan's voice. But the hair, the shades, the jacket, the jeans?

In the distance, the sound of the helicopter holds steady. It's accompanied now by a distant, almost inaudible wail of sirens. No telling how far away they might be. This new incarnation of Declan inclines his head at the sound, then refocuses on JD.

JD gawks at Declan.

"Get back in the truck," says Declan.

JD gawks a moment longer, then flings the keys across the barn in the direction of the horse stalls. The keys fall well short, clatter on the floor. It's a lame gesture. They both know it. Declan shakes his head.

He says, "You went, you saw, you did God knows what to Ronnie. Now you're back here to conquer, after a fashion. And conquer you will. Conquer you will. With some minor adjustments to the plan."

Declan takes a few steps forward. He's positioned himself beside the front of the Charger, passenger side. He keeps JD covered with the automatic. Then he opens the passenger door, leans in, and withdraws something from the glovebox. Whatever it is, it's small enough for Declan to conceal in his hand.

"Into the truck, my friend."

Dry-mouthed, JD complies. He clambers up into the driver's seat. He positions himself on the seat, as if he's about to start the truck. Even grips the wheel with both hands. He sees Declan in his peripheral vision, standing beside the open door.

"Richard," says JD, "sir, I believe this was all a misunderstanding."

Declan holds something up to JD. It's whatever he took from the glovebox. "Take this," he says.

JD reaches out to take it, thinking it might somehow be a spare truck key. Instead, he sees it's a plastic zip-tie. JD feels like a horse has kicked him in the stomach.

JD dumbly complies when Declan tells him to use the zip-tie to secure his own right hand to the steering wheel. The zip-tie isn't long enough for both his hands, but that seems of little concern to Declan. One hand is enough.

"Pull it tight. Tight as can be. No need to worry about your circulation."

JD pulls the end of the zip-tie until the plastic bites hard into the skin of his wrist. His right hand has already taken on a dark, swollen appearance. He recalls a horror movie he and Lil once watched. Two men in a filthy industrial bathroom, both of them shackled in place. Their captor had given the men a hacksaw. The hacksaw wouldn't cut the shackles, but it would cut through flesh and bone. And a clock, of course, was ticking.

In the world outside the barn, the sirens are louder now. Sirens layered on sirens, punctuated by the helicopter.

Declan closes the driver side door of the ice cream truck from outside. He starts to make his way around the front of the vehicle.

JD paws lamely at himself with his left hand. He longs for his lost baton. The burner is in his inside pocket, and the camcorder is still stuffed into his righthand patch pocket. He twists hard to reach the camcorder, as if he might use it for ... for what?

As he and Lil watched that horror movie, JD proselytized on the thousand ways he would have escaped the situation, the shackles in the filthy bathroom. How he would have turned the tables on the sadistic captor. How he would have emerged victorious. All without having to use the hacksaw on himself, until Lil finally told him to shut up and watch the fuckin movie.

Funny, he can't come up with a single idea now. All he can do is desperately finger the top of the camcorder in his pocket.

Declan opens the passenger side door and climbs up and sits. He sets the automatic pistol in his lap, then lifts his hands to the gray metal box on the dashboard. The failsafe. The face of the box is hinged at the bottom. Declan opens it gently. The inside of the box contains several loops of delicate wire, bound together by electrical tape. Among the wires is a cellphone. An exact match for JD's own burner, in fact, except the faceplate has been removed to allow the wires to connect to the motherboard.

Beside the cellphone is a Timex digital watch without the wrist straps. It's not the big red LED display from the thriller movie, but it's not far off.

Declan rubs his fingertips, inhales. Then he takes hold of the Timex, as delicate as a surgeon. JD can't see the display, but he can hear the beeping as Declan sets it. JD struggles harder for the camcorder in his pocket. Outside, the sirens and the helicopter have become louder.

JD manages to get his fingers into the narrow strap of the camcorder. He pulls it out of his pocket, grunting against the pain of the way his body is twisted. But as soon as the camcorder is free, he sees his gesture for the absolute futility it is. He can't even hurl it.

Declan sees this too. He's been watching JD for the last few seconds. Now he smiles. He reaches across the space between the seats.

It's a gentle gesture, almost loving, almost a light caress of JD's face, until Declan takes hold of JD's injured ear and gives it a vicious yank.

The pain is explosive. JD hears himself shrieking, feels fresh blood flowing down his face and neck. He drops the camcorder, clamps his hand to his ear.

Declan steps out of the truck. He tucks the automatic into the waist of his slimfit jeans and pulls the suede jacket down to conceal it. He starts to close the door, then stops.

"Woe to that man who betrays the Prophet of Righteousness. It would be better for him if he had not been born. You can think about that, my friend, for the next one minute and twenty—make that two minutes and fifteen seconds."

"I'm not," JD pants, but he doesn't know how to finish that statement.

"Oh yes you are," says Declan. "You and however many of Caesar's Legion get here first. It's not what I wanted, but I'll take it. The more the merrier. Goodbye."

"Where are you going, Richard? Where's Becca?"

"I'm joining the rest of the patriot network," says Declan. "The whereabouts of which are classified."

"You really believe that," says JD. "Don't you."

"Coming from the guy with the tinfoil hat," says Declan.

"Where's Becca?"

But Declan slams shut the passenger door. JD watches as Declan jogs over to the open barn doors. Declan gazes out the doors, shading his eyes with his hand, looking to the front of the property. The sirens are growing louder by the second. Maybe the police cars are already in sight, in which case Declan can take the back way off the property.

Let the cops come. Caesar's Legion. That's the idea now, with the Van Lathan Building still standing. Let them come by the score, surround the Judas in the ice cream truck, just as the time on the failsafe runs out.

One minute now. Not even one minute.

JD watches as Declan turns back from the open doors, jogs over to the Charger. He picks up the third gym bag and brings it around to the trunk. JD starts to cry.

He can't bear to look at Declan any more. He pulls his eyes away, and through his tear-blurred vision, he catches sight of himself in the in the sideview mirror. He sees his ruined trilby. He sees the burned remnants of his hair, his mangled, bleeding half-ear. His face streaked with blood and dirt and now with tears. He sees his hollow cheeks, the lines at the sides of his eyes.

He sees his mother expiring on the couch, the needle in her arm.

He sees Lil tiring of his joblessness, throwing him out.

He sees his brother and the Harpy Herself, surveying the destroyed apartment.

He sees Granddad, dead in the arms of one of his favourite ladyfriends at the Imperial Arms. Acute, final, complete liver failure. Early June of this very year.

Through it all JD wants to see Them (or the globalists or the deep state or the illuminati or whoever) pulling the strings, using their mind control, authoring the conspiracy. Eliminating the just because. But They are absent. More absent now than ever.

Outside, Declan hastens over to the Charger.

JD has no idea how the failsafe works, if setting the Timex has somehow cancelled out or overridden that other device nestled in the wires. Maybe it doesn't matter. It's the gesture that counts. He's already holding up the burner with his left hand. This entire time, the burner was freely accessible. It's at 6% battery. He thumbs his way to the contact list. To the only contact.

Declan is lowering himself into the driver's seat.

JD twists his purple, lifeless right hand into the horn. It wails out across the barn. He sees Declan stiffen, half in half out of the Charger. Declan's head whips around.

JD has selected Tyrant. He settles his thumb on the call button, not quite pushing, not yet, and turns the phone forward. Holds it up so it's in plain view over the dashboard.

It's impossible to see what Declan's eyes are doing behind the aviator shades, but his mouth drops open. For a second he is frozen in place. Then he tumbles the rest of the way into the car, not even closing the door behind him. JD hears the Charger roar to life. It heaves forward.

The car fishtails into the barn doorframe and drags against the timber. Declan must be standing on the accelerator, but it's not enough.

It's not enough to get him away.

JD laughs, closes his eyes. He pushes the button.

Between 1984 and 1994 ... Canada became the centre of the whole new world order operation, one huge research laboratory ... Vancouver was gradually made to resemble a never land in the setting Lemurian sun while, according to one prognosis, Toronto became the 'centre' of a vast Satanic conspiracy, the eye of a tornado where the forces of evil contend with the forces of good for domination of the planet during the next 1,000 years.

—Dr Robert Driscoll, Ottawa: The Occult
Capital of the New World Order

5: The Time for Dialogue is Now Over

Transcribed from *Full Disclosure with Gilbert Emmerich*, AM 710, November 14, 2015.

Gilbert Emmerich: My job, fellow truthers, is to ask the hard questions. The questions the lamestream media won't touch. The questions they don't want you to even think about. The abnormal, the paranormal, cover-ups, conspiracies. That's the whole point of Full Disclosure. I'm proud as hell of what we do.

But sometimes I get carried away, okay? My producer, Paul, he knows all about it. It's Paul's job – and a thankless job at that – to try to bring me back down to earth once in a while.

These last few weeks, truthers, we've been talking to one repeat caller in particular. You know who I mean. JD, Johnny D, John Doe # 2. The self-styled 11/3/11 insider. The response to my conversations with Johnny has been crazy. Crazy. There are believers, there are haters, there's everybody in between. We've never had this kind of traffic on our forums. Makes our advertisers happy, let me tell you.

That's why it hurts so bad to say this. We won't be taking any more calls from John Doe # 2.

Everything related to JD is way outta hand. On top of that – and this is coming from a show about conspiracies and coverups, mind you – I don't know how much Johnny D can be trusted. You know? There are a lot of coincidences in his side of the story, fellow truthers. A lot of convenient facts. Our JD might be something of an attention-whore, you know?

Now what do we know about the outcome of 11/3/11? I mean, what's the rest of the official story?

Well, yes, the official story tells us there was an undercover cop in the mix. Detective-Sergeant Dominic Grillo. He'd been working inside the Patriot Bloc for six months, under the name Gage Terry. We know his cover was blown by a skinhead sympathizer, old pal of Ronnie Fortin's, inside the Bayfield Police Services. That's a whole other story for a whole other day. This Detective-Sergeant Grillo, well, they think that's his body they found two years ago, all burned up, in the basement of a vacant house way outside of town. Leaves behind a wife and three kids.

Speaking of Ronnie Fortin, the official story says he's a total vegetable now. Quadriplegic, severe brain trauma, the whole works. Apparently just sits around messing himself and drooling all day. Never gonna get out of a wheelchair for the rest of his life.

I don't have to tell you truthers this, but here's where it gets murky. If Ronnie Fortin fell down those stairs at reservoir hill ... who drove the truck back to the farmhouse?

In the official version, the experts say – the experts admit – they don't know how the truck got back to the farmhouse.

Could've been Becca Sears, they say. They say she got cold feet about the whole thing. They found her in that big-ass jacuzzi with cut wrists and enough valium in her bloodstream to knock out a dinosaur. Well, what was left of her bloodstream, what didn't drain out into the jacuzzi.

The experts say it could've been Richard Declan who drove the truck back, though they don't have any idea why he would've done that, since the whole operation was his idea in the first place.

Either way, we know what happened next. The gray truck ended back at the farmhouse, in the barn. A whole lot of cops showed up – we've all seen that helicopter footage online – which was Declan's Plan B. Round up a bunch of cops and blow them all to hell ...

But nothing happened.

Nothing happened. All of that supposed ammonium nitrate fertilizer was totally inert. A false flag. Something the dead undercover cop had set up to bring the Patriot Bloc down. Too bad they got to him before he got to them.

So whether it was down in front of the Van Lathan Building or up at the farmhouse, that truck was never going to blow up. Man, try to wrap your head around that little factoid.

Either way, the fallout from the whole thing has been very real. Maybe that's the reason I still talk about it so much, years later. I call it fascism. I call it a police-state. I call it government overreach. If you live in Bayfield, you know exactly what I mean. You can't park on Monarch Avenue anymore. You can't even idle there. Cops give out loitering tickets like they're ... well ... candy or something. Our rights are being trampled on, all because of what?

Nothing.

A con job. A decoy. One of the biggest acts of so-called domestic terror turns out to be a total con job. A conspiracy. It was, they tell us, part of a bigger plan to nab the Patriot Bloc. Catch them in the act of planning something. Build up a big case against them, then throw them all in jail and chuck away the key. That's what we do to patriots in this country. Anyway, it all went off the rails when the undercover cop got ratted out. That was when Richard Declan decided he needed to kick everything into high-gear.

And through it all, despite all these hard questions you and I and everybody else has been asking, the experts and their official story tell us the same thing.

There was no John Doe # 2.

Which of course is what they would say, because as you and I both know, truthers, there's always more to it than the official version. I just personally don't know how much more there is in this case, because I don't know if the guy we've been talking to for the last couple weeks is a total crackpot. My producer thinks he is. So does my lawyer. And you know what, truthers? So do I.

That's why we're not taking his calls anymore. Full Disclosure with Gilbert Emmerich gets enough craziness as it is. We're hard-hitting independent journalists uncovering real conspiracies. We've got a reputation to maintain.

Okay, we're gonna change the subject, but before we do that, a word from our sponsors. You've heard me talk about Guardian Angel child-sized body armour before. I love it. Big believer in this stuff. But now Guardian Angel has introduced a nanotech bulletproof plate meant to fit inside your child's school backpack ...

In most cases, experts can provide persuasive answers. But sometimes, the truth is that we simply don't know. The world is a complicated place, and some aspects of even the most heavily scrutinized historical events always will remain fissures in society's intellectual foundations.

—Jonathan Kay, *Among the Truthers*

Nowhere is the dreamer or the misfit so alone.

—Rush, *Subdivisions*

6: In Geometric Order

Transcribed from *Full Disclosure with Gilbert Emmerich*, AM 710, January 17, 2016.

Gilbert Emmerich: Alright, truthers, we're back. We've been having a hell of a discussion about the Deepwater Horizon oil spill. Equipment malfunction, or crazy Green Peace sabotage? I know where I stand on the matter. Right, we've got our next caller. Okay, caller, your thoughts on the Deepwater Horizon?

Caller: I've got thoughts, Mr Emmerich, but they're not about the Deepwater Horizon.

...

GE: ... I think I know that voice.

Caller: Hello, kind sir. You're hard to get through to.

GE: Well, Johnny, I had to stop taking your calls. It was getting a bit crazy.

Caller: I know, Mr Emmerich. I heard what you had to say. You told all your listeners I was an attention-whore.

GE, chuckling: Well, John, sometimes we use colourful language on the radio. No offense was intended.

Caller: I didn't take offense about that, even if I was just telling you the truth. What really bothered me, Mr Emmerich, is you called me a crackpot. You made it sound like I couldn't be trusted.

GE: I did, that's true, but the thing is, John, your whole story seemed pretty farfetched. And it was unreliable. We did some digging. Couldn't verify anything you said. That was the problem. You know what sets Full

Disclosure apart from the mainstream media? We're responsible, John. We're committed to the truth.

Caller: So are you going to hang up on me?

GE: ... I know what my producer would do, but you know what? Oil spills are boring. It's good to hear from you, Johnny. What did you want to talk about?

Caller: Well, I'm better now, Mr Emmerich. I'm in a better place. I'm doing what I'm supposed to do, you see? And I've realized a few things, and I wanted to share them with you and all the truthers out there.

H ey man," says the young guy, "do you have the time by chance?"

They're in a food court at Alliance College. It's a weeknight evening and most of the fast food kiosks are closed. Only a KFC and a café and a pizza place remain open. For the past twenty-five minutes JD has been sitting at a table by himself, eating some French fries, reading part of a thick course package. He's got a gym bag on the floor beside him. He glances at his cellphone and says, "Yes, kind sir, it's ten minutes to eight."

The young guy nods, says thanks, and goes back to studying some handwritten notes on a scratchpad. He can't be older than thirty. That would make JD almost fifteen years his senior. JD hasn't encountered more than a handful of other students in the forty-plus age category at Alliance, but you're never too old to hit the reset button.

That's one of Dr Casey-Ramos's favourite pearls of wisdom. JD has heard her say it more times than he can count. But that's okay – Dr Casey-Ramos is quite tolerable, all things considered. She's even got JD halfway convinced that the whole field of psychiatry is not, in fact, a gigantic con, as he used to suspect.

JD eats a couple of fries and turns back to his course package. The reading assigned for this week is about direct action. He tries to find his place in the text again: ... nonviolent collective action operates outside the realm of standard political channels, and often takes the form of grassroots protests ...

He smiles, thinking fondly about 99Together. He'll always be proud of their accomplishments in Civic Park. Some of JD's greatest allies from those days – Tiny Tim, for one – are still caught up in the system. As far as JD's heard, Tim is out of jail, but his lengthy legal battle hasn't ended. If JD could do more to help him out, he would.

But meaningful change takes time, dedication, and above all patience. That's another one of Dr Casey-Ramos's sayings.

The text JD is reading is for a course called Social Justice and Nurturing Communities. It's an elective – he didn't even have to sign up for it. He's taking it purely out of interest ... and the off-chance he might see a certain Simone again.

He hasn't seen her yet. He hasn't seen her since, well, That Night, but you never know when Fate is going to intervene on your behalf. That's not one of Dr Casey-Ramos's sayings. That's all JD.

He looks at the text again, reads: Examples of successful grassroots protests include the Salt Satyagraha of 1930 and the march on Washington of1963 ... 99Together should be in there too, he thinks. There were ten thousand of them in Civic Park. Maybe a hundred thousand. And JD was at the forefront. He'll always have that.

These days, JD uses the internet from time to time, but he doesn't look up anything about 11/3/11. He only read the official report once, just after it was made public. JD never listens to Full Disclosure with Gilbert Emmerich anymore. Dr Casey-Ramos has helped him get past all that. The meds help too.

The meds block out the ELF. Which he doesn't believe in anyway.

Without ELF to worry about, he doesn't need to wear a faraday shield on his head anymore. He's grown his hair long, mainly so he can wear it down. Hide his mangled ear. He still likes to dress sharp, wear Sunday-go-to-meeting outfits, channel Bogart. Dressing sharp seems to fit well with going to college. Sometimes he thinks he could pass as a professor. The idea amuses him. He wonders if he, too, could get his PhD from the prestigious International Institute of Grand Cayman.

JD's cellphone buzzes. He glances at it. It's a text message from his brother's wife, saying she'll pick him up at 9:30, when JD's final evening lecture lets out. When she says 9:30, she means 9:30 exactly. No dilly-dallying. If JD is so much as two minutes late getting to the car, she'll go up one side of him and down the other.

She says it's because she's got a lot to do in the evening. Make the kids' lunches, take the laundry out of the dryer, go over JD's brother's work receipts. But JD knows it's her way of keeping an eye on him. Keeping him accountable. Thanks for that concept are due, once again, to Dr Casey-Ramos.

Not that any of JD's sister-in-law's efforts are necessary. JD is efficient. JD is organized. JD is the most accountable person you'll ever meet.

JD is doing well in his dual program at Alliance, where he'll get both his high school diploma and some college credits. He's working twenty hours a week at the Foodmart on Oswalde Street. He's hanging out with Daniel every second weekend, and even managing to kick Lil some of the money she obsesses over.

JD never misses an appointment with Dr Casey-Ramos, or a check-in with the Authorities. JD even managed to help his brother finish building the basement bedroom last fall. He texts his sister-in-law back and tells her he'll see her at 9:30. These are the rules nowadays. The meds help JD stick to the rules, and he never skips his meds.

The young guy who asked JD for the time gathers up his notes and stands up and stretches. Before he leaves the food court, he gives JD a little head-nod. JD smiles in reply. JD smiles a lot these days, or tries too. He's got a lot to smile about.

A lot to smile about.

Doesn't he?

For one thing, his name was never attached to the events of That Night. To 11/3/11. To this day, the common people have no knowledge of JD's connection to the events in question at all. Never mind the endless news articles. The internet forums. All his attempts to tell his side of things on Full Disclosure.

All the conspiracy theories surrounding John Doe # 2.

JD has been written out of the official story. Redacted, is the word. In many ways, he has Gage to thank for that. No, not Gage, Dominic Grillo. The undercover cop. Even now, Gage or Grillo or whoever he is (whoever he was) doesn't seem quite real to JD. But all of the man's notes and reports and files were real enough. He always maintained JD was not a credible threat, not a central component of Declan's plan.

Gage-Grillo even went so far as to say JD showed several signs of mental illness.

And in the aftermath of 11/3/11, the Authorities ended up sending JD to a hospital for a long time.

Now that JD is out of the hospital, he takes his meds and never skips them. Never skips his appointments with Dr Casey-Ramos. Never skips his mandated check-ins with the Authorities. He's otherwise free to live among the common people and take his dual program at Alliance College and work his parttime job at Foodmart. He's free to be accountable.

He's also free to listen to look up the John Doe # 2 stories on the internet. Or to listen to Full Disclosure. But he doesn't. Ever.

JD did watch the Declan video when it was leaked onto the internet seven months ago. He couldn't help himself.

The Declan video is taken from a camera on a helicopter, so the picture quality is poor. Jolts and shudders and rapid zooms in and out. The lingering patches of fog at ground level don't help the picture quality either. The video shows a long stretch of rural road. Late autumn bareness in the trees and farm fields on either side of the road.

A car comes into view, barrelling along the road at high speed. The camera does one of its rapid, inexpert zoom-ins, briefly losing the car, then finding it again. Close up like this, it's clear the speeding vehicle is a muscle car. Dodge Charger by the look of it. The license plates aren't visible. The image stays tight on the Charger for a few moments. It's going fast enough to weave a little, as if the driver has it floored but is not in full control of the 300 horses under the hood.

The camera zooms back out - way out - and now three police cruisers in pursuit are visible. They're a good half-mile behind the Charger, trying to match its speed. It's possible the Charger could outpace the cruisers, but then the rural road ends in a T-junction at another rural road.

There's a roadblock already in place.

The camera zooms out. For a moment, the roadblock and the cars are all lost as the helicopter circles over foggy bush. Then the roadblock is recaptured. Another shaky zoom-in. The Charger is stopped fifty yards short of the roadblock. A darkhaired man in a suede jacket has gotten out of the muscle car.

The man false-starts left, then right, as if he's a runningback trying to fake out an oncoming tackler. Then he stops, plants his feet, and hauls something out of his jacket. The image is too grainy to be completely sure what it is, but it's small and dark and he's lifting it with both hands.

What happens next is over in mere seconds. There are half a dozen cops in half a dozen different positions around the roadblock. One, two, three, maybe all six engage the man from the muscle car with their service weapons. The man doesn't go flying, or dance and spin with the impact of each round. He just pitches over sideways, undramatically. Slides down the ditch by the side of the road. He ends up facefirst in the muck and leaves at the bottom of the ditch. He does not move again.

That's the end of the revolution for Richard Declan, aka Dr Richard Declan, aka Reverend Richie.

That's the end of Patriot Alpha One.

Yes, JD watched the video when it was leaked onto the internet. But he only watched it once. And no, he doesn't think about it anymore.

This coming weekend, JD has plans to go with his brother to the cemetery where their mother is buried. It's been a long, long time since JD has visited her headstone. They're taking JD's brother's sons, and they're taking Daniel.

JD has been told that Granddad is buried there too, and that it's time he goes to pay his respects. JD doesn't much care for the plan, but he's agreed to it. Partly because it means he can skip a shift at the Foodmart.

As for Country Club Estate, he has no idea what's become of the little slice of heaven in seven-seven. The Westinghouse radio, the vintage Playmates in their gilt frames, even the mountain of laundry JD never had the time to do. He has time to do his laundry now. His brother's wife makes sure he has the time.

Inert.

That's the word the Authorities use to describe the fertilizer that was supposed to have been in the plastic drums. The fertilizer was inert. The primer cord was fake. The failsafe was a decoy. That was all Gage-Grillo's doing. Part of the whole case the Authorities were building against the Patriot Bloc.

Still, the look on Declan's face when he saw JD making the call. The way he threw himself into the car and hightailed it out of there. No dignity, no composure. None of what had made Declan what he was up until then.

JD will always have that moment.

He gets up from the table in the food court, stretches, and picks up his course package. He drops the course package into the gym bag. The gym bag is new. He bought it with his Foodmart earnings at Gibson's Surplus & More on Westway Boulevard. The gym bag isn't the only thing he bought at Gibson's.

JD's lecture doesn't start until 8:30. He's got some time to wander around.

He wanders out of the food court. He's not going in the direction of the lecture hall. He wanders through the exit, gym bag in hand. It's a cold evening. Reminds him of his time as a man of no fixed address, living in Civic Park, defending himself from hordes of thieves every night. He turns his collar up.

He cuts through the shopping plaza. There's an off-campus bookstore in the plaza. A place where you can get used course packages and textbooks at a slight discount. Once, not long after JD started his program at Alliance, he thought he saw Simone at the bookstore. The style of clothes, the curves, the close-cropped hair.

He rushed into the store, heart pounding, to see if it was her. But the place was so crowded with new students he could barely navigate among the shelves and stacks. He did what he could, elbowed and shouldered his way around.

Then he turned a corner. Through the bookstore's window, he saw the curves and the close-cropped hair getting into a car in the parking lot. The car was long gone before JD could get himself out of the bookstore.

He holds out hope that he'll see Simone again. Maybe by fate, maybe not. He's not sure about fate anymore.

JD is at the far edge of the shopping plaza now. The knoll comes into view, as does the one-storey brick building. The red and white radio tower rising behind it.

Whenever Simone comes to mind, so too does Becca. JD knows what the Authorities have said about Becca. All that valium in her system, her wrists cut in the bathtub. Nobody will ever know if that was Declan's doing. For some reason, JD doesn't think it was Declan. JD thinks Becca did it to herself. One last final act of clarity. He's not sure why, but the idea brings him some comfort.

It's better than choking to death on the couch while your kids are locked up in the basement.

These days JD never skips his meds. The meds block out the ELF. Which he doesn't believe in anyway.

He sets the gym bag down. He kneels beside it, unzips it, reaches inside. Grasps that other thing he bought at Gibson's Surplus & More. At the same time, he takes his cellphone out of his pocket and makes a call.

Caller: I'm doing what I'm supposed to do, Mr Emmerich. These are good times in my life, and I believe in them.

Gilbert Emmerich: Well, I'm sure happy to hear that, Johnny. Sounds like you're really knocking it out of the park. Good for you.

Caller: Thank you, kind sir.

GE: Okay, it was good to catch up, but I'm gonna have to let you go now, John. Switch to our next caller. Back to the Deepwater Horizon cover-up. Next on the line we've got Bob. Bob, you're on Full Disclosure. Go ahead.

…

GE: Bob?

Caller: Still me, Mr Emmerich. Still John Doe # 2.

GE: Let's call this a technical diff—

Caller: I shouldn't think about it, you see, but I do. I do think about it.

GE: Paul, are you in the booth?

Caller: And what I've come to understand, Mr Emmerich, is there is a Them. I've done a lot of work with Dr Casey-Ramos, and she says there's no Them. There's no ELF, there's no conspiracy. There is no Them. But she's wrong. And I can't stop thinking about it. And do you know who They are?

GE: … Paul? Come on, man, don't tell me you're out for a smoke right now.

Caller: They are you, Mr Emmerich. You see? They are you. It took me a long time to figure this out. But now I know. And I've decided to do something about. Maybe nobody knows what the truth is about John Doe #2, but everybody is going to know about you.

GE: Alright, this is crazy. First thing is I'm going to fire my produ—

Caller: Don't worry about your producer, Mr Emmerich. Maybe he just went outside for a cigarette. Maybe that's where him and myself happened to meet up with each other. Maybe he saw the gift I bought for myself from the surplus store over the weekend. Bought with my own money, might I add. A katana, kind sir. You know what that is? A samurai sword from the days of ancient Japan. Beautiful craftsmanship. A very honourable weapon. I had one in high school.

GE: You, ah, you're carrying a goddamn samurai sword, Johnny?

Caller: Maybe I am, Mr Emmerich. Maybe I'm walking through the front of your studio right now. Maybe your producer's still outside. There's nobody else here, is there? Except for you. All by yourself. You're at your microphone there, telling all your listeners the secret reasons for all the bad things that happen to them, when maybe there's no reason at all.

I read online, good sir, that this show makes a lot of money. More than all the other shows on AM 710 combined. I read that you just got a deal. Syndic—, synd—, syndication. That's the word. Syndication. Very good, Mr Emmerich. But maybe you should have used some of that money for extra security around here. The world is full of the abnormal and the paranormal and cover-ups and conspiracies, after all. Isn't it.

Maybe I'm on the other side of the door to the recording room now, Mr Emmerich. Should we see if the door is locked? On the other hand, maybe—

GE: I … oh Christ … I'm sorry, John. I'm sorry. This is just a show is all it is. It's just, it's just entertainment, okay? I don't know about any of this stuff. I don't know anything, except I'm sorry. Okay? John?

Caller: On the other hand, maybe not. Maybe I'm not here at all. Maybe there's nobody with a katana outside your recording room. Maybe your producer just went outside for a longer cigarette break than usual. Maybe it's all in your head, and we just needed to hear it.

GE: … Why? Jesus Christ, John. Why would you do this?

Caller: Why, Mr Emmerich? Just because, good sir. Just because.

About the Author

A.E. Merrick is a Toronto-based dilettante who has experimented with a number of different identities, occupations, and pastimes. They are uncomfortable with publicly searchable databases of personal information. They write truth rather than fiction. This is their first novel.

www.ingramcontent.com/pod-product-compliance
Lightning Source LLC
Chambersburg PA
CBHW070442200726
48293CB00007B/2106